# ON
# SARPY
# CREEK

# ON SARPY CREEK

## IRA STEPHENS NELSON

*A Novel*

RIVERBEND PUBLISHING
&
BEDROCK EDITIONS

Copyright © 1938 by Ira Stephens Nelson

Original elements of this edition copyright © 2003 by Riverbend Publishing and Bedrock Editions

Co-published by Riverbend Publishing and Bedrock Editions, Helena, Montana

Printed in the United States of America.

2  3  4  5  6  7  8  9  0  BP  08 07  06  05

Cover painting: *Moon over Willow Creek* by Dale Livezey (oil on canvas, 48 x 60 inches, 1999)

Cover design by Patricia Borneman, Bedrock Editions

Text design by Suzan Glosser, Riverbend Publishing

ISBN 1-931832-36-6

Cataloging-in-Publication data is on file at the Library of Congress.

| Riverbend Publishing | Bedrock Editions |
|---|---|
| P.O. Box 5833 | 2 N Last Chance Gulch |
| Helena, MT 59604 | Helena, MT 59601 |
| 1-866-787-2363 | 406-449-5135 |
| www.riverbendpublishing.com | www.bedrockbooks.com |

*From the dust jacket of the 1938 edition of On Sarpy Creek.*

# CHAPTER I

IN THE second year of the drought, Herman Leidermen set out to call his neighbors together that they might pray for rain.

One day in June he drove across the little valley, over the bridge of Sarpy Creek's feeble waters, and into the hills beyond. Already the early summer heat was parching the earth. Wheat fields beside the road drooped in great patches of yellow. The grass was gray. The sun pouring down its heat from a sky of cloudless blue, day after day, week after week, and the gentle hot winds caressing across the mountains, the open range and the barbed-wire-fenced farms . . . it was all leaving desolation. Even the wild roses that clustered in low places would not hold their petals.

At the top of the hills he let the horses stop for a breathing space. He was driving old Rone and Tobey; and Tobey was always mindful of the habit of years and never failed to pause hopefully of his own accord at the summit of each little knoll. He knew his master was indulgent and as fully aware as he himself of the silent understanding between them.

From here, Herman could see for miles in all directions. Either way, the horizon was always tipped with mountains. But Herman looked only down the dusty road that curved in and out among the dry farms, past the homes of the people he loved. He thought: "If it would only rain."

He drove deeper among the hills, stopping at the crude homes scattered over the lonely land, telling them the prayer meeting would be a week from this day, on Thursday; and

1

the minister would plead with God for rain. Some of the farmers he found in the fields and they looked at him with dubious expression; plainly their eyes were a little awed and questioning of a power they neither doubted nor believed, that they had looked at from afar but never tested.

In the cool of the evening, Case Gyler and his young wife Sareeny made camp under a cluster of cottonwoods, forty miles up Sarpy Creek.

Case was powerful worried.

He wished, with a strong wish that made him desperate, that he had waited until after Sareeny's baby was born, and then made this journey. But they had both believed they would surely have time to reach her folks' old home on Sarpy, and Sareeny had wanted her Ma to be with her when this first one came. They had not counted on the baby's being due for a week yet. Because this was their first, they had failed to accept or understand certain signs that warn a woman when her time draws near. Poor little Sareeny was not to blame, young as she was. Case felt that Sareeny had been an unknowing little woman when she had married him a year ago, and she was an unknowing little woman now.

All day long, sitting beside him on the jolting wagon seat, she had felt sharp pains running through her body, and each time she had caught her breath with the fear the baby might not wait until she reached her mother's home. She would not be afraid of the baby's coming if her own mother stood beside the bed; if her own mother's understanding hands were working over her.

She knew Case was scared, too, though he would never let on to her. She could see it in the quick turning of his eyes to her when she breathed a little differently, or even so much as moved her legs or arms. She could see it in the soft tenderness that had hovered around his lips all day. Camped out here alone with Case, miles from any house they knew of, she might die. She was a-scared, and he was a-scared, but they would never let on to each other.

Before sundown Case had began to watch about for a likely place to camp. A place by the Creek, for water, and where he could find wood for a fire. He had no tent, and he would have to lay their bed upon the ground with nothing closing them in from the open night. But that was no worry. The night would be warm and clear. For once Case was thankful there would be no rain.

He saw ahead of them the place he wanted. It was a cove, so close beside the Creek the grass was green and thick. There was wood and water.

He turned the horses away from the road and the wagon rattled across the uneven sod to a stop under the trees.

The first thing Case did was take the pile of quilts and the feather bed from the wagon and spread them on the ground for Sareeny to lie on. Maybe, when she rested awhile the pains would leave and she would feel better, and they would see there was nothing to be a-feared of, after all.

It only took him a short time to unhitch the horses from the wagon, strip the harness from them, and stake them to eat their fill of grass and water. He had no grain to feed them. The old milk cow, tied and led behind the wagon, had already stretched her rope to the limit to reach the trickle of water and drink long and deeply of it.

He gathered wood from the underbrush. Sareeny lay quietly and watched him build the fire between the stones that he had dropped just so that the coffeepot and frying pan would set without tipping over. His sun-browned callused hands broke the wood easily. Smoke rose.

It was just getting twilight. You still could look a long ways off across the hills, and see them blending into one another. But now they were blurred with dusk. There was just enough breeze to move the leaves of the cottonwoods. A few feet away the Creek made little tinkling sounds, and Sareeny could hear the crickets down there along the banks. All the night noises were beginning to wake. It was almost like she and Case had a world to themselves, and it was a lonesome world. Never before had this rough and lonely land seemed so quiet and unpeopled, so smothered with the hush of solitude.

Pain caused her to catch her breath and open her mouth to call his name involuntarily.

He stood up suddenly from the fire and looked towards her:—

"You all right, Sareeny?"

The pain, sharper, agonizing, had crushed through her body. He was at her side in an instant. She did not answer him at once. The pain was straining within her. Now she knew it would be born tonight. She waited a moment until the pain had slowed before answering him.

She tried to make her voice natural:—

"Go gather more wood and get things ready now, Case. I want you here beside me when dark comes."

He stood there as if he feared to leave her, his eyes dark with expression. She threw back the blanket he had spread over her, and stood up. She knew she must not lie down yet. She must keep moving, as she had heard her mother, mother of five children, tell.

For the moment Case stood there watching her he did not breathe. When he turned to go for wood he cursed himself. For a hundred things. Even for marrying Sareeny, a year ago, when he had no money to buy land for a home or to stock it with cows for meat and milk, and horses to breed and sell. For taking her off a hundred miles from her folks, because she was his wife, to live on a place and watch the crops he had planted in the spring wither back to bare upturned soil;

till he had finally to give up in despair to her longing to be back close to her Ma.

Everything they owned in the world was in that wagon, or around it. The few things they had kept house with; the two horses he had staked out here in the long green grass close to the creek; the cow who stood near by contentedly chewing her cud, her sides bulging from having drunk so deep of the cool water, her milk bag dripping, waiting. But she would not be milked now. Case gathered his armload of wood and went back to Sareeny by the fire.

For what seemed hours he walked with her, back and forth, back and forth. He had thought he knew what pain was. But here was his little wife Sareeny, racked with agony, her muscles knotted, her face twisted and wet with sweat, often banging on his arms and looking at him with eyes like he was a stranger she had never seen before. Case knew enough about death. He knew too much about death. He had spent a year in war, and he had seen blood and death and dying men till it had left such a mark on his soul never would he speak of it. But never before had he felt such an awful nearness of death, or known that it lurked so jealously around each new life. Unknowing tears blinded Sareeny's eyes, so that she could not have seen him anyway, even had her look been able to tell him she knew he was there. A time passed, and she grew worse, and he knew that now she would not be able to help him in his efforts to help her. He must, in his blundering fear, bring the child to birth before it was too late.

A cool breeze sprung up in the west and swept through the night. A quarter-moon tilted among the stars in the dark sky. Case threw more wood on the fire.

It was long past midnight when the baby gave its first cry into the air of earth. Case cut the cord through which the first life had crept in Sareeny's creation of this new life. He wrapped the child in a blanket and laid it close against its mother's side under the covers he drew over them. In the bright light of the fire he noticed only that it was red as rose color, and wrinkled-like, its tiny knees drawn up to its body. He did not wonder if it was boy or girl.

Sareeny lay there weak and white as she could ever be. He laid more quilts over her, and she looked up at him and he could feel her smile rather than see it. He went back to the fire with tears in his eyes and a great song of thanksgiving in his heart. He felt humbled. Sareeny would be all right. She couldn't have looked like that if she wasn't going to be all right.

For a few minutes he went and stood by the fire in silence. He was moved by some deep feeling he could not have named. In the last two or three hours he had been sure Sareeny was going to die in his hands. Never again in his life would he come so near to getting down on his knees and saying with all the meaning in him, "Thank you, God, thank you." He came nearer to doing it because there was no one to watch him, or see him. But in another minute the nearness had passed, and he was too human to let go of himself like that. It was like a door slamming shut in his mind. He built up the fire to leaping red flames and went down the Creek to wash the blood-stain from his hands.

# CHAPTER 2

BETWEEN the time of an hour past midnight and the hour before dawn are what we might call the still hours of the night, out here in the West. For it is then the coyotes stop their howling, and the night birds don't call any more, and about the only sound is the little breeze rustling the leaves of trees or the blades of grass against each other. And the breeze brings with it the odor of sage. Like on this night in June there is the odor of wild roses mingled, too.

Case sat cross-legged beside the fire, feeding it wood, and sometimes staring deep into the heart of it thinking, while the quarter-moon slowly slanted to silence on the mountains outlined on the west. Sareeny moved restlessly now and then, and he was always quick at her side, looking anxiously into her face, pulling the covers closer about her shoulders. The baby never made a sound. It was so still that three times during the night Case went to the bed with a queer catch in his throat and ran his hand under the covers to feel it. It was warm as toast. It was living. When he laid his callused hand on the soft flesh he could almost feel the blood beating through its veins, and slowly he began to wonder what a miracle all life was. His wonder over Sareeny was no less.

Lord, he had not known he loved Sareeny so much, he thought, as he sat before the fire. He had not known till now that any man could love any woman so much, or feel so tender towards her. He would not hurt Sareeny for all the world.

There were things that would hurt Sareeny, too, if she knew. Sareeny had never been over fifty miles from her father's door, until she had married Case and gone with him up on Broadview Prairies to live. But Case had traveled much, because his own mother had died so long ago he could never remember her and he had ever been dissatisfied and restless alone with his father. Case had run away when he was yet a boy and had been batted about by the world, learning things about the people in it and the way they lived and the hidden things that went on beneath the surface of their lives. Case understood people. So many of the hidden things about them he had learned . . . Then in war, too, as a soldier, he had seen so much of the hidden things rush to the surface, and people forgot to be ashamed like in times of peace. The easy giving of woman to man with the thought that what did it matter when tomorrow might never come . . . yet that was not really the reason, Case knew now, for such things as that and many more are hidden among all the good in all the world, waiting only for an excuse to come out into the bright light of day. Yes, there were many things in all that part of his life to hurt Sareeny, if she knew.

And there was the Indian woman, Letitia.

Only his father knew about that. One day the old man had been riding the range, hunting out his cows, and he had come upon his son and the Indian woman lying on the thick green grass of a glade sheltered by trees and high wild-cherry bushes. The old man turned his horse homeward, sick at heart. With the twilight Case had come home, silent and careless before his father. In a few words the old man had told him what was what. Case did not answer.

Throughout all that summer and the winter following, he and Letitia had carried on with each other. When he had not gone to her, she had come to him. He had mighty nigh been fool enough to marry Letitia. In the beginning, Letitia had believed he meant to marry her. And yet, later, when she knew that he would not, she had come to him the same, and he had ever found her waiting when he went to her. Case had ignored his father's almost sullen silence. Only one night when he returned home and undressed to lie down beside him the old man had raised up in bed and said angrily:

If ye've no notion of marrying her, better had ye never come home to Sarpy from the war."

From the darkness Case had answered lightly: "Would you like me to marry her? Have neighbors calling me a squaw man?"

The old man's words were heavy with feeling.

". . . She's too good fer ye . . ."

And Case had not gone to sleep. He had lain there, pondering. Hell, why were people always lying, hiding, covering up? He knew enough about people. Men especially . . . and women as well. He knew enough about his father, too. A man is a man and a woman is woman and—well, there was too much foolishness and pretending and silence over facts that are as unalterable and blinding in their truth as the sudden brilliant sun. He believed there should be no shame.

Letitia was not like the other Indian women or girls on the Crow Reservation. Though she was all Indian, from the tips of her little feet to the heavy, dusky black braids of her hair, she was better educated. She knew more of the white man's ways of laughter and civilized, subtle things. She was prettier, whether she dressed in the clothes of a white woman or in the soft white, beaded doeskin the Indians were so proud to wear. She was strangely beautiful with her dark ruddy face and eyes that were smoky-agate color. What Case did not know was that Letitia loved him the way many a woman loves a man for many years. Nor did he know that Letitia had borne him a child.

In December of that winter he had gone to a neighborhood dance; and Sareeny, whom he had known all his life, now grown up to a small, quiet woman, was in his arms. In the spring he had married Sareeny, who had lived all her life on her father's farm that bordered his father's place where Sarpy Creek twisted lazily through the hills to a distant river. Letitia, with all the silence of her race, had stayed in the mountains. She would be silent and his father would be silent. Sareeny would never know. Letitia gave birth to the child and was silent after that, too, for never would she tell Case of it.

As Case mulled by the fire the thought struck him suddenly: Letitia would be there near his old home—willing, mostly likely, if he wanted her. . . . But that thought was with him only a split second. He shoved a chunk of wood into the fire with such force a shower of sparks rose in the dark. There weren't no better woman on earth than Sareeny, yonder with the child that was his'n and her'n. No better woman on earth. He went to her and smoothed her covers, his hands clumsy in their sudden desire for tenderness. She was sleeping, weak and drugged with pain.

He hunted among the things in the wagon until he found a bucket, and went to milk the cow. She looked around at him almost reproachfully when he put his head against her warm flank, for her bag was so full of milk that thin streams of it were forced from her teats. The sound of the milk hitting the bottom of the bucket sounded loud in the silence.

When he had finished, daylight was just beginning to seep into the blackness over all the land. In the east the sky would soon turn pink. Sareeny called to him.

He hurried up to where she lay beside the wagon. She was smiling. Her gray eyes were warm and bright, and though there was no color in her face, she looked prettier than he had ever seen her. Her long brown hair that he had always thought a lot nicer than any other woman's was loose and down and spread out over the pillow in fine waves soft as the feel of silk. Sareeny was not pretty like a lot of these babyish women, but he had always believed she would be a fine-looking person even when she got old. For her face wasn't too long, or too broad, or too round, and her mouth was firm and kind. She had ever been to him a pleasing little woman. Her eyebrows were slender and black, curving above her eyes like fine pencil marks, the lashes long and thick.

"It's a girl, Case," she said.

He dropped down on his knees beside her with laughter in his throat but tears were close to his eyes.

"I hadn't thought till now, Sareeny."

There were tears in her eyes, too. Pride was rising up in her till it shone in her voice and face and even in the movement of her hands.

"Do you like it?"

He answered seriously.

"Of course. It didn't really make any difference to me if it wasn't a boy."

She laughed at him. She scolded because he had not fixed himself something to eat during the night. He set about to prepare breakfast. For her he meant to cook some oatmeal gruel and soft-boil some eggs if she wanted them. And there was the baby, still unwashed. After breakfast he would have to heat water, and when the sun warmed up a-plenty, give the little woman baby her first bath.

He took the pail and went down the Creek to a deeper place he had seen yesterday. There the water was cold and clear, shaded all day from the heat of the sun by an old, old cottonwood tree. A tangled wilderness of wild-rose bushes grew all about, drooping over the rippling surface, their petals falling into it to be slowly carried away. Case had to

11

brush off a handful of the deep pink patches from the pail he carried.

After breakfast, he washed the baby. It was a laughable sight to watch and Sareeny had to laugh sometimes even though she was close to worried crying for fear he would drop it or hurt it in his clumsy hands. And the little woman child voiced her indignation with loud wails. Case was secretly astonished that a thing, so silent yesterday could make so much noise today. When he had finished, Sareeny took it back under the covers, talking to it with a soft new tone of voice Case had never heard her use before. She gave it her breasts and it hushed its crying. Case stood in silent awe. Danged if the little thing didn't seem to be actually enjoying its breakfast. Sareeny was different, too. The same and yet different. She wasn't only his now. It was kinda like she might have grown up overnight, somehow, with a new look in her face and a new touch to her hands that had never been there before.

Case knew he ought to stay here today, at least, and let Sareeny rest. There was danger in lifting her in the wagon, moving her about. Yet there was danger in staying here, too. This would be another scorching day. Before it was over, swift thunder and lightning could come with cold rain. He had enough worry on his mind, now, wondering how he could get set to make a living for the three of them.

He walked away from the wagon, climbing the nearest hill above the valley. From this high place he could look away yonder across the hills, his eyes following the twisting, turning ways of Sarpy Creek by the trees that were bunched along its valley. The valley curved from sight again and again in its path through the crumpled land, always to re-appear, a cluster of green. Forty miles along its distance lay the spot that was home to Sareeny and himself. The spot where now they both felt they should settle on and stay to live. They'd find a place and get settled there somehow. Because that was what they wanted to do. They had been away a year and they had learned to know they loved this place. They loved all the places here they knew so well: the old wagon roads they had traveled so many times in their childhood; the neighbors whose faces were as familiar as those of their own folks. A poor man, having to scratch for a living, never has it too easy, nohow, and Case reckoned it would be a heap easier to fasten a solid home to solid ground here among friends than to try it again in some other strange place.

Before noon Case had a soft bed made in the wagon box, arranged with all the quilts and feather pillows he and Sareeny owned. As carefully as he ever did anything in his life he lifted Sareeny and placed her on it, then laid the baby beside her. He stretched a blanket above them to shade them from the sun.

They could be home tonight, if he kept the horses going at a steady pace, and it didn't get too hot. The road for the most part ran close along the Creek, and big trees threw a lot of shade.

Sareeny relaxed against the soft pillows. The baby lay in the curve of her arm. The horses plodded along the dry road, the wagon creaked softly as the wheels rolled over the soft sand. Sareeny was thinking she would name this girl-baby Ellen, after its grandmother. That would please her old Ma, because this was the first grandchild. Not one of Sareeny's brothers was married, as yet.

It was good to be getting close to home. She would go with Case anywhere in the world he wanted to take her, but never would she be so contented as when she was here, where everything all around was dear because she had lived with it so long; and at times hated it with rebellion because she had been so young, the world had been so big and interesting and she couldn't get away to do as she pleased. But that was before she married Case. After that, things just seemed to settle into one long peaceful living. She had stopped wishing so crazily for one thing one day and a different, impossible thing the next day. Now the time to come was settled. She was a married woman. She had a baby. Her life was laid ahead of her as a road. A friendly, homey road. Her and Case would go on living and living in a home of their own, glad to be with and have each other. Making the best living they could, all the money they could, maybe someday even being a little rich.

She looked at Case up there on the wagon seat and smiled to herself. Oh but he was good-looking, with his broad shoulders, his brown eyes and jet-black hair, the fine way he held his head. This morning he had told her stubbornly that he intended to see they had no more babies. Ho ho! Well, she wanted a boy. A boy with Case's black hair and bright brown eyes and chin that said he was a little set in his ways. She intended to see they had one.

Already the memory of last night's pain was dulled, misted over with newer plans, new pleasures . . . and the wonder and magic of the child beside her which would grow . . . and grow. . . . Sareeny was such a simple and unworldly-wise little woman.

She rested quietly. She even felt soft satisfaction in listening to the dull thud of the horses' plodding feet, in watching the dust that rose in slow clouds behind the wagon and settled slower, touchless, back to earth.

The wagon creaked on. They passed a large herd of cattle bearing the brand ◊4–, the biggest ranch in the country. Over on a hill they saw a cowboy on his pony. Case waved, and the cowboy's spurs and silver-mounted saddle flashed in the sun when he turned to wave back gaily.

The old milk cow, tied with Case's lariat rope behind the wagon, hung back a moment and mooed as the wagon pulled her on.

14

# CHAPTER 3

THERE WERE few families living close around the old
homes of Sareeny and Case. But these few were rooted there
with their years of living, by births and deaths. And by something deeper even than that. The Leidermans, the Gores,
the Frys had lived for a quarter of a century in their homes
along Sarpy's small wooded valley hemmed in by rising hills.
Eden and his blind son, Felix, had lived for twenty years in
the big house that was the friendly envy of every neighbor.
Old Man Mills had hunted deer and antelope when the
narrow valley was an uncleared wilderness of underbrush and
wild cherry bushes, before ever a house or a fence was built.
And in the summer before the war had ended, when the
time came for him to stand by and see his wife's body laid
forever away, he left the ranch house he had long ago built
with his own hands, and he moved into the village of Sarpy.
By common consent of his neighbors he became their minister, their leader to a vague, yet ultimate goal. When a young
man he had been an ordained minister, and had papers to
prove it. By the way he talked they could never have even
guessed that he profited from any book learning or book
study. He was a neighbor, talking as they talked, living as
they lived. They wanted him for their minister because they
knew he was a mortal good old man, a godly man, and wise.
He was not goody-goody. He was not saintly. Most likely, in
his younger days, if he had caught some young fellow stealing a horse from him, he would have talked with him and
reasoned with him, and had that done no good he would

have doubled up his fist and smacked him one, whaling the daylights out of him; then he would have said, "Now damn ye, come on in and have supper with us. Ye may as well start the right kind of life with a full belly."

Every neighbor loved Old Man Mills.

Their daily lives were knit too closely together to be named "community." Each knew all the others, so well. Neighbors, through the long slow beat of summer after summer; through the fierce grip of winter's after winter's freezing cold.

Strange indeed, how intangible things could be hidden away in the heart and the mind and the home of one, that not another among them could guess. These stark, intangible things, undisclosed, made even more appalling by the utter silence of the way they were concealed. For twenty years, Eden had lived among them, his secret hidden, shared only by old Herman Leidermen. For nigh about half that long, Dorcy Fry had coldly concealed, admitting not even to herself, the smoldering hate that ever grew each year within her, bitter, bitter.

With Sareeny and her mother there was a silent bond of understanding and sympathy that held them closer than the mere state of mother and child. Of all the family, Sareeny alone truly realized how hard her mother worked; how swiftly her old face was ageing, her hair graying; and how many things had been lacking from her mother's life. The mother knew the daughter's mind and often talked to her of secret things she never worded to anyone else. Thus Sareeny knew her mother's mind as no other did—not even the father.

That bond had sprung into being one winter night long ago, when Sareeny was twelve. The bringing of it had brought an invisible barrier to Sareeny and her father. She would remember that night as long as she lived, and she would never forgive him for it if she lived to be a hundred.

Her father had struck her mother and drawn blood from her mother's mouth.

It was her mother's eyes she remembered most. Hurt and stricken as they could ever be. Shrinking back there against the wall, uttering one cry, then holding the back of her hand to where the blood dripped off her chin.

Sareeny cried a long while into her pillow that night, while her brothers Ranny and Jacob and Chris slept in the same room as peacefully as though there were nothing wrong in the whole wide world. Sareeny had been quite sure that her mother and father would never make up or be friendly or speak to each other again, and it was all her father's fault. No wonder her mother's hands were rough and brown as old leather, with so much washing to be done by hand, on a board; and cooking, cooking, working in summers to preserve food for winters; sewing . . . for never one of the children had store bought, ready made clothes. Even the boys' shirts and little blue denim overalls were made from long yards of material carefully selected by her mother in the little one-store town. There was garden work to help with, and chickens to manage, and cream to churn with a long dash, up and down, in the glass churn, until it separated into little golden globes of good sweet butter. But never was her mother too busy, in the years the children were growing young-uns, to stop for any one of them and soothe a bruised finger or other petty hurt, with an understanding face.

What matter if her father was sorry afterward. He had done it and that was that.

To save her life Sareeny could not help but have always a tiny thought of it pushing up somewhere in her mind when she looked at him.

It was there tonight, when the wagon rattled into the yard of the old log house and her father came out cursing the dogs to stop their barking. It was there when he kissed her and she saw the starlight glint on unshed tears in his eyes because he was so glad it was her come home again.

His voice was unnatural when he called loudly back into the house:—

"My God, Ellen, it's Sareeny and Case. And they got a baby."

Her mother came out, wearing a long white flannel nightgown. Her hair hung in one thick braid down her back, the way she had always fixed it for the night as long as Sareeny could remember.

They cried a little, Sareeny with her face pressed against her mother's wrinkled old neck where she could feel the muscles tightened and the blood beating hard through the veins. Inside the house there was shouting and the sound of bare feet running down the stairs. Chris bumped around in the darkness of the room upstairs trying to find his pants. Sareeny, there in the wagon, seemed to realize of a sudden all that she had endured alone with Case in the hills last night. Case was everything in the world to her; he filled her life; a thought of him stood somewhere close to every other thought. But here was her family gathering round her, like coming back from childhood with a million memories that couldn't all be remembered or forgotten. Her oldest brother, Randolph, came out the door, tall and homely as ever. Then Jacob, smiling in his careless way. Then sixteen year old Chris, his face soft with boyish tenderness, and a certain pride over this thing happened to Sareeny.

They lifted her from under all the covers Case had tucked around her against the chill night air and carried her into the house. Sareeny's mother took the baby in her arms with a no greater, but a newer, different, tenderness from that with which she held her own littlest ones. Now she, Ellen Alice Gore, was a grandmother. Mother of a mother.

She put Sareeny in the high old walnut bedstead in the downstairs bedroom. Little Tana, youngest of all the Gore family, stared over the foot of it with wide open fascinated eyes.

Ellen shooed them all out. There were countless things she knew to do for Sareeny, and the first was peace and quiet.

Oil lamps burned late that night in the old Gore house, out in Sarpy land. Case and the men sat long around the table in the kitchen, talking and talking about the drought and the hot winds. Surely the world must be headed straight for destruction, with the rich men hogging it all from the poor men, and Congress doing nothing but make long speeches that never said anything. The President sitting behind his big desk yonder in Washington and not even beginning to realize how things actually were. Let the President and the Congressmen live out here a few years. Let 'em live on beans and salt pork, if they had the guts to make it out of this dry, rocky, windy land. Let 'em see their kids running around in ragged shoes when snow stood knee deep on the ground. Yeh! Ha! They'd go back to Washington and take their jobs mighty serious, they would, then!

Ellen, coming back and forth through the room, heard it all as so much chaff blown about by the wind. Men were all alike. They had to run off at the mouth just so much, and like the sap coming up in spring, there weren't no help for it except let it come. Like the sap, it served its purpose, maybe, for a man to blow off his opinions like steam.

With Jim Gore, especially. Jim's mind was full of cure-alls for every ill thing imagined or otherwise, that marred the world. He always had an idea. He was full of ideas. Ellen would move about a room, doing up her work, and without really listening to him she would hear him describing, explaining, intense in his beliefs and seriousness, just where

19

the mistakes lay and how they should be righted. Sometimes she would smile, secretly, silently within herself. She would think: "My poor old man. Raggedy old farmer that he is." At other times she would hear with weariness and a kind of aggravated patience. She was getting old, he was getting old. Ever since she had married him she had pinched pennies, and been saving with sugar and flour, and sewed patches as big as dinner plates on his old overalls. Now listen to him talk with such a positive knowing look! She wondered when and where he did all of his serious thinking.

She worked about the kitchen, cleaning up after the late supper she had fixed for them. Little Tana fell asleep in her chair by the kitchen table, yet refused obstinately to go to bed, mildly excited over Sareeny and Case and the new baby. There was something softer than a smile about Ellen's lips. She washed clean the faded oilcloth and straightened the dishes in the cupboard, but her mind was with Sareeny yonder in the bedroom. One early morning a year ago, Sareeny had stood beside Case while the minister said the words that made them man and wife . . . an hour later she drove away with him, a hundred miles, to a little house she had never seen. Now she had returned. Sareeny was home again, where, to Ellen, it would ever seem the natural place Sareeny belonged.

She called twice for Chris before he came to dry the dishes. Because he was just at that age when he could be a big help to her, she depended on him, though he grumbled with resentment. Chris felt that he was already a man and out of place in the kitchen. He was husky and good looking, with light hair and blue eyes. He hated drying dishes more than anything else.

"Why can't you leave a fellow alone?" he said angrily.

Then with its usual suddenness the heart attack struck Ellen. It was not new to her. It was the second attack in the month. She felt it coming, her breath shortened, the pain rose in her chest. No one knew she had these spells. She wanted to hide it. She picked up the water bucket and went out into the dark yard towards the well. She could feel her heart seeming to swell with pain, yet pausing in its beat to lie stilled in her breast.

She knew she was going to fall. She turned her face to the cool wind, trying to breathe deep of it. Always, in one of these spells, she was stricken with the fear she was going to die. Afterwards she would marvel over what happened in her mind in that instant before falling. It was the same now. Everything she saw was like a flash . . . the old log house, dark, and through the lighted window she could see Chris, resentment still in his face. She heard the jumble of men's voices, a chair scraped across the rough floor, the breathing whisper of the night wind against the dry wheat beyond the house. Then a burst of complete darkness.

She opened her eyes to find Chris bending over her. His face was like a scared rabbit. She could feel his surprise and terror at coming out and finding her here, like this. In another minute he would be yelping for his father.

She forced herself to speak:—

"Chris, help me up."

He lifted her, supporting her with his arm.

"Gosh, Ma," he said uncertainly, "what's the matter?"

"I guess I fainted, Chris. I'm all right now."

She thought swiftly. Chris would be running to tell his father in a minute. They'd all be a worrying over her. She didn't want them a worrying over her. Not as long as they could do nothing to help her, anyway. She'd been to a doctor, last fall. None of the family must know the doctor had said no medicine could help her.

She could breathe natural now, though she still was weak and dizzy. She said crossly:—

21

"Now, Chris, don't run in the house blabbin' this, to worry yore Pa. And you know how Sareeny would feel. Jest keep yore mouth shut."

He eyed her. Worried, still not over his scare.

"You are sick, Mom. Else you wouldn't of fainted."

She knew she could make him promise to keep his mouth shut, if he was not too scared. She was over the spell now. She made Chris walk around with her, and she breathed the cool air, so she could go in the house looking as though nothing had happened. Maybe she wouldn't have another spell for months.

He promised. It would be a long time before he grumbled again when she asked him to do some little thing.

She entered the house quietly, and finished her work in the kitchen. Then she went in the room where Sareeny lay, and closed the door, shutting away the men with their idle talk of this thing and that.

To Sareeny it seemed that after this year's absence only her mother remained almost the same. Pa's hair had grown just a little more gray, his eyes a little more squinting, crinkly in their expression. Tana and Chris had grown until it was a surprise. And Ranny and Jacob, grown men, had hardened, more mature, stalwart. Her brother Jacob had turned out to be the best looking one of the family after all. But Ma had not changed, Sareeny thought, when Ellen said good night with the lamp in her hand and went out to close the door.

Sareeny lay in the dark room, only half asleep. She had heard her father say that just yesterday old Herman Leidermen had come by bringing word everyone should come to town to a prayer meeting next Thursday and pray for rain. Funny old Herman, she wanted to see him and his fat little wife, Birdie. Birdie was nigh about as round as a dumpling, and always cracking some joke, in spite of her everlasting religion and touchy ways. As many years as Sareeny could remember, Birdie had been expecting a lost brother to come home. Brother Jack. He was Birdie's only relative, and she talked so much of him.

Sareeny let her mind muse over old friends.

She wanted to see Case's father, and all the other people she had known all her life. Eden, and blind Felix, who lived alone in the big house close to town. She and Felix had played together a thousand times, when they were kids, before his father had sent him away to school. It had been a school where blind people were taught to read by running their fingers over little raised dots and dashes. Felix had been blind all his life. She could remember long ago when he had said:—

"What is the sky like, Sareeny?"

She had been a little girl, and explaining something as huge as the sky was pretty difficult. She had told him it was just awful, awful big. And it was a funny thing; in the day-time you could look and look and there was nothing there when the weather was nice, except the sun; in storms it was filled with queer things called clouds that boiled into one another or drifted about like so much fluffy cotton. At night there was most a million stars a-sparkling. The sky was blue color.

He had said:—

"But what is blue color, Sareeny?"

She hadn't been able to tell Felix what blue color was. She thought now, Lordy but kids has got a lot to learn. Whether or not they have two good eyes. Anyway, Felix and his father wouldn't be hurt overmuch with the drought. Many a time folks had said if old Eden ever took all his money from the bank, the bank would have to close its doors.

After a while, Case came and crept into bed beside her, ever so quietly, thinking she was asleep. When he went to sleep, the palm of his hand, rough and coarse from hard working, rested lightly against her face.

In another room, Ellen did not sleep. In the darkness her eyes were wide awake. As a woman just turned grandmother, she realized how old she was getting to be; and a body can think of many things after living sixty years on this earth.

# CHAPTER 4

ARLY the next morning Jacob got up from bed and dressed quietly in the upstairs room he shared with Ranny. He moved carefully, so that his footsteps would not wake his mother and father sleeping in the room directly below him. They would be up soon, but Jacob wanted to be alone with himself and think awhile, before he cornered his father down at the barn and talked to him.

Sareeny's homecoming had forced a sudden decision in Jacob's mind. This thing had to be done. It had to be settled, and it couldn't wait much longer. He dreaded it more than he had ever before dreaded anything. Not because he was ashamed. Nor because he was afraid of what his father would think or say. Like his other brothers, and Sareeny too, he was not afraid of his father, but he simply could not be comfortable while deadly serious before him. With their mother they could admit and confess and laugh with natural ease. Yet before their father they had never been able to seem to themselves either as grown-up people able to do their own thinking, or as children who looked to him for advice.

Jacob knew these things he had to tell his father would be sudden and unforeseen.

And too well he knew why he dreaded this whole business.

He would say: "I guess I'll have to marry Frace Cristan." Frace Cristan. Already he almost hated her. But in the past weeks he had thought it all out, and he had understood that he had not hated her until he had learned that the only thing he could do was marry her. Before then he had thought she was the finest woman he could ever meet. She was so different from any other woman he had seen. Honest, educated, friendly, there was something about her that could win over any person, old or young. He had not meant to get into any trouble over her. Now he hated the thought of marrying her, and hated her because he would have to marry her, and because there was no way out of it. And marriage itself is like a seal on a man's life, but the child, when it came, would be as a chain binding his life to her life, welding him to these ways of living that he hated a hundredfold more than he hated her. He had not seen her for several days now. As on time and time again in those days he thought of her; a young, pleasant-appearing woman, with brown hair and blue eyes. She made everyone like her. She was too educated, she had traveled too much, she had met too many people. She was too smart, that was it. She ought never to have come to teach school in this back-woodsy country.

He rolled a cigarette and sat by the window, waiting. As soon as Pa got up and went down to the barn, he would follow him. Jacob didn't want Ranny or Chris or Case or anyone around, when he told the old man. He knew the old man would blow up and raise thunder.

Daylight was coming. The air was heavy with the pungent, unexplainable scents of early morning in this lonely land. In spite of the drought night seemed to loose a thin dampness with its dark, sharpening the odors of new wheat struggling to grow, of grass and sage and dusty wind.

Jacob had got up from bed with a kind of vague anger and recklessness in his mind. Sitting by the window, thinking, his anger gave way slowly to resentment and something like despair. He could look at things squarely, honestly. He knew this mess was all of his own making. But God, why did it have to happen? He didn't want to marry Frace. He didn't want his life to be trapped here. He had planned on so many things for the next few years. He wanted to be a farmer. That was all he ever wanted to be. But before he settled, he wanted to do so many things. This was all of his own doing. Remembering, he could place no blame on Frace. He knew Frace loved him.

Now there was nothing to do except marry her, live with her, do the best he could.

He heard his Pa up. He waited until the old man had built a fire in the kitchen stove and gone out of the house towards the barn. Then he followed.

Once Jacob decided to do a thing he would not hem or haw, beating about the bush. He found his father cleaning mangers. Inside, the barn was still dark. Jacob found a pitch-fork and went to help. He said at once:—

"Pa, I'm going to marry Frace Cristan today. No need to lie or try to hide something you will learn anyway. I *have* to marry her."

Old Jim stopped his work and stood stock-still. He was silent for a full half-minute. Darkness hid his face.

He spoke slowly:

"So you have to marry her. How long since she told you that?"

"Four months."

"You took plenty of time makin' up your mind . . . while she waited."

Jacob thought with quick anger: I won't stand for much preaching. Aloud he said:—

"I'm not wantin' to marry her now. I don't feel any love for her."

Silence.

"What was it you felt when you was havin' your own way with her?" Old Jim asked. He leaned his pitchfork against the barn stall and came out to the doorway and light. Jacob

27

was surprised when he saw his Pa's face. Why, the old man was not going to raise hell, he just looked sober and old, sober and sort of hurt.

Jacob wanted to say: "What man could stand up and say he wouldn't have done the same thing—alone with her, believing he could? I wonder if you could have said that your own self, twenty years ago—or even now." But he knew the least said the better. He muttered: "There's no saints living on this earth, Pa. I reckon we're all pretty much the same."

Old Jim kept his back turned. Oh, what was the use of talking, wasting words? He knew Jacob would never give a minute's thought to anything he said. Nothing he could say would touch Jacob's mind one whit. This was the man his second boy had grown into.

He'd just as well say nothing, and go on up to the house for the milk buckets, and get at the morning's chores. He spoke without turning around:—

"If you are goin' to be married, I reckon you'll want me to give you some horses and cows and the like. Well, you can have 'em. I ain't goin' to cuss you, Jacob. Frace is a mighty fine woman. I ought to flatten you out for makin' her wait four months."

He turned his face and looked suddenly at Jacob. There were other things he wanted to say but he hardly knew how to put them into words. Without thinking he added quickly:—

"It's not that I'm too surprised or hurt over you doin' this thing, Jacob. But in all your life there's been a streak o' meanness and selfishness growin' ever' year in you, that none o' the others had. I reckon I'm the only one that's noticed it, as yet. I want you to live right. You will learn just what I mean, some day."

Jim broke the news at the breakfast table.

28

"There won't be no need in tryin' to keep it still. He should have married her four months ago."

Case kept his eyes on his plate. Through the open door of the bedroom Sareeny heard her father's words.

Jacob sat in silence. He could have cursed his Pa's gruff way of saying things.

After one instant, Ellen had gone on dishing hot cakes at the stove. She picked up the coffeepot and came to fill Ranny's and Case's and old Jim's cup. When she came to Jacob she stood there a moment, one hand resting on his shoulders, the pressure of her fingers a firm caress.

She said simply:—

"I'm glad for you, Jacob."

The others said nothing. Ranny went on buttering his hot cakes, refusing even to look up from his plate. Jim went on eating, though he did not relish his food, speaking only when he gruffly asked for something. His face still was flushed with anger.

Only Chris showed surprise. He could not keep his eyes off Jacob's dark-skinned face that was flushed now clear to the roots of his black hair because of this heavy silence so full of meaning.

Sareeny would have called Jacob to her and said something to him, but she did not know Frace Cristan. Until now she had never heard of her. She could think of nothing to say that would sound right. So she too was silent.

After breakfast, Jim hitched a team of horses to the old two-seated buggy. He and Ellen and Jacob got in and drove over the road towards Sarpy.

Frace Cristan lived in a little building furnished by the county for the teacher. Neighbors had wondered, that spring when the school term was finished, why Frace planned on living the time between terms in that little one-room shack, instead of spending her vacation in a pleasanter place.

29

When Jacob drove up to her yard with his father and mother, she came out the door to greet them. Her face was flushed. There was doubt in her eyes.

Jacob left no time for embarrassed silence. He jumped down from the buggy with the words:—

"I brought my folks along to witness our marriage, Frace."

She looked quickly from them to him. The muscles around her mouth quivered, so that she forced a smile she did not feel to steady them. Her eyes filled with tears.

"Oh, Jacob." Her voice was low.

To cover their own embarrassment, Ellen made slow work of getting down from the buggy, and Jim was busy with the make-believe difficulty of fitting the buggy whip into its socket.

They went into the clean, quiet, one room.

Jacob helped her find the marriage license he had bought, halfheartedly, four months ago. Jim went to fetch the minister. It was all happening so quietly, so quickly, that it cut Frace more than all the doubt and hurt she had endured secretly. Jacob knew she was waiting to marry him, of course. But what must he really think of her, to treat her like this?

Ellen came and put both arms around her, saying simply and honestly:—

"From the first time I met you, I've liked you, Frace. I'm proud you're marryin' my Jacob." Her eyes looked down into Frace's face, seeing and understanding all Frace felt. Oh, why were Jacob and his father such fools, barging in here like this? She said with strange gentleness: "Why not wait till evenin' and have a better weddin' over at home, with no one there but our own folks? Sareeny and Case are home now." She turned to Jacob.

He frowned. "Why wait?"

Frace's eyes were suddenly cold and hard. Without looking toward Ellen she spoke to her.

"As Jacob says, there's no need of waiting longer."

Riding home, Frace sat beside Jacob on the back seat of the buggy. Jacob had tried to talk, making conversation because he felt he should, but she saw through his efforts and did not encourage them. Most of the way she sat in silence, thinking. A year ago, when she had come to this place to teach school, she could not have foreseen all this. But if she could have foreseen it, would she have turned and gone away, she wondered? All her life she had been orphaned, alone. Now she was one of the Gores, of Sarpy Creek. This strong, dark-skinned man beside her was her husband, if she could hold him. And she would hold him, she told herself, because she loved him, because she was already heavy with his child.

She sat quietly beside him. As they neared home, the doubt and worry left her face; and secretively, just as quietly, she began to feel a kind of peace. She seemed a very ordinary little woman, with brown hair and blue eyes and a rather plain face. Her one charm lay in the frank, friendly way she could win trust and confidence, when her natural self. Her eyes turned to Jacob's dark face, seeking silent satisfaction in the strength she saw there and in the thick spread of his shoulders.

Now for the first time in four months, he turned his brown eyes to look full into hers. His thoughts were veiled. She knew his mind was set against her.

She looked away again. Thoughts rose in her mind like a swift prayer. I'll show him. I want to love this life. I want them all to love me. Yet, withal, had she been deeply honest with herself, she would have known that she was a fool to love him and become his wife. Had she chosen she could have done much better with her life. Now her back was deliberately turned to things that might have been. She faced life here in a hilly land of solitude and sweeping winds, stormy, changing, hard. She would need patience, and she knew it could only come from within her self.

# CHAPTER 5

JACOB'S marriage seemed hardly to stir a ripple in their daily way of things. He, Ranny, and old Jim, Case with them, went right on cutting and curing the sparse hay in the north pasture. Ellen went right ahead with her canning and sealing of gooseberry preserves. In one day the neighbors heard of it and got over their surprise. In two days it was like yesterday's news. Jacob Gore and Frace Cristan had married sudden-like. They were going to live with Jacob's folks, for a year, and Jacob would farm with his father. Frace was already four months or more with Jacob's child, but they were married. Even now neighbors were beginning to slowly forget that Jacob and Frace had been as man and wife before wedlock. This drought was too big a worry for them to give much thought to idle gossip. Wheat was yellowing with slow death in the fields. If it did not rain soon, winter would find pastures bare of grass for livestock; and it would find many a pocketbook bare of money, too. Money that was needed even in good years, to buy all the things they could not grow or save in summers.

That first morning, Ellen had drawn Frace into the room where Sareeny lay. Frace's blue eyes met the long look in Sareeny's gray eyes before and while Ellen spoke.

"This is Jacob's wife, Sareeny. Her name is Frace."

Frace held Sareeny's hand and looked down at her. She had thought Jacob's family strange, seeming ever to hide their true thoughts. But there was no doubting Sareeny's friendliness.

33

When the buggy had stopped in the yard of this old log house Jacob had jumped out, and speaking to Frace as though she were a child he had said: "You go on in the house, Frace." And then he had walked away towards the barns, leaving his father to unhitch and care for the horses.

Sareeny was saying: "I hope you will like every one of us, Frace."

Frace thrust her uneasiness from her, determined. She smiled down at Sareeny and Sareeny's baby. She said simply:—

"I do like you, all of you. I want you all to learn to like me, more and more. I want you all to love me. Your mother knows I grew up in a home for orphaned children. I've never known what it was to have a family."

Jacob kept out of Frace's way as much as he could. When he could not keep out of her way he eyed her secretly. He could see she was winning them all over, completely, as one rakes in winnings in a shrewd game. She'd lit right in to helping Ellen with the work. It was all seeming different than Jacob had expected it, somehow. The second day found Frace her old self. She was not being meek, chilled by his treatment of her, as he had expected she would be. If she was hurt she hid it. She went right ahead, talking and acting as if there were not a thing wrong. She could cleverly bring laughter to the lips of any of them, and she laughed as much as anyone. It caused Jacob dull anger, so that he was learning to hate her more than ever. He swore to himself that he would never live with her. Because she had been willing to let him have his way with her, now she bore his child, binding him to her with strong bonds no mortal man could break. He could not run away because ever would these bonds be here when he returned. He forgot that having his way with her had not been easy. Now she worked, side by side with his old Mom, shoving her hands into greasy suds of dishwater,

34

or rubbing his Pa's old blue shirts on the washboard, as if she were not a high educated woman used to earning money to buy any pretty thing she wanted. Frace had more nice clothes than Jacob would ever believe a woman could need. Even her underwear was smooth shimmering silk, a thing unheard of in his mother's—or even Sareeny's—life. Because he did not want her and hated her being his wife, Jacob could find fault with everything she did, everything she wore, even the very things that had first drawn him to her, before.

Now that Sareeny was recovering from the birth of her first child, she longed to be up and about, doing something to help. She and Case were both worried over what they were going to do. They did not like the thought of staying in her father's house too long. Neighbors had dropped in to see them, some bringing presents for the baby. With simple sincerity every neighbor who came wished Jacob and Frace good luck and good living. Sareeny had seen everyone—except Felix Eden and his father; and Dorcy Fry. She would be glad to see Felix and his old Dad. In Dorcy Fry she had not much interest. She did not know Dorcy very well. She disliked Dorcy's husband, Olen, a big brute of a man lazy as all get out. Ellen had never been overly friendly with the Frys.

Ellen would not let Sareeny up from bed until the right time for her to be up and around. Sareeny weren't no heathen woman, she said, to have a baby and in no time at all be up as if nothing had happened. She must take care of herself. There was enough unexpected things happened already, for one month. Ellen said as long as she had lived on Sarpy this was the way it had been. A long spell of just common workaday way of things, then a short spell of sudden unexpected things. For a year . . . two years, nothing would happen; then . . . Bingo!

The very next day seemed to bear out the truth of her words.

It was the day before the prayer meeting.

Old Man Eden was killed by a two-year-old bronco horse he was breaking to work in the fields. Thus Sareeny did not get to see him ever again.

The horse was a pretty thing. Sorrel color, as smooth and shining as rich velvet. But it had eaten some of the wild loco that flowered out in wide creamy-colored patches on the open range, and the weed had made it crazy as a loon.

Because he had worked the horse earlier in the day and the animal had gone along calm and steady as an old field mare, Eden had decided to use it for cultivating the strip of corn growing close to the house.

The horse had balked.

Olen Fry, who lived in the house across the road, sat on his porch in the shade like the lazy good-for-nothing man he was, and watched it all.

He saw Eden come around in front of the horse and the locoed beast rear suddenly on its hind legs, knocking the old man down, trampling him and crushing the bones in his chest. By the time Olen could run shouting across the road the horse was away towards the far side of the field, dragging the cultivator, tearing a jagged, crazy streak through the drought-stunted corn.

Ellen and Jim, Herman and Birdie Leidermen, all the neighbors, hurried to Eden's home as soon as they heard of it, wanting to do anything that could be done. The old man would die. They all knew that. He breathed blood from his nose and coughed it from his broken chest. The doctor came as quick as they could get him from the big town on Yellowstone River; he went in the room where they had laid Eden on the bed. The doctor gave him medicine to ease his pain and make breathing easier, but he knew there weren't no use.

Felix was gone far up into the mountains with the artist fellow who had lived here less than a year and spent all his time painting pictures of the West. Someone mentioned sending riders to hunt Felix out, up there in the timbered canyons. But Eden turned his face sideways on the pillow and muttered:—

"No, no . . . leave Felix be."

He had been hurt in the late afternoon. The sun set with pale red and twilight turned to summer night. Still he lived. He lay on the bed in Felix's room of the house he had lived so many years with. His mind was as clear as the most peaceful moment he could have remembered. And because he knew he would not be here when daylight came again, he was remembering many things; little happenings sweeping back out of long, long stretches of time, like years blending into minutes. Felix, playing about the yard, barelegged and bare-footed, in knee-breeches, laughing sometimes till the sound of him made others laugh over something that tickled his boy mind; turning his soft and merry eyes up to your face—or tilting his head back till they looked up at the sky and the sun they could never see. Felix going away to school and coming home with his big thick boots a yard square, the pages clean white with little bulging dots and dashes he read with his finger tips.

Felix, now a young man restless and unhappy in his dark world. Oh, his father had seen it.

Towards midnight Eden roused and opened his eyes. He saw the doctor leaning over him. He felt no pain. The drugs had soothed his whole broken body with a dull numbness. It seemed to him that he might have just wakened from a long sleep. But even while sleeping his mind had been busy, deciding for him things that must be done. He heard the hushed voices of his neighbors beyond the closed door. He spoke to the doctor and his voice was almost natural. He knew he was about to die.

"Bring Herman Leidermen in here."

As the doctor went to open the door, Dorcy Fry came in with cold, clean cloths. She came to the bed and leaned over him, brushing the red froth blood from his nostrils and mouth. He looked up at her gratefully. She was bony, thin-faced, homely. Her lips were a stern straight line, as though unused to smiling. Dorcy never would show what she felt. Now, the pity in his face stung her more than ever, because he was dying.

He said: "You're a good woman, Dorcy."

She did not answer, and he added slowly: "I've heard him beatin' you . . . abusin' you for no reason. Many a night it was near more than Felix and me could stand . . . listenin' to what was goin' on and nuthin' but the road between his place and our'n. No man should treat a woman as he treats you."

Her hands stopped their movement with the white cloths. She stood motionless a moment before looking down, directly at him.

"I reckon me and my kids will shore miss you, neighbor."

Beyond the closed door neighbors' low voices halted. The doctor came in with Herman. Herman was a small man, Dutchy-looking, as good as gold. Eden told him to get pen and ink and paper.

Herman wrote down what Eden spoke in slow words.

"All my lands, all my livestock, my moneys in the bank, everything I own in the world belongs to my son Felix—to be shared equally in the benefits of by him and his mother, Arminta Potter - provided - she comes here to live with him and makes his home her home as long as she shall live."

Dorcy and the doctor signed their names as witnesses.

Eden turned his eyes, now strangely haggard, up to Herman's.

"You know where you can look for her, Herman. I'm doin' what I feel I should do. You find her and bring her here. And I name you to look after Felix's interests and lease his land and see that things make money."

The neighbors, now standing silently in this bedroom or yonder in the big log-beamed room that was the kitchen, listened in surprised wonder. They had not known that Eden had a wife, Felix a living mother, somewhere. So long they had believed Eden to be a widower. So many times they had passed him on the road, or opened their doors to him in winter, and put another plate for him on their supper tables. Truth to tell, as they often said in later years when speaking of this night, you can never say you know a man completely. Not in ten years, or twenty, or many more.

Eden told Dorcy to go in the kitchen and make coffee for these neighbors who had come hoping to be of help to him. And those were the last words he spoke. He lay back on his pillow with relieved satisfaction. He'd be leaving his house in order now.

Leave Felix be, he had said. Let no man go to fetch him. Let Herman be the first to tell him when the blind son came down from the mountains home again.

Later, the doctor helped Dorcy cover the bruised and broken body with sheets.

It was the young doctor's first call from far out in this remote and thinly settled land. He had rushed across a seventy-mile distance by train until the railroad ended; then, met by a guide and furnished with a horse, he had ridden until it seemed the distance would never end. He had never before realized that this rugged country spread so far. To him it was akin to an unexplored wilderness, almost as it must have been long ago, yet hiding among its deep hills actual homes of hard-working people, like a soft hum of life in its silence.

Startled now, he listened to them. They were going to build a coffin for this old man's body. The baking, oppressive heat of the sun would not give them time to travel that long distance for a boughten coffin, with all the nicer things they did not have.

Later in the morning the men folks sawed and smoothed the white pine lumber for the plain box. The women lined it with snowy white sheeting. Old Man Mills was there, ready and waiting to do his part. Solemn feeling, and the knowledge death always brings to reveal the futile, foolish struggles always indulged in during life on this earth, was their farewell to this neighbor who had lived among them so long. Later in the afternoon of that same day they buried the body in the sandy slope of the cemetery just west of the little town. Only friends stood about the grave.

What, Mills said, speaks with greater meaning than the silence of a cemetery, whose markers bear the names of people who have lived and loved and gone again through the far last doors of life, that open but one way and then close with swift silence?

And blind Felix, somewhere in yonder mountains, knew nothing of all this that had struck like lightning.

Herman Leidermen's fat little wife, Birdie, sat on the buggy seat and cried all the way home from the funeral. She thought Felix ought to have been there and she said so to Herman.

"And what about his wife?" she went on. "Where was she?"

Herman stared straight on down the road

"I reckon I'll have to go fetch her, soon as Felix comes home to go with me."

Birdie looked at him with puzzled irritation.

"How long did you know Eden's wife was still alive?"

"Twenty years."

"You never said anything. Why didn't they live together?"

"That's their own business."

"But Felix thought his mother was dead."

Herman's eyes hardened. "And well she might be, to him."

Birdie's blue eyes grew dark with interest and she looked at him closely. "Herman, what in the name of tarnation are you so close-mouthed about? I don't like the sound of what you just said. What do you mean?"

He squirmed in his seat and reached out with his buggy whip to crack old Tobey smartly on the rump. Tobey flicked his tail resentfully.

"Hang it all Birdie, there can't be no easy explainin' of all the whys and wherefores of us humans' actions. Now shut your mouth about it, honey. And don't never ask me no more questions."

Birdie hushed, but there was something about it all she did not know, and her woman's mind would never let her rest until she did.

Herman would never tell her. Birdie was a fine little woman, but she talked too easy, and not one human being alive in the world but what likes to find out something secretive and hidden about the other fellow. Herman's religion made him believe simply that God Almighty forever has His own ways of working things out, and who are we to throw a monkey wrench in His plans?

He started thinking of that time he had seen Eden's wife. He and Eden had driven a bunch of cattle, over five hundred of the dumb critters, from here to the railroad at the big town on Yellowstone River. That had been in the fall of 1900. Lord, what a long time gone. Here it was now, over twenty years later, a big war had come and gone, people were talking drought, and all that remained of Eden was back yonder buried in dirt. When you stopped to remember, this drought was no worse than others that had been.

He and Eden had bunched the cattle at night and slept beside campfires. Antelopes had roamed about in herds then, as the buffalo had so long ceased to do even before that time.

Coyotes had been a sight thicker than now. He remembered the frosty mornings and Eden straddling a half-broke bronc. How that feller could ride in his day! A horse had mighty near to buck out of its own skin to throw Eden, then.

And there had been the saloon in the big town. The clink of glasses, the smell of whisky. Smoke, and loud voices, and talk like is always heard where men are just men.

She had come down the stairway. A fine-looking woman, in spite of all her paint, a-wearing a silver dress. She stopped on the stairway and stood stock-still before coming on down and over to their table.

"Well, here I am, Fred," she had said to Eden.

Herman remembered Eden's face, for it had been a terrible thing. The muscles in Eden's jaws had stood out in little quivering knots when he answered her.

"Yeh, here you are. Feel right at home, I guess."

Eden had taken a ten-dollar bill from his pocket and waved it before her eyes. "I got ten dollars, my own self. . . ."

She hadn't said anything in answer to that direct insult. But she had leaned forward and half-whispered:—

"Fred, how is the baby?"

Eden was in misery. It had been in his eyes with tears and hatred and a look of murder.

"You will never see him," he had answered. "You will never get a dime of my money—if you were the last woman on earth. You damned whore!"

No, many a time there's no explaining the ways and actions of us humans. For instance, Old Eden changing his mind. But Eden had made him promise years ago to keep his mouth shut, and keep it shut he would.

Now this business of looking after the lands, the livestock, and the money belonging to Felix was a serious business, when you so wanted to do the thing right and make no mistake. First he would have to get it all down on papers, listing every single and last thing Felix owned in the world, with what the law said it was worth. Then he must help Felix to manage it all so that every year there would be some money made, little or much according to the sun, the wind, and the rain of each changing season.

Herman meant to get Case Gyler and his wife Sareeny to live there with Felix. Case was a good worker. Sareeny was a good woman. Felix should be happy enough with them, because they were young people, too. Herman was worried in his own mind over the coming of Felix's mother. What manner of woman would she be, with a host of such things as she could remember and look back on? Oh, she knew what suffering was, for he had noticed the marks of it stamped in the flesh of her face that one time he had seen her.

But it is a ticklish business, too, a-putting women like her and Sareeny together. Now Sareeny, there weren't no purer woman on God's earth. She was pretty-like, too, with her quiet, kind, easygoin' ways, that made all the people like her. He had known her always—from the time she had been a baby, a-nursing at her own mother's breasts. She had been a bashful, shy little woman, growing up, until she had started going to neighborhood dances and parties, meeting other young people. More than one young fellow had been uneasy with love for Sareeny, before she married Case. Now with a youngster of her own . . . Herman could well imagine how powerful proud she was of it.

There weren't no easy life for a woman out here in this lonesome windswept part of Montana. The sun blistered in summer, its hot glare hurting your eyes. In winter the snow walled out the rest of the world and winds roamed their frozen ways, gusting around the corners of the house till the very sound of it made you think your own home, however humble, was a wonderful thing.

Herman thought what a glory it was some young women would live a life as life was here because they loved a man. So many young people, old ones, too, went a-seeking down long roads' lengths, answering a call of street lights a-sparkling, or a living painted with brighter, ever different colors. Happiness is where you find it.

At home that night, he and Birdie ate the cold supper she fixed, neither of them talking much.

As always, Herman was the first to bed. Birdie blew out the oil lamp, and then as always with her everlasting religion she stood there in the darkness a moment and whispered a little prayer. So long had this been a habit that Herman scarcely noticed it. It was something neither of them ever mentioned. A little fact in their lives that never came into the light of day.

"God, wherever my brother Jack is in this world, please take care of him. Watch over him with your great wisdom and lead him to live a good life. Send him home someday to us, this I ask in the name of Almighty God, Amen."

Neither of them knew, or would ever know, that Jack had long ago died, penniless, in a little town far to the south. And the people there, not knowing his name or from where he came, had buried him in a nameless grave.

And his bones and flesh had long since rotted away.

Tonight Herman listened. The thought burst suddenly upon his mind that maybe Birdie was a making a plumb fool of herself a-standing there talking to God every night. God never gave no sign or sound that He had heard. There was only silence, with the wind a whish-sh-sh-sh-ing through the pine trees that stood in the dark yard. But the next second Herman was ashamed. He reckoned he should never question a human's pitiful faith in the only thing a human has to pin his faith on; you had to have faith to have hope, and the greater your faith, the stronger your hope.

A half-hour later Birdie woke him and asked him to "Stop that *snoring!*"

# CHAPTER 6

O N SUNDAY, Felix and his friend, Caleb the artist fellow, started their downward trip out of the mountains, towards home.

Felix did not want to go. He had never before so wanted to linger on and on up here where the cool breezes fanned away the summer's heat, and you could lie for hours on the thick beds of pine needles that padded the earth; doing nothing, thinking easily. And you could hear from near and far the thundering tinkle of rushing water leaping to spray against the rocks. Ice water, clearer than any crystal, and hugging in its lively depths gleaming rainbow trout. Off in the distance somewhere the soft roar of a waterfall, and sometimes the shrill call of an eagle from the sky.

It is good for a man's soul. Felix could but listen and that he did. His thoughts were busy, and he beat down the restless dissatisfaction within himself.

Caleb had painted pictures, sometimes working tensely for hours, then flinging the thing away with sick disgust because it did not please him. Caleb was more than forty years old, but he acted like a child, sometimes, when his work was not easy. If Felix talked or if he was silent it made no difference. Caleb would curse, loudly, fluently, easily. The words he used would have made the old devil himself hide his face in shame.

"If a painting is good," Caleb would say, "it's got to say something. Why did I ever start all this, anyway? Why didn't I get me a peaceful, respectful job and live like a human being?"

Felix would laugh to himself. A few hours later Caleb would be busy with brush and colors again. Caleb was a funny man, without any effort at being so, or even realizing it himself. His loud, rasping voice most always held a mournful, complaining note. And there was ever that why, why, why. "Why do I work like a slave and worry myself bald and lay awake nights to work at picturing the wicked expression in a wild horse's eyes? Why do I want to be an artist anyway? Why don't I get married and forget it? Because I'm too smart to get married, that is why. I'd rather lay awake and worry about the wild horse, at least he don't talk back." Caleb's three favorite things to complain about were marriage, and artists that were fools, and critics that were worse. But it was all bluster. He was not a good artist and he knew it. And he didn't blame the critics for telling him so. The truth of it was he got enough satisfaction out of life to do three men. He had traveled to some of the most interesting, out-of-the-way places on earth, and stored up in his mind were enough fascinating things to make you forget all about sleep and bed, if you could get him by a warm fireside on a long winter evening.

He had bought a comfortable, old-fashioned house a mile from Felix's home. He had hired a good stout Norwegian woman who kept it as neat as a pin and did his laundry and cooked finer meals for him than he could have bought anywhere. Yet many a time he looked up at her after a hearty meal, his blue eyes opened wide, and rasped slowly: "Why don't you learn to cook?"

Beneath his habits there was plenty of goodness, and Felix knew it well.

The trails they followed were sometimes tortuous, twisting downward between high rock walls and around boulders as big as houses. Often they curved through friendly pine forests, under the great knarred or stately old trees.

Little tender young pines were growing here and there like silent children.

Felix had raised his saddle horse from a colt. The animal was as gentle and affectionate as any pet can be. Its name was Master. Felix's father had named it that, for always the horse had been so proud, as if conscious of its snowy beauty, and born to wear a fine saddle.

The old pack mare was the middle horse on the trail. She trudged along, carrying her load dutifully. Caleb led the way, most often staring ahead of himself with silent thinking. He had the makings of a picture in his mind, and he felt that it would be good, for this picture would say something.

It had happened this morning at camp.

They were up with the dawn. Caleb had fried the trout to a flaky brown and turned them out on a plate. He realized of a sudden that Felix had been gone overly long down there by the stream. . . .

Felix had stood in a little clearing near the swift waters. His face was touched with sadness as it so often was when he was alone with his thoughts. Up, off yonder, mountain peaks shouldered their wild beauty into the sky, and the mighty sun peered above them driving away the soft bright colors that had announced its near approach. That light touched Felix's face and made his fair hair fairer. To the south, across many canyons, beyond miles and miles of thickly wooded foothills, lay Sarpy land like a gray mystery. There flowered around Felix's feet patches of blue wild forget-me-nots and long crimson sprays of Indian paintbrush. The mountainous background aloft against the sky had been a beautiful sight to see.

Caleb would paint that picture: Felix standing in the midst of all that beauty; and he would call it simply "The Blind Man."

They traveled leisurely, resting the horses. In late afternoon of the third day they were in the foothills. They found signs of Indians camping. Tepee poles, fire-blackened stones, and once a papoose's crude doll fashioned by some squaw mother's fingers. The trail followed closely by a stream now. Wild currant and gooseberry bushes grew thick and high under the cottonwoods and willows and aspen. Spread out over all the foothills on all sides were the greenish black of cedar, spruce, and pine. But down here along the passage of the water all was varying shades of bright green, spotted here and there with the quivering silver of shining aspen leaves.

A black cloud rose up in the west and spread, its gray mists clinging around the high mountain peaks, hiding them. Down through the piney woods came an easy wind with the scent of rain. Caleb shouted over his shoulder:

"We may get wet, Felix!"

Felix turned his face upward and breathed the pungent odor. Let the rain come. Lord, let it come, and fall on every hopeful farmer's field. Let it sweep on across the foothills, to Sarpy. Felix smiled to himself, and thought. . . . Dad is probably watching the clouds too, hoping it will rain, worrying that it won't. . . .

Drought was an ugly thing, thought Felix. It spread into the land silently, treacherously, cheating good folks of all they asked from earth and life. When their crops in the fields fail, good farmers do not only have to do without the things money buys. Good simple folks like these on Sarpy were cheated of something else, too. Felix knew that the very lives of these people here were intermingled with the lives of the things they planted and the things they grew, to be stored away for comfort against want and cold need. It was a good life, too. Simple and good and real. A man grown up found himself a wife and they lived together and loved each other and begot children. They worked hard and earned simple pleasures. They never asked too much from life. The years brought on a kind of peace, and content seemed easy to find. Felix's thinking, as on countless times before, could turn so easily to an altar of poignant thought. . . . If only my eyes could see. . . .

The rain began to fall in light, quick drops. Caleb spurred his horse into a gallop and the others followed. Thunder rumbled like a great landslide deep in the earth. Around a curve of the thicketed trail they came suddenly upon the lone white tepee of an Indian camp. A herd of sheep, brought here to graze for the summer in the foothills' richer pastures, were bunched for the night in a near-by crude corral.

It was the summer home of Letitia and her father.

Letitia's mother had died fourteen years before, when Letitia was a chubby, shabbily dressed, unclean little Indian girl of seven.

Ever would Letitia turn from the sick memory of that death. Never could she forget that last look at her mother's body, her mother's face, and her mother's hands. A thousand hard hoofs of stampeding cattle had trampled over the body and crushed the life from it, beating its broken bones and bleeding flesh into the soil.

There would come times when Letitia could not force back thoughts of that day; and she would remember standing on a hilltop and screaming with terrified tears, watching her mother run to escape the path of the mad beasts. She would remember her father off yonder switching his horse into a wild race to rescue her; then the cattle sweeping on, the dull roar of their hoofs pounding the soil and finally passing by.

Down there in the billowing, choking dust lay her mother. Letitia had found her father kneeling beside the body, his snorting horse panting and backed away; her father had said nothing, but after a while he had stood up and walked away a little distance, his bare arms folded on his chest, and he had stood looking into the Southland a long time without a sound. Letitia had crept forward to look into her mother's face.

After that, the father had taken Letitia to the Indian agency to live and she had made her home among the whites. He had gone back to his tepee alone, and tended his herds alone, and alone he rode the range in silence, shunning even the members of his tribe. Letitia never would know of his thoughts in those long days of the long years she had lived in white men's cities. She did not know how he sat beside his lone campfire in nights of summer and nights of winter, pondering. Sometimes he rode his horse on some high pinnacle of the crumpled land and sat like a bronzed statue, staring off into miraged distance.

The Indian's world was ended.

At his rare visits to see his daughter he would watch her inscrutably. She wore white girls' dresses, she laughed and talked and arranged her hair as white girls do, and always she was scented like the flowers of the hills. She was pretty. He was pleased. Thus he said to her once:—

"Be white. Do not be a squaw."

They had told him she was quick to learn. He did not know she had an alert, brilliant mind. He had all the wisdom of his race but he would not have understood. Letitia was gifted had she chosen to use her gifts. But she did not choose to use them. Something in her mind had sent her back to the peace of her father's tepee; to the calm hills and the herds and the untreacherous sky. She was proud of and pampered her own beauty. She was carefree and happy . . . until Case Gyler had come and gone. Her child by Case was born in the same week that Case had married Sareeny. So quiet had Letitia been over the child's birth that everything about it had been cloaked in silence. The little black-haired, chubby boy lived half the time with Letitia's aunt, and

Letitia's aunt was a fat, lazy, true-to-type squaw, good-natured and sensible with the raising of a child; she let him run naked and grow in natural health. But Letitia had many plans for her son. She planned silently that he should be educated and trained and grown into a fine man. And because Letitia loved Case, she would never tell Case of the child's birth. Or such were Letitia's plans.

Now when Felix and Caleb sat in her father's tepee she served them food and drink with the dignity and easy grace of a charming hostess. To Caleb she was politely friendly. To Felix she was warmly kind, turning her smoky-agate colored eyes to him with silent friendship. She had known Felix for many years, and yesterday she had learned of his father's death.

A slow fire burned outside the tepee, spitting at the drowsy rain that teased the glowing coals. Letitia watched Caleb's face with expressionless amusement when her father turned away without a word and crawled between blankets to sleep. She waited until Caleb had taken his own blankets under the sloping sides of the tepee, before she said to Felix:—

"Sit with me by the fire, Felix. I will talk with you."

His blue eyes smiled towards her, pleased. He wore a gray silk shirt, unbuttoned at the neck, and his shoulders spread beneath it with thick strength.

"I'd like that, Letitia."

Her eyes never left his face. "I came up from Sarpy land just yesterday, Felix. There is a change . . . for you . . . I find it hard, hard to tell you, Felix."

"A change in Sarpy land?" he laughed. "It's unbelievable."

Silently she looked at him, as though wondering whether to tell him, after all. "Yes, Felix. But then time always brings changes. I went first to the post office, and I learned that your friends Case Gyler and his wife Sareeny have returned to make their home on Sarpy. And they have a baby."

He said with simple gladness: "I can about imagine how happy Sareeny is with that. She is like a sister to me. I'm going to see them the first thing when I get home."

Letitia sat staring with steady eyes at the fire. Her thoughts saw Case's eyes, brown and tender, close there looking into her own, and she remembered his arms reaching for her with confident strength. You Case . . . making me love you . . . do you think I am only a squaw, forgetting all the things you said to me . . .

Felix spoke to her.

"But what did you mean about the change, Letitia?"

She told him; stumbling a little over her words, for it is not easy to tell a young man his father is dead and buried, when only a few days ago the father was going about his life and they were riding the range together.

She told him all as she had learned it yesterday: people were talking of his mother and father having been parted all these years; and the father had said with almost his dying breath that the mother should come here and live the rest of her life with Felix. Herman Leidermen was going to fetch her, as soon as Felix returned to go with him. Herman Leidermen wanted Case Gyler to live with Felix and farm the land. . . .

Felix had said nothing after the shock of first understanding the truth of her words. When he stood up from his place by the fire, the cool rainy needles of a pine branch brushed his face, and his groping fingers found the branch and clutched it tight. He knew he must believe what Letitia was telling him, unbelievable as it was.

Rain and wind whispers went on about their wide, freedom-swept way above the earth. The stream down there, that had been a carefree crystal clear this morning, was now muddled and littered. It would go on that way for days, until the water slowly cleared again, forgetting and crystal clear.

Felix was a grown man, and a grown man meets grief with a solid front. No need to hurry on home now. There was nothing there, except the house. Tomorrow he would find it there, just as it had always been to him; something he could not see, but could feel the nearness of as he rode closer, and seeming to put touchless, invisible arms around him when he entered the door. The house would be waiting, silent and understanding, just as it was waiting now, emptied of human soul, alone in the rain and dark.

He was not too shocked at Letitia's words of his mother. He had known long ago there must be something back of his father's silence. He had never been able to break through that silence of his father. But the world he had shared with him had been so complete, that he had only wondered about his mother now and then. Now it was like that world was gone with his father; and he was entering another world where his father never would walk or talk and new people came close to fill out his life.

His thoughts turned to his mother. He could in no way imagine her, or what had caused her and his father to part. Now if she came here to live, what kind of woman would she prove to be? He would learn to know her. Until he did know her he would not know what to think about her or what was back of all his father's silence.

Tomorrow he would ride down into Sarpy land with Caleb. How many times, when they had been returning from similar trips like this, had he said to Caleb when they reached the big hills overlooking Sarpy Creek:—

"Do you see Dad working in the fields?"

That single thought brought him the complete realization

54

of his loss. He bowed his head on his hands. Letitia moved from her silent place by the fire to lay more wood on the flames.

# CHAPTER 7

SAREENY and Case moved into Felix's home on a sultry, tight-aired day in July. Since that blessed rain that had come in on a night of June, it seemed that each day whimsical nature must express itself in some determined way. A sudden drenching shower of cold rain, or in some late afternoon a swift darkening of the skies with lightning flashing blue-white along the hilly horizons, and thunder breaking loud and sharp.

On this day it seemed as though everything on earth stood still and silent in the heat. All over the range land the cattle and horses had retreated to the nearest shade, where they stood flicking their tails or slinging their heads to rout the flies that tormented them.

When Sareeny's and Case's wagon topped the big hill overlooking Felix's father's place they looked down and saw the little town with its one short dirt street running east and west; a few wooden houses sat unevenly beside each other along the boardwalk; the big building, with its high second-story false front, was all the more outstanding because of its clean white coat of paint. Each summer, Clyde Parker, the owner, pridefully renewed that coat. There was a dance hall, long and rough and ugly, minus a few windows. At the far end of the street, facing east and next door to the schoolhouse, was a friendly little white church with a bell in the steeple.

Down the westward road a piece, stood the house that would be Sareeny's home. It looked to the south, and for some reason she scarcely knew, herself, Sareeny was glad. It may be that the north blows down the cold of winter, and the east wind ever means dark weather; and the west is the land of the setting sun. But the south . . . a house that looks toward the south faces a land of eternal warmth and balmy winds; and there is ever the bright yellow sunshine about the door as the sun makes its way across the clear sky of any season.

The house was built of big solid logs. Sarpy Creek flowed almost across the yard, and there was plenty of long green grass and sturdy stout-limbed cottonwoods to cool the breeze and shade. Half-acre patches of wild-cherry and wild-rose bushes clustered on the bottom land behind the house. Even a dozen apple trees were there, that Felix's father had planted long ago, coaxing their growth these many years.

Sareeny looked down at the house and the yard and the trees. Inside of her, silent, she felt she wanted to cry. Because she felt she had about everything she wanted now. A house that would be a home in a land that was home. And a husband she could never tell in words how much she loved . . . even if she would try; she smiled to herself now, her face turned down to the baby in her lap, and thought: "There is only one way I can ever tell Case how *much* I love him and that's by daily living . . . a long, long time from now maybe he will know." She wouldn't want Case to know what she was thinking, though. She just wouldn't, that's all. There are some things a man and wife know perfectly well are true, but they don't talk about them. Like Case's eyes when he looked at her. Never once had he looked at her that his eyes didn't love her silently, often times without him realizing it.

They passed the little church. The wagon rumbled across the Creek's old bridge and turned off the main road. Case jumped down and opened the squeaky pole gate. Sareeny drove through, into the yard, holding the lines of the horses in one hand while the other arm held the bundled baby close to her breast.

The first thing Sareeny did after entering the house and putting the sleeping baby on the center of the big bed was open all the windows of all the rooms and let the still sultry air seep through if it would.

Oh, this was a nice house. The windows even had weights and little ropes concealed in the casing so that all you had to do to raise or lower them was give them a flip of your hand. (Sareeny's mother's windows had to be raised and propped open with a stick.) There was even smooth, gaily patterned linoleum on the floors of the front room, the dining room, and kitchen. (Sareeny's mother had never had a rug and not a foot of all her floors but was splintery from her scrubbing and her children's long-ago playing, romping feet.)

Winter cold would have a hard time creeping through the thick log walls of this house. There were seven rooms; two bedrooms upstairs, the stairway turning in its upward strength from the dining room. A west bedroom opened off the kitchen, and there Sareeny and Case would sleep; there the baby lay now, a sleeping bundle with pink hands and face and feet uncovered on the white spread.

The southern half of the ground floor held the living room in the southwest corner. Long and high with its big polished log beams running the full length, it was light and airy with its many paned windows opening into the west. A natural stone fireplace spread across the back end. There were two long rows of books lined neatly on built-in shelves; Sareeny ran her hand over them almost lovingly; she loved to read, but never had she been in the same house with so many books, before. A piano stood straight and proud across a corner. Sareeny went to it . . . how she wished she could play. . . . be able to sit down and take the music from it in gay or restful sounds, or as she felt inside. Maybe Felix would teach her. Felix could make that thing talk. And in his room was a violin, too, that he could play. Making mellow music that could turn away your thoughts from the worries of every day. Eden had spent many a dollar on Felix's learning of all these things.

"If my boy can't have sight he shall have knowledge a-plenty." And Felix had gone to schools a long ways off, studying, learning; the languages of people in faraway lands around the earth; music; and in evenings when Felix was home again, his father had read to him from the books. The best in fiction and fact, Felix had said.

. . . And Case stopped going to school even while he was yet a boy . . . he did not finish the eighth grade . . . and I've never been inside the door of a high school . . . Sareeny turned away from the books and the piano and her thoughts. She and Case were happy. There was a heap of things to live for, even though a person wasn't brimful of book learning.

The dining room came next. It had only one window and that looked out into the cool shadows of the porch. But the window was high and wide and opened on hinges, like doors. The room that had always been Felix's, and would always continue to be, was in the southeast corner. That long open front porch was pleasant and inviting with a glassed door on one end opening into the living room, and a glassed door on the other end opening into Felix's room, and the great bay window of the dining room in the center.

Oh, Sareeny was glad of this home. Everything in it was as clean as soap and water could make it; because only yesterday she and her mother and Jacob's wife Frace had finished scrubbing and dusting it. All the curtains were washed fresh and smoothly ironed. Every floor was spotless and free of dust. Later, when she got spare time, Sareeny would knit colorful, oval-shaped rag rugs for all the bedrooms. Felix would never be sorry he had let this good fortune come to her and Case.

Soon now Felix would be returning from the big town on Yellowstone River, where he had gone with old Herman to find Felix's mother. They would bring her back here to live. Sareeny had talked little about it, but she had wondered over Felix's mother. She hoped the mother would like her and that they would be better friends with each other. They could all live together happy in this house.

Down at the barns Case had put the horses away for the night with their helping of grain and hay. Now he stood beside the corral fence, one foot resting on the bottom rail and his arms on the top rail, looking across the fields he would farm. He would have to feed his work horses well, because there was plenty of work waiting to be done. There would be some harvesting, in spite of the early drought. All the Creek bottom land was covered with alfalfa to be cut and cured for hay. There was wood to be hauled down from the foothills for winter fuel. He could work and work and always the next day would be crowded with things to do. But he was glad, with a deep and solid content that comes from security and calm confidence.

So often a man may dream of doing things, but he is so helpless without the means. Now he had the means. Felix and old Herman had come to him and the three of them had drawn up a contract. Case was to work the farm, he was to breed and manage the stock as though they were his own. And each year three fifths of all the produce would be his, the other two fifths, Felix's. After they had all signed their names on the contract, over at Sareeny's father's place, Sareeny had turned to Felix with her quiet voice:—

"I believe there is a host of good things waiting ahead for all of us, Felix."

Somehow that had seemed to move again in Felix that old honest friendliness that had been shocked into silence with his father's death.

Now with hard work and planning ahead there was plenty for Sareeny and that tiny mite of a baby girl to look forward to. Case was mighty proud of that baby. When he and Sareeny had lived in that hut upon Broadview Prairies and she had first told him they were going to have a baby he had hoped it would be a boy. Sareeny could not know how he had begun to worry then. Because he had no money, and there seemed no way of making any in this place he had chosen for their home. Day after day he had watched the little green blades of his wheat wither and yellow. Day after day he had worried more and more over the money for their next sack of flour and the things that Sareeny wished for silently, uncomplainingly. Almost then, he had wished he had not married her. Oh, not because of himself. But for her. It seemed so impossible ever to do the things he had planned to do. A man loses his grip when he is hemmed in on all sides by forces over which he has no control. For he cannot make the rain come or his crops grow without moisture. Thank God he had come back to Sarpy Creek.

What did it matter that he had wished for a boy? He could not be one bit more proud of it than he was of this one, when he took it on his lap of an evening after supper. Sareeny had named it Ellen Peggy, after its grandmother. But he reckoned they would ever call it Peggy, because he liked the name. Little Peggy.

By and by, though, in a long-off unbelievable time she would not be little Peggy. She would be a grown woman. . . even as her mother and mother's mother was; thinking a woman's thoughts, even putting the whole trust of her life in some man's hands; living out another span of time, and no one could say what it would hold for her before it ended. It made a man wonder, when he stopped to think. . . .

Case turned and walked slowly to the house. He did not like such heavy thought. A man has enough to think of when he takes care of this present life. But sometimes in a still minute such thoughts will come in your mind unawares, one leading to another. Just let the time gone by be gone by and never think over ten years ahead, that is the way to be.

The sandy path to the house wound straight on under the low-branched cottonwoods, and over the loose soil around the bushy trees of the apple orchard, where little green apples gleamed almost white in the rich floodlight of the setting sun.

"Let the time gone by be gone by," thought Case. But he knew in his own mind that a man can never do that completely. For thoughts would come. Like they came to himself. Some memory of wartime in France . . . walking past silent forms of dead men . . . and groaning writhing wounded men, in a dead city torn to terrible ruin with great guns and bombs. Or a thought of some happening pushed aside to be unthought of . . . like that Indian woman, Letitia. . . .

He opened the screen door and stepped into the kitchen. Sareeny was frying ham at the big stove in the corner. Her face was red from the stove's heat. Supper was waiting on a nearby table.

Case did an unexpected thing. He had never been one for much kissing or making show of his love or speaking his innermost thoughts point-blank. But now when Sareeny passed him on her way to the table he stopped her with his arms around her and kissed her on the lips. He asked her, point-blank:—

"How happy are you, Sareeny?"

62

Sareeny was mightily surprised and just as pleased. She felt like dropping the plate of ham and putting her arms around his neck. She said simply:—

"There's not a more contented woman in the world, Case."

"I want you to always be that, Sareeny."

She put the ham on the table and went into the bedroom where the baby lay, wide awake, on the bed. Already it was beginning to notice things, seemed like. Its little eyes looking toward some object with what Sareeny fondly imagined was unblinking curiosity . . . This little Peggy was a good baby. Seldom did she cry or fret as so many babies did. Though Sareeny felt it was foolish to think it, at times like this it was as though this little being were straight from God Himself; as though it were her and Case's life taken root to grow as all living things on earth must grow to reach maturity and the end.

She knew herself to be a mighty lucky woman. Not because of all these things she could name one by one, or touch with her hands. But more because of things felt and not named . . . things beyond the limits of her power to name or describe—except, maybe, that her life and Case's life were tuned together, creating, as it were, a separate little world of their own making and kept alive by things all folks feel and cannot name. She reckoned that was it. She was as lucky in one way as Frace was unlucky in another.

The very Devil had laid a-hold of Jacob. He was causing Pa and Ma no end of worry. Sareeny worried even more, because she knew when Pa grew tired of Jacob's sulling and flaring around he would forget Jacob was a grown man and light into him. Not one of them would side with Jacob in whatever way he felt, because he should be man enough to drink the tea he had brewed for himself.

Not one of them ever knew what lay in Frace's mind. But they could guess. She worked until Ellen worried that she would overdo herself. But she was brave enough to smile and hide from them all what she was really thinking; spunky enough to keep her mouth still to Jacob's short words and hateful actions. They only saw her, time and again, grit her teeth on her lower lip and turn her eyes to the floor to hide her feeling.

Only Ellen tried to think out an understanding of Jacob in this matter. Jacob had ever been set on having his own way, even as a boy. Ellen remembered now that they had most always let him have it, too. He had ever been stubborn and high strung. He was different than any other of her children. Yet he had his good points, too! . . . Jacob had never told a lie to his old Ma—never pretended to her, or anyone, something he did not feel. Above all he was honest. Jacob was the only one of her children born with *gifts*. In Jacob there was something of the feeling of music, something of the color and fire and stubborn honesty of that which creates art. And something of the saint and the old Devil's workery, too. Ellen knew all these things, now that Jacob was a man.

His Pa could never do anything with him.

Once Ellen had gone to the well in the dark, not knowing that Jacob and Frace were there. She had heard Frace say:—

"You must have loved me then, Jacob."

After one second of fearing they would see her and think she was spying on them, Ellen had stood deliberately listening in the dark, hoping to hear something that would help her to help them.

Jacob had said shortly:—

"No use talking. We're man and wife now, we'll try to have a home, and I'll never mistreat you."

"I've been thinking, Jacob. After the baby is born, you can leave. I won't try to hold you. I can still teach, if I want to. I'll stay here. I can stay right here with your folks. I think they're truly the finest people I've ever known. Your mother is a saint and you know it."

He was silent.

And suddenly Frace was crying. She raised her voice, not caring at the moment who heard.

"How can you be so rotten, Jacob! You made me believe like a fool you wanted to marry me. You told me . . ." She stopped. She was letting herself go in the very way she had determined not to. As much as possible she wanted to keep all this hidden, in the background. Already her life had blended quietly into all their lives, and she was ashamed in the midst of them. If she could help it, whatever happened between her and Jacob would be clouded over and shadowed by all the life on Sarpy; by his mother's and his father's daily life, his neighbors, and his sweet womanly sister, Sareeny.

# CHAPTER 8

WILD CHERRIES hung juicy sweet and black on their bushes behind Felix Eden's house. They had ripened earlier this year because of the hot, dry weather. Sareeny wanted to pick some of them for jelly. Case liked the good tangy flavor of them with hot biscuits.

But Sareeny could work from early morning till long past dark, now, with little time to spare. Sometimes it seemed there were a thousand things she meant to do, or had to do, before winter set in. Each morning she got up from bed glad that she had the means to do with, and gladder still, when after breakfast there was an hour of fun in bathing the baby in water that must be just right; and dressing its little body in garments that she washed and ironed each day as carefully as she ever did anything in her life.

While she got breakfast, Case milked the cows. After eating, he put the milk through the cream separator. The busy hum of it filled the kitchen; the milk came out one spout, a snowy, foamy white; the cream came out the other, a thick, golden stream, ready with all its wholesome goodness for any way Sareeny chose to use it on her eating table. Say, it was a grand thing to have all these things waiting at your finger tips to be used in cooking good meals. Sareeny found time to gather the eggs each evening, and each time she gathered more than they could use even when Felix and his mother would come home. That flock would pay well for every bit of good care it got, and Case would see that they were well tended.

Eden had been a rough and plain old pioneer rancher. He had been a good man and he had worked hard all his life. But that wasn't all, thought Sareeny. He had plenty of brains and he had known how to use them.

Her own father could have had just as much success, if he had just decided he was going to have it, or if he had any pride. But no, he didn't have any pride. That old log house her father and mother lived in was just as it had been twenty-two years ago when she was born to them. Never had anything inside or outside of it been painted. Never would it be either, as long as her father had the say of things. Her father lived by the rough and common ways of the young new country he had grown up with. The country had kept on growing and he had not. That was it. He had been born at old Fort Custer, long back yonder even before the Indians had massacred every one of Custer's little army of men. That massacre was all history, now. But it was not history when you listened to some of these old timers tell about it.

As if you were there almost, you could see the land beside the Big Horn and Little Horn Rivers that day in June. Long buffalo grass waving in the wind; the hills rising up from the curving river's wooded shores and stretching away and away into the distance until they met some mountain's hazy slope. In the battle you could nigh about see the screeching Indians milling about the hilltop, their horses rearing and plunging, completely encircling Custer's men. Some of the Indians wore their hideous war paint, some wore the brilliant feather headdress, and some were stark naked except for a breechcloth. Men had died by bullets and arrows, or the stab of knives, or bloody hatchets sunk deep in the brain. People told that the Indians scalped every man except Custer. In savage respect they rode away and left his silent body unmarred. On that grassy hilltop battlefield now marble slabs stood in neat, silent rows, or rested away a little distance on some opposite slope, for every man was buried where he fell. Those slabs stood near a great smooth highway that stretched a thousand miles across the nation. They were mute reminders.

Now driving along the peaceful, fenced lane of a country road, you passed the Indians driving. It was hard to believe that not so very long ago they were a dangerous race to be feared and reckoned with. The fat and lazy squaws, wrapped in their bright blankets, were seldom anything but sullen and stubborn; a hoglike grunt was the only answer you were apt to get for a question. But they were not all like that. Some of the younger educated ones could put the whites to shame.

Sareeny remembered an Indian girl she had first seen two years ago, just after the World War ended. There had been a big doings that lasted three days in the little town. Every rancher for miles around had donated free beef for the barbecue, and wild range horses for the rodeo. People had come from as far as even a hundred miles away. There had been racing, and horse bucking, and all kinds of trick riding. This Indian girl had taken part in everything and had won many prizes. With her first appearance the band had burst out with a blare of music, the whole crowd had applauded with pleased surprise, and Sareeny had thought there could never be a prettier girl. Snow white, soft paper thin leather formed the girl's garments and they were trimmed in a rich red that set off her dark beauty. Her slender skirt was fringed, her little black boots glistened no blacker than her hair. She had been the favorite of the whole crowd. Her name was Letitia.

How Sareeny's mother did enjoy that day! Only on rare occasions did she get away from the close, endless drudgery of her home. Never did she have any money. When there was wheat or oats or cattle or a horse to be sold, Jim Gore sold it; and he kept the money. Every cent of it would be spent on the needs of his family. But the only times they ever saw any of the jingling silver or soiled crumpled bills was when he took them from his old billfold to pay a debt, or count out the exact change that Ellen asked for.

"There's some real pretty yard goods down at Clyde Parker's store, Jim. I'd like to get some of it and make Tana a dress."

Jim might give it grudgingly. Or he might ask simply how much she wanted. Then he would take his greasy, soiled old pocketbook from his overall pocket and count out the amount. On rare occasions he would lay another bill almost roughly in front of her:

"You might want a new dress, your own self."

And then with a frown he would pretend there was something he must hurry to do out in the fields or down by the barn. Ellen's face would flush with happiness and her eyes would shine with tenderness. If she went and laid her arms on his shoulders to kiss him he would draw back like a bashful boy, away from his children's eyes, his face red. But once, when he had gone out the door, Sareeny caught a look into his face and his eyes were shining even as her mother's had.

Sareeny's brother Ranny came over to help Case mow and cure the hay. Every day they worked until the sun had set and the field turned shadowy with dusk; for Case feared the black clouds that piled up each afternoon in the west or north, threatening rain. He was glad when the storm clouds blew away over the horizon and the sun would set from a clear rose colored sky. Rain would rot and mold the new hay. From the kitchen window Sareeny could see the fields and the long, low ticks of dark green alfalfa. Some of it would soon be ready to build into neat stacks and cover, for winter. Warm helpful breezes blew in from the south. Case guided the clattering mowing machine, and Ranny followed with the rake.

Felix had promised to let Sareeny know when he would arrive home with his mother. Sareeny watched anxiously the mail box at the road in front of the house. Quietly, within herself, she was almost as excited over the coming of Felix's mother as Felix himself could be.

The letter came on a Friday. It was addressed to Case, but Sareeny opened it right there on the road beside the mail box that still bore Felix's father's name. It was just a short note, written by old Herman.

Tell Sareeny we have found Felix's mother (he wrote with large old fashioned scrawl) and we will be home Saturday night. It would do your heart good to see how happy he is. He seems to be just beginning to realize that he actually has a mother. She is happy too, in her way. . . .

Sareeny put the letter back in the envelope with glad relief. Glad because it was true and relieved because there had been a fear in her own mind that something might have happened to this woman that no one could know or guess during all the years she had been parted from her husband and son. Sareeny thought it was none of her own business what had caused Eden and his wife to part long ago. Parted and divorced, old Herman had said. Living apart and never seeing each other, two separate people with two separate lives, but still held together by the bond of another life they had created. A man and wife did not always cleave together for a lifetime. But what parted these two was no other person's business, now. Sareeny vowed that never by word or action would she make it her business.

Dorcy Fry, Olen Fry's wife, came out in the yard of the Fry home across the road and waved. Sareeny waved back to her. She didn't know Dorcy very well. She wasn't sure she wanted to know her, either. Everyone talked about them and always had as long as Sareeny could remember. Even Ellen had called them a dirty outfit. Olen Fry was more often drunk than sober. Folks said he would come home drunk and beat Dorcy. A bottle of whisky could make him crazy as a loon. His children roamed about over the fields and in people's gardens, a ragged dirty sassy lot, stealing anything they could lay their fingers on. Dorcy was a tall, thin, bitter faced woman, but never had she been heard to utter a complaining word against Olen. She acted now like she wanted to talk, but Sareeny turned and went through the gate into her own yard.

All the next day Sareeny worked about the house, dusting, arranging the furniture. She wanted everything just right, and she wanted the best meal she could put together. No woman on any neighboring farm was a better cook than Sareeny, young as Sareeny was. Long ago she had commenced to learn. Ellen had said to her: "The real important things of any woman's life can be numbered on one hand. Cookin' is one of them. Not a human bein' on earth but what likes to eat. Make up your mind to be a good cook and start learnin' now." Sareeny had learned, and many a meal she had cooked for Case's satisfaction when he came a-courting her.

Felix had always liked fresh-baked light bread. Early this morning she had kneaded the flour into the dough and set it to rise. She molded it into loaves and buns and set it to rise again. All afternoon she baked, taking the hot crusted loaves from the oven, their delicious homey odor filling the whole house. She had a week's supply, just as her mother always did on baking day. She buttered the light brown crust and wrapped each loaf in waxed paper before putting it in the big bread drawer.

Many times she went to the front door, and shading her eyes against the sun, looked down the long road that ran straight into the west. Soon the sun would set. Its low, late beams poured the bright orange light over all the land, and because the road ran straight into the brilliance she could not see the horses and buggy coming slowly nearer.

71

Case and Ranny would finish the haymaking today. They had twelve long rounded stacks of it down by the barn; and there would be another cutting before fall.

Sareeny went back into the kitchen. She had been holding the baby on her arm, carrying it about with her as she worked; now it was asleep, and she laid it on the center of her bed. Case was going to make it a cradle soon as he finished with the hay. Tomorrow, maybe. Ranny had scolded her, saying if she didn't stop toting it about with her it would be the spoiledest young-un on earth. A lot for him to say! If she laid it down for just a minute he or Case was sure to pick it up.

There was a girl ten miles up in the hills that Ranny went with. Her name was Beth. Ranny loved her, too, it was easy to see. Nothing much had been said, but the folks all sort of expected he'd marry her, this fall. Beth was as plain as a mud fence, but if Ranny loved her and she loved him that was enough. . . If it were only that way with Jacob and Frace. . . Ranny told how Frace was busy sewing, making a baby's little clothing, and how proud she was of each little garment when it was finished and laid away. . . . ready. . . . Frace was a great help to Ma, Ranny said. Sareeny thought now if Ranny married and got off to a home of his own, it would double ease the load on their Ma. These last four or five years had seemed to bear harder on Ma than all the years before, graying her hair, changing her face so quick with lines and sagging muscles, the expression of the old. . . . Lord knows it was time her load was lightened.

There was the sound of horses' heavy trotting down the road in front of the house, and Herman's old dust covered buggy turned in at the gate. Sareeny hurried out and was waiting when they stopped beside the door.

Felix jumped down lightly from the buggy. He heard her step and turned, his hands found her shoulders to grip them in glad welcome. Sareeny's pure friendliness brought tears to her own eyes when she saw the new joy in his face and the way his blind blue eyes held honest pride.

"Here is my mother, Sareeny," he said.

Herman spoke: "Just call her Minty, Sareeny. Minty, this is Sareeny."

Sareeny stepped close to the buggy with words of welcome ready for the woman who waited there.

Old, weary eyes looked down at her with a look that said so much plainer than words:—

"I want you to like me, child."

And Sareeny said simply: "Get down and come in, Minty. Supper's ready."

Herman made light talk while he helped the middle-aged woman from the buggy and held out her cheap suitcase to Felix's hand. But all the while he was thinking and his thoughts were never separate or clear, but were of one thing and another at the same time. You have come home now, old mother, to live with the son you gave birth to. . . . This is all a strange bit of life. . . . No word of what I know of it must I ever say. Yes Felix it's God's blessing you were blind when we found the place your mother lived. . . .

It was getting dark when he drove down the road towards home. Birdie would be a waiting for him, a-looking down the dark road to see if he was coming. She would be listening for the sounds of horses' trotting feet and buggy wheels a-turning. Night was mighty lonesome out here in the hills.

Sareeny and Minty and Felix were in the pleasant warmth of the long kitchen. Now Sareeny looked to see this mother's face, and the woman who looked through the eyes, or little things about her that might hint of the woman unknown now but to be discovered and known in time to come, as they came to know each other.

Minty stood close to the warm cookstove, for even the summer nights, here so near the mountains, were chilly. Felix, tall and strong, stood with one arm across her shoulders as he talked. And when his mother spoke, her eyes would turn up to his face half-surprised, silent love.

Sareeny watched their faces. She had expected Felix's mother to be an old woman, yet now she was surprised. There were wrinkles and silent unchangeable expressions in Minty's face that a lifetime of living could not have put there. Minty had lived through a lifetime of trouble, thought Sareeny. Maybe no one could even guess the trouble this woman had lived through. And sorrow, too. Being parted from the man you married and living off somewhere from the child you mothered might be sorrow enough. Trouble and sorrow can change a face, too, leaving their marks in lines and wrinkles, changing even the very flesh.

Minty's hair was gray, and she wore it braided and coiled at the back of her head. Its smooth thick gray curved above her cheeks, hiding her ears. Her teeth were false.

To Sareeny, this reunion of mother and son after twenty-two years was a sad thing. The best years of a boy's life for the woman who mothered him are the years that boy is growing from a helpless, unknowing youngster, growing slowly to a man. It seemed to Sareeny that a mother, mature woman though she be, would grow in some faint and satisfying way as she so slowly raised up her boy each year to a bigger man in body and mind and soul.

Minty was a middle-aged, slender woman, far older than her years. She was taller than Sareeny, and her flesh was thin—it seemed to stretch tightly over the bones of her pale white hands; her shoulders were rounded and small. Out of the strange hardness in her face her eyes looked out at you, blue and kind as Felix's were. She went into the bedroom where Sareeny's little Peggy lay on the bed, and she took the child in her arms, its little face resting against her flat breast, patting it softly on the back and talking to it.

There were tears in her eyes. It might have been that Felix was no older than that when she was parted from him, Sareeny thought.

At the supper table Felix said the chore of milking the cows and putting the milk through the cream separator was his own work. He had always taken care of those things, and he had always tended the chickens, too. Those were chores Case could leave to him.

Minty spoke up a little hesitantly, saying they must lay out some work for her; and her eyes turned down to her plate with soft silence when she added:—

"I want to do something to help."

It was a good supper and everyone was happy. There was so much to talk about and so many new things to think of that the talk moved swiftly from one thing to another. Ranny left the table long before the others, because he wanted to clean and dress himself up to go see his Beth, ten miles north in the hills.

When Case and Felix had taken the milk buckets on their arms and gone off down to the cow barns, Sareeny and Minty were alone in the big kitchen. Sareeny was scraping and stacking the dishes and putting the leftover food away while Minty washed the dishes in the hot soapy water. Sareeny's eyes were warm with awakened friendship when she said simply:—

"It's been a happy day. You will like it here, Minty."

Minty did not pause in her work or took up from the steaming suds. "All the rest of my life is going to be happy, and I know it, somehow. I never liked it in the city. From now on let's all just forget that I was ever there."

# CHAPTER 9

SEPTEMBER had come, bringing Indian summer. The earth changed with the magic of color and white frost. The sun's August heat mellowed to drowsy warmth, flooding the cropped fields in its lazy light. It was a perfect fall. Off in the unknown, impatient winter waited, but now the warm sun and breezes scented with drying fodder and cured hay held full sway. The air was heavy with the odor of ripened things, harvested and threshed; like the stubbled fields with their piles of clean white straw.

Everywhere there was evidence of work done and work finished neatly and laid away until another year would pass. But as a farmer's work is never done, so it was with Sareeny and Case. Always there were tasks ahead. Now that the harvest was over, wood had to be hauled down from the foothills and cut for winter. Case made two trips each day. With each return load, the stack by the kitchen door grew in width and height. But it took a small mountain of wood to keep any house warm all the long winter, and this was a big house.

Now Sareeny was "at home" completely. No house was a home until you had lived in it awhile, and eaten many a meal in it, and slept in it, going to your beds some nights so tired you wished the night was twice as long.

Sareeny liked to see Case coming home with his wagon heaped high with rich pine stumps and cedar logs. Let the winter come with all the deep snow and freezing winds it wanted. This house and this family would be ready for it. On the shelves of the cool, shadowy cellar were rows of jars, sealed food gathered and stored away. There were bins of potatoes; another bin filled with the red gold of carrots. There were cabbage, and a barrel of kraut, and a pile of dark green Hubbard squash her father had brought over last week from his own field.

Minty was worth her weight in gold. She had stepped right into the daily scheme of things, taking over and claiming certain work for herself. She was becoming almost a second mother to Sareeny. Sareeny was learning to love her; not as she loved her own mother, for she loved Ellen with a deep tenderness and silent understanding that needed no words, no proof, no thought to make it grow. But Minty was so good with such an old homely goodness, and so quietly happy to be here in a home that was a home with Felix and them all, that it done your heart good to see her. And Felix went about his daily chores with quiet content. In the busy, pleasant way of things, he forgot, as they all often did, that he was blind.

There was much travel on the road in front of the house these days. Farmers went by hauling loads of grain to the little railroad town twenty miles to the west. Because there was no railroad here this place had no buyer of grain, and it weren't no more than a wide spot in the road, nohow, with just Clyde Parker's old store and a little post office, a school, a dance hall and a church. Someday a railroad would come here, maybe. But Sareeny could remember folks talking that when she was a little girl nearly twenty years ago, and never a train had come here yet.

On Saturday nights after the day's work and the chores were done, they would all sit in the cool darkness of the porch and listen to the dance music at the hall. It made Sareeny wish a little she could go, as she and Case had gone so much in the year before they were married. Law, what a heap of fun they had had then! Dancing all night and laughing your way home in the gray dawn of a morning, with never a worry to mind. Her father had grumbled at what he called her giddy ways. But her mother had many times said quietly:—

"Don't you take what he says too much to mind. It's only a short time of your life you're young and not married."

On Sundays they could hear the churchbell ringing out loudly and clearly, like a summons. Old Man Mills came one day and asked them all to come to church. He stayed for dinner, and Sareeny and Minty had fried chicken. After he left, Case said of course Mills wasn't like the usual preacher, but preachers did dote on chicken dinners, and being invited out to big feeds was as much a part of their lives as teaching people religion. It was a wicked thing to say, and Sareeny knew it. Though she had never thought much about God, she had always kind of taken it for granted there must be one, somewhere. The talk went on, wondering over different religions and different beliefs. It ended as such things usually do, in midair, with no one any wiser.

Old Minty had the last word:—

"God is where you find him."

A car came down the road one day, stopping and posting signs on fenceposts and all the bridges, advertising a Fair at the big town on Yellowstone River. "SIX GLORIOUS DAYS AND NIGHTS!" the signs said. "RACING!" "RODEO!" "CARNIVAL!" "FIREWORKS!" *"Come one, come all and have the time of your lives!"* The biggest sign of all was on the road right in front of Dorcy Fry's house. Dorcy's kids swarmed out like a band of excited monkeys and stood around the men while they tacked up the cardboards. Sareeny was hanging out washed clothes, and she came around in the front yard to see what all the shouting was about. She stood wishing for a long minute that they all might go. She had never been to a Fair but she had heard tell of all the fun people had. Ranny had gone once, two years ago. He had told all about it. The bands a-playing, and the flags a-flying, and all manner of excitement, with more people milling about than you could shake a stick at. Ranny had come home flat broke, for he had spent every nickel he had and borrowed some to boot. Pa had been powerful mad, because all Ranny had to show for his money gone was a silly little toy monkey on a rubber string that bounced up and down when you shook the string. Ranny admitted sheepishly that the thing had cost him three dollars and he had won it by throwing baseballs at a nigger's head stuck out of a canvas. He had hit the nigger. Oh, the Fair was an easy place to spend money, all right.

Case had gone after his last load of wood. It was a sleepy afternoon. Felix had rode off on his white horse, Master, over to Caleb's. You couldn't blame Felix for loving that horse the way he did. Almost as if he realized the kind man he carried was blind, Master went stepping off down the road careful and proud, his beautiful neck arched. Minty was out on the front porch with the baby in her lap. Minty made over that baby more than anyone else in the house did. Always she was going to its cradle, or picking it up, talking to it, coaxing it to laugh. Little Peggy would grow up a spoiled young-un, no doubt of that.

Sareeny had got the notion she wanted to go and meet Case. She had seen him coming far off on a hilltop, his wagon and horses a black speck in the distance. He did not come through the village, but cut right across the open range until he reached the fenced pastures and came through a little used gate, into the fields. That saved time. It was a mile to the far side of the field, and another hour before he would reach there, but what did she care? Minty was here to see after the baby; and it was a long time since she had been away by herself, alone and free.

She went across the stubbled hayfield, where little green shoots of alfalfa were growing up in a race with each night's frost. She was bareheaded, for the sun was not hot, and gentle winds blew in from the south.

Sareeny was almost pretty, now. Her warm tanned face was as clear and healthy as simplicity could make it; her gray eyes bright. She wore her thick, wavy brown hair coiled loosely where the light tan of her neck curved to straight girlish shoulders. Her dress was pink and long, the smooth starched gingham sleeves puffing out to cover just half of her rounded, perfect arms.

She reached the edge of the alfalfa field and climbed the sloping hill, out of the Creek bottom land. Before her lay the fenced pastures. She sat down to rest awhile and look around her.

The sky was blue, blue. Piled high in the south were white clouds shining silver in the sun. This was the nicest time of year. Too bad winter had to come. She could see for miles off through the hazy air. Away yonder, four miles to the east her mother lived, the house hidden by the distances of hills rising and falling to rise again, larger, higher. A mile down the long westward road was Caleb's house; and a little farther on Herman's and Birdie's home was plunked down on a piney hilltop for all the world like it had squatted there with stubborn aggravation and refused to go on to a better place. Old Herman had built it years ago when he and Birdie had homesteaded the land, thinking to build a better one in time to come. Now it was safe to say he never would; and that little flat-roofed, sprawling building would ever be his and Birdie's home until they died.

Her eyes turned down to her own home, with its setting of big shady trees. It was a pretty sight from up here. All the leaves of the cottonwoods were yellowing. The wild-cherry bushes were scarlet patches, here and there, some in the very yard, some following closely along the turning, meandering Creek's water as far as the eyes could see. Dorcy's home was an ugly spot on the other side of the road. For her yard was cluttered up, with nary a blade of grass or tree for shade. Her chickens and hogs prowled about the very door, and her children played there each summer, their bare feet wearing the bit of earth down to naked, hard-packed soil. When you sat up here on the hill and looked down at that house and yard and all the cluttered-up things, you could really wonder what Dorcy's life was like. The little house was gray from winter after winter's hard beat against its low walls; the old shingles were warped and curled from many summers' heat and countless rains that had rolled off the wide eaves to the ground. Dorcy had lived there ever since she and Olen had married. . . . That was a long time ago—nigh around twenty years. Now she had seven children. Anyway, Dorcy was a neighbor, with every right to be treated like one. And before very long she was going to be asked in a neighborly way to come over to the big brown house across the road, too.

All the land, even out in the far-reaching stretches of the open range, was quiet and lazylike, as though nature set back and rested after a busy summer's work. It was a lucky thing the drought had broke when it did or the world would have been a dreary-looking place by now. Yonder on the sandy slope of the hill just west of the little town, halfway between Dorcy's house and the little church, was the graveyard. Looking from here it was hard for your eyes to find the spot where Eden was buried, for the mound of sandy earth was settled and washed down by rains and baked by the sun. But there it was, nearest the road, just a spot where the grass was cleared away, with a granite marker that was a pretty thing when you saw it up close. Twice old Minty had slipped away all by herself and gone there; and many an evening Felix had gone his slow careful way down the little distance of the road to find his father's grave.

Sareeny heard Case's creaking wagon coming slowly nearer and louder. Now it stopped. That would be his stopping at the gate on the far side of the pasture. She got up and started across the half-mile space to meet him.

He saw her coming, her idle steps pausing here and there along the faint traces of the old grassy road. Her pink dress was bright gay color against the gray slope. He knew she had left Minty with the baby and come to meet him, and in a certain way he was pleased; for he had two things in his mind to tell her.

He stopped the wagon and held his hand down to her, half-lifting her up over the high wheel to the flat board seat. When the wagon moved on, his brown eyes looked at her, tender and proud, loving her silently as they always did.

"Tired?" he asked

She returned his look. "No, I'm not tired. There was nothing much to do, 'cept the housework."

His clothes were scented with cedar and pine. His hands were sticky with the resin sap that oozed from pine stumps and logs. His old everyday Stetson hat was wilted and loose and could never again be known as a twin brother to the crisp creamy-colored one he kept at the house for Sunday and dress-up wear. Sareeny was secretly proud of his strength and good looks. When Case washed up fresh and clean, and parted his jet-black hair on the side and put on a white shirt with his blue serge suit, you never set your eyes on a handsomer man! He would boast that he never had an ache or pain in his life. Sometimes Sareeny would think of his being over in France and the awful war, and marvel that he had come home without being hit by a bullet or any hurt.

He asked her suddenly:—

"Do you remember that Indian woman—the pretty one—that was away in school all her life until about three years ago? Her name is Letitia."

"I know the one you mean. Why?"

His face was blood red.

"I thought it best I tell you before some-un else heard it and told you. She's struck on me, Sareeny."

Sareeny stared at him, wanting to laugh. "Do you mean she is in love with you?"

He stared straight on over the trudging horses. "I reckon so. She's been coming to me every day I got wood in the foothills. She tries to make me love her."

Sareeny asked blankly: "How?"

He squirmed miserably on the flat seat. "Oh you know how a woman can do . . . Come up close to you and look at you and say things . . . ever'thing to make a man want to put his arms around her . . ."

Sareeny's eyes held little hard gray lights. "Did you want to put your arms around her?"

He turned his eyes straight to hers.

"Whether I did or not, you are the only woman I want or will ever want. I don't know myself why I went and told you on her. Anyway, this is the last load of wood. We'll forget it. I got something else to tell you."

That Letitia was a wise one, thought Sareeny; she knew a heap that couldn't be learned in schoolbooks. . . .

Case went on:—

"I was talking to Minty and Felix, last night, and we all decided to manage things so as I could take you to the Fair. We counted on surprising you."

He was smiling down at her, expecting her to be surprised and glad. Looking up into his face and seeing only honest thoughts of her own self there, she could throw any other thought of any other woman out of her mind as easily as drawing her breath. If some other woman wanted to run after him and make a tarnal fool out of herself, let her. That's all it would amount to.

Case said he reckoned they could spend ten dollars. And Caleb was lending them his car to make the trip in. Sareeny did look pleased at that. She had often thought it would be many a year before she and Case could own a car, if ever; and now they would have this car for two days the same as if it were their own. The more her mind dwelt on the trip and the things she would see, the more quietly happy she became.

"I've never been anywhere," she thought. "Here I am a grown woman with a husband and baby and I've never been away from out here in the sticks, with the coyotes and prairie dogs and rattlesnakes. I haven't seen anything. I haven't been anywhere."

That thought was still with her when she was ready for bed, that night. Case was already in bed, and asleep, she guessed, from the way his long legs were sprawled out. Case always slept like that, and she did have a time with him, getting him to wake up and move over before he crowded her completely off. She went for a last look at the baby before putting out the oil light. The cradle stood close by the side of her bed where she could reach out in any hour of the dark night and touch it with her hand, or sleep with her hand resting on it.

Little Peggy's eyes were as wide awake and bright and as far away from sleep as they could be. She had squirmed from under the covers, laying with her little knees up in the air, kicking with both feet. She laughed as her mother, watching her, laughed.

Sareeny blew out the oil lamp, then took the child on her lap for a few minutes, sitting in the rocker beside the window. She liked to sit here in the quiet dark when the house was stilled of all talk and movement. At such times she would sit even after the baby had nursed and closed its eyes in limp sleep. And she would let her thoughts drift on to where they would; to far away pleasant things that can never be on the mind during the busy turn of day. It was at such times, it seemed to her, that she really thought things out, and understood them as they were.

There are many deep under-thoughts a wife does not tell even to her husband; and had she known it, many deep under-thoughts a husband does not tell even to his wife.

When she came to bed Case turned and squirmed in his sleep. She put her hand on his thick shoulder and shook it gently.

She said hesitantly:—

"Case, I was wondering if we could take Ma with us to the Fair. She's never been to one, either . . . and she don't have much pleasure, after working hard all her life."

He lay motionless yet half-awake under the covers. His sleep-drugged mind heard what she said and formed thoughts vaguely. . . . The good in you is always showing itself in some way . . . if I were only half as good . . . yes, your mother would never see a Fair if she waited for Jim Gore or one of her grown sons to take her. . . .

He spoke drowsily:—

"Sure, if you want her to go, Sareeny."

# CHAPTER 10

F RACE'S baby was born ahead of its time. It came on the night of September the twelfth. Because of its premature birth, they were all a-feared that it would not live. Old Ellen shushed their fears away. She knew how to take care of it, she said. But she was only saying that to make them all feel better and to make things easier for Frace. Ellen was really more a-feared than any of them that the baby would never live and nourish and grow. When she took the red, pitiful little thing in her arms she could have cried for Frace's sake. And for Jacob's, too, when she saw how he felt about it.

It had been a cool night, but because of the hot fire needed in the stoves, inside the old log house had been hot and close and still. The only sounds were those of Frace's low-voiced pain, ashamed somehow, even in this pain, before Jacob's eyes. And the sound of Ellen's voice when she spoke now and then, steady, confident, controlled. The air was charged with all the tense things, not easily explained, that are felt in their soundless power in such a home at such a time.

Even in the birth the thought had come to Jacob, and he could not get it out of his mind: "If the child dies, I can send Frace away . . . and it will write finish for her and for me with each other . . . for there will be nothing more holding us together. Frace was now in his own bed. He watched her twisting and turning with live pain. For the first time he realized what it meant to wonder how your own life started.

For the first time he felt pity for Frace. And finally, when the child was birthed, and wrapped in the blanket, and laid in his arms, he was ashamed, for his thinking. How very small and strange his child seemed, laid in the warm fuzzy blanket and in his arms. He could not wish it dead. He knew he could not. The longer he held the child the stronger the feeling that came in him. When Ellen came and took the blanketed child from him, he was sick . . . sickened at his own self. He cursed himself, and he felt like a man that is cursed, unable to make himself buckle down and do what is decent and right, as Pa or Ranny or any other man would have done. The feeling burned in him. How would he ever end up, anyhow, if he couldn't make a change in his self, somehow? He had stood and watched the child come into life and hoped that it would die. And not only that, but all the other things that were a part of himself—that made himself. He could not form into clear thoughts all that he was feeling. But he was sickened with the vague realization that as a man or as a human he was not much good; he was not worth much. He could change, but always he would be himself, Jacob. Unless a man can make himself over, and a man would have to be inspired to do that. But it must give a man a powerful feeling to *know* he is a good man, to know all his friends know it; to have his own life give him complete satisfaction. Could any man do that? Jacob wondered.

Frace had not looked at him, or called his name, through all her pain. When it was over, she lay with her head turned on the pillow, her face turned to the wall, as though he were not in the room.

But early the next morning she sent Chris and little Tana over to Sareeny's, to tell Sareeny the baby was here, and it was a boy, and she had named it Keith.

Three days later Ellen brightened with her first hope and belief that the child would live.

Case's father sent word he was coming over someday for one of Sareeny's fried chicken dinners with hot biscuits and chicken gravy and whipped cream pumpkin pie.

Chris brought that word, together with the fat young turkey hens and a proud glistening gobbler Ellen had sent to Sareeny. Sareeny was pleased and surprised. She stood by while Chris unwired the old crate on the wagon box and set them free in the barnyard. The hens flew out heavily, stretching their long necks and chirping their surprise and curiosity. They were bronzed color, sleek and shining. The old gobbler came out angrily; the minute his feet touched the ground he expressed his rage and injured dignity, hunching his fiery red head down till it seemed he had no neck, strutting about slowly with his tail spread wide, his wing feathers dragging the dust, noising his supremacy and importance; Chris said he looked like a mad Irishman.

Of all her brothers, Chris was Sareeny's favorite. Not that she ever said so in words, or even marked him so in her thoughts. But he was so different from Ranny, or Jacob. Ranny was a fine young man, tall and homely; a steady worker. In Ranny was about the same good and the same bad of every man who was just ordinary. There had never been, and would never be, anything deep or surprising or different in Ranny. He would make Beth a good husband. Jacob would be all right, too, once he got sort of straightened out and lined up in his life. Sareeny believed that Jacob must be a puzzle even to himself. She could not understand him the way you should understand a person you have known all your life. Jacob could make himself so miserable. He could be so honestly good; so utterly aggravating; so down-right mean. And then again he could be so that everyone of them would feel that they had misjudged him. Oh, Jacob was good, he meant well, he tried often times when they did not realize it to do what was right. But he was ever like a wind arrow pivoted in some high place of changing wind, never quieting to point some straight and definite way, solid-like, as Pa and Ranny and Case—as all ordinary men do. It must be as Mom said: if a woman had a dozen children, each and every one of them would grow up to be different from all the others.

Now Chris was sixteen, and just beginning to grow up, like a man.

He stayed for the noon meal. Sareeny wanted to ride with him over to her Ma's place; and he promised to bring her home again before sundown. Case and Felix had ridden away on saddle horses, early this morning, out into the wide range-land that lay to the west. All of Felix's cattle had to be rounded up and driven nearer home, where they could be looked after this winter. And any day or night now might bring a deep snow. Each dawn found the frost thicker, whiter. The trees around the house had dropped their yellow leaves into the yard, where Minty raked and burned them. Now the trees threw no shade, and no shaded place was needed, for the sunlight was warm and welcome. You could step off the front porch and look up into the clear sky that seemed so much bigger through the skeleton branches of the tall trees; the house set nakedly under them, exposed to the sun and wind and deep frosts that came silently in the dark.

Minty never wanted to leave home, even for short neighborly visits up or down the road. Neighbors came and met her and went away liking this woman who was Felix's mother; they said among themselves that she was as common as an old shoe, not a bit stuck up because Felix had money in the bank and lands and stock to make them rich. She was as friendly and good as any soul could be, they told. As for her and old Eden being divorced, there was always two sides to any story and who could tell where the most blame lay.

Chris drove the team slowly over the four-mile distance to his home. He loved Sareeny's presence on the flat seat beside him. With Sareeny he could just let go on his thoughts and talk and talk, and it seemed she could do the same with him. She never laughed or looked at him with the condescending eyes of a grown person when he spoke of something he meant to do or planned to do. Ranny might say: "Oh, go on and chase yourself—you are just a kid." Or Jacob rasp out: "Wait till you are dry behind the ears, fella!" But Sareeny would talk with him and turn her calm gray eyes to him with common interest. If she disapproved of some plan she said so simply, and told him why.

The wagon rattled along the bumpy, twisting road. The horses were lazy, trudging along with eyes half-closed, not needing to watch the road any more than the humans in the wagon needed to watch it, for memory knew every curve and turn from a hundred trips before. The air was hazy, any direction you looked, from some mountain forest fire away off yonder that sent its odor of smoke and burning pine across miles of drifting wind. Once, two years ago, Ranny had let Chris go deer hunting with him, up in the mountains. And a forest fire had broke out. He and Ranny had been mighty nigh caught. The fire had been swept on by a high wind and smoke had been so thick you choked for breath. Flames and flying sparks rode on the wind from canyon to canyon and tree to tree, and roared across thickly timbered mountain-sides. Nothing on earth could have been more terrible. Wild things of the forest ran crazy scared trying to get away; but some didn't get away. Chris could imagine them, the pretty soft-eyed does, the proud, swift bucks, even a powerful, lazy old grizzly, caught in the high walls of flames, breathing the awful heat, running, running, this way and that, and finding no way out. They would be scared just as a human being would be scared; crying for help, clawing at the smoke for air to breathe, fire catching to their coats. . . .

The wagon went through a gate and into Jim Gore's field. A half-mile away was Jim's old log house set at the foot of a long slope; surrounded by the land he had worked and pastured and harvested from for a quarter of a century. Yonder was Ranny, in the field south of the house, seeding the winter wheat.

Sareeny wished, now that she was married and in a home of her own, that she could come over here and visit Mom without feeling sad and happy, too. Frace was a blessing, the way she had lightened the load on Mom. But never could Sareeny ride through that gate and look down across the field to the old home without thinking: "Mom is probably plum wore out from overworking and doing for them all. How much longer is that going to last—she's earned a rest— can't they realize Ma is getting old?"

Maybe the boys should not be blamed. Ranny and Jacob just didn't realize anything, much, except themselves or what they were going to do. Oh, they were good enough to Mom in their way. When they worked and made money they showed their feeling for her. Jacob would buy some little trinket to please her. Ranny would come quietly around to slip some silver into her work-darkened hand. Pa was the one that should be made to wake up. His own life was as full and complete as he wanted it to be, with his farming and stock raising. But Mom was different; she was happy and had always been; and it was not that she worked so, doing things for them all that she loved more than life, because that was what she wanted to do; but it was like little things she talked of only now and then on a quiet homey evening: Some day I'll have rugs on all my floors. And her eyes would warm with some imaginary hope, letting her believe for the moment it would really come true: "I'll have a set of as fine a furniture as anybody could want. . . . Our table will be laid with white linen and pure silver and dishes that will make you hungry to see. . . ." She loved pretty things. Like the lavender lilacs and yellow roses she had planted around her house. Each year she had taken up more roots and reset them, close around the high log walls of the house and here and there about the barns and granaries and sheds. In Maytime, lavender lilacs were everywhere, some bushes growing higher than her head with heavy sweet-scented flower clusters. In Junetime, rose banks of lemon yellow hid every ugly spot and gave her quiet satisfaction.

There was no grass in Ellen's yard. And feet coming and going in work and play these last twenty-five years had packed it down to solid old earth, hard as concrete. Her feet, as she carried water from the well, or went the way to the garden or chickenhouse, or washed clothes in the shed near by, or hurried to answer some child's cry of hurt. Jim's heavy step, as he came in from the fields to his meals or his bed at night. Now little Tana was there to play, shouting running . . . Sareeny thought her mother would never be rewarded with the peace and rest she had earned.

And her mother's secret heart yearned to Tana's blond little head and bright blue child's eyes, because this would be the last she would have. Even it had come surprisingly late in her life, disputing even the old doctor who had helped bring Chris into the world. It was a last wonder created from her life and Jim's life, in her feeling for it.

When the sun was less than an hour high and Sareeny was almost ready for Chris to take her home again, she went to look for her father down by the barn. She found him mending the rails of a corral fence where some half-wild bronc had broken through.

He paused when he saw her coming, and pushed his hat back to wipe the sweat from his forehead. His clothes were ragged and dirty and torn. Never could Ellen keep him clean, not if she laid out fresh patched clothes for him each morning. If during the day his hands were soiled, he wiped them on his pants. If a task was made easier by his kneeling to work at it in the mushy bog of the cowpen, he knelt in it.

His shoulders were stooped a little from a lifetime of endless toil. His hair was gray. His strong blue eyes met Sareeny's, loving her with simple pride.

She said bluntly:—

"Case is going to take me to the Fair. He said I could ask Mom to go along with us. I thought she'd enjoy it."

He straightened up slowly with surprise.

"Well now, do you think she'd want to go?"

"I don't see why not. It's the first chance she ever had."

His hand fumbled at the rail and his back was turned.

He did not answer for a full half-minute, but pretended to be studying where the rail must fit into place. When he did answer he did not look around, and his face was hurt.

"Your Mom has never cared for much gadding about the country, Sareeny. She was satisfied to be at home, with us."

Sareeny noticed the back of his hand was bleeding from a deep bruise. The blood ran down his old brown knotted fingers and dried there with dirt and stain and sticky resin that oozed from the pine rail.

Without thinking her words she said: "You ought not to do this heavy work, Pa. Not when Ranny or Jacob are home. And Chris could be helping."

He turned and sat down on the bottom rail, then moved over to make a place for her beside him. Never had the stoop of his shoulders, nor the turn of his head, nor the look of his eyes seemed so old to her.

"There can be no complaint over the work of my boys," he said thoughtfully. "That is, with Ranny and Jacob. But Chris. . . . He shook his head slowly. "I'll be danged if I can figure that boy out. He mopes around, seeming to always have a chip on his shoulder. When some one of us want him to do something, he's gone, off down by the Creek or rode off in the hills by his self. A man's kids are all different."

He chuckled suddenly:—

"You know when I was busy down here a while ago and I looked up and saw you coming across the field with the baby in your arms, I wished for a minute you were back home with us again. To stay, and live with us. I was remembering things you did a long time ago. I looked up and there you were —a grown woman. When you were no higher than my knees and just learning to walk good, your Mommy used to take you with us when we went down to the cowpens to milk. You was the only young-un we had then, but Ranny was on the way. We tried to teach you to call all the cows by name but you called them all 'Cowbulls.'. . . One old cow we had then was a regular pet, as gentle as she could be. We lifted you up on her back and you would ride from here to the house. You liked that. You would go to bed at night and cry: 'I wanta ride my cowbull. . . . I wanta ride my cowbull. . . .' "

He chuckled at the memory of that.

Sareeny put her arm through his and hugged it against her side. "Can't you go to the Fair with us, Pa? Say, we'd have fun! Mom and you and Case and I."

"I don't have any hankering to go, Sareeny. I'd ruther stay home. But you take you Ma."

"It won't do for me to ask her. She'd find a thousand reasons why she must stay home, even though she was aching to go. You ask her. . . ."

Ellen's eyes widened and brightened and shone. But maybe she oughtn't to go, she said; there was little Tana sniffling in a chair by the kitchen table, crying because her

mother had never before even thought of going away and
not taking her; she folded her arms on the table and put her
tangled blond head on them, crying silently; her little bare
feet and slender legs, tanned brown as a Mexican, dangled
from the chair, too short to touch the floor. Jim picked her
up in his arms. Sareeny wished, so much that tears were in
her own eyes, they could take the little tike with them. It
would cost so little more money, when you didn't have it
you just didn't. She had a guilty feeling Case was being reck-
less and extravagant in going, anyhow. But Lord, a human
being has a right to some such pleasure.

Frace got right up and argued that Mom was going and
that was that. Now when she was here she meant to see that
Ellen had some time of her own. Jacob agreed with her,
matter-of-factly. He sat by the table, holding his baby on
his knees. He had hardly talked all the afternoon. He was
proud of the baby; but it was a strange pride with no glow of
actual life or feeling.

Sareeny said with Caleb's car they could drive the seventy
miles to Yellowstone River in two and a half hours, easy.
Case had said they could make it in an hour and a half, but
Ellen set her foot down there. This weren't no race, she said,
and she'd ruther stay home than be laying upside down in a
ditch somewhere along the way with ever' bone in her body
broke.

They were going on Friday; and bright and early on the
morning of that day, Jim brought Ellen over. She was primped
up, the tight-waisted old black silk dress she was wearing
made her seem shorter, heavier. It had a high lace neck that
fitted closely under her chin, and long sleeves tight at the
wrists with ruffled cuffs of the same creamy lace. The dress
was twenty years old.

A body would have thought she was going away for six
months, the way she had given last-minute advice and

instructions to Jim and Frace. The fresh-churned butter was on the second shelf of the cellar; bread a-plenty was baked, and cookies, too; don't let Tana eat too many; don't let Tana play with matches. Watch Tana.

In the bosom of Ellen's dress three silver dollars were tied up in a handkerchief and placed there where she could feel the weight of them against her breast. It was the first money Jim had ever given her without her asking for it. And the weight of the silver was there like a weight of love and thought of him she wanted to keep always. Jim was a mortal good man. He had emptied his pocketbook to give her that money. She had seen him do it. And she hadn't wanted to take anything, but he had forced it on her with his face red and eyes that wouldn't meet hers. And she had felt nigh about ashamed to be going away and leaving him, and guilty because she wanted to go where there weren't no real reason on earth for her going. Shucks, no pleasure in God's world is more satisfying to a woman than keeping things as they ought to be in her own home. A woman may live and die after a whole lifetime and all she's done is make a home for her man and her children. But weren't that enough? Now they would all tote her off to this Fair whether she changed her mind or not about wanting to go. But it would be a sight nicer if there was money for all to go.

She reckoned it was childish, but she did wish she was either staying home with them or taking them all with her.

It was seventy miles over windblown, grassy range, across cedar ridges and past piney slopes, to Yellowstone River. This main traveled road reached on, up and down long slopes and across wide treeless plateaus, around high, naked, yellowish buttes, as was the nature of the land. Cattle grazed in scattered herds. Miles farther along the way, sheep bands covered whole hillsides; moving so slow in their browsing for grass they looked like dusty motionless patches, guarded by the peaceful herder and his faithful dogs.

Autumn haze doubled the beauty of every nature's landscape. To the east and the west and the north and the south, mountains bulged up in the distance, crested white with snow.

Long before noon Case had pitched their little tent among the dozens of others almost a stone's throw from the very grounds of the Fair. Crowds were milling about all the buildings and moving up and down the midway like a restless river. Bands were playing, drums throbbed like excitement, and so many men were shouting and calling that only now and then could one be understood as he raised his voice above all the others:—

"Step right over here, Folks! See the greatest array of wonders ever gathered under one tent. Only a dime. On-leeee a dime!"

Case said things didn't really get started over there until in the afternoon. Ellen and Sareeny could rest with the baby, here at the tent, until dinner; or if they wanted to go downtown with him, there was plenty to see, even though none of them had money to spend.

They walked downtown, Case carrying the baby. It was a mile, but Sareeny and Ellen said they would both rather walk than ride in the car and have to dodge a hundred other drivers that were darting this way and that. Case had said they would just bum around, looking in the big store windows, and that's what they did. Sareeny saw things she would gladly have worked her whole life for, if she could just have them. There were dresses, that made her catch her breath, ashamed for a minute of the one she wore. But there weren't no use being a fool. Of course there were a thousand things—no, a million million things, that we would like to have, and could have if we had stacks of money. All this just made you realize what money was and what it could do, that's all. But when you are poor, things like this might just as well never have been made, as far as you are concerned your own self.

Someday—maybe. . . .

The Fair beckoned and called and lured. The barkers shouted their games of chance; the merry-go-round's music twinkled in strange gay contrast to the band's throbbing match. Bright blanketed squaws, with squalling brown papooses riding their backs, passed in the crowd.

There were horse races, when you got so excited wanting a certain horse to win you stood up and shouted without realizing it. There was horse bucking, and steer riding, and men were thrown and pawed by sharp hoofs in a swirl of dust. You watched from your safe place in the grandstand, unable to keep your mouth from crying out with fear and excitement.

Only Case saw Letitia near them, quiet in the crowd, and she had never been more strangely beautiful. And for him and for her it was like the din and clamor around them suddenly quieted—their eyes met with a secret message, each for the other. . . . If he came again to the place on Sarpy, she would be waiting. . . . Their quick secret message was the same and yet different. She moved on in the jostling, eager crowd, and the message lingered in her eyes' soft expression. He turned to Sareeny, who was bright and laughing with excitement; and the message in his eyes slid hidden behind his presence with her. Without ever actually thinking it, he believed himself clever. He thought: "What harm in a man's natural pleasure, if no one knows of it, to make it wrong with their own way of thinking?"

In nearby buildings were all manner of things made by people's hands and brought here with the hope they would be neat enough, or pretty enough, or clever enough to win a prize. There were pickles, preserves, and jelly and cheese, that made your mouth water just to see. There were quilts every woman envied.

But the prettiest thing of all, to Sareeny's and Ellen's notion, was the fireworks that night. All but a few of the big floodlights were turned off, and the people had crowded into the grandstand, only now the seats were free. You could sit anywhere you were lucky enough to find a place empty.

Sareeny and Ellen hardly knew what to expect, when the first shower of sparks burst in the dark sky. And it formed a living picture of Niagara Falls, so real they held their breath until the picture slowly faded into the black night. Again and again the fireworks rose and burst, hiding the stars behind this nearer brilliance, forming a colored likeness of some startling, pretty thing, showers of sparks quivering and turning in a cascade to the night earth.

It was a beautiful sight to see.

When they were finally in bed on the straw in their tent, after talking Case to sleep, the silence was a thousand times different than ever before. It seemed sudden and black and awful. A little ways to the east the Yellowstone River swished over its gravelly bed, curving around a high bluff and under two long and graceful bridges, railroad and highway.

Ellen wished she were home.

The silver weight of the three silver dollars was pushed under her pillow. Tomorrow she would spend a part of it for something to take home to Tana and Frace and them all. And a little gift for Sareeny and Case and baby Peggy. God bless them all.

# CHAPTER 11

BY THE time baby Peggy was nearing two years old, many things had happened. Little things, commonplace and seemingly unimportant, but rounding out the hours and days and weeks with the subtle quality of life. If there be a book of life it is the human soul, and every long day of living is recorded there, building up and tearing down, putting and taking away, silently and ever so softly forming self toward a final reckoning.

March hesitated between wet spring and slushy winter. Blustery winds spread gray mists over all the sky; rain that was half snow, drizzled. The dawns and darks blended so well together that each came almost imperceptibly, slowly shutting or opening the cold world.

Every morning at four Case got up from his warm bed to build fires. He did not dress yet, but lit the oil lamp and went to the kitchen in his undershirt and drawers. As quick as he could he cleaned the ashes from the big cookstove and started the fire, filling the firebox with chunks of pine and cedar. Then he went back to bed until the stove heated and warmed the big kitchen. The bottoms of his feet would be like solid ice, and if they touched Sareeny's warm ones under the covers she would gasp in her sleep and jerk her own feet away.

The pine and cedar blazed swiftly. Its crackling heat turned the top of the stove rose-red, melting the chill in the kitchen's every corner. Sareeny and Case came there to put on their shoes by its pleasant warmth. Often Minty was there before them, her chair drawn close to the wide oven while she drew on her stockings and warmed each shoe before setting her foot in it.

Minty was a good woman. Loving her was something you just could not help doing. She was ever near in her quiet way, a silent, living comfort. They respected her opinions; because they knew that she knew, and her knowledge was not from books or taught by careful teachers. Felix worshiped her. And not even he ever questioned her about her life gone by. Sometimes during a quiet talk she would tell them of some little happening, and it kindled with interest, a brief moment of her life for them to see and wonder at. She let them wonder.

Time gone by is dead and only the soul holds the record of its passing.

More and more she could let her thoughts turn to that record and along the path her life had followed, and her thinking was with less of the feeling of hopeless shame. At first, when Felix had come near her, loving and proud, laying his arm across her shoulders, his blind blue eyes tender, she had hurt inside. Quick, hot tears welled up, unshed. She had wanted to cry for no reason that she could name. And sometimes, long after the house was steeped in dark and silence of sleep, she had let herself cry; because this thing or that thing had been done in time gone by, and could ever after only be carried about in memory, regretted and sorrowed, never undone. She was ashamed and touched because this life was so good in this house with these people; and she would live here until she died. Her thoughts lay with her memories, silent and unspoken, each expressed only in her content and the ways she made every neighbor woman and man think kindly of her.

Sareeny was busied with new thoughts and new desires and the making of little new clothes, for a baby due in

August. A boy, maybe. How Sareeny hoped it would be a boy; all her thoughts and all her plans were for this little son forming so slowly and mysteriously under some secret, sacred guidance. A love already borne him caused her to see and imagine him, growing and learning as little Peggy was. She liked to think of him most at that sweetest time—he would just be learning to walk with faltering, uncertain steps from arms to outstretched, waiting arms. She would call him Robert Case. Robert Case Gyler, that was a good name. A good name for a doctor, lawyer, or anything he chose to be after twenty or twenty-five years of growing up to a man and learning, learning.

Case said not to count her chickens before they were hatched. It might not be a boy. It might be a girl. Or even twin girls. Who could say, yet?

But he was not fooling Sareeny. He was planning on Robert Case just as much as she was, and she knew it. Case was never one to say much, anyway. He went on about his work, and you could never know what he was thinking. He was quiet and good. Because she knew him so well, and loved him so much, she could guess some of the thoughts he had. Now he would never talk to her of the war or things that had happened there, but he thought back over it, and no wonder, with so much death and suffering he had seen.

But where Robert Case was concerned there was nothing to do but wait. Time would pass with flowering spring and ripening summer, with sun's heat and work, and slow pains quickening and heartbeats adding life to life. If a man child were on its way to her, a Robert Case Gyler, some dawn or dark of an August day would find it in her arms, nursing at her breasts, started on its little unknown living journey; with all a good mother's hopes and fears and joys and tears. If it were a boy, she would have no more children.

Little Peggy was live mischief, now. She ran with wobbling steps from room to room in her playing; she climbed tables and chairs and upset things; say, she was a spoiled one! How could she help it with Minty and Felix humoring her every whim? She lay on the floor and kicked and squealed if she didn't get what she wanted; until sometimes Sareeny had to pick her up and spank her little hind end until it was red. Minty would watch with a pained face. They all spoiled her. Grandpa and Grandma Gore made over her. It don't take a young-un long to learn it can rule the roost.

She liked to climb up on a chair and look out the kitchen window, pressing her little face against the cold pane to watch Felix or Case crossing the Creek to the chickenhouse or barn. She was a sweet baby, so sweet with her little round face, her tangled brown curls and laughtered gray eyes that often Sareeny could not help but reach out with a rush of tenderness to seize and love her.

If this baby on its way was Robert Case, it would be the last. Let all this talk of woman's sin in managing to have no more children be just fools' talk. Nowadays a child growing up to a man or woman needed a thousand times more. The world was changing. In this generation education and training must be had as a fighting chance. A boy or girl had to have a thousand things more, now, that their grandparents never even thought of. It took money. It took all the work and time you could give, if you were not rich. Sareeny had seen and known and grown up with the children of crowded families. Like herself and Case, now they all had to take what they could get from life, instead of a fair chance at earning what they wanted. No sir. No one could tell her where the sin was and where it was not. She knew. She wanted a son, and after it was born, there would be no more.

It was her secret.

Case began his spring plowing the first of April. It was a late spring. Long after the frost had gone out of the ground, rain and snow kept all the fields sloppy. Water trickled down every hillside, and every gully was a baby brook hunting out its way to Sarpy. In April, Sarpy Creek was a muddy, churning torrent that it had not been in years, littered with sticks and trash it had picked up along the way. The dirty water slowly lowered under brightening skies and warming sun, leaving high-water marks along its banks. Sareeny, with fear and worry, kept close watch over Peggy playing in the yard. The swift, ugly water slid silently back of the house, sweeping thigh-deep over the little arched footbridge that led to the barns and chickenhouses. At first they had feared it might rise to the level of the chickenhouse, and make them move all the chickens to a safe place; but as luck would have it, the apple orchard caught the overflow; and the bare-limbed, bushy trees, yellowing with the rising of sap and life, stood in a motionless pond. It was a fine thing for the apples. This was certainly not going to be a drought year, but even if it rained no more all summer, moisture was seeping down to the very deepest, darkest roots where the sun's rays could never reach. This fall there ought to be plenty of apples, for canning, for cider, or to make juicy, spicy pies or store away in the cellar for next winter's cold days that were as inevitable as the coming of day or night, or the sun's crossing the sky each day to vanish in the west. Summer would ripen and mature what spring began; fall completed and finished the whole great work with the crash of color and silvered sparkling frost, and as is just of anything so great, a climax of beauty and the harvest and all the forces used.

Felix tended all the chickens. He put the cranky, touchous old setting hens in a place by themselves and let them have the eggs to hatch. As spring came on his flock of baby chicks grew, ranging in size from gawky, greedy ones, just growing good wing and tailfeathers, to soft downy babies still wet from their mysterious growth in the shell.

Felix loved those chickens, just as he loved every living thing he fed and touched and cared for. He was far more tenderhearted than a man has a business to be. He loved to go out at morning and evening to feed them, and have them gather so thickly around his feet he must slide each foot carefully along the ground for fear of crushing his cheeping, clucking, pecking friends. He loved to go among his cows standing silent for him to give them hay and grain; or get his stool and sit to milk them. Trust won from a dumb animal is the most honest thing on earth.

Felix tried not to think of his being blind. Long ago he had brooded over it for days at a time, trying to find with his thoughts someone to blame and hate for it. It had taken time and much learning, and several good, intelligent friends to make him accept simply the fact he was born without sight and nothing on earth would ever cause his eyes to see. Among his earliest memories were the many times his father had taken him from one doctor to another, anxiously and hopefully. And in later years Felix by himself had gone secretly, to a great doctor here, or a specialist there, and they all explained to him that he had been born without sight in his eyes and there was nothing they could do. They could explain why he could not see, but with all their skill they could not give him sight when God or Nature had not given him the natural power to see with.

Down at the cowbarns he was silent as the cows were silent while he milked; and his light hair pressed against the hair on the cow's warm flank, and his blue eyes, turned down to the sound of milk streaming into milk, were not alert with a ready cheerfulness as they ever were at the house. Here was no one to care whether he was glad or just honest with himself. Here the things that hurt him came back to life, and in the silence of mute, complete trust he thought the hurt out. And then he could go back to the house that set on this little spot of an unseen world with no pretense in his contentment. The same old Felix.

Case seeded the spring wheat the last week in April. He worked six horses to the big wheat drill, and he was in the field before the sun rose above the sky line in the east. At noon he changed his horses and ate a quick dinner, then back to the seeding he went, to work until the sun had set. Every day counted for the wheat to sprout and grow, and the more it could grow before the summer heat set in, so much the better for it.

Sareeny and Minty planted their garden in the back yard between the house and apple orchard. The soil was moist and rich, ready with its eternal patience to take the seed and turn them to living things.

Now on these mornings of spring the air was soft with the sun's warm light and scented with the odor of buds bursting overnight to flakes of green, tender leaves. Meadow larks sat on fence posts and tilted their heads up from yellow breasts to answer the song of a mate. Bluebirds flashed into view to poise on some slender footing of a twig or wire and watch curiously while man worked. The farmers in their fields, and cowboys busy on the open range rounding up the cattle herds . . . . Cowboys with bright shirts and flapping chaps, and Stetson hats and jingling spurs. Nine out of every ten of them one hundred per cent good fellows: happy-go-lucky, honest-hearted men. Riding the West's open range and sleeping under the open sky at night, with a saddle for a pillow, and a million stars lighting the way for the moon; the night wind's breathing on every tree and bush and blade of grass, the coyote's lonesome call— that will nourish the best in any man. And the cowboy's home on the range is his life.

In May, Dorcy Fry's oldest boy, Benson, took sick with a fever. When he came in the house, complaining, Dorcy first thought it was only a touch of the flu, or caused from something he had eaten. She gave him a good dose of physic and put him to bed.

That night Benson died.

And that night Dorcy murdered her husband, Olen.

Benson was just sixteen. Dorcy worried over him all that day he took sick. The fever burned in his young face, hot against her hand. She did everything she knew to do, or could do to help him. She put him in the back bedroom and made the other children go play where their noise would not disturb him.

He lay stretched silently in the bed. He was almost as tall as his father. But still just a boy. Height don't make a man, Dorcy thought. His face was a boy's soft-skinned face, his mouth a boy's young mouth that hasn't yet learned hardness. His hands were slender and tanned brown, without the grasp of a man.

Dorcy was a good mother, loving her children with a tenderness that was surprising when compared with her unsmiling face and silent ways. She sat on the bedside and caressed her boy's hair back from his forehead. Benson needed a hair cut. She'd been trying to get Olen to cut the boy's hair, for a month. Maybe she could get him to do it tomorrow or the next day.

Sitting there on the bed, Dorcy thought to herself that she would like to see all her children dressed up fine, just once at least. Benson with a new suit—blue serge, as blue was his favorite color; and a light-colored shirt and silky tie; a pair of shiny black dress shoes, too, that just fit. He would be nice-looking. His brown hair was just curly enough for a boy.

It was hot in the bedroom. Benson stirred restlessly under the thin blanket. He was not breathing natural. Dorcy brought a piece of cardboard and fanned a faint cool breeze about his face. It was so quiet in the house she could hear the faraway chatter of the children playing down by the barn. She let her thoughts run idly, dwelling on her children. Always, when thoughts of them crowded all other thoughts from her mind, and she relaxed, it was like a strength in her had wilted. Then could be seen her real self, the true Dorcy. The sternness, the hardness would melt from her face and eyes and mouth, and it could be seen how unhappy her life had been. Only it was not unhappiness. It was deeper than that. Her mere unhappiness had ended when she accepted it, bowed her will to it, took her cup of bitterness and drank it, surrendering, then went on stolidly living in the face of it. There her unhappiness, like futile flutterings and railing and resentment, had ended. Surrendering to something stronger than patience, as quiet and powerful as pillars of cold steel. Long ago Dorcy had surrendered to her unhappiness.

Her oldest girl, Rose, was twelve. Rose had always wanted a pink silk dress. Rose would soon be sixteen; four years could go by so quick. Yes, Rose would want nice clothes then, too. Because she would begin to think of going about with a fellow, then. The other children did not matter so much yet, for they were too young to be ashamed of what they wore, Dorcy thought. Denver was ten, and a boy of ten doesn't worry if his overalls are made-over and patched. Sid would be eight years old the seventeenth of September. Silver would start to school next fall, and that six-year-old would certainly expect a new dress—bless her vain little heart! Silver was always trying to pretty herself up in some outlandish game of make-believe, where she colored her face with beet juice and flour. As for them two little-est young-uns, Inez and June, why they just didn't know there was such a thing as worry in the world!

Dorcy heard Olen drawing water from the well. She fluffed the pillow under Benson's head, and went out through the kitchen to the back yard.

Olen was drinking water from the battered old well-bucket. The bucket leaked in a dozen places, and when he held it to his lips it wet his shirt. The cold water ran down and splattered off his rough shoes to the hard-packed earth.

Dorcy waited. She was going to ask him if he would get a doctor for Benson. Benson's fever was rising and he was almost out of his head.

Olen drank with noisy gulps. He had pulled off his old hat and tossed it in the shade of the kitchen. His hair was blond and tangled. He looked younger than Dorcy. At forty he was handsome, insolent, hateful.

He lowered the bucket and dropped it back into the well, where it dangled on the rope, banging against the rock walls. His glance at Dorcy was angry, threatening.

"Where's that boy?"

Dorcy replaced the old plank lid on the well shaft before answering him. Silver had almost fallen in there once and the water was ten feet deep.

"He's sick, Olen. And runnin' a high fever. I want you to go get a doctor."

Olen looked at her as though she had turned suddenly crazy.

"Hell! That boy ain't sick. He jest don't want to plant, that's all. He don't need a doctor. I reckon I can cure him, my own self. Go tell him I'll give him twenty minutes to get out in the field."

Dorcy moved over to the kitchen door. Olen was always hard to get along with and meaner than ever when he had a little work to do.

"Benson is sick, I tell you. Now Olen go send for a doctor."

"If you think I'm going to ride horseback twenty miles jest to please you, you are crazy. That big overgrown kid ain't sick."

She said patiently:—

"Olen, you won't have to ride twenty miles. You can go down to Clyde Parker's store and telephone."

Olen stretched out in the shade and pillowed his head on his arm.

Dorcy stood looking down at him silently. An old thought that she had never put into words came to her mind. Someday I'm going to leave you, Olen Fry. . . . else someday I may hate you so much I will kill you. . . .

She said aloud:—

"If you won't go, then I'm going over to Sareeny's and send Felix or Case."

He raised up with a curse.

"Stay away from that outfit. I mean now and from now on.

Dorcy stood leaning against the doorjamb and said nothing for a moment. He went on sneeringly:—

"I suppose you want to tell Case Gyler my kid is sick and I won't go get a doctor. Is that it?"

"Oh, I reckon Case Gyler don't need to be told anything about you."

Olen's face reddened with anger, and then he laughed loudly, his eyes shining.

"I don't need to be told anything about Case Gyler, either. No sir. Not a thing. Not after I've seen him twice with the fancy squaw of his, and watched them half an hour in the bushes up Sarpy Creek. He meets her there, ever' so often."

"That makes you just one of two things," Dorcy said slowly. "Either a rotten liar or a sneaking, filthy peeping Tom.

He was on his feet so quickly she was shocked with fright and couldn't move. His finger closed over her arm, pinching the flesh. He jerked her out the door.

"You homely bitch. After twenty years of lookin' at that sour face do you think I'll let you call me that? I thought I'd learnt you . . . .

His fist struck her squarely in the mouth. She staggered back, her nose spurting blood. He turned and walked down the pathway to the barn.

Dorcy went in and lay beside Benson in the back room. She was sobbing; great dry sobs, without a tear. After a while she went to the back door and called Rose. She gave the girl a note and sent her to Parker's store. Parker would trust her for the twenty cents long-distance call.

It was five o'clock in the afternoon. Benson was worse. He turned and twisted in the bed, talking out of his head. Dorcy could not soothe him, and she was frightened. She sent Silver across the road to ask Sareeny to come over.

Silver found no one home. Sareeny had gone to spend the day with her mother and taken old Minty with her. Rose came home, and Parker had sent a note saying he had telephoned, but the doctor was away from his office on another call; and the doctor's wife had promised to send him on as soon as possible.

Dorcy fixed a lunch for the other children. As soon as they ate, she put them to bed. Dark came, and still Olen did not return to the house.

The house was still except for the children's regular breathing and Benson's boyish voice muttering words that had no sense. She lit the oil lamp and sat beside his bed.

Maybe Benson would be all right in the morning. Maybe he would get up with a clear head, and eat a big breakfast, and go to the field to work.

It was while she was brushing back the hair from his

forehead with a damp cloth that she found the wood tick, fastened firmly in his scalp.

Four hours later Benson was dead with spotted fever.

Dorcy had not known when he died. She had lifted his hand and found it limp, and felt his face and found the life gone from it. When she knew, then, that he was dead, she had not wept, but bowed her head on the thin cotton blanket that covered his breast, and she had suffered as only death can make the living suffer.

A few minutes later Olen had entered the house. He fumbled around in the kitchen and lit the oil lamp there to find something to eat. When Dorcy came there he was sitting at the table eating cold biscuits and milk.

He looked at her oddly, struck by her expression. Her thin black hair was loose over her bony shoulders; her dark gray eyes almost black. She was holding Benson's overalls that he had taken off when she put him to bed. In her left hand was a large rasp she had taken from the overall pocket. She said calmly and yet strangely:—

"Go look in the bedroom."

He got up from the table with a curse. She followed him. He paused in the bedroom door, frowning angrily towards the bed. He went and stood a brief moment looking down. "Come out of it!" he said gruffly. And he fastened his fingers in the thick brown hair, yanking the head up roughly.

Dorcy cried out with agony: "Olen! Don't!" She flashed across the room with the heavy steel rasp upraised, and brought it down on his head. It sank in his brain, and he fell. He lay face downward on the plank floor, and blood streamed from the deep gash in his brain to silently form a red puddle under his face. She knew he was dead.

It was three o'clock in the morning when Dorcy crossed the road to wake Sareeny, and tell her of Benson's death.

112

These darkest hours of the night were still except for the winds brushing through the bright new leaves of the sturdy cottonwoods about Sareeny's yard.

Dorcy walked blindly. She was trembling so she could scarcely open the little yard gate. She could still hear the splash of Olen's body as it hit the glistening deep surface of the water in the old well.

One thought raced ahead of all other thoughts: There are two sticks of dynamite buried down by the barn . . . . tomorrow I shall use them to blow that old well in . . . . no one shall ever know . . . no one shall ever know. . . .

Every neighbor for miles around came to Benson's funeral. No one wondered greatly where Olen Fry was, because he always had a habit of making sudden and unforeseen trips to near-by towns and staying till his last dollar was gone.

Now Dorcy told them he had left her, never to come back.

God alone could tell what Dorcy suffered in this time. Her neighbors pitied her because she was alone in this time of trouble, and they silently cursed the man they knew had abused her all these years. They told that Dorcy had believed her boy died of typhoid fever, caught from the drinking water, and she had filled her well in, using dynamite to cave in its rocked wall, refusing ever to drink that water again. But the doctor had come later and said the boy died of spotted fever, caused by a wood-tick bite.

Well, if Olen Fry had gone away and left his wife, maybe she was better off without him, they said. But he had picked a wrong time to leave her. The neighbors talked, and everything about them said it would be mighty unhealthy for Olen Fry when and if he ever showed his face around here again.

They must never find out, thought Dorcy.

Sareeny wept over Dorcy's trouble, and vowed those six

113

little children would never go hungry as long as there was plenty to eat in this big brown house across the road.

# CHAPTER 12

SOMETIMES Jacob wondered how Frace could have held up under their life these last two years, the way it had been; and still be able to smile as strong as ever, to push right ahead and get as much satisfaction from each day, on and on, as any one of them did. She was a strange woman. He had to admit to himself, even though he had never loved her and the very sight of her aggravated him, that she had more honest worth than he would ever be able to understand. He hadn't been able to drive her away. He hadn't been able to break her down. After the baby was born he hadn't even been able to hurt her. At last he understood why.

When Frace was a very small child, her own folks had died. (Jacob had heard Frace telling Ma all about these things.) And Frace was put in a place for orphaned children. She had never had a home. All her childhood life she had been shifted about, from one strange place to another, among strange people, no one really wanting her. To really understand it, you would have to listen to Frace tell about it. More than the words she used, her eyes and face and manner recalled it all so truly as it had been. Frace could sit and recount it from her memory, and to listen and watch her as she talked it was all so real. . . . You went with her when she was a child, from place to place, thinking the things her child mind had thought, feeling as a child felt. Frace knew she had been a strange child; too sensitive, too cowed, too afraid of strange faces. But she had got over it, learning, and by the time she had grown up to call herself a woman, she could hold her own with anyone. She could decide what she wanted to do—and do it!

Never in all her life did she have a home, where people lived together, ate together, kept their own fire, and in a certain way lived all their lives as one complete life. Where a quarrel may rage swiftly and then is as quickly forgotten, because it is home.

Jacob understood that in the beginning Frace had loved him. Later, still because she had loved him, she had married him. But she had stayed on in this house, unchanged, because she was home at last and she loved it. She might as well have been a blood sister to Sareeny and Tana and Ranny and Chris, the way she felt towards them, the way they felt towards her. She was a favorite of them all; though Ranny had long since married Beth and moved away to live. And Jacob reckoned his old Pa and Mom would as soon lose anything else they had on earth as lose Frace. Frace had stayed on here because at last here was something solid in her life, likened to a foundation. She loved all this life. She was a queer one. She loved the windy days, and the white, glittering winter mornings, and the black thunderous evenings that could come in mid-summer. She loved the damp rich odor of fresh plowed garden soil, in every spring; even the crying loneliness of windy cold January nights that are so dark and long. She even loved these damned hills that stood up in everything, rain, snow, heat, cold, winter, summer, forever and ever, unbudged, not caring what went on in folks' lives who lived here. She was a queer one. Jacob just let her alone, but he watched her, and she was most always in his mind. He couldn't ever stop thinking about her.

He couldn't figure out if she still loved him, or not. Yet he knew that whether she loved him or whether she didn't, that was not the reason she had not packed up and taken little

Keith and gone away. She had stayed on here only because she wanted to.

A week after Keith was born, she had made her bed in another room, and never since had she slept with Jacob, or kissed him, or touched him with her hands.

Jacob could not understand her.

She had Keith. All her life centered, and was bound, and bloomed forth again in the child.

From the first, Keith had been hers. That was the bitterest thing of all to Jacob. He worshiped the child, too. For the first time in his life, something great and overwhelming was brought to feeling in him. His love for his boy. He did not try to understand it, or try to understand why it kept him from feeling too strong a hate for Frace. He could have killed Frace for hogging little Keith away from him.

She was so sly about it, he thought. She would say to the child: "Go to your Daddy, Keith. See, he wants you to come to him." Yet when Keith remained at her side, tugging at her skirt, she would pick him up and say no more, loving him with her lips and eyes and jealous arms. If she wouldn't be infernally making over Keith, trying to teach him this and that, playing with him, Keith would not be so crazy over her, Jacob thought.

Now, spring work crowded in upon them all. Even Chris was as steady in the field as Jacob or his old Pa. Frace and Ellen were busy all day long, marking off and planting straight rows in the garden, and trying to remember which of the hens had been setting on eggs two weeks, and which had first started to set last week, or which batch of eggs was due to hatch tomorrow, or which was due to hatch Saturday; it was a grand mix-up, because Tana had lost the paper Frace kept track of it on, so now they didn't know which old hen was which. And as Tana said, the dumb old biddies could only set on the eggs, pecking at your hands like old fools, not knowing a thing about it themselves until the first egg cracked under them with a wiggle and yeep. Frace loved to tend the chickens. Anything she did was no work, because she made it fun for herself. Keith tagged at her heels, in the garden and about the chicken pens. She would give him a soft downy chick to hold and pet, teaching him not to squeeze the life out of it as he had the first ones he picked up.

It happened one day in late May, a silly, trifling thing, that brought matters to a head for Frace and Jacob.

Early that morning Sareeny came over, and ever afterwards she wished that she had stayed home that day of all days, and kept her mouth shut and minded her own business. Frace and Jacob were surely no business of hers. Their lives were no one's but their own separate affair, to work out in their own way. Later, when Sareeny mulled over the day's swift happenings, she felt like slapping her own face because she had opened her mouth in such a biggety way and butted in, to speak and quarrel where she had no reason except that Jacob was her brother. She never blamed Jacob for flaring up and turning on her—he ought to have grabbed a-hold of her and shook her till she couldn't see straight, and sent her home to Case till she had learned to keep her mouth shut.

The day was hot. Ellen and Sareeny were in the far end of the garden, picking the first cooking of new peas. Peg was there with them. Jacob, seeding a near field with oats, had tied his team to the fence and come to the well at the house for a drink. Frace, with Keith, was close by in the chicken yard that was alive with baby chickens and cranky, quarrelsome old mother hens.

Suddenly an old hen, angry because the child was in the midst of her brood, flew at Keith's face. Clucking and squawking with rage, her wings spread, she knocked the child down, scaring him into wild terror. He screamed like a war-whooping

Indian, scaring even Ellen and Sareeny so that they ran across the garden to see what on earth was the matter.

Jacob came a-running. He was in the chicken yard in an instant, to see Frace lifting up the screaming child whose face was bleeding from a few pecks and scratches that were hardly more than skin-deep. The blood and the sudden uproar struck alarm in Jacob. He did not know what had happened. The long strain of his brooding, his restless misery, was beginning to tell on him, anyway. He had not been happy for so long. It was true that even his own family, beyond his mother, seemed quietly sided against him, blaming him without real understanding. He had worried and studied so long in his mind, alone, wondering how he could in some way get his life righted again, untangled . . . and it seemed he was in a bog so deep he would have to stay there, ever the same.

He was growing more and more restless.

Lately he had thought he could not stand it much longer.

Sareeny and her mother came up just as he pulled Keith roughly from Frace's arms. His voice was hoarse and harsh, unnatural:—

"What have you been doing to him?"

Frace said with surprise: "Why, Jacob! He's only frightened. He'll be all right, soon as I get him quiet."

Rage, or hatred, or some other such thing, moved in every muscle of Jacob's face. Feelings of strange conflicting emotions were so strong in him that even Ellen and Sareeny could sense the turmoil in his mind, though they could have never put it into words. Everything was in him—rage, hurt, and despair a man feels when he is ready to throw up his hands and let everything, himself included, go to hell.

Ellen was thinking: Jacob you never could reason and view anything like you should, whatever you see and do and feel, big or little, you view it like it meant your whole body and

119

soul . . . if you would only take your whole life and everything you live a little more lightly . . .

He flared at Frace:—

"That's all you know. Soon as you do this or soon as you
do that. That's the way you been ever since you first opened
your eyes and looked at him. Oh, I'm sick of it! I'm sick of
you and the way you go just hunting around for something
to be cheerful over . . . hiding what you must be really thinking. . . "

Fury burst from Frace, so unexpected, so intense, it took
possession of her body. Jacob had hardly hushed before she
lashed out at him, her voice uncontrolled.

"How do you think I feel? Do you think I'm happy living
this way? I didn't ask to come here and live here in this place
in this house. I've done the best I could with a bad bargain—a mighty bad bargain!" Her voice broke and she strove
to keep from crying. Her words seemed all the more strong
and intense because they had grown used to her kindness. .
. . "Oh, I could call you every dirty name I could lay tongue
to, because I remember every thing you ever did with me
since we met! Do you think I've forgot how I come to let you
stay that first night with me, or the things you said, or how
I let you lay your filthy hands on me because I believed you
loved me? You didn't love me, but you knew I loved you and
if you worked it right you'd sleep in my bed that night and
other nights till you found another woman that suited you.
Knowing you like I do now, I ought to hate you and everything about you! You won't throw anything up to me, Jacob
Gore! "

Her blue eyes burned in their look at him.

Jacob's teeth were clenched, his lips loose; angrier still
because Sareeny and his mother were here to listen while
Frace said these things, and because Sareeny's gray eyes
were narrowed and burned at him with a look akin to Frace's.

He moved Keith from one arm to the other and looked at Frace.

"This is my kid, too. It's about time you begin to remember that, ever' day."

She scorned: "I wish I could forget it—and teach him to—"

He turned and walked across the yard, into the field, carrying Keith in his arms.

The yard and old log house seemed quieted, solidly indifferent. Sareeny was thinking: "If only Jacob wouldn't be such a fool . . . he could at least try to make a go of it with Frace, now that it's too late to do anything else. . . ."

Ellen went and stood silently beside Frace, and looked at her with a vague kind of pity. She had long ago tried to stop worrying over Frace and Jacob. Worry would do no good. Time would have to straighten things out for them in some way. Time and God.

These last two years had aged Ellen, terribly. She yet hid the secret of her dangerous heart attacks. No need to have them all a-worrying over her when it would do no good and no doctor could cure her. Chris had forgot about that one time, she reckoned. She knew, and any doctor would know, that someday the heart pains would come, sharp and unexpected, and she would fall, dying. But my God, why tell them all about it, and have them all a-worrying over her, ever thinking she might drop dead at their feet.

She was a thin, gray-haired old woman. She turned to look at Jacob working in the field, and said sadly to Frace:

"I reckon you must hate him."

Frace was still trembling with anger. This thing was not finished yet, Sareeny thought. Frace drew a deep breath and did not look up from the ground when she answered with set bitterness.

"How do I know? Right now I could say I hate him like

green poison. Sometimes I think I love him, and I want to go to him and put my hands on his face and tell him so. I'm a fool woman. But when I try to understand Jacob I know that he is not like he seems. You know it, too."

She was silent a moment, then added:—

"The best thing for me to do is pack up my clothes and take Keith and get away from everything in this place."

Sareeny said quickly: "Not a one of us would let you do that, Frace. Jacob will come to his senses and behave his self. He's just stubborn and peculiar-humored and teetered-up to. He needs someone to tell him a few things, that's all."

Frace did not answer. She needed to go somewhere by herself and cry, but she was not going to let herself do it. She was too angry. She thought with acid bitterness that there were two ways for her to follow. She could take Keith and leave; or she could stay here and try to control her life with good sense, trying to make the best of things. She knew that as long as she could choose, she would stay here. She turned her head to look at Jacob yonder in the field with the dust and the team and the seeder and the bright spot of green that was little Keith in the sweater his Grandma Gore had knitted for him. She thought: "I'm his wife, Frace. But I'll die before I ever go to him for anything, unless he comes to me first. I've been a goody-goody too long. I've taken too much from him. From now on I'll take no more. I'll let him know I've got a mind of my own— that I'm no goody-goody fool!"

Jacob had set Keith on the grain box of the seeder. He had wiped away the blood-stains and tears with his big, none-too-clean, red bandanna handkerchief. Keith shut up his crying in the interest of this strange new trip to the field. He was a sturdy, chubby-built little fellow. He could already talk good, and no wonder, with the whole family his constant teacher.

Driving around the field, Jacob let him ride on the grain box. The boy looked like him, he thought proudly. Keith's hair was as jetty-black as his father's; his sturdy little body and quick growth promised Jacob's same thick-shouldered strength and height. But he had Frace's clear blue eyes. When the seed drill neared the house again, Keith looked up and saw his mother, with Sareeny and Ellen, still standing in the yard. He wanted to go to his mother. Mostly because he was so rotten spoilt, he set up his squalling again. Jacob meant to drive right on past the house. It wouldn't hurt the kid to squall. Let him holler. He'd shut up as soon as they got past the house.

Frace knew that, too. But anger and aroused stubbornness made her feel great satisfaction that she had an excuse to go take Keith. When Jacob reached the edge of the field closest to the yard she stepped out and was waiting. And the contrary satisfaction was so clear in her face that it started Jacob off all over again.

Sareeny, like a fool, followed Frace across the yard. It was as plain as anything that Jacob and Frace were going to flare up with each other again. There had been enough of this foolishness. Pa was just coming up from the barnyard, towards the house, and it would never do for him to hear Jacob. He was hard against Jacob, anyway, these last two years. Pa had no patience—things might be said and done that would take a long time to mend.

Sareeny turned a little ahead of Frace to reach Jacob first. Keith shut up as soon as Sareeny lifted him down in her arms. The spoiled young-un had ought to have his hind end blistered with the palm of her hand! And Pa ought to knock some sense into Jacob! Sareeny was so aggravated and so filled with nervous dread she spoke to Jacob with harsh anger. She could remember—Ellen could, too!—How Jacob and Pa were when they got riled up—

and how easily they could turn that way. She said angrily:—

"Keep your mouth shut, Jacob. There's been enough said, already."

He turned his eyes, bright brown and determined, to look straight at her, warning her to mind her own business.

"The trouble is, nothing has been said. Ever'thing has drifted for two years. We'll forget everything that's been said this morning—but now's as good a time as any for some understanding between Frace and me."

Sareeny said quickly: "Well, go about it with some sense, Jacob. You know how it hurts Ma to have Pa riled up and in a ruckus. Here they come now. Stop acting like a fool!"

Then he turned on her.

"Keep out of this, Sareeny. I reckon I'm not the only fool in this family. You don't do so bad your own self."

Frace and Ellen and Jim heard him. It was too late now to stop anything being said. As though he had not paused in his talking Jacob added bitterly to Sareeny:

"You are the biggest fool of all—a simple, trusting fool, unable to see what's going on before your very eyes. But by God, I won't be the one to tell you!"

Old Jim had quickened his steps towards them. He was frowning—he had a temper even worse than Jacob's, when aroused. One word now, and all the harbored resentment he felt against Jacob would come out.

Frace could see there was going to be trouble. Jacob and his Pa were too much alike to turn men's unreasoning anger on each other. This was all her fault. She thought: Oh, what good did all this do—it has only made things worse for Jacob and myself. . . . Her fury left her as suddenly as it had come, leaving her white and sick, able to think with good sense and a kind of calm accepting despair.

Old Jim came up without a word, searching them from one to the other with his eyes.

Frace said at once, almost without thinking, because she knew it was right: "I'm going to part from Jacob, Pa."

They all stared at her.

Her eyes silenced anything Jacob might say, bending him to acceptance of anything she might say. She went on talking calmly, as though they had discussed and agreed on their plans.

"I could take Keith and leave. But even then, Jacob would not be happy here. It's best that I stay and he go. If you will help me, I can get the Sarpy school to teach. Yes, it's best that I stay and he go. He is leaving this afternoon."

She raised her eyes and looked directly at him. "Aren't you, Jacob?"

He did not answer for a long moment. But stood looking straight at her, as she looked at him, as though each in surrendering to the other had stopped for one last moment of wondering over one another.

Softer, yet in the same tone she had used, he answered: "Yes. I'll leave today."

And then to get away from them he started up the horses and drove the seeder for one last trip around the field. He shouted to the horses and the wind caught and lifted back to them the strangeness in his voice.

Her face set in its calmness, Frace came and took Keith from Sareeny's arms and went without a word into the house.

Sareeny turned and walked into the yard, away from her father and mother. Let them talk this thing over without her.

How ever would Jacob turn out now?

Sareeny often wondered how they all went through the strange ordinariness of that dinner—Jacob's last dinner at home. At first they were all still and tight-lipped. Whatever

125

Ellen and Jim had spoke between themselves over this thing, they had accepted it, believing that Time would surely work things right. Old Jim did hardly look up from his plate as he ate slowly. Ellen did not eat, but took a piece of the meat Frace had cooked, and left it on her plate untouched. Sareeny would never have believed her Ma could control feeling the way she did now. They all knew, they could all see, Mom was plum sick and broken-up over this thing, but she was bending to it, facing it, because it was the best thing. Jacob would have to learn and how was he to do it except for them to stand back and let him blunder and fumble and live and learn.

Unknown to each other, Ellen's and Frace's thoughts were closely the same. Now and then in the uncomfortable silence the look of their eyes fell upon Jacob's black handsome head bent towards his plate, and each was suddenly sorry for him, some deep inner knowledge of Jacob that they alone had, caused each to think in her own way: I understand why you do the things you do. . . . You have not lived enough, you have not experienced enough—all your young life you lived cut away from the world in this place, with no more grasp of the world and the strange world's ways than a hand has of the wind. You will stand and look, amazed. . . . Frace's knowledge formed of its self a strange thought: Slow fires burned in Jacob. He would not be honestly human until those fires were quenched, until they were tempered with learning more of life. Jacob was not really bad and no good. He was restless and dissatisfied and he could not have told you why. But Frace could tell why. These things were in Jacob and they would have to be worn away by his actual living. Until he learned how to measure, with simplicity, value for value in monotonous old life on this earth as we all live it, day by day. . . .

Chris and Tana were gone, off to a neighbor's.

Frace leaned over Keith's highchair to mash and butter the vegetables on his plate. In tenderness her bright brown head rested against his bright black child's head that was for all the world exactly like Jacob's except that Keith's eyes were exactly like Frace's eyes, bright blue as corn-flowers in the sun. Jacob looked up at them and then looked away again quickly, and no one could know what he was thinking.

Sareeny was sorry as she could ever be, that she had opened her mouth and butted in so hateful where she had no busi-ness. She told Jacob so, when dinner was over and he came and found her alone by the lilacs in the yard. She asked him point-blank what he had meant by saying she was a simple, trusting fool.

He reddened and would not look her in the face.

"You had best forget all about it, Sareeny. I was only say-ing anything that popped in my mind."

And he would say no more about it. He would not tell her of the night he had sat in the darkness away yonder on Cedar Ridge, and Case and Letitia had come so close to him. And because he had not wanted to give himself away and let them know of his presence he had been forced to sit and listen, with them not a stone's throw away. And by God Almighty! Sareeny would never learn from him that Letitia had a son secreted yonder in the mountains; a son by Case, and even Case was unknowing that it had ever been born, for the boy was three years old in this summer. Letitia had never told Case. And the boy had been born in the very week Case had married Sareeny. Now Case, still unknowing, was carrying on with Letitia again—that lurky, too wise, Crow Indian squaw, with eyes like strangely colored velvet—she seemed never to be all In-dian or all white! Though Jacob had hated Case Gyler's very guts ever since that night, he'd kept his mouth shut for nigh onto two years. He'd leave and still keep it shut.

He wanted to make up in some way for the harsh words he had spoken to Sareeny. She had ever been his favorite. He believed she had more actual, honest, pure goodness than any other person among all the hills of Sarpy.

She laughed when he told her so, and confided to him that if she always let herself go, just as on this morning, he could never say that. She tried to tell him something of herself that she had never before and even now could not easily put into words. Some long time ago, when she was yet hardly more than a child, she reckoned, with her quiet ways and spells of deep thinking, there had come out of her mind a profound desire to be a good woman—to live her life, long through to the finish, with kindness, and gentleness, and hands that would comfort any other person's suffering, and year by year build herself to learn to forgive and overlook wrong and understand life. All this had become as an aim in her own life, so that more than anything else she wanted people to talk among themselves that she was a good woman. It sounded sickly and foolish when she tried to explain it with words, and she hushed, a little ashamed. But she had told a part of herself that was there inside of her, pulsing with life, slowly molding her into the woman she most wanted to be.

When Jacob was gone, Sareeny and Frace went to the garden and finished picking the new peas for supper. Everything was as though nothing had happened. Except that Ma was in the house, crying, with old Jim blundering around trying to comfort her. And Frace was white and tight-lipped, her eyes not thinking or seeing what her hands did.

. . . Of course she still loved Jacob, foolish as they both were. If you are a woman, and love a man, can you stop loving him when your first child is born and grows small and dependent and lovable, with a small face like its father's face, small lips that quirk in its father's laugh, hair like that of its father's head—and eyes like your own?

Outwardly everything was the same. Hot sunshine warmed all the land, and warmed the west wind that blew softly, making the earth a pleasant place to live and be free on. Sarpy's hills never are moody with loneliness in bright springtime, as they seem to be in windy fall weather, or dark winter, or on thunderous summer evenings. Springtime in this remote and quiet country is as though the Lord looks down and smiles, pleased with all the minute wonders that burst forth in creation.

But there was a silence—Jacob's silence—now that he was gone.

Case said nary a word when in the early evening Sareeny came home and told him all that had happened and been said.

At the time he couldn't say a word. His tongue was paralyzed with worry and fear over the jolt of realizing that Jacob knew about Letitia.

Case understood well enough what Jacob had meant in calling Sareeny a simple, trusting fool.

Now surely in time Sareeny would learn all about it. And what would she do when she learned he was not anyways near the kind of man he had made her believe him to be?

He sat at supper with Sareeny and Minty and Felix, and he was unable to think much over what they were talking. Peg sat in her high chair beside him and jabbered and clomped her feet noisily against the table and he was glad he could turn his attention to making her behave.

He didn't feel hungry, himself.

He felt the too sudden shock of realizing what a complete fool a man can be.

And it had all seemed so simple, so easily explained, actually and honestly so harmless, in his mind up to now. Hell's fire, go out in the world, anywhere in the world, look at people and men and study them, get below the surface, and what do you find? Plenty of what the Bible teaches you, of course, among the opposite things—but don't you truly see that a heap of the wrong and the sin and all such is formed in folks' ways of thinking and forming beliefs? But no, that was only his own fool's way of thinking. All the time that had been only his weak and sickly way to find an excuse for his—adultery, that was the word—with Letitia.

If Sareeny found out she would leave him!

That thought burned like fire in Case's mind.

A man is a fool to think he can secret such a thing in his life, Case knew now. In the beginning his father had known, even now he might be suspicious. Now Jacob knew. And lately, Dorcy Fry's eyes had held a strange expression when she looked at him, though she was such a puzzling woman it would take Christ Himself to figure her out or what she might be thinking. But the silence of her wordless look worried Case. Though how in the world could Dorcy know anything about it?

And all because of the hidden, closeted pleasure of Letitia being like a second wife to him. All because she had come to him and he had wanted her, and he had thought it was something he could hide away as safe from other folks' knowledge as a thought that is never looked or spoken.

Before ever he left the supper table, while Sareeny still talked of Jacob, Case made up his mind he was through with Letitia. As soon as he could he would break with her and give her to understand she was not to come back to him ever again. It would take a little time and he would have to be careful. Letitia loved him, and because of that, this matter did not prove her cheap and weak and foolish, as it did him. She was a new Indian, able to hold her own in a changed world. In a certain way he loved Letitia, but not in the eternal, foreverly way he loved Sareeny. He knew in his own mind that when Sareeny left him, in death, or any other way, something in his life would be as dead. In any lonely region set away from the balance of the world, a man's love for his wife is even more as the anchor and the realization to which his life is rooted.

After supper Case left the house and walked away alone across the fields.

How in tarnation had Jacob learned about Letitia, anyway? By spying on them, most likely! There always had been something uncertain and sly-footed about Jacob. Now, before the summer passed, Jacob would no doubt come home again and settle down with Frace, and sooner or later he would up and tell Sareeny all that he had seen in his spying. Case could curse himself, his thoughts writhing in torment because he had no defending reason—not even in his own secret thinking, now.

The wonder of it was the pleasure it gave him to be with Letitia, alone with her in some thickly wooded place hidden in the hills. He would often lie flat on his back beside where she sat, and they would not even talk much; her hands, tender in their touch as any woman's could be, were always about his face or smoothing his black hair, or silencing any worrying words of his lips. . . . Oh, Letitia loved him, she loved him so much she dwelled upon every stolen hour with him; and every word she said, everything she wore, was with a thought of him. Case knew that now. She had loved him since that summer before ever he had married Sareeny.

Letitia would lean above him with her strange dark beauty that she knew so well how to set off to advantage by her choice of rich color and cloth. She was like a child—beautiful and girl-like—but she was a woman, too—able to talk deeply and wisely, seeming even more educated and worldly than Felix, who had traveled and spent years at Eastern schools. All her young life Letitia had studied and planned and worked, learning, always with the thought that she would show people what an Indian could do! An Indian woman could be just as beautiful, dress as stylishly, talk as brightly and intelligently as any white woman. She'd show them!

She met Case, and loved him, and slowly the importance of her eager plans faded.

Someday, perhaps, she *would* tell Case of the boy she had birthed for him three years ago. Perhaps she might not tell him for a long time, if ever. It was better that he did not know. Though many times when they were alone in the hills she would look close in Case's dark brown eyes and smile to herself and think: "What would he say if I told him? If I told him he was a father to my little half-Indian, half-white boy before he was ever a father to the girl baby his own wife gave him?" She had named the boy Hosea. She had liked that name, though she could never remember where she had heard it. Hosea Gyler.

But she did not tell Case, because she knew that if ever he learned of it, the shock and surprise of his learning would mean a crisis.

Case was half-afraid of what Letitia might do, if he suddenly refused to meet her. No, he must go at this matter carefully. He would get it settled and finished and past, but quietly. The more he thought about it the more disgusted he was with himself. But it was a relief to him to know he was turning his back on the whole thing; he knew he'd never be such a fool again!

Thinking, he stayed in the field until dark had come. When he came at last to the house, Sareeny and Minty and Felix were waiting for him on the big front porch.

And Dorcy sat there with them.

They were all a little tired and were not in a talkative mood, and the warm night was restful.

# CHAPTER 13

THIS summer, Sareeny finally talked Case into joining the Church. He was stubborn about it; not because he did not believe in God, he said; but he believed in letting his life take care of its self, too.

At first he would not listen seriously when she talked. He did not yet believe she was serious.

"Your life can't take care of its self, Case," Sareeny told him.

He was ever a little short-tempered and grouchy this summer.

"Why can't it?"

She thought out her words and said simply:—

"Because you must live it, your own self."

He got up and left the house. Sareeny would be glad when he finished cultivating the corn in the west eighty. It was a mile from that field to the house, and that made four miles each day going to and from work and meals. When he finished that work he would have a week to rest before the hay season started.

Felix sat at the table by the kitchen window. He was typing a letter. Sareeny liked to watch him. One time he had told her he used his finger tips to see with, and she could almost believe it, the way his fingers flashed over the typewriter keys stamping out a letter with every word just right.

Now he finished, and as he folded the letter, he turned to her. With Sareeny his blue eyes were always gentle and his face warm with friendship. He loved Sareeny twice as much as he would a sister and he didn't care who knew it.

Felix thought it would be a fine thing if they all joined the Church. He had thought about it many times, he said, and in all truth a person could live a good life and never enter a church door. He told Sareeny about a time he had lived in New York City, knowing not one person there and in all those millions of people he had known not one friend. For six months he had lived in a room across the street from a great cathedral. And in the mornings and in the evenings he had sat by his window and listened to the crowds come to worship and pay tribute to a God. They lifted their voices in song and murmured prayers to a glory too great for earth. He had thought then: "Wherever in the world one may go there are churches. There must be a God."

Sareeny liked to hear Felix talk, for he had a way of describing things he had never seen, yet he could make her see as though she had been to that place with him. Often he would ask her to describe something to him. The colors of a flower, or sunset, or the way the mountains looked off in the distance. And she would grope in her mind for words to picture for him the fiery brilliance of the sunset's reds and blues and golds.

More often he went with his mother on long hikes over the hills and up and down Sarpy Creek's twisting little valley. It was hard to tell which did Minty the more good, those long walks in the warm outdoors, or the close, deep companionship of Felix. They learned from each other many things. Minty's cheeks filled out and her eyes brightened with a clearness and sparkle. Only once did she come home with an expression of her old, quiet sadness.

Felix had questioned her about her life in the city; about all her life up to the time he had come with old Herman to find her.

Minty had lied to him, completely and convincingly.

Felix believed her, and never again would he question her or wonder over those twenty years she had lived apart from his father.

But a few days later, she and Felix went over to Herman's and Birdie's for dinner. Birdie had never ceased to be curious over the true story of Minty; and when Felix innocently gave her an opening, Birdie had the whole pack of lies out of him within thirty minutes' time.

Birdie thought to herself: "So that's why she and old Eden were divorced. They just couldn't get along with each other and be happy. Well, that's not the whole truth and I still don't understand it all, but anyway I found out that much." She allowed herself a quick look at Herman. A look that said, "There now, do you think you can keep me from finding out anything I want to know?"

Minty, tight-lipped and hard-eyed, looked up from her plate and across the table to old Herman. Herman's eyes said very plainly: "Don't you worry a bit. The truth about you is safe."

Secretly, in the silence of her own upstairs room at home, Minty sometimes lay awake in her bed, or sat in her rocker by the window, her thoughts heavy with guilt and shame. Not but it was best for her to lie to Felix and them all. It hurts to deceive someone whose reason for trusting you is loving you. Nor would it hurt so much could she have lied just once and no more. But now, perhaps again and again she would have to repeat that story, and perhaps enlarge upon it with each retelling. Each time she might be leading them nearer to learning the truth.

They all went to church the next Sunday. And they were all accepted as members, promising to live as God Himself would have them live. Mills the minister was a

136

plain, simply educated ex-rancher. His beliefs were simple:

"Ye all know the difference between right and wrong. Yore joining of the Church is proof ye are turning away from all wrong, to henceforth do what ye know is right."

There was no confession of sins. As Mills said, from this time forward they were to do right, to live each day believing in an Almighty God, Creator of the earth and everything upon it. God was not to be feared, but trusted. Their sins, if they had any, they would bury away, as one buries away tainted meat in the soil for the soil to change back to clean, rain-washed earth. And they would sin no more.

Mills preached a good sermon. As his beliefs were plain, so his words were plain. To be a Christian one had only to treat his neighbors and friends and fellow men with goodness and never refuse a helping hand; to believe in God and acknowledge him as the Creator of the earth and the source of all the things by which we are able to live. Was that such a hard thing to do, he demanded of them? He looked down from his pulpit and smiled, thinking to himself that there was not one among them heavy-laden with sin. They were the farmers and the ranchers and the neighbor-families he had known for years. Not one among them, he would vow, was a thief, or a murderer, or dwelt upon adultery.

They were his neighbors.

Sareeny prepared dinner for twenty people that day. Never before had the wide, high-ceilinged dining room of Felix's father's house held so many laughing, talking people, or the long table been so loaded with good things to eat. Sareeny and Minty and Frace stood long over the hot stove, frying chicken, so that their own faces were red from the heat.

Dorcy was there, with her six shy shabbily-dressed children. Dorcy was a changed woman these last few months. As Birdie said, it was as though something frozen in her face had melted and she had at last decided to let herself enjoy life. Well, she was certainly a thousand times better off since that worthless man of hers had left her.

Throughout all the summer months, neighbors had come to Dorcy's house. They brought gifts. A sack of new potatoes, or a chunk of fresh beef. Neighbor men had gathered and dug a new well, higher up on the hillside; they repaired her house; even the artist fellow, Caleb, who seemed a mite stuck-uppity and queer till you got to know him, had sent over a wagonload of oldish furniture that was as good as new to Dorcy.

Oh, the world must seem a better place to Dorcy, now. For she was a changed woman in more ways than one.

She had stepped right out and took a-hold of things, so to speak, and she was making more money right now than Olen Fry had ever made. She had traded off four of them worthless old plug horses for four good milk cows. She sold cream and butter. She had worked like a nigger, fixing that place up, cleaning out the cluttered-up yard and planting flowers. Her back yard was a pretty sight with scarlet poppy blooms and tall white shasta daisies, and a rock garden where the old well used to be. Everything over there sure looked different, and as Birdie said, it all just went to prove the fact it was that worthless Olen Fry who had give the family such a bad name.

Dorcy ought to be glad he was gone.

Never would Dorcy speak a word about Olen up and leaving her like he did. When anyone mentioned his name, her lips clamped shut tight as a bench vise, and her eyes, turning to look away, were hard as gray flint rock.

Late in July, Case cut the alfalfa on the far side of the big hill west of the house. Many a bucket of wild cherries Sareeny had picked there, standing in the midst of a wilderness of wild-rose bushes as high as her waist, scattered over with the cherry bushes darker green. It was a place of cool shadows, where cottontail rabbits birthed their young and scampered away from her feet down sandy, scented paths. Marshy in places, where Sarpy Creek's clear water overflowed, it was the nesting place of hundreds of red-winged blackbirds, their little ebony bodies and crimson wings reflecting every bright ray of summer sun. The clinking notes of their glad twinkling song quivered in the air on every side. Away yonder, on past the hayfield, was the open range. The range land stretched for miles and miles to the west as wild and untamed as it had been a hundred years ago, except that now there were cattle herds instead of buffalo herds, and cowboys instead of naked, savage Indians. The range was greenish gray and inviting, a far-reaching distance of high, rounded, grassy hills, with the grass knee-high and swelling and moving in the wind like waves on the sea. A pleasant place, with so much bright blue sky, and purple shadows hiding distant mountains, many steep canyons and sheer cliffs; but a greenhorn could get lost out there as easy as rolling off a log. If he got lost in the winter, with snows white dazzling and deceiving distance, and that cold Montana wind whistling around every hill, he would be done for, that's all.

Sareeny now was burdened and slowed with her unborn child that would enter life next month. Felix and Minty had scolded her when she took the bucket and went to pick the half-green cherries, for she ought to stay near home, and they knew it. But Sareeny had ever liked to walk out over the fields and the pastures alone, free to let her thoughts turn where they would, and these last few weeks she had been moody and strangely silent.

The sun was not so hot this morning. It was one of those times when the wind and sun and clear blue vaulted height of sky all combine to make a perfect day; and the earth, lusty and rich with ripening crops, waits in peace for the harvest.

Case's mowing machine clattered across the hayfield, cutting neat, straight strips from the dark green alfalfa. Old sage hens mustered their young together and led them away, slipping silently through the high green forest of alfalfa stalks and purple blossoms. Now and then a snake moved, softly as velvet, away from the threatening noise and the horse's sharp shod hoofs.

Sareeny moved leisurely along the sun and shadow-specked pathway that curved this way and that around the cherry bushes. There was no need for her to hurry. Minty would get the dinner ready; and little Peggy was as well off there with old Minty as she could ever be on her mother's lap. The cherries were extra fine this year, large and juicy; though they were only half-ripe, so that they were red, not yet turning black. They hung in heavy red clusters from every twig. They would make fine jelly. She could fill her bucket in no time. Then when Case came around to this side of the field she could talk to him awhile.

She fell to thinking of Ranny. None of them had seen Ranny for nearly two years now. Not since he and Beth had married and gone off to Stillwater County to live, nearly two hundred miles away. There hadn't been any sense in Ranny going so far away. An ordinary man was always like that, it seemed. As soon as he got married he wanted to take his woman and get plum away, if he could, and have her all to himself. That's the way Case had done her; taking her up on them God forsaken Broadview Prairies to live where they had mighty nigh starved to death. Because of all that, their first baby, Peggy, had been born out in the hills with no one but Case and herself. She could have died.

But she hadn't died, she told herself with great satisfaction, and then laughed inwardly at her own foolishness. Here she was, on a day over two years later, picking cherries while Case mowed hay in a nearby field; and little Peggy was a healthy child, started toward her three-year birthday; as noisy as any young-un could be.

And another baby would be in her arms before the next snowfall.

She was very much alive, she told herself.

Mills had preached a good sermon, last Sunday. The three parts of life, he had said, were birth, and the actual living of life . . . and death. Well, she had two of the three parts practically in the palm of her hand, right now. And somewhere in the time to come, death was the surest thing on earth.

Mills had said: "How can ye be shore there is a God?"

Sareeny reckoned there were a hundred ways one could be sure. The bright red cherries hanging in heavy clusters above her head were one answer, if when she dropped them in her bucket she stopped to look at them closely, and studied every vein that made up the fruit around the small hard seed. And the seed itself was an answer, for you had only to drop it in the earth and leave it be. A tree would come up, growing swiftly, yet too slow for the eyes to follow, growing bark and wooden branches; the wood and bark would send out flowers, and the flowers would fall to reveal the fruit.

Often as she worked about the house or garden on a summer afternoon, and Felix was home, a sudden gleaming ripple of music would come to her on the still air; and as Felix played the piano or violin she would pause in her work to listen, for, ever had it seemed to her, music must be a breath of God Himself. Was there one human being on earth who would not pause to listen when he heard music, making him remember or forget?

Sareeny had her bucket nearly full of cherries and was about ready to quit, when Case stopped his mowing and came walking down the crooked path towards her. She watched him as he took long slow steps, turning his broad shoulders sideways to go through the narrow places where thorny runners of wild rose curved downward over sandy banks.

Case had been working too hard, she thought. Else he would never look so worried, and be so silent, as though he never had any rest. At home here lately, after the day's work was done, he would go and sit on the long front porch; talking only when some one of them asked a question. He didn't relish his meals as he used to do, either.

She took her pail and set it down carefully, then made a place to sit on the grassy bank. Case came and dropped down heavily beside her.

His face, under the wide brim of the coarse straw hat, was tanned brown as pine bark. It made his hair look blacker, his teeth whiter. Sareeny leaned over and kissed him. Her mind, her face, the expression in her eyes, held a thought she so seldom put into words: I love you so much, Case.

Case said, half-scolding:—

"You ought not to walk way over here, Sareeny."

She smiled to herself, quickly. If she lived with him a hundred years it would still please her when he showed worry over her.

"I like to get out like this. And I won't be able to go for a while after the baby is born."

He said proudly:—

"This baby can be born in a hospital if you want it to be. If you will let me, I'll take you there when you are ready to go. Then we will know everything is going to be all right."

She gasped and stared at him, then laughed. "Why, Case! I don't have to go to any hospital!"

"No, you don't have to. But I thought you might want to. . . . They could make it a heap easier for you there."

"But it would cost a pile of money."

"It would be worth it."

She thought a moment, then shook her head, smiling at him, understanding what he had tried to say. "No, I'd rather stay home. Where I can have you and Mom—and Minty. And Frace and Dorcy will do anything they can to help.

He walked to the top of the hill with her and carried the bucket of cherries. Sareeny breathed heavily from the steep climb.

Case frowned: "There'll be no more walks for you, lady. Not for a while."

Sareeny breathed deeply. It was hard for her to catch up on her breath. She looked at Case and laughed and said:—

"No, not till there's another man to go with me. . . ."

Case put out his arm and hugged her shoulders to him. She could feel his arm quiver, and the tone of his voice surprised her. He said strangely:—

"God bless you, Sareeny—" His arm dropped slowly from her shoulders. "You'd better go on home, now."

Case came in early from the field that night. Without a word to any of them he saddled a horse and rode away up Sarpy Creek across the far stretches of the fields, and into the open range.

And he found Letitia there.

There was a place where a multitude of scrubby cedar swarmed over a long hillside looking to the west. Even on the stillest days the wind was never silent there. In some unimagined way, wisps of breeze were caught down from the high blue freedom of the sky, and hung in the spicy scented branches. The cedars sheltered countless winding, crooked paths, and the hoary trunks formed cornices for many a low room of sandy floors, walled in with dusky green twilight.

Letitia had waited for him there in days of winter, when

snows heavy-white blanketed all the land and every bush and twig and tree leaned under its weight of softly heaped snow crystals. In the summer she would often bring a book to read, and she read and lay and waited in some thick shade; while her horse browsed about near by, cropping choicest bits of green grass that sprouted from some hidden spring.

This day when she saw Case walking and leading his horse up the long slope towards her she ran to meet him and put her arms around his neck. She was always so pitifully glad to see him. She was like a child, her eyes sparkling with joy and half-tears. But her eyes were wise, too, with the trained intelligence of a person taught that cleverness will win them anything wanted in life.

She was clothed in a riding habit of soft gray, with tiny buttons as black as her hair. This summer she had bobbed her hair, and with every movement of her little head the smooth black surface caught sheens of light; and the way her hair curved down her cheeks formed of her face a heart shape with red mouth and white teeth and eyes wise in ways God never meant an Indian to be.

Case pulled her arms from his shoulders. He said swiftly, as though it were something he dreaded:—

"I'm not coming here any more, Letitia."

Her face changed slowly. Her eyes stopped their laughing. She studied his face and knew that he meant it and she could not change him. When she spoke her voice was almost gentle.

"And you were half-afraid of what I might say to that, weren't you? Do not worry, Case. I knew that someday you would not come any more."

He said nothing. He took tobacco and papers from his shirt pocket and rolled a cigarette with unsteady fingers. . . . For the first time in his life, he was ashamed. He was angry with himself. God knowed he was no angel! He'd lived through as much dirt as any man. But he'd never before tried to understand anything—like this thing that had drawn him on into this mess. He knowed right from wrong, same as anyone did. But like everyone else, he reckoned, he'd had to live a lot and learn a little, till all of a sudden he'd got wise to himself, that's all. A thousand voices could shout and whisper and talk to you all the first forty years of your life, saying: This thing is wrong. You know it is wrong. You must not do this thing. . . . And though we know it is wrong, never do we fully understand all the whys and wherefores of that law of life until we have lived it. You had to learn to think about such things.

His face was flushed. He knew suddenly that this was not mere dirt, his carrying on with Letitia when Sareeny was back yonder at the house, believing in him.

Letitia was thinking: "Now I should tell him. Now I should tell him everything."

But she could not. She stood with her lips closed, and looked at him. She did not want to tell him, now. Later she would see that he knew all there was to know. But not yet.

She stood very still and looked at him, thinking very slowly and clearly, studying him out. She had always known that he was most likely using her for a fool, conceal it as he would. And she had known this was coming. Last week, and the week before that, every week since early spring, she had seen that he was planning to be rid of her.

She suddenly saw him exactly as he was—for what he was—exactly as he had always felt towards her. She raised the quirt that hung from her wrist, to strike him across the face with it. She let it drop again, even before he had understood what she was about to do. Nothing in the look of her face had changed.

She said quietly:—

145

"I loved you, Case. From the time you first began to notice me when I came home to the reservation."

He said something, but she paid no attention to him, for she was thinking: A hundred times you have slipped away and met me here and took me even as though you were married to me and I was your willing squaw. Now you think you can say "good-bye" and that is the end of it. You fool, you fool.

Let him go on home, thinking with smug satisfaction this thing was settled and neatly ended and forever past.

He was a fool. He believed she was a fool, too, an ignorant, fool Indian, never able to forget he was a white man.

She stood perfectly composed, perfectly dressed, a beautiful, intelligent Indian woman. She scorned him and his white wife, and scorned herself because she had let herself love him. He was not even a fit man for his white, simple wife, Sareeny.

But Letitia loved him, she knew even now she loved him while she loathed him for the worst that was in him. He was just another man, poor, as good as he was bad, and what was she but another low Indian woman, educated and trained and pushed back within the bounds of her obscure reservation?

She forced herself to control her thoughts and talk with him.

When they parted this time, never would she come near him again.

But he would learn that such a thing as this can never be finished!—or forgotten.

And as long as she lived, Letitia never saw Case's face again, after this day.

On this evening they spoke their last words to each other.

As so often happens on the open range, a swift west wind came down suddenly from nowhere. It streamed through

146

the bushy cedars, lonesomely lulling a thousand unseen things to peace. Case wanted to get away, to be quickly rid of this thing that had hung on his soul so long, a dead weight to be hidden and carried in the presence of Sareeny and everyone he knew.

The sun had set. He rode his horse home slowly, and he was consciously free of a shame that had rose up in his mind every time he had looked at Sareeny, until he had feared she must surely see and guess. He thought to himself now that he was free of this he would never again look after another woman or carry on with her as he had Letitia. As all men must learn in time, that some things are not to be taken lightly, so he had learned. In his mind there was no thought of the word "sin," for it was a word Case had not used twice in his life. But there was thought of Sareeny, quiet in her ways, almost as this country twilight was quiet, the harsh sounds of day life muted softly over every dusky hill and low place. She was as good a wife as any man ever claimed. And there was only one of her; he could look the wide world over and he would never find another of her. And there was thought of the long time to come and their being together; and he could go on loving her, taking care of her, making her life as pleasant as he could so long as her life was in his hands. He loved Sareeny. He loved Sareeny the way any man loves the woman who was meant for him.

Letitia had said she would marry Charley Wilson, a young educated Indian on the reservation. Well, that was the best thing for her. And left alone, everything would right itself in time, for that is the way of the world.

Letitia, at home that night, took off the soft gray riding habit and clothed herself in the softer, doeskin garments her people wore. She replaced her boots with small beaded moccasins.

She burned the clothes she had been so proud of because they set off her pretty face and slender body. One by one she dropped them on the fire; the gray riding habit, the stylish dresses she had selected so carefully from mail order catalogues, the trim, neat little shoes.

There was hatred in her face. Her father watched with quiet satisfaction. Long ago he had seen his mistake in expecting Letitia to take a white girl's place among the whites. It could not be done. Not yet. Sometime, in years to come, perhaps, an Indian would not be treated as the whites treat the people who work for them. But that time was not yet. Now, when an Indian girl tried to dress and tried to act as white girls do, low white men were quick to believe she was cheap and no good. It was well she was burning those clothes that made every man, even Indians, turn to look at her.

And that was Letitia's way of telling him that never again would she wear other than the usual garments of a Crow Indian squaw.

That same night she led Charley Wilson on until he asked her to marry him. Charley knew she had a son over three years old, and that the father was a white man living somewhere along Sarpy. Charley did not know the man's name, and he did not care. The boy would not live with Letitia all the time, but would continue to divide each year between time with her and long summer vacations with Letitia's father. But if Letitia wanted the boy with her all the time, she could have him. Charley was a good man. Letitia knew that. He had wanted to marry her since the time they had met in college, and they had studied together, and sat in the same schoolrooms, and each had learned the other's plans and hopes. Charley's black eyes worshiped Letitia with humble, doglike devotion. Letitia knew he would forgive what was to come, because he was good, and loved her so. He would be her refuge.

They were married the next day. Old Man Mills came out to the reservation to perform the marriage ceremony, and later he said it was the biggest wedding among the Indians that he had ever seen. That Charley Wilson was a handsome fellow—a smart businessman!— with an educated wife, he ought to do a lot for the tribe.

A week after she was married, Letitia told Charley that the middle of winter would bring her another child, and the father was the same white man who lived on Sarpy.

The three days following were like a blank in their lives. Everything hung in the balance, with their misery, their hot words, their hatred, their bitter silence, the shame and uncertainty. Charley might have whipped her. Anything he might have done would have been upheld by the tribe. But at the end of the three days he understood her misery and, because he loved her, he came to forgive and comfort her. Her refuge, just as she had known he would be. His steadfast kindness went on the same, and never was there a Crow Indian who treated his wife better, or was as proud to have her always with him, or loved her more.

Letitia was not his squaw. She was his wife.

As fall came on, he said not one word about what she had told him. His gentleness with her never changed. But as he watched her growing heavy and burdened with another child that was not his, his thoughts tortured him. He was not jealous over this part of Letitia's life he had not shared. He loved her too much for that, and neither of them were dull, slow-thinking Indians out of place in an up-to-date world.

He thought with quick hatred of some white man laughing to himself and saying Oh, it was only an Indian squaw. . . .

Letitia had not yet offered to tell him the white man's name. He would not force her to tell him. There were other ways of learning. He would not kill the man. Only a fool would do that. But there were other ways of punishment, too.

Different plans drifted through his mind as to how he might punish that man without hurting Letitia. For a time he wished that he might take both the children, when this one came, and push them in the white man's door and say: "Here. They are yours—may God damn your soul. You take them and feed them and raise them up. They are part of your own life. Not mine." But he could not do that. Before this unborn child could ever be one breath in its father's time it was love and pain and care in its mother's. Even now she was making ready for it, sewing little garments this little half-Indian and half-white would wear. No, he could not do that.

But his love for Letitia prevented him doing anything. As she had said, the middle of winter brought the second child. A cold night when east Montana wind drove the snow to deep drifts against the walls of Charley's new house. When morning came, and he had seen the little black-haired boy baby, Letitia told him Case's name.

And Charley promised her he would go down to Sarpy land and find Case and tell him, without anger, of each child. And that Hosea Gyler had been three years old this last month of June.

Letitia's eyes smoldered as she told Charlie just what to say. She meant this to be the last time she ever spoke Case's name, or brought thought of him into words.

Now would Case take this lightly? Now would he see that there are some things a man does he cannot wash his hands of so simply, or turn to forget so easily?

Charley's greater concern now was that Letitia be well and strong again.

As Sareeny's mother said, it never rains but what it pours. In August, she had come and stayed two weeks with Sareeny, the crew of harvesters came to be fed and waited on, with Sareeny having a baby in the midst of all that bustle and confusion.

The day after the baby was born the whole family had gathered around proud and happy; and old Jim said he'd be durned if Sareeny didn't pick the very worst time for the stork to come. He hoped she wouldn't wait next time till she was stranded out in the hills, or till twenty men had come to harvest a summer's crop.

Sareeny smiled to herself, resting her back on the pile of fluffed pillows her mother's work-darkened hands had arranged. Case would look at her and his eyes were warmly lit with a love that was ever as new as endless water running in clear depths over a sandy bed. When he looked at the baby boy, pride would break out all over his face, and by the way he acted Ellen said you'd think he'd had the baby his own self, 'stead of Sareeny.

Sareeny said nothing. But she thought to herself, Now that this baby is born a boy, there will be no more.

Every one of them, Ellen and Minty and Jim and Felix, suggested a name for him. Even Frace and Chris and Tana argued that Frederick was a fine name for any man. They could call him Freddie till he growed up a little, then shorten it to Fred.

But yonder in the field busy harvest waited for the men to work, and dollars in the form of wheat poured from the thresher's spout in a copper-colored stream. And noon-time would bring the men in, thirsty and dusty, hungry enough to eat a dozen platters of fried chicken. As Jim said, it would be a long time before this new fellow would give a dang what they called him, or anything else so long as he eat regular.

Sareeny let them talk and argue and remember every name they had ever heard, because she knew they enjoyed it.

But she named him, and his name was Robert Case.

With September came the frosts. The nights settled down colder, blacker. Wind blew, whirling up dust from stubbled fields, rolling giant tumbleweeds on and on and on till they struck a fence and piled up there, covered with the tiny hulls of a billion billion seeds they had strewn along their way— Schools opened. Schoolrooms, scattered here and there over the lonely land, were dusted and swept. Almost always it was a new teacher to come. Last year's teacher was married, in her own home now. Teachers never lasted long. They came, young and eager and more or less excited, from a college that had taught them how to teach others. They were young women, starting their careers. By the time another summer had rolled around, some young fellow had snatched them up. . . Their careers had changed, pleasantly, to what they had hoped it would be in the first place.

Frace returned to her work of teaching Sarpy School. She loved this work, with its interest and concentration, its alternating periods of boisterous play and silent study. The work and the children did not let her have so much time to think of her own self, or Jacob, or wonder where Jacob was or what he was doing.

For Jacob had never written a line.

For some reason Frace did not worry over Jacob, or even feel grieved. Honestly, she was much happier, now that time had accustomed her to his being gone. But on every day she could not help but wonder where he was, which way he had taken, and if anything had happened to him, to change him.

She was too contented over the fullness of life here, to mull with deep worry over any of Jacob's bullheadedness. As Frace saw them all their lives here were complete and full with quiet content. It seemed to Frace that the old sandy road they all traveled on nearly every day, except in winter, could be compared to an artery along which all the contentment, the friendliness, the deep satisfaction of their living flowed from one home to another. Even though life was hard here, with scant luxury, especially for a wife and mother. The sandy road turned from Sareeny's yard, and Dorcy's yard, to meet and blend into one lazylike, slumberous way across the little valley and over the hills, past lonely homes, to finally turn in at Ellen's carefully tended yard of old lilacs and flower shrubbery. Frace, with Tana, hurried home there each night. A whole day seemed a long time for Frace to be away from little Keith.

Dorcy washed and scrubbed and dressed up her four oldest young-uns in better clothes than they had ever before had in their lives. She sent them down the road to school and Frace. This was six-year-old Silver's first year. In two more years, Rose would be ready for high school. Sid and Denver, the ornery little scamps, would never finish the eighth grade unless she could make them get down and study. Dorcy wished she could have gone further in school, her own self. Then she could help them more, and not show them how ignorant she was every time they asked her how to do a fraction problem. Sid and Denver did have a time with their problems.

God in heaven, they would never have a problem like hers, she thought. A problem that would be a dead weight on her mind ever' hour of her life, whispering to her out of the walls at night, dogging her feet with ever' step she took by day. That old well was just a patch of scattered rock, now that the frost had killed the flowers. Every time she passed it she could not keep her eyes from turning there with fear, as though she half-expected Olen to pop up through the dirt and lunge at her. Sometimes she would stop an everlasting battle in her mind not to think about it. And she pondered the whole thing, until she could be calm, and talk to the children and neighbors, easily hiding tell-tale thought. At such times she would think honestly and simply: I'm not sorry. . . . I'm not sorry. God knows I stood enough. I've got to go right on without saying anything . . . make people think he left me. I've got my children to think of. . . .

She knew she must not worry or fight too much against her thoughts, or she would turn insane. She must not imagine things, like she had first done. That made her dream. Horrible dreams, when he loomed up suddenly in the dark door of her bedroom, his clothes rotted away to rags, his face seeming both dead and alive, but frozen into the awful expression he had when he died. She might dream again that he came to stand over her bed. . . .

Now on these blowy days of late fall the house was silent, for the two younger children napped in the afternoon, and there was no sound but that of the wind pressing against the outer walls as it passed. Many an afternoon Dorcy bundled up the two babies and went across the road to Sareeny's.

Case cleared two thousand dollars that fall. He deposited the money in a bank. For a long time there was hardly a day passed that Sareeny did not go and get the little leathern book to look at the neat figures. She gloated over them. Never had she believed they would have that much money so soon and all at one time. Now they had it so easily. But no!—it was not had easily. There was not one penny of that money they had not sweated and worked for; their hands and fingers had done drudgery, their bodies bent and leaned at hard work till many a tired day was over. But here was pay. It was not great riches, but it turned away the need and want and hurt of being poor as a door is shut against the wind.

In midwinter Charley Wilson came and went away quietly, leaving with Case the message Letitia had sent. Charley rode away, his black eyes glowing with satisfaction, for in

154

the few minutes he had taken to put Letitia's message into words he had understood the punishment would right itself. Even though Case Gyler kept this secret, everything about his life would work together to punish him. If he was a man completely no good, nothing would punish him except bodily pain. But this man was like so many men of his white race. Half very good and half very bad. And all his life the good half battled with the bad half, because he wanted his people to think he was a good man, a United States Citizen of good character.

The good in him would make him think of and be sorry for Letitia's sons that were also his sons. He would wonder over them from time to time. He would someday want to see them. But he would hide it all in shame from everyone he knew. Already he had begun doing that. There was his wife and his children by her, his friends and his church, all would be tools. And he would punish himself, because he was half good.

Charley was satisfied.

Jacob made no friends in his new life. True, there was the waitress in the waterfront cafe who served him his breakfast every morning at four o'clock, long before daylight. She recognized him as a steady customer, and talked to him in a disinterested, desultory fashion. She did not know who he was, or where he came from, or where he went, and she cared less. There were the men he knew because he worked with them, impersonal yet not unfriendly men, strong and unextraordinary, who, like himself, were doing this work because they were uneducated and untrained for something better, whose environment of life had shaped them as they were. Some of these men were old, even past middle age. They worked hard. They talked rough and laughed loud and ate their food with dirty hands and gulping mouths of honest hunger. They told lurid jokes about women, and in their raucous laughter no thought was concealed. Many of them had lived all their lives in these streets close by the sea, working where great ships came from afar and anchored at wharves to dump strange cargoes on the land. These men knew only the waterfront, with its crowding noise, and vaguely curtained vice, fish markets, the dank smell of sea water, the cheap glitter by night. Any kind of human being may be found on such a street.

Jacob knew his landlady—though he had changed his room when he began this later job. His first landlady had been a sour-faced, pinch-nosed woman who eyed him with virginly disgust, distrusting him merely because he was a man and therefore nasty, in her opinion; she was a religious woman, though she wouldn't have trusted Jesus Christ Himself had He stepped down from heaven and laid His hand on her brow. Now, this second landlady was more friendly; she called a greeting to Jacob when he came in from work at night, and sang out hello to him whenever she passed down the hall and the door to his room was open. She would have trusted him for his rent, now that she knew he would work and was honest. She even hinted that as long as he paid his rent, his room was his, and if a different woman slept in his bed every night—his room was his!—Wasn't it?

But Jacob made no friends.

He was not lonely, and he wanted no friends. There were too many other interests. He understood now, partly, why he had been so restless and dissatisfied and unhappy, back home. It had not been all because of Frace. Much of it had been caused from his own weariness of year after year of the sameness of that narrow world. Some people can stand a thing like that, but not Jacob. His restless, quick mind was unhappy under a stale unchanging outlook on unchanging scenes, on people who, if they had anything different or vital

156

or dramatic in their lives, so hid it behind the common-place facts of their daily existence that even the closest neighbor was unknowing of it.

Jacob thought that here was everything—everything! To forever freshen up the interest, to make a man wonder, never to let him grow restless or ingrown upon himself. Back home their world had been like a tea cup, known so well to the few of them who lived there, overshadowed by mountainous edges above which news and glitter of a vast world beyond had spilled occasionally. Here, for Jacob, the world was something in which he lived confident that each new day or night would never be stale or dull or dead with unchange.

How Jacob reveled in all the change, the rush, the turbulent spirit of this city by the sea! Even in the sleepy, black hour when Jacob went to his work on the boat and the boat turned out on the dark sea, he could look back as the distance grew and the city glittered and sparkled like a great jewel in the night, hiding in its glitter so many many things. And by day the little boat, sturdy and courageous, pushed her valiant way over the deep water, and the water slapped against her sides with petty resentment. In bright weather the sea was bluer than a summer sky in Montana. In slow wind, waves rolled, capped white and lovely. Always in a storm or before it, the sea was green, paler, yet as beautiful as the shade of an emerald's green. And in black darkness the water hissed and rolled, surging with sinuous movement.

Oh, the sea was a lovely thing!—A restless, mighty thing— a threatening, mysterious thing! Seeing it, listening to it, riding and working upon it, it struck some answering, kindred note in Jacob's soul. How he loved and feared and loved the sea.

He wished that someday he might have a farm near it, with cattle grazing on green slopes that reached down to shore, and windows in his house to look across the moving water. He knew he could never be anything much, except a farmer, and that was what he wanted to be. But he wanted to look around a little, first.

Frace, and the folks at home, wondered why he did not write. It was not that he had no thought of them. But it was not yet definite in his mind what he would say to them.

It was midwinter before he decided.

Many times he wished that his old Ma could have gone on one of those long walks with him. She would have just stood and looked, open-mouthed, with hushed wonder, at the incredible beauty of a sunken rose-garden's riot of color; or great cathedrals lighted by the weird soft beauty of many stained and colored windows bearing pictures of Christ in agony on the Cross, Christ with gentle face and outstretched hand to forgive and relieve the woman fallen in misery and despair at His feet. Jacob liked to look at those huge colored windows. Sometimes, on a Sunday, when worship was over, the people would flock from the cathedral, crowding the street about him, and Jacob reckoned nigh over a thousand people had been there in just this one cathedral. Why had many of them come? Because of habit, or because they thought it was the proper thing to do in society?—Or because in their hearts they wanted to? Jacob reckoned he would never go to church until he wanted to. He would never want to, until long time taught him to wonder over his own end, until something in his heart turned him there to that which voices eternity and the ultimate end and hope of every human self.

In midwinter Jacob wrote letters home. He asked Frace to divorce him. His letter to Frace was long and painstaking. Frace wept over the depth and feeling that struggled through the simple expression of that letter, but never would Jacob know that she cried over it. He sent money and gifts for little Keith. After the letter was stamped and dropped in the mail, his thinking of Keith made him miserable and un-happy. He did not want to think of Keith, except to send Frace money now and then, to buy things. . . . A drink of hard, stinging whisky would keep him from thinking. . . . Two hours after that letter was mailed Jacob stood giddy on his feet by a speakeasy bar.

Frace's answering letter was short, but simple and friendly. If Jacob wanted a divorce, he could have it. In his mother's letter, in all of the letters from home, Jacob sensed something withheld, as opinions or feelings concealed behind the friendliness and loyalty of his folks. They did not even criticize him, or write one word of disapproval.

For Jacob, this was vaguely disturbing.

Frace was granted the divorce in late spring.

Now, by law, she and Jacob were free of each other. Free to turn away, to forget, each to do as pleased them, with no thought of the other.

Jacob found a better-paying boat to work on. The year had subtly taught him many things. And even more subtly brought to life many things that were in him. He meant to save his money, and when he had enough he would buy a farm. He'd find and buy just the place he wanted. Hopes and thoughts in his mind shaped slowly into plans. A man could do anything he set his mind to, if he worked and was careful, and didn't let himself get sidetracked.

Another year passed.

Up and down the long varied distance of the Pacific Coast, Jacob had gone from one boat to another, always with the hope of bettering himself.

This year had wrought changes in him that were not subtle. He was all a man, now. The sea had seemed to de-velop and harden him, giving him greater strength, greater determination and stubbornness. He had many a fight, for he was afraid of no one. He was sure of himself, sure of everything about him. Sure of his good looks, knowing that his strong shoulders and tanned, handsome face, his brown, clear eyes, with brows and lashes as black as his hair, made many a woman turn to look at him. Nice women, well-dressed, with gentleness and purity in their faces. . . . Gay, foolish women, with warped minds, divertedly seeking nothing more than imagined thrills in life—and cheap, open women who belonged to any man for a handful of silver. Jacob was conceited, he thought he knew them all. He knew he could take one good look into a woman's face, and mark her in his mind for which of the three she was. He was so conceited he dressed overcarefully and well, selecting his clothes with thoughtful decision.

But he was not always happy. Many a night he drank and puked and drank at some dim and ribald bar close by the sea. And his mind turned in on himself so that he was aware of his own foolishness and ficklety. He knew that he was not a fool, and yet he could not make his life sane and solid and simple—it was like as though he needed a great rock chained to him, binding him down to earth and plain sense. Ma had not raised him to be what he was. That would make him think of Ellen, and he would stand wobbly on his feet and stare vacantly across the bar, vowing silently in his mind that someday he would send her something. Something nice. Something that would make her catch her breath. Something that seemed beyond the power of her life ever yet the likes of which she had always wanted to possess.

Yet never did he write to her.

Another year passed.

A letter came from Sareeny, saying they were all alive and well. The letter reached Jacob in midwinter, and found him in San Francisco. It said there had been no drought. Heavy crops had paid big money. Felix and Case had shared the expense and put a telephone in the house. He would never

160

recognize Keith who had grown so; and Frace was well, still teaching Sarpy school.

This mention of Frace brought her to Jacob's mind for the first time in months.

The letter went on to tell, though Mom was all right now, how on one day Frace had came in a room and found Mom laying like dead on the floor with no beat of her heart and no color in her face—Mom looked awful old. . . .

Jacob entered a place where a glittering window display had caught his eye. Never had his Ma had a jewel, though always she had loved them.

He stood pondering above the black velvet trays the soft-voiced, eager owner held before him. What would Ma like most? A diamond? A ruby? An emerald? Or a pearl? Any one of them cost a powerful lot of money. But he did not care. Wasn't she worth all the jewels on earth, he thought? . . . All this priceless sparkle before him made him think more strongly of her, somehow, and his eyes were suddenly blurred. . . . He bent his head so the man would not see.

The diamonds were like chipped and carved bits of ice, a-fire with colored sparkle. The ruby was like a single drop of hard, polished blood. He did not like the deep poison-green of the emerald. But the pearl shimmered between the tips of his long brown fingers. It was light as a feather and perfectly round, so indescribably delicate, hard and solid between his fingers, yet soft to the touch. It held the shimmering beauty of the sea. He bought it in a ring for his Mom's finger, and mailed it to her in the small velvet box.

Jacob frequented the better bars, now that he made more money. Here the people were of a higher caste. They were educated, accustomed to better things. They could even get very drunk, to a certain limit, with dignity.

In such a place, Jacob met Eunice Maylain.

161

He saw her first in the noon hour. She was tall and very well dressed in a tailored fashion. They were drinking at the circular bar, he had been watching her, hoping that she would look at him.

She did. She was pretty. She sat looking at him deliberately; and then, perhaps because she liked him, or perhaps because she knew that he had been watching her, she smiled very honestly and frankly.

Then, like a dash of cold water for Jacob, she turned away and forgot him.

She seemed to forget him completely, for days. And always he was near. Next she found that she could not keep herself from looking at him, and always his eyes met hers. He was so physically attractive.

She was always well dressed, though never too expensively. She drank a great deal, sometimes just a trifle too much. But she was always coldly intelligent. She was a woman who could weigh matters, make up her mind, and demand—*demand* what she considered due.

Her hair was brown and bobbed long. It was straight where it smoothed down over her head, then softened to waves where it rested on her shoulders. Her eyes were gray, her skin smooth white. She was a very pretty woman.

She hated and feared the sea.

One evening she surrendered suddenly to herself and to the look in Jacob's eyes.

She came and sat at his table.

# CHAPTER 14

IT SEEMED to Sareeny that nothing on earth ever remained the same for long. A constant change is always taking place, in every last thing. Each year everything upon earth, and everything in life, is in some way different than it was the year before. So much so, that the happenings of each day, as they are left behind in times passing, are looked back on with homesickness or relief, according to how good or bad they be.

She told this to Caleb, the artist, one day while he was waiting for Felix to get ready for a sudden fishing trip to the mountains. Caleb laughed at her.

Look at the hills, he said. Didn't they stand just as they had stood for a thousand years? Couldn't you look to the west and see the Rocky Mountains' Great Divide stretched like a high wall across the distance? Well, the Indians had looked at them, too; and the Lewis and Clark Expedition had looked and seen them just as they were now; those mountains had stood there when the earth was young, God alone knows how many years ago.

It might be, the only thing that changes is ourselves, thought Sareeny. The good, solid old earth remains ever the same; and men change only the surface of it, as they live through the changes of their own lives; changes that begin the moment your heart first beats, and continue until you are dead and buried and rotted away.

Certainly this Sarpy land was not the same to her, or her neighbors. There had been a time, when she was a child, that the hills reaching for miles and miles in every direction had been a vast land unexplored for her. Then she had liked to climb the highest hills nearest her Mom's house; she had liked to look as far as her eyes could see and wonder, for beyond that distance there were a thousand big cities, and oceans thousands of miles across. Lo! What an appallingly big thing the earth had been, then. Later the hills were hateful things, lonesome things, penning her in, making her prisoner away from every imagined thing she wanted in life. Then again, later, they had seemed to silently welcome her back, and she had come gladly, because they were home. Now through all that time the hills had never changed; it was only within herself. This country would be home to her as long as she lived, and she knew it. Even if Case should some day decide to pick up and move to the Oregon coast, like he talked now and then of doing. If ever she moved away, and no matter how she changed, she would always feel a homesickness for this land, as long as she lived.

Now it was a place made different by thousands of dollars the state spent each year on the roads. Cars were forever passing with dust and noise, honking their horns to shoo Sareeny's and Dorcy's chickens or turkeys off the way. The last two years had seen a railroad laid, and noontime of each day found the passenger train thundering over its smooth rails that followed closely along Sarpy Creek. Night's quiet dark was shattered by the long drawn, eerie screech of freight trains' whistles. It had taken Sareeny weeks to grow used to that awful sound. Case had laughed at her many a time, when the lonely whistle had brought her straight up in bed, wide awake. This was only a little spur of a great railroad, he said, with just two trains passing every twenty-four hours. The railroad ran straight across Dorcy's wide farm, from end to end. The Company had paid Dorcy two thousand dollars to let them put the railroad there. Two thousand dollars! That was enough to keep Dorcy and her children in comfort for a long time to come. But the money was in a bank and Dorcy could not touch it nor see it nor spend one penny of it, until the law courts got a lot of unnecessary foolishness straightened out to their own satisfaction, and proved that worthless Olen Fry was legally dead, so that he would have no claim on the money.

Now what would Olen Fry think of that, thought Sareeny, if he came back someday and found himself declared legally dead, and his wife a rich woman?

It would serve him right. If he had not abused Dorcy all those years and run off and left her with a patchel of young-uns, they would both have all that money, and be happy with it.

The railroad had bred a hundred changes. The little town now had a doctor. A drugstore stood new and proud, directly across the street from Clyde Parker's old place. Next door to the dance hall, a brick building housed a garage and filling station. Down by the Church was the railroad station, and the homey white house the Company had built for its agent.

As some neighbors said proudly, this was progress. Crowding and making way for a better day, an easier life. But progress, like life, never stopped growing or crowding or changing. Relax a little and you find a strangeness has crept in. . . . A child you knew is a youth in school, a girl you knew is a woman married. . . . A man you knew is dead. . . .

The last Thursday in June, Sareeny was in bed again with another new baby and proud as Lucifer over it, too. It was a boy, and to please Case, she named it Amos Alexander, silly as the name sounded for such a little fellow. She decided ever they would call it Alex.

Case was a worry to her, sometimes. It did beat all how a man could act. So good one day, so shut-mouthed and sullen the next, as if he were worrying and pondering over something he was too stubborn to talk about. What was there to worry about? Times were good . . . crops were good. Life was good. . . . Oh not always too good, for some aggravating things are bound to happen. Still they had no great trouble that she could think of, and life was satisfying, if you had sense enough to see it that way. There were times when she would have lost patience with Case if she hadn't kept a grip on herself. He would not even explain to her what the trouble with his Dad had been over.

Case's father rarely came to see them, though he was fond of Sareeny. And Sareeny always tried herself to be good to him, because he was the only relative Case had. He was a queerish old man, hard and rough-spoken and good. For all of his being nigh onto sixty years old, he could work in the field beside Case or any younger man any day. He seldom left his place where he lived by himself, and often Sareeny wondered how he could stand being alone all the time.

After the trouble with Case, he never once came again to see them, though he lived close onto fifteen years.

He came riding into the yard early one morning, mad as a hornet. He looked grim and sick. His eyes looked like he could kill someone.

Case and he walked over to the orchard, talking by themselves where no one could hear. Sareeny knew something was wrong. She watched them through the kitchen window, wondering.

The old man called Case every stinging, filthy name he could lay tongue to; and he threatened to kill him.

Case had stood still with no word or movement, except that his hands, brown and clenched, twitched at the wrists. He would not look in his father's eyes, because his father's eyes hated him with raw shame, man's shame that is gross and terrible.

"I wish ye had came dead from yore mother's womb!"

When he saw that Case would speak no word back at him, the old man said:—

"A neighbor told me—and till then I did not know it was bein' joked about among the men, whispered among the wimmin. I went up to the mountains and I learned for myself. Two boys, as fine as I ever seed. My God, did ye think ye could secret such a thing forever?"

Whatever Case thought about that, he did not say.

And his father knew that to talk any longer would not help matters. But he went on, because he could not hold the words in him. His face and voice were sick.

"A squaw! I could have forgived it in ye as a man, before ye had a wife, a woman of yore own. I could have forgive ye the first child, because it was pregnanted before ye married Sareeny. But because of this second child and all that it means, some one of us ought to kill ye for what ye be. Why don't ye go and tell Sareeny, before she hears it from a neighbor?"

Sareeny came again to the kitchen window, anxious, and looked out at them.

She saw the old man knock Case flat on his back, and blood ran from Case's mouth.

She might have screamed; afterwards she could not remember what she did. Trying to keep from crying she ran through the house and out the front door. By the time she came out to the porch, the old man was crossing the yard. His face was as white as her own. He stopped and stared at her, then came quickly to her, his mouth opened to speak. But he changed his mind, and only let his hand fall heavily on her shoulder. In a way that she did not understand, he said:—

"God bless ye fer a good little woman, Sareeny."

167

Before she reached Case, his father was gone on the faunching, pawing horse he had ridden into the yard.

Case got up and tried to brush the dirt from his old hat, then slapped it against his knee until the dirt was free.

At first he would not look in Sareeny's eyes.

She wiped the blood from his lips with her handkerchief. She was trembling all over. Out of the silence she asked:—

"What ever was the matter, Case?"

Then he looked at her, deep and direct in her eyes. There was hurt and worry and something so piteous in the love of his brown eyes for her that she cried out his name and put her hands against his face.

She had but one week to go with this last child.

He said brokenly:—

"Oh, I've been a fool, Sareeny!"

His face was close to hers. His lips were close to her lips, tender with his love as a husband for her, tender with her love as a wife for him.

He spoke in a way he never had before. Hoarsely: "I could kill any man for touching you—anyone for hurting you. I'd die for you, Sareeny. I love you more than I love my own life."

He turned away from her, like as though he wanted to turn away from his own self, too; and he went down to the barn and on to his work in the fields without explaining to her or to Minty or to Felix one word of what the trouble had been about.

Sareeny mulled over the whole thing, strange doubt in her mind over why Case refused to explain it. Only once he spoke of it, and that was to make her promise never to question his father.

Case held to the desperate hope that no neighbor's talk would reach Sareeny's ears. Maybe she would not learn of it. It was the neighbors farther to the south who were talking,

168

and they only came down to Sarpy on Sunday visits. These close neighbors, Herman and Birdie, Dorcy and Caleb, they would breathe no word of it to Sareeny, even if they knew. And certainly old Minty or blind Felix would strive to keep it from her.

Case was sure if Sareeny ever learned of this, she would take Peg and Robert Case and the little-est one and part from him. If ever she did it, she would not come back. Sareeny was like that.

Case could no more go to her and tell her of this thing, than he could wish and depend on his wish coming true— that she would never learn of it. He would nigh about be willing to lay down and die, rather than go to her and tell her with his own mouth, to her own face.

This month of June grew, the child came and was named, and as no knowing looks or whispers mixed in the neighbor- hood friendliness of Sarpy, Case's tension eased.

It was quiet summertime.

The Saturday after Sareeny's baby was born Ellen and Frace came to stay over Sunday with her.

Frace was quieter than she used to be. Subdued. Some force in her was gone, yet it had gone so softly none of them realized a change in her. She was a quiet, mature woman, with a good head for business. She could do things with management of money that mystified them all. Her savings account grew, and grew, slowly and with small sums, yet steadily. She dressed as well as ever, Keith had everything he needed; and many a pleasant, surprising thing she bought in mail order catalogues and gave to Ellen. Proof enough of Frace's goodness and levelheadedness was the way old Jim felt towards her. Seldom did he take to anyone. He said many a time that Frace was as good a woman as ever set her feet upon the earth. He meant it, too. And Frace was good. She was no angel—she had a temper, if she ever needed it, she could get aggravated and cross, same as any human. But she was a sweet, blue-eyed brown-haired woman, kindhearted and unselfish—and wise.

Keith was a beautiful child.

On Sunday afternoon Dorcy came over. She was changed, deeply, profoundly. Her own utter determination had battled within her, silencing what she wanted to silence, breaking down the habits and the slow-built character of her life, changing her to warm friendliness, a good neighbor. Only at times, in unguarded moments, her white face would relax into indescribable weariness. That two thousand dollars in the bank that she could not have was always on Dorcy's mind. It haunted her. She needed money so badly. She talked of it, and lay awake nights thinking of it, and what countless things she could do with it if she had it and wanted to spend it. But she would not spend it, she thought, but she would save it for her children. . . . How easily she could prove Olen Fry was dead!—Not only legally—but actually!—If she but dared to prove it. That money!—that money!—Two thousand silver dollars. Dorcy knew she must force herself not to talk of it too much. But she could never force herself to stop thinking of it. Not when she needed it so badly. Two thousand dollars was indeed a vast sum to Dorcy.

Only the women were in the house. They sat in the kitchen, to be near the room where Sareeny yet lay in childbed. The kitchen door was open, and warm summer afternoon sunlight cast across the floor.

The phone rang.

Ellen answered it.

They were in no way prepared for the startling, totally unheard-of thing that happened.

The receiver clicked. A girl's voice repeated in a monotone: "Long distance . . . San Francisco calling . . . San Francisco . . ."

170

At first Ellen did not clearly understand. When in a few moments Jacob's voice sounded in her ear, she was trembling all over.

His voice sped to her over the wire's distance.

"I'm going to be married, Mom."

Quick tears came to Ellen's old eyes. She leaned closer to the phone.

"Oh, Jacob—who to . . .?"

"It's a girl from the East. Clear from New York City, Mom. She's a peach. Her name is Eunice (Ellen faintly heard his voice aside.) "Say a few words to her, Eunice . . ."

Far away, Eunice was crowded into the narrow telephone booth with Jacob. She was more than a little drunk. She leaned forward foolishly and half-barked "Hello!" Even now in her face and actions there was a note of condescension. She held her face up close by the phone and Jacob kissed her. He was a little wobbly, himself.

It seemed to Ellen that they talked only a few seconds. Jacob and Eunice would live in New York. How are you, Mom, God bless you. Yes, I'll write—I'll write regular now—good-by—good-by. . . .

Ellen stood and wept by the phone in Sareeny's kitchen. Yonder in the bedroom Sareeny cried, partly because she understood how her mother felt. And Ellen cried because Jacob had married a woman they had never seen, because here sat Frace, wordless and still. Because even in some surer way now, there was only Chris and Tana left . . . and because of a dozen other reasons only an old mother can think of at such a time.

Frace sat stiffly in the straight-backed chair by the kitchen door. She knew she should say something. She should say something. But she could not. She did not try. Keith ran past the door and she called to him so sharply that he turned and came to her slowly, his blue eyes wondering. His black hair was like Jacob's, his face was exactly like Jacob's. . . .

She spoke in her natural tone.

"Put your hat on, Keith. Don't run and play bareheaded in the hot sun."

Dorcy went out the front door and across the road to her home, to see after her own children. Keith followed her.

Frace said to Ellen:—

"I'd always planned on Jacob coming home to me, someday. I believe he will, yet . . . unless he has found exactly the right woman for himself. I have looked pretty deep into Jacob. You will see."

Sareeny, in her own mind, thought no one could ever be sure of anything in Jacob.

From her bedroom window Sareeny could look out and see Peg and Robert Case playing in the yard. Peg was growing like a weed. She would be five years old next Tuesday. And she was already confidently planning on the big cake with five candles old Minty had promised her. Trust Minty to make Peg's birthday party a solemn duty, with ice cream and surprises and anything else Peg might expect. Frace's Keith would be five years old, too, on the twelfth of this coming September.

This bright June day was thick with flying cotton from every cottonwood tree. The tiny seed pods loosened the fluffy stuff, and it floated down on every furling breeze, to light and carpet the heavy green grass, as hoary frost out of place on a summer day.

Next year, Sareeny was thinking, I'll have to take Peg by the hand and lead her off to school; and Frace's Keith will be starting to school; time goes by so fast you can hardly keep up with it. . . .

Robert Case was not making one bit less noise than his sister, out there in the yard. His Dad had rigged him up a make-believe horse, and now Robert sat astride it, his pudgy little legs moving like pistons when he spurred his imaginary beast on in a mad race with Peg's. Peg passed him with shouts of victory and the loud whack of wood against wood, for her horse was a broomstick and could dart this way and that with her own flying feet. But Robert always won, in his own smug satisfaction.

His eyes were brown as Case's, and looked out upon everything with assured audacity. He bossed Peg about with gusty importance. His hair, under the little specially made cowboy hat Felix had gave him, was as straight and black as an Indian's. Oh, Case was proud of that boy. His eyes, when he looked at Robert, were almost as smug in their pride as that very young fellow's own satisfaction.

Ellen was glad to get back to her own home again. If she were away for one day and night, she began to worry. Jim was just like any other man; you couldn't depend on him, when Frace was not there, either, to see after things. Jim done his best to keep things going, and Chris would help Tana manage the cooking and housework. But never yet had Ellen took Frace and stayed away from home overnight, without returning to find some kind of a mess, or something they had forgotten to do. She couldn't help but smile to herself. She'd just bet she had hardly got over the hill away from home, yesterday, before Tana was busy trying to cook up some fancy doodad from a printed recipe. And it usually ended in a mess for Tana and Chris. Or else a good old-fashioned bellyache. Seldom did Tana try out her experiments in fancy pies and salads and tarts on her father. When he came in for his meals he found good sensible food, like potatoes and meat and gravy. Then after he left the house Tana would proudly bring out her surprise for herself and Chris. She knew her father would probably put a stop to such tomfoolery. If Chris wasn't such a big overgrown kid, he'd be more dependable, too. Chris would be twenty-one this coming November. Tana was fifteen, last March.

Of all the Gore family, Chris was the homeliest. And the most appealing. His face was ugly, in spite of his good complexion and clear blue eyes and white teeth that showed in his quick grin. But give Chris ten minutes with any stranger and the stranger was his friend. He was not so tall as Ranny or Jacob. Ranny was a good two inches over six feet, and so slender he looked even taller. Jacob was just six feet, and strong as a young horse. Many a time, in thinking over her family, Ellen wondered that Jacob with his dark-skinned face and dark brown eyes could be so much like Sareeny in his quiet ways and thoughts hidden behind a shield of silence. And yet so unlike her in other ways. Oh, Jacob was good, too. It was not that. But not in the ways of Sareeny. Ellen could understand, yet not think out clearly, that Sareeny's goodness was like the quiet comfort of a warm fireside on a still winter evening. If you were worn with pain and worry, you leaned to it for comfort, and its warmth enfolded you; for the worry and pain and discouragement to ease away. The unseen being of herself within herself shone out in the straight trust of her gray eyes, and lurked in the voice that had never lost her a friend.

Time and time again Ellen was glad this woman was her child.

Now Ranny, who resembled Sareeny with his face that was like her face, his gray eyes, and Sareeny's way of laughing, was as different from her as black and white. Ranny was a big noise, from the time he stepped in a door till he went out again. He liked to brag. A few years ago he had been like a careless wind, climbing up to dizzy heights with one get-rich-quick scheme after another, shifting plans and ideas as only the young can. First a wheat farmer, but on a big, big scale. Starting out moderately, he would use the profits of each year to double his produce the next. Thousands of acres of good rich soil would take the seed he planted, and when the harvest was over, even if wheat were only one dollar a bushel, he'd have more money than Pa ever dreamed of making. Rancher, chain-store groceryman, or homesteading land he was sure concealed a fortune in oil—it all passed through Ranny's mind.

Oh, many a wild tale he had up and spoken at neighborly gatherings. Men hard-bitten and a little weary with endless struggle for a living, and a life that is never too easy no matter how or where on earth you live it, laughed up their sleeve and egged him on.

Ellen reckoned about all Ranny and Beth had to brag about now was the new baby that came each year, steady as a clock's ticking. They had four children, and Beth's last letter said another was on the way.

As is the way of all mothers, Ellen believed she knew every one of her children, inside out. But she did not know Chris. None of them knew Chris, except Tana.

Tana and Chris would ride in close companionship, miles away from home, out into the grassy, windy rangeland, or sometimes even to the clusters of mountains far down Sarpy. They discussed many a deep subject while they spent a day exploring, or whiled the time away.

They liked to climb up on some high hill, where they could see for miles in all directions; and sit there for hours in the quiet sunlight that was never hot with the free wind never idling in restless roaming. The saddled horses browsed about lazily, for a Western horse will never think of wandering away when the reins are dropped over its head to the ground.

They would take potatoes and eggs and some of Mom's good smoked bacon. They cooked their meals over a campfire built beside some hill's deep-sprouting spring or mountain's clear tumbling stream of melted snow and ice. Eggs and bacon cooked like that will make the sleepiest appetite come to life like the quick ringing of a bell.

There were a thousand things to see. Curious old jack rabbits, as gray in summer as the bunches of sage where they hid when danger passed, sat off somewhere on their haunches and watched, their soft, slate-colored eyes not missing a single human movement. Birds hovered around a moment disdainfully, before winging away, back to the importance of their own nests and babies' wide-open hungry mouths. Sometimes a bald eagle rose high, high, in the sky, and poised there on some upper wave of wind, the wide spread of his motionless wings riding the thin air like a light feather.

With an old telescope that had belonged to Jacob, they could watch a hundred wild things of the hills, feeding or resting or playing even as children play. Sometimes, deep back in the hills, they spotted a straggling band of antelope; and it was a pitiful thing that only a few of these remained of the once great herds. The telescope brought them so close that Tana would unthinkingly put out her hand to stroke their soft-haired shoulders and smooth, rounded backs. They were as light and graceful on their slender tapering legs as deer, and just as pretty. A buck would lay his beautiful, antlered head across his mate's shoulder, and nuzzle her with his black, dainty nose, and Tana would laugh and declare his eyes were as tender as a lover's. Little fawns slept, concealed cunningly by their mothers in high sagebrush and deep grass; or they played, bouncing about on their four tiny hoofs, sniffing at everything, their eyes looking out on the world with sprightly innocence.

Now Tana loved this Western country. With a wise content that was strange in a youngster fifteen years old, she never longed to start out and see a thousand things that lay for thousands of miles farther than the eyes could see. She would be perfectly satisfied to live here all her life, she said. And read from books about the rest of the world. A home here was good enough for anyone, if they were smart enough to appreciate just half of the things. The hills; and the mountains so thickly timbered and woven with dark canyons and high cliffs and bright peaks. There must be a million square miles of skies, from day to day never quite the same in color or form of clouds. She would be satisfied to do her exploring in a book, by a cozy fire on a winter night, letting the wind, lonesome around the eaves of the house, help her imagination along. When the right man came along, in three or four or five years, she'd grab him, and they would make their home right here in old Montana.

But not so with Chris. Some one of these days he was going to take a few clothes and a little money, and he would hop a freight train. He'd travel a little and learn a lot. He would learn something about this land and that land, the Southern climate, and the Eastern seaboard. He spoke almost gloatingly of this thing and that thing he would see. . . . Fields of white cotton spread out under a warm Southern sun, with darkies black as crow birds moving slowly down the long, straight rows, picking the white fleece. . . . Cities and ships and lakes . . . and the ocean. It had ever seemed to Chris that the ocean must be the strangest thing on earth. Salt water over a mile deep—think of it!—ever moving, surging, tumbling; it could take the biggest ships and toss them about like a chip in a whirlwind. It had fish that could swallow the biggest man—think of that!—As easily as he swallowed a gulp of water. Deep under the everlasting unrest of its surface, age-old secrets lay in dark as thick as midnight; like old ships that had gone down with every slave chained to his rowing place aboard. The wide depth of the ocean held a million secrets, some of them as old as time itself. Chris would talk of all these things and the look in his eyes said he could hardly wait to go.

For as long as Mom lived, he would never leave her. Tana would hardly listen to him, then, but sat in silence, hushed by the sadness in a strange thought of an unbelievable time when Mom would not be here and home would never again be as home.

Jim would fuss because Chris was such a big overgrown kid, and would not act like a youth going on twenty-one should act. It was time he sat up to a little serious thought and stopped gadding about over the hills like a schoolboy. A man had to learn to be a little stern, a little hard-boiled, and leave all the goody-goody stuff to the womenfolks. Chris's hands were a lot quicker at comforting or easing a pain or any little hurt, than they were at laying a red-hot branding iron on a calf's rump, or breaking a young horse to work in the field. Chris had every last thing on the place following like pets at his heels, every time he crossed the yard. And he petted his Ma—she enjoyed it, too!

But Chris was a good boy, Jim would fend quickly.

Last fall, Chris had worked like a nigger from the last of July till the first of November. He had traveled with a harvesting crew from one end of the neighborhood to the other and back again, working in the harvests. He had helped to bind and shock the grain. The slick handle of the pitchfork had put calluses as thick as shoe leather on his hands. The hot sun had painted health on his face, tinting his fair skin with a ruddy glow. The heavy lifting had broadened his shoulders with thick muscle. Three times a day he had sat down to a table loaded with the finest food on earth, for it is an old truthful story that every farm wife tries herself when cooking for harvesters.

Chris came home with four hundred and eighty-five dollars in cash. He spent three hundred and fifty of it on his mother.

Lord, never would Ellen forget that day! Even yet she was proud and talked over it. And talk about love being something you could see!—Why her old eyes fairly blessed that boy when she looked at him.

Ellen would never know how it came about. But Tana knew.

The day after Chris came home, he and Tana saddled their horses and rode away. Out there in the hills he began talking about Ellen, and Tana had been startled because tears came to his eyes. But after he talked awhile, Tana understood, because he made her see a lot of things she had never really noticed before.

He hadn't seen Ellen during all those weeks he was away at work. Towards the last, he got kinda homesick for her, he said. He knew as well as anything that she'd be worrying, because he had to sleep out in a haystack, rain or shine, like all harvesters did; or that maybe he would get careless, beings as he was so young, and get caught in the machinery of the thresher. Nearly every year some man was killed in the harvest, caught in the big moving belts and crushed, or killed by a runaway team. Oh, Mom could think of a dozen things that might happen, when she commenced to worry. Before he left, you would have thought he was a six-year-old, the way she cautioned a hundred times against this thing or that thing a-happening.

He got to where he would think of her, sometimes, if he lay awake after the other men were asleep. They lay wrapped in their blankets in places rounded out to fit their bodies. It was fun sleeping like that, Chris agreed with Tana, except when hay straw got down your back or up your nose. The last thing you see at night are the stars and the yellow moon, quiet in the sky as we be quiet when we hold our breath to listen for a faint sound. But crickets sing all through the night, a horse in a barn stall will stamp its hoof and snort

179

sleepily, now and then a dog barks lonesomely; and if you don't go right to sleep you think and think and think.

Good old Mom. Off yonder at home she would be sleeping; her tired old body stretched beside Pa's in the bed. Mom was always tired, nowadays. She would catch her breath in the night and moan so quiet-like that Pa never once heard her, though he slept right beside her. But Chris had heard her, more than once. Sometimes in her sleep Mom would lose her breath and raise up from her pillow, gasping. Once she had told Chris that after one of those spells she was half a-feared to go back to sleep again, for fear she would lose her breath and not get it back. And once, long ago, Chris had came out in the dark yard by the well and found her fallen on the ground as though she were dead, just as Frace had come in a room and found her on the floor, not so long ago. Mom was not well. Chris knew it; and he felt that she could live but a few years more.

No one ever came in Ellen Gore's house that she didn't offer something to eat. If it was mealtime she put a plate for them on the table. If it was not mealtime she fixed a lunch anyway. No neighbor had ever taken sick that she was not there to help in any way she could. It must be hard on a woman to live like Mom had, Chris thought uncertainly. He had never before thought of his mother as just another woman, because she was his mother. She was not just a woman who had married his father nearly thirty years ago, when she was young, and lived with him ever since, working and ageing. She was the first face he ever remembered seeing, smiling, loving, talking. All his life she had been beside him, or behind him, or before him, ever and always doing something for his own good. She had carried him about in her arms, in what seemed a long time ago, and he had not been much bigger than her two hands. She had carried him before that, too; before ever her hands had touched him;

180

before ever he had came into the world to grow into another, a separate human being. It was the same with Sareeny, and Ranny, and Jacob, and Tana. Oh no, he couldn't ever think of Ellen Gore as just another woman. She was his old Mom.

After Chris and Tana came home that day they took Frace and went over to Sareeny's. Sareeny's mouth fell open when they told her what Chris meant to do. They got out the mail-order catalogues and gathered around the table in the kitchen. Minty and Felix and Case joined in, all offering suggestions. They were all about as happy and excited as a patchel of kids on Christmas eve. For what is more fun, when you have been poor all your life, then to sit down and spend money like you had it by the tubfuls? Sareeny said later that they had spent that hard-earned money of Chris's like it was mere water.

It took a heap of scheming, to get Ellen away from home for three days. But Jim was brought in on the secret, and Sareeny played sick, sending word that Mom would just have to come over and stay for a few days. For Minty would not be home, and Peg and Robert would need someone to look after them when their own mother was in bed with the flu.

Minty slipped over to Ellen's, then, and set to work with Frace and Tana and Chris and old Jim. They painted the woodwork in the old house. Chris put light, cheerful paper on all the walls. Mom had scrubbed those old wood walls with soap and water a thousand times, he reckoned. She had scrubbed them her last time, now. They laid shining, bright-colored linoleum on every inch of the floors. The old pine boards were worn deep in spots, where she had scrubbed, and where feet had stepped a million times. Jim had to fill in those places with clean white sand before they could lay this new covering. Minty and Tana and Frace hung fluffy, filmy new curtains at every window. Then last of all they brought in the new furniture. They had the leather daven-port and chairs in every corner and on every side of the living room before they decided which place showed it off the best.

When it was all ready, here came Sareeny, bringing Mom home. Mom had little crinkly, puzzled lines all around her eyes and mouth, for as she said later, she smelt a nigger in the woodpile, somewhere. Sareeny pretending to be sick and forgetting where the pain was till it was in a different place ever' time you asked her!

For ten minutes after Ellen entered the house she had hardly said a word; just went from room to room, her eyes shining and turning from one thing to another; her old brown hands, deformed by thirty years of hard work, smoothing over the cheerful surfaces of the walls. Wherever she went, the others followed, and Chris tagged right at her heels, his eyes fairly dancing with pride and excitement.

Then because she was so happy Ellen had to cry.

Chris was only five-and-a-half feet tall, but he weighed as much as either Ranny or Jacob. His wide shoulders and thick neck were too big even for his own Pa's shirts. His legs were stout and solid with hard muscle. Healthy red was always mixed in the tan of his face. His complexion was about the only thing perfect in Chris's looks. Tana would laugh and tease him, saying she sure hoped her complexion would al-ways stay as perfect as Chris's. Chris would get a little dis-gusted with himself when she commenced that. She would pretend to be half serious, saying:—

"It will happen some day. A girl will take a good look into those blue eyes of yours and her heart will go—kerplunk! It's not fair. I ought to be the good-looking one in this fam-ily."

More than once Chris had doused her head in the water trough when she wouldn't hush her mouth. But she would come up laughing, her mouth taunting him good-naturedly. Chris thought his little sister would never have to worry much over her good looks, but he would as soon bite his own tongue as tell her so. She wasn't little, anyway. She was nigh about as tall as he was. She had quarreled and nagged at Mom and Pa all summer, but they wouldn't let her bob her hair. Girls could get the silliest notions, thought Chris. If Tana ever acted as silly as some girls he'd grab a-hold of her and shake some sense into her, he would. Sometimes of a Saturday he would pass a group of girls knotted on a street corner in Sarpy. When he would approach they would huddle together in close, secret conversation, pretending not to see him, but casting quick, cute glances in his direction as he passed. It did beat all, how a bunch of girls could get so interested and giggling in something so much of a sudden. They giggled furtively when he passed, and he went on down the boardwalk with his cheeks burning. The darned fools!

Tana teased and laughed and joked and wheedled. You could get as mad as the devil at her, yet pretty soon here you would be, doing just what she wanted you to do. But she could fly off the handle, too, and come at you like a mad steer, slapping your face before you could say "Jack Robinson." Then afterwards she would try to make up for it; without ever letting on, she would give you the biggest piece of pie every night for a week, and jump to wait on you every time you looked up.

Tana was a sly, sweet imp, that's what. She could get more out of Pa than any of them could, if she toadied up to him a little.

Her hair was like Chris's: flaxen color. She had blue eyes and little feet, and a voice that Chris said should have belonged to a hog caller. . . . She could make that much noise with it.

The crops grew and ripened slowly. Winter wheat sent up tall bearded heads, lush with soft kernels. The fields spread in stretches of swaying green. The hot sun worked silently with the deep stillness of the earth, and the green became tinted with faint smatterings of yellow. Then, as if that were a foothold, the yellow deepened and spread swiftly with each day, until finally no dark color marred the richness of living gold. It swayed in the harvest wind, completed, waiting.

Sareeny, Minty, Dorcy, and Frace worked together canning and preserving food. The shelves in their cellars were loaded with everything Sareeny could think of and find to can. Minty laughed, saying they would open a boarding house this winter, if there was anyone to board. Talk about a table groaning under a weight of good things to eat—theirs ought to do it this winter! By next springtime the men folks might be so fat they would be slow in planting the crops. But say, it was a comfortable feeling to know there was not the slightest danger of going hungry. All they would have to do in this cold winter was go to the cellar; if they wanted three kinds of vegetables and three kinds of fruit, there it was. Beside jams, jellies, pickles, and most anything else you could name. For meat they would have chicken any time they wanted it. Turkey whenever they were hungry for it. And beef and pork when Case butchered. He would butcher for Dorcy, too. The three young shoats and the steer she had been fattening all summer.

Often there came to Sareeny's mind those words of God: "Trust in me and you shall not want. Everything you need shall be given unto you. Ask and you shall receive."

As Mills said, it was so easy to live a good life, and so much more satisfying, that the wonder was every human being on earth could not see it. Sareeny could not understand how a person deep-dyed in sin could go on living and laughing, looking their fellow men in the eyes as though nothing was wrong. Surely they must get mortally weary sometimes, with lying and hiding things in their mind. They must wonder, "How will it ever end?" And they must try at times to turn away and do better, for never is there a person, good or bad, who wants to die without having done something good, somewhere.

Now if a person lets go on all holds, and decides to live out the rest of his life without trying to do better, he is as good as dead, thought Sareeny. He might as well die then, because from then on he is going to be something that just lives and walks and breathes, yet a dead weight on the world, of no use whatsoever. Now take the whores (Sareeny did not like the word); they had just decided to give themselves up to a complete world of sin, and that, in a way of speaking, was letting the world go on without them. Last year, when she and Case had gone to the Fair, they had walked down through the part of town Case had told her was the red light district. Never had Sareeny really believed there could be such a place. Women sat in windows of houses close by the street, and they had beckoned to every passing man, or called to him. Bold and brazen, without shame. The little houses set side by side, with doors thrown open in mute invitation. The women's faces at the windows were strange, different than the face of any woman she had ever seen. Sometimes the light in the window or the light above the door threw a red glow upon the head that was ever turned to the street.

It was a strange world, that she had never seen. It sickened her, so that she hurried to get away from it. She had the thought that these were not woman at all, but only women's faces and women's bodies, going on living after the women in them had died. Something in them had died, or they could never abandon themselves in such a world. Maybe it was their woman's soul.

185

But no, the soul does not die. It is the only thing that lives. The actual we, it lives on everlasting, even after the body is dead and buried and rotted away. The soul cannot die, for it is life, and life cannot die. It can only leave the body or form which held it.

Old Man Mills, white-haired and white-bearded, stood up in the pulpit of his church every Sunday and preached down upon them the greatest truths of life. "Go yore way," he said. "Forget that there is a hereafter. But remember that there is hell here, if we are not careful. And it is misery. And the only true remedy for that misery is our bein' able to say somethin' like this at the end of each day: "Well, I hain't done any thing mean today. I hain't hurt anyone's feelin's, but I could have. I could have told Neighbor Brown a few acrid truths about his self; but I let him go, because I reckon it would caused nothin' 'cept trouble, anyhow, and he'll find out in time about his self, anyway. So I lent him my plow, and my horse, and the five dollars in cash he asked for, because I knew he needed it—and I did have it and more, too. And I wished him luck and I meant it! Today I have done no cheatin', committed no murder, done no thievin'. I have been a pretty good man today, and what's more I found it was easy and I enjoyed it." Old Man Mills drove home his thoughts with a few sentences that made them all smile. "And then ye will go to yore bed for the most peaceful, restin' sleep ye can have while on this earth. If ye can say ever' day in yore life some words like I jest told ye, by the time ye are old ye will have so many friends that ye will wish ye could live all over again. And if yore time ends before ye are old ye won't mind half so much a-dyin'."

Dorcy, murderess, would sit with never a sound and look up to his face. Her lips were set in a straight line; her eyes seemed to blink while he talked and she listened. Minty (past Jezebel), would sit there by Felix, and as she listened, her face said she enjoyed every word. As for old Herman Leidermen, Birdie had to keep pinching him to keep him awake. Birdie had said many a time that it wouldn't surprise her a bit if old Herman snored at his own funeral.

Case, lecherist, fornicator, sat way back at the end of the churchroom, where he could have a little control over Peg's whispering and Robert's squirming. All around him sat his neighbors from the south. He would look up, listening, his brown eyes veiled in expression.

"There is one sin," Mills said, "that only the good can have. If ye try hard to live right ye are apt to think of yoreself as little less than a saint. Ye can see another feller doin' wrong, but ye never try to understand why. And there is always a heap of whys and wherefores about every blame."

Sareeny would move little Alex gently in her arms to still his squirminess. Never again would she let herself think a black thought over this or that baby being the last to come to her and Case. It was murder, that's what it was. A feeling of half awful fear would raise up in her breast when she looked at this baby and thought: "If I had not changed my way of thinking you would not be here now. Dear Lord, how could I ever have felt I didn't want another like you." It was not meant for a human to meddle too deep with life. If a baby came as steady as every summer rolled around, it would be again and again, life, as unceasing as the ticking of a clock that never runs down, as steady as endless time and with the same powerful forces.

It was two months now, since Jacob had married a strange woman and talked to them from away off yonder. Still they had not heard from him. Ellen fretted and worried, plum hurt. It would be so easy for Jacob to sit down and write her a few words. He might be sick. Lord only knowed what might be the matter with him. What kind of a woman had he married that would let him treat his old Ma like this? Whenever

Ellen talked of Jacob she would move her right hand and her eyes would turn down to—the satin luster of the pearl that shimmered in the ring on her gnarled finger. Her gentle, old, sweet face held many a worried thought for Jacob. She wore her gray hair grandmotherish, parting it in the middle, combing it lightly down over her ears to the back of her neck, to a neat flat coil. Secretly Ellen prayed that Jacob would come home, that she would see him again before she died. The secret pains in her breast were sharper, frequent, now. She did not expect to live long. One, two years, maybe. But that was her secret, too, hers alone, until someday it burst upon them, shattering all their daily lives until they would grow used to her absence. She loved them so. They loved her so. . . . She was real, as the touch of their hands, or as the air they breathed. . . . It was only natural that it would be unnatural for them to stop short and think of an actual time when she would not be among them. No, she would say no word to bring this vague thing to realness for them. . . . She would hide it softly in every day she had yet to live—hide it softly in the very touch of her hands, in every word she spoke.

A hundred times she would have written to Jacob, had she only known which street he lived on, yonder among New York's millions of humans. But she knew no exact place to send the letter. So she could only go on worrying and watching the mail. Tomorrow, he might write.

Frace comforted her. They all tried to shush her fears away. Jacob was somewhere on his honeymoon. And he'd know she oughtn't to worry. Besides, she'd probably get a letter, next week.

But winter had come, before they heard from Jacob.

This year, Felix just about bundled his mother up and forced her to go to the Fair with Sareeny and Case. She had always before flatly refused to go. She did not want to go now. She was perfectly satisfied to stay at home, because she could think of no nicer place she would rather be. Felix insisted that she go and enjoy herself. And she could not tell him she had hoped never to see that city by the river again.

Thus Felix was alone in his father's house for the first time since before his father's death. Even Sareeny did not like to go away and leave him there. But Dorcy promised to come over each of the three days they would be away, and help him cook his meals. Felix laughed away their fears that he would be lonesome. Looking after the cows and chickens would take a big part of his time, as it always did.

Something happened while he was there alone that Felix would remember all his life.

He was alone three nights. And each of those three nights he dreamed that he could see.

He dreamed that he woke in a dark room, and opening the door of that room, he stepped out into a world of light.

For a moment the light had stung his eyes, hurting him. He stood outside the doorway of the dark house and looked about him with surprise. He thought: "Why, it must be day."

But then his eyes grew accustomed to the suddenness of light after black night, and he could see clearly; and he saw that it was not day, for there were stars in the sky, and a moon hung motionless high above the hills in the east. He stood and looked and listened. It seemed that all the earth was so still the sound of his own breathing was loud.

A little pathway led away from where his feet stood, and curved on down the hillside. For this house stood on a high hill, and he saw that it was not his home but he did not care. He turned and closed the door behind him.

The pathway curved this way and that; Felix crossed a wide meadow, where a thousand silent things were living— long grass, green and thick, as grows on the soft, wet land of a marsh; and clusters of underbrush, or shubbery; small blue flowers, seeming to grow on long runners of vines reached sometimes across the sandy path, and he stopped to look at them because they were so perfect, so fragrant, and mute evidence of something he knew, and could not understand, nor put into words, nor describe.

Looking up, the sky seemed very high to him, and yet the stars were near. They were like a million sparks flung there with a careful hand, to tremble and expand and quiver with the force of their own glittering; the moon was white; white and sparkling as a plate of pure frost; yet it shed a light that was faintly blue. Away yonder was a creek, its water like pale blue silver threading its way along a valley, and great trees stood thereabouts in silent, shadowy splendor. To the west, beyond miles and miles of stony hills and grassy prairie, stood the mountains. They were a beautiful sight to see. Even across that distance, he had to look up to see their cone peaks and wide sweeps of plateau. In color, they were sea lavender.

Dorcy came over quietly the next morning and cooked his breakfast. When Felix came back from the cow barns, carrying the big buckets of steaming milk, he smelled coffee boiling and bacon frying. Dorcy opened the door for him with a friendly good morning. She was as pleased over doing this thing for him as he was to have her do it.

Dorcy was as good and neighborly a woman as any family could be proud to know.

Later in the day she came over and baked an apple pie for him. Felix had said more than once that Dorcy's apple pie always made his mouth water, especially if he could open the oven door while it was cooking and take a good whiff of the hot cinnamon and apple juice bubbling through the rich crust.

She brought some sewing, too, and worked there all the afternoon, because she thought Felix might be lonesome, and she was a little lonesome herself, with Sareeny and Minty gone. This fall weather was akin to lonesomeness, anyhow, with the wind ever a-blowing. However bright the day might be, the air was hazy, and the far-off places you looked to see were blurred with a faint fogginess that was not fog, but only a peculiar way, a being, of autumn's own. It belonged with this time of bright falling leaves, and harvested fields, and lonesome wind that swirled around corners to press against a window.

Dorcy lowered her gray head to the sewing machine that she might see better to thread the needle. Her eyes were beginning to fail her these last few years. She reckoned she'd have to get herself a pair of spectacles and wear them, else soon she couldn't see a thing. But there were so many things to buy. Even when she managed to make a good living for herself and the children, there was never much left when they were all clothed and fed. It was no wonder Dorcy brooded over that two thousand dollars and was haunted with the wanting of it. Six pairs of shoes, twice a year. Seven pairs, counting herself. One pair of shoes was enough for her. She could buy a new pair and save them for kinda dress-up wear, and take the next to the newest ones for everyday. That Sid and Silver were the ones to kick out shoes—theirs had to be resoled twice to Rose's and Denver's once. It took many a hard day's work, many a tired hour of lifting and sowing and reaping, just to get the clothes to cover your nakedness in this world.

So ran Dorcy's thoughts, as she worked and talked to Felix of other things. Never had a neighbor heard Dorcy complain or give one word that her life was hard.

All day Felix could not help but think of his dream, and his mind mulled over it. The dream was a regrettable thing to him because it destroyed his peace and made him hate his eyes that had never let him see.

And because of his thinking, he dreamed again the second and third nights. In the third dream there were people. But he was sick with bewilderment because he could not see them. They passed on the path and spoke to him. . . .

"Hello Felix." "How are you, Felix?" "Well, by golly," and here they would grasp his hand or lay an arm heavily across his shoulder,—"look who is here! Why don't you ever come around and visit us, Felix?"

Dazed, he would make some answer, then go on his way. "I am not blind," he would think half-angrily. "I can see." Yet he would pass some home set close beside the pathway, and he would hear children's voices at noisy play; someone would call out a friendly greeting, and though he might be quick to recognize the voice, he could see no faces or no shape of hand that reached out of mystery to grasp his own.

He came back to the open, black doorway of the little house on the high hill. He entered and the door closed. The blackness closed around him, and half-terrified he tried to find the door again, to open it. He called to the voices he could hear, outside. He could not see.

He woke; and Minty was sitting at the side of his bed. She was brushing her hands over his face and hair, trying to wake him up. She said: "Felix, we're home!" He heard Sareeny's voice in mild teasing: "You were dreaming, Felix. It must have been caused from your cooking." Peg and Robert Case came and bounced on his bed, talking to him. Case came, like as though they had all been away a month, and grasped his hand in friendliness.

But ever after, Felix could not turn away the feeling he was in the dark room and the door would never open.

# CHAPTER 15

JACOB'S letter was short. And it was just as aggravating as Jacob himself, Sareeny thought. For it told them little, but made them wonder and guess at all the things he could have written and did not. But it was just like him. Even if Jacob were here, it would be mighty unusual if he up and told them all about himself without having to be asked a hundred pumping questions. There was just no sense in his being so shut-mouthed with his own folks.

The letter was one short paragraph, written in his high dashing way across a sheet of stationery.

Well Mom, I'll be stepping in your door at home, around Christmas time. Tell Pa to cheer up right now and be in a welcoming mood when I come. Tell Keith his daddy is coming to see him. Tell Sareeny and Chris and Tana I'll be glad to see them all. I hope Ranny will be there with his little horde of offspring. Polish up a plate for me, and find a turkey with three legs and two gizzards if you can. Lordy, I'm wanting to see you, Mom.

That was all. Except his name, flung across the bottom of the page as only Jacob could write it. There was not one word for Frace. There was not one word about Eunice, or whether she would come with him, or whether she even so much as thought of sending them a wish-you-well and "Merry Christmas."

Ellen would have given almost anything to see Eunice. Yet what if Jacob did bring her here! What thin ice over deep water that would be! With Frace under the same roof, and sitting at the same table, and hers and Jacob's child in noisy play about the house. Ellen nodded her head sideways slowly, completely at loss to imagine the reality in this happening. In the span of her life such a thing did not happen with the seriousness of a man and a woman in marriage. Now in the newspapers you read about situations even more outlandish than that. But seldom with the old marriages. A new day, a marked change, had moved into the world's ways; and the change was yet growing, driving out strict and grim and harsh old-fashioned manners of life. Lord! Lord! Wasn't it time the world woke up to a little sense on its outlook of human beings? Time was, when a woman married a man for better or for worse she was stuck with him, no matter how worse the worse was. Time was, when a respectable God-fearing man and woman found unhappiness, even misery or hate, in their years together, they endured it if they could, if they could not endure it they parted, and most likely if they were young enough each waited and hoped the other would die first and soon, leaving the other free; for divorces were a shameful thing, almost unheard of. Now the world said: Bosh! Why be so narrow-minded and silly? Think of marriage as sacred and serious—but remember it is meant for and founded on happiness and fulfillment. If truly you have made a mistake, is not the life of each of you rightfully of greater importance to the self of each of you? Even if there be a child, is it not more sane to cut the vows asunder, and leave you free to seek where and what you will in your time on earth? Ellen thought sadly that no human on earth is above making a mistake. Even in marriage . . . especially when we are all so deceiving and pretentious and treacherous with each other when we meet as strangers—so much so that sometimes even love does not melt clean these things away, to naked us starkly as we are. Oh! Ellen thought, living is a ponderous thing. When you look too deep, it is better not to have looked at all, but to have gone on lightly, simply. Freedom.

Frace said: "If Eunice comes, she'll come. We will welcome her and be pleased to know her. Maybe we will love her. Maybe she is a good wife. Maybe she is the very woman for Jacob. If he brings her here for Christmastime I will greet her with true friendliness. Nothing I feel would want to make me do differently."

And so Frace lied. Ellen knew Frace lied. You could see it in the very set of Frace's mouth, in the look of her eyes, in the subtle flutter of her hands over Keith's face. Why was it that Frace still loved Jacob, no less than the way she had loved him before Keith was born, when she came to live in this old log house? Were the truth known, she loved Jacob so much that thought of him was curtained tenderly in her mind. Had he come home to her on some stilled day, she would have cried out his name involuntarily and run to meet him, to know the reality of his arms and lips, the pressure of his strong body. But Frace was no saint woman. You could see she hated Eunice, conceal it as she would. You could see that if she would let herself go, she would have railed out against Jacob with hard and bitter words. How could she say what she would feel if Jacob stepped in the door with his new wife!

But Frace had won her place in Jacob's family. Always she would be there between them and their whole acceptance of Eunice.

Now Ellen and Frace planned together, planning the biggest Christmas the Gores and Gylers and Edens ever had. A Christmas such as older folks spoke of with happy rememberings. A dinner such as people liked to talk about. What would it matter if the tree was not loaded with presents that were nice because they cost a pocketful of silver? For Ellen, all the children would be home again, and these

195

children's children would fill that still emptiness left in her house and daily life by Ranny's and Sareeny's and Jacob's growing off to married lives of their own. If she missed those three so much, what would she do if she were yet alive when Chris and Tana married off in turn and went to another house, another life, another world almost? She thought: "An old woman is an old fool. She likes to see her daughters stepping off with fine young men. She likes to see a young man worried and jealous, chasing after her girl like there weren't another in the world. She likes to see her fine big boys feeling that way over some other woman's daughters. She will even help them on a little, liking to feel it all her own important doings, instead of something that has been old ever since Eve eat the apple and hunted up Adam." A woman knows, as her children marry off one by one, how lonesome her house is going to be when the last one is gone. She knows how still her house is going to be, and made even quieter because she can remember most everything her young-uns ever done. She knows how she is going to feel some morning when her old man comes down alone to breakfast, and they sit down to the table alone. At any of her children's weddings, she stands away like a part of the background, a yesterday, and smiles because she is happy and would seldom admit to herself that she is sad.

Chris and Tana bickered their Pa and Mom into going over to Sareeny's almost every Saturday night, though it didn't take much bickering. This Saturday, when Jacob's letter came, was a dark, blustery day as though winter might be tired of playing about and was settling down to serious business. It was going to snow.

Chris and Felix carried in big armfuls of wood and stacked it by the fireplace. Old Jim was somewhere down by the barns, helping Case throw hay to the horses and cattle. Sareeny and Minty and Ellen and Frace worked in the kitchen, all four of them talking as happy as they had every right to be when all is well and the world is good. Good food simmered in kettles on the stove, the supper table was set, the house was warm and could be kept that way all winter. At last a letter had come from Jacob, and at least he was alive and well. The world was good enough.

Tana went about the house, lighting lamps. Peg and Robert Case tagged at her heels, and she liked to have them follow her about. Their "Aunt Tana" made her feel grown-up and nigh about as old as Sareeny. She thought to herself: "Well, I am very nearly grown-up. I'll be sixteen, next March. Lots of women are married when they are sixteen."

She liked to take Sareeny's youngest, Alex, and go sit alone in the big living room, away from all the women's intimate talk in the kitchen and the men's passing in and out there as they did the night chores.

She did not light the lamps in the living room, because the fireplace threw enough light, and she liked the half light and half darkness. She sat in the big chair close beside the fire, with the baby snuggled in her arms. She could love him half to death, he was so cute. He was almost as fat and round as a butterball. Tana could understand why it is a mother never loses patience with a baby. If it keeps her awake half the night with crying colic, and wearies her half-dead with its weight on her arm by day, and keeps her washing diapers till she's blue in the face, she don't seem to mind overmuch. For she can sit down in the quiet of an evening with the baby quiet in her arms, and she don't give a hoot for anything else.

While she was sitting there with the baby asleep on her lap, Felix came in the room. She was quiet and he did not notice her when he came and leaned against the mantel. The firelight caught his shadow and moved it as the flames in the fireplace moved with every faint draft. He was smiling a little, as though pleased over the neighbors and the friendliness in his house.

He was tall and broad-shouldered as Jacob. And he was just as good-looking. He looked better-natured, Tana thought.

Now anyone could take a good look at the grip of Jacob's jaw and tell you Jacob was as stubborn as the very devil—or at the calculating expression of his eyes and tell you he was a little selfish. But Felix was kind. Even if Tana had not heard everyone say so a dozen times, she would have known he was good. He was a good guy and you knew it when you looked at him. One time Mom had said: "If you hear tell that such and such a person looks honest you can make up your mind he is homelier than a mud fence." Felix looked honest, yet he was the best-looking man on Sarpy, too. He was as strong as Case, or Ranny, or even Jacob—who could lay two thick mail-order catalogues one on the other and tear them in halves with his hands. From the expression in Felix's eyes when he listened or spoke in conversation, strangers never knew he was blind.

From this minute, Tana loved Felix—with a love that grew so slowly she did not herself know of it, until a year later. But she did know, at this minute, that she had never before really looked at him.

Minty called from the doorway: "Supper is ready, Felix." And then she came to the fireplace and stood a moment beside him on the hearth. He put his arm across her shoulders. She said quietly:—

"Felix, do you really know how nice this room is? I've always liked it, but just now—when I came to the door I never saw it look so cozy and homey. The wind sounding down the chimney, the fire lit, and everything."

He turned his head, his blue eyes looking around as though he could see every corner of the room he knew by heart.

"If I lost everything we own I'd miss this spot the most."

Minty smiled at Tana: "Tana, you're as still as a mouse."

"Where is she?" Felix demanded.

She reached out her foot and touched him.

"Right here, and I've been here since before you came in. I'm playing nursemaid to Amos Alexander the First."

"It's snowing like sixty outside," Minty said, with so much satisfaction they laughed. "I've been hoping it would, all day. It makes a person enjoy the evening and the fire twice as much."

Felix spoke half-seriously. "Mother, you are getting younger every day. I suppose you'll want to pop corn and make candy tonight."

"Well, I do," Tana spoke up promptly.

Minty laughed, just a little.

"I wish I were getting younger, Felix. Tana, tell Felix just how young I look."

Tana responded with blunt honesty. "You don't look over fifty-five. Sometimes you look younger, sometimes older. When you came here your hair was gray, now it's white—"

"That's enough," Minty said, laughing. "Tana you are growing up, you are not a child any longer, when you can look a sixty-three-year-old woman in the eyes and tell her she doesn't look over fifty-five."

Supper was not over when other folks began to come. First Herman and Birdie arrived, and they had with them Mills, the preacher. Case went out and helped old Herman bed down the horses for the night, for what was the sense of Herman and Birdie driving home again in this storm? There were plenty of beds in the house.

It was bitter cold. The snow was fine, almost like frost, and a hard wind drove it in from the east. East wind meant the storm would not let up till it blew itself out. Birdie came in the warm kitchen with her round face as red as buffalo berries, and, during the long ride in the wind and snow, a miniature snowbank had piled up on the broad slope of her fat behind. Every winter, Birdie gained weight and put on fat like a sleek heifer waiting in the butchering pen, but in summers, with her gardening and caring for several hundred baby chicks, she worked it off again.

Tonight, even though Birdie was her usual cheerful, good self, there was an air of deep anger, a depressed thoughtfulness, about her.

Caleb came next. To Case's remark that they had been expecting him but thought he might have frozen to death on the way over Caleb answered mournfully, "I'll most likely live a couple more years yet." He turned his wide, unblinking blue eyes down the long length of the supper table that did not have one vacant chair, and demanded with doleful hopelessness: "Anything left to eat?"

They all liked Caleb. He was a good neighbor, once you got used to his funny ways.

Dorcy came in quietly with her six children. Rose and Sid and Silver went into the dining room and sat down. Even the two youngest behaved themselves in the finest way, Birdie thought, watching them. Dorcy had done wonders with those kids since they were completely under her own wing, and Olen Fry was not there to ball things up. The two youngest, June and Inez, stood beside Dorcy's chair and looked so wishfully at the thick chocolate-frosted cake on the table that Sareeny made them come and eat all they wanted of it. Denver sat on the floor and listened to the men folks talk.

Dorcy was happier, these last few months. She was getting rid of the constant fear of being found out. She could even think with hard pride that she would never let a word slip, or any little thing happen, that would make them wonder why Olen had left her so suddenly. She had even stopped

200

hearing that silent voice that had screamed over and over in her mind! *"Murderer! You have—murdered your husband!"* And then like a maddening whisper—"If they catch you—you will hang!"

It was ever on her mind, so that she had to keep a firm grip on herself, else she took spells when she would tremble as though with the ague. Sometimes at home, she would think half wildly: "Why did I do it? What made me do it? I could have taken the children and left him. . . . I didn't have to live with him . . . when my Benson died I went crazy. . . I'll go crazy again if I don't stop thinking. . . ." Something in her mind, something as hard and unbreaking as steel, would come to her aid. She wasn't going to let anything happen to these children of hers. It wasn't their fault she had married a drunkard and brought them into the world. Then she could go out among people as calmly as she sat now. She sat with her long hands clasped loosely on her lap, her gray head turned attentively to something Minty was saying.

High winter pelted against the outer log walls of old Eden's house. They sat about the long living room that was warmed to its furtherest corner by the lively fire. One by one the men told stories, and even the children sat round, wide-awakened wide-eyed, listening. Caleb was by far the best storyteller, because he had traveled in his day to almost every land on earth, and he could tell a story about a foreign, far-away land that would make your mouth pop open. But old Herman told a good one.

A long time ago there lived a man in the state of Iowa who had never been lucky enough, or unlucky enough, to find himself a wife. Being a little past middle age and not knowing any ladies that might be suitable or willing, he gets the idea of advertising for a mate. In due time an answer comes to his advertisement, and a picture of a very sweet and motherly lady. A little more time and she has accepted his proposal our Uncle Sam delivered, and is on her way to her new husband and home.

The man was overjoyed. He remodeled his house, and bought new furniture. He met the train that delivered his mail-order bride, and all went well through the introductions, the marriage license bureau, the simple wedding, and the trip home. But at the supper table there came a hitch.

"Do you believe in Spirits, Abe?" the new wife asked very seriously.

Abe was a little dumb on the subject, till his new wife explained to him, and went on to add that she, herself, was a Spiritualist.

"Do you mean to say that you can call Spirits to you and talk to them, any time you want to?" Abe asked superstitiously.

"I don't have to call them," she answered proudly. "They come to me. I am gifted."

Abe thought it was just something else he didn't know about wimmin.

Late in the night he woke, with his wife punching him nervously under the covers.

"Abe," she whispered hoarsely. "Look!"

He sat up and looked. It was so dark in the room he couldn't see the edge of the bed.

"The Spirits!" she whispered. "See them?"

"I can't see a thing," he quavered.

"Oh, but you will. They're gatherin' all around our bed, Abe. There is my second husband—Oh Henry my dear!— Your poor head is bleeding where the mule kicked and killed you. There is Aunt Edna. Hello Aunt Edna! There is Grandma . . . and here comes Uncle Eli. . . ."

Abe said later he wasn't sure his hair stood on end, but he could feel it raise up from his head.

"See them come!" his wife exclaimed loudly.

. . .Here old Herman paused to light his pipe before finishing his story.

"Abe could only stand for three nights of the family reunion. I hear-tell he is a bachelor now, down in Wyoming. I hear-tell he is kinda crazy. Does all his own cookin' and laundry and won't allow a woman on his ranch."

Caleb, with a little coaxing, let them push the guitar into his hands, and Frace brought Felix the violin. Everybody there had a favorite song they wanted to hear. Dorcy liked that great song of the West: "Home on the Range." Felix had a good voice, and while Caleb was not so gifted, he didn't hurt the song any if he joined in now and then. He could play that guitar like nobody's business. The violin in Felix's hands became a voice that was the most beautiful thing on earth. The mellow, rich tones were like something alive. Felix could take that violin and make you want to cry with homesickness, even though you were sitting here on your own hearth. He could make you feel as gay and lighthearted as though there were not one worry in the world, and nothing to do all your life but laugh and rest easy. Sareeny liked to watch him. His strong chin held the violin, his head leaned down as if he must listen to make the right sounds. His smooth light hair caught sheens of firelight, and she had the strange feeling his blind blue eyes could see the things he was telling in music.

There was one song old Herman liked in particular, because it reminded him of his younger days when he had moseyed from one big cattle ranch to another, all over Montana and Wyoming. Those were the days before he got married, he said, and all he had to worry about then was Texas longhorn cattle goring him to death; and wild-eyed broncs, bucking till your breath got tangled up somewhere in your stomach and you landed flat on your face in the dust.

Caleb's sad voice just fitted this song, somehow, and even old Herman joined in on the chorus:—

Go to sleep,
My little buckaroo.
And we will ride the range
Like grown-up cowboys do.
Now it's time you rounded up
Another dream or two. . . .

As the evening grew, Birdie was even more strangely silent and thoughtful. She was not like her usual self. She was a little saddened and yet looked as though she might be a little miffed about something. Herman tried several times to draw her out of herself and get her into the mood of the evening.

He knew well what was the matter with her.

And knowing her, he was afraid, for Birdie could never keep her mouth shut and tend her own business. She was a high-wrought little woman, there was a world of good in her, but she was so emotional that any sudden, unexpected turn of events could make her go to pieces. For Birdie would see, in her emotional mind, not only the facts, but all the clear details and vivid scenes, and her imaginative mind would work like a busitive ant, conjuring them up for her. After a while the reaction would set in, and that was what Herman feared. For it would cause Birdie to be either too generously sympathetic, or too angry at injustice, or too righteously indignant or downright angry and spiteful, whatever the case would be. And she could not keep her mouth shut. Herman believed that at such a time she would have grumbled and fussed in the very face of the Devil. Yet was that not a woman for you!

The stormy winter evening grew, the clock struck the hours and half-hours, the children were sleepy by the open fire. . .

Birdie sat on the piano stool, her fat shoulder resting against the polished, glinting wood of the piano.

Out of a momentary silence she spoke.

Old Herman could have throttled her with his quick hands—he could have cursed her for the way she was—she looked right at Case who was leaning at the fireplace to put more wood on the fire—clearly she was speaking to him—

Herman said sharply, without thinking: "Hush Birdie, my God . . ."

She said clearly:—

"I plum forgot to mention it, but a terrible thing happened on the reservation today. A neighbor to the south happened by our house and told us—an Indian's house caught fire . . a can of gasoline exploded, and the house was burned to the ground. The Indian was Charley Wilson. The terrible thing was his wife and baby were trapped in the house."

Case dropped the wood on the fire in a shower of sparks. He straightened up slowly from his leaning towards it.

A hush struck the room.

It was only a second of time—Sareeny's interest had turned to Birdie—but the eyes of all the others had turned to Case, he felt and saw the look of all their eyes upon him.

They all knew. *Christ, they all knew.*

Ellen's old face expressed the horror she felt, as did Frace's. And Dorcy's strange look held many things. . . . Old Jim's teeth clamped shut and his eyes squinted at Case.

Birdie went on talking. . . .

"The woman and child were burned to a cinder. Oh it was the pitifullest thing. The woman must have snatched the child, she ran upstairs, and she and the child were both clothed with fire, and she wept and screamed. . . . They last saw her at the window with her arms about the child. It all happened so quickly! The Indian and his hired man were running from the barn to the house. They saw her fall, then

205

her hand came up and clutched the sill of the window she had broken out, she tried to pull herself up. And the little boy screamed, blazing at the open window, stretching his little arms out towards them. The whole house was in flames and rolling smoke. . . ."

Birdie's voice trembled and was husky with feeling. A little fearful of her own words, she turned her eyes down to her lap and ended swiftly:—

"And what must the father feel? Or is he glad, maybe? There is a story the father is a married white man, living not too far away. The father of the dead child, and the father of the older one who yet lives. I lay a curse on that man's head. He ought to be stripped, and tied to a post and whipped. Him with a good trusting wife! Neighbors ought to tar and feather him, and ride him on a rail out of the hills. And maybe they would were it not for his sweet wife!"

Case's chest rose and fell with quick breaths, the flesh of his face was as though it had hardened to mask the inferno of his mind; he stood silently, close to the fire, close to the couch where Sareeny sat.

Ellen said quickly:

"It's a sad thing to happen."

Frace added hurriedly: "You must have known them, Mr. Mills. You are so well acquainted among the Indians."

Old Man Mills recalled the day Charley Wilson had came to Sarpy seeking a minister to speak a marriage ceremony. The Indian bride, Mills remembered, was pretty as a picture, and educated, too. Mills went on talking: Only last summer he had visited them again. The youngest child was round about two years old, a sweet little boy, a mortal sweet little boy. The oldest boy, who yet lived, was around six years old—he was a fine-looking little feller, too—and smart as a whip!

206

Case stood and listened, not daring to trust his voice to say one word. Sareeny reached out and got his hand and pulled him down on the couch beside her.

He felt sick. He wanted to get out of the room, where he could not hear their talk, away from their eyes.

He went out through the kitchen and into the yard. The night was so black he could not even see the dark hulk of the barns and stock buildings across the frozen creek. The cold east wind blew the stinging snow against his face. He tried to think.

He did not hear the door open and close, as Old Jim came out into the yard.

Old Jim came to him and said roughly:—

"So it's true, then."

After a silence Case answered.

"You know it's true."

They stood in the dark shelter of the house. Old Jim's thoughts were heavy and despairing in him. How was a man to meet and cope with such a thing as this? He was only an old man, a tired old man, worn out with the troubles and the hardships he'd lived in his own life. All the best part of his own life was gone, burned down to only a stub of the candle and paler flame that is left, and still he must worry; over money that is hard to get, money so hard to get that he must wear faded and patched clothes, and push away thoughts of a thousand things he would like to give his old woman—God bless her! Now in their old days their children's troubles were flung back in their faces, they must worry and share them, too.

Freezing cold wind laden with snow roared through the treetops above them and above the house. It swept over all the land, in raging possession of the night.

Old Jim thought, a heathen man with trouble in his simple life, will fall to his knees upon the ground and turn his face

207

to heaven and stretch his black arms to heaven and wail his troubles to his God, calling on his God for pity and mercy; but a poor civilized white man works and worries, doing his poor best all through his life, and in times of trouble he says, "Well I got to face it, somehow."

Case had made this trouble for them all. None of them wanted Sareeny to up and leave Case, breaking her heart because she loved him. She could not rightfully be blamed for leaving him, and leave him she would, when she learned of this, if it were not handled wisely.

He said to Case:—

"How old is the other boy?"

Case pretended to study a minute, but he did not need to think; he had thought many a time before; he knew exactly how old Hosea was.

"He's about six years old, I reckon."

"What do you think of doing about him?"

Case could only shake his head and not answer. He asked back:

"Do you think Birdie has told Sareeny?"

What did that matter, old Jim demanded? Sareeny would have to know. But Birdie had not and would not tell her. Herman would shut Birdie up.

Case was set in his mind that surely they could tide this thing over, with Sareeny never knowing. From where he stood close by the kitchen window, he could look in the house, and Sareeny had come in the kitchen with a lamp in her hand—Case turned and made old Jim promise that they would all keep this hidden from her. Old Jim, not knowing that Jacob had been the first to learn of it, promised that no one of them would tell Sareeny. He went heavily in the house and left Case alone in the dark winter yard.

Case leaned against the house and thought over and again: Letitia is dead. It's sorry I am now, Letitia, for the hurt I caused you. . . . I must do something for that boy of mine, but what can I do? Charley Wilson will not keep it now. . . What will become of it? . . . A six-year-old boy Indian.

The Indian agent might put it in an orphanage . . . but no, by God!

He would not let them do that. He was still too much a man to stand by and let that happen. If it were not for Sareeny's being so good he would go to her simply and tell her the truth; but never as long as he lived would he let a thing like this hurt her. He felt, and could understand, that if he could weather this, doing as near right as he could by the boy Hosea, the crisis would be over, and the remainder of his life with Sareeny would never again be threatened by any foolish act of his.

Inside the house, in an upstairs room, Herman and Birdie were getting ready for bed. Herman had stripped off his pants and was standing in his drawers, unbuttoning his shirt. He was saying in a low voice, angrily:

"You thought you was bein' nobly smart, didn't you?"

In the same low voice she retorted just as angrily:—

"Why shouldn't I say what I think? If I had my way we wouldn't stay here tonight, even. I got no use for Case Gyler and I intend to let him know it!"

Herman turned, before blowing out the oil lamp, to glare at her. He said with strong conviction:—

"You'll keep you mouth shut. And I mean what I say. What can a man do with a woman like you, but slap your jaw till your ears ring, and you learn to use some sense. You tend your own business."

And Birdie shut up.


Three days later Case still had not formed a plan in his mind. And the problem was settled for him by the simple wisdom of Letitia's Crow Indian father.

It was a bright, cold day when the old man came driving down the road in a warmly curtained buggy. Winter had blanketed the earth with a foot-deep cover of snow that sparkled in the thin sunlight. Letitia's father was a strange combination of half-modern and half-ancient Indian. He wore a large gray Stetson hat that was at least three years old. His hair hung in two long braids down his back. New, black, four-buckle overshoes covered his moccasined feet.

He stopped the buggy at the road gate and shouted for Case to come out. When Case came from the house and out to where he was waiting, the old man offered no word of greeting. But he loosened the side curtain of the buggy and flung back a blanket with the blunt words:—

"I bring your papoose to its own home."

Hosea, with the pathetic defiance of a six-year-old boy, sat very stiff and straight on the buggy seat. His brown eyes stared straight at Case with curious antagonism. He wore a neat little suit, and black boots that Case knew were of Letitia's own buying. Coal-black hair contrasted sharply with his little pure white Stetson and hatband woven of scarlet beads.

He only stared at Case a moment, then his look turned down to his small feet and the bundle of clothing beside them. Plainly he was close to crying. His muscles jerked, and he was trembling.

The old man said simply:—

"If you want him you take him now. If you no take him now you never take him. And I will take him away with me and know him as my son. But I will not teach him untruths. He knows you are his father."

Case could not speak; nor turn his eyes away from the little boy who sat on the bright blanket and would not look towards him.

Letitia's father said gruffly:—

"You keep, or I take?"

Case's eyes filled with tears; his mouth twisted when he spoke.

"You take. And sometime soon I will bring you money to keep—to send him to school. . . ."

Without a word the old man started up his horses and turned them back the way he had come. He drove away down the road.

Case walked slowly across the yard and on towards the barns. When he passed the house, Sareeny called to him from the kitchen window.

But he did not answer.

# CHAPTER 16

IT WAS a lonesome winter. From the time of that first heavy snowfall the brown soil was not bared to the winds until spring blew in, four months later. Four months of wind and snow and bitter cold was a weary stretch of time. Their world narrowed down till it seemed the old log house and snow-swept yard penned them in. As Minty said, they had too much time to think. Try as they would to find work to do, there would be long afternoons when time seemed to drag; and longer evenings, after the night chores were done, when it seemed nine o'clock would never come. If they went to bed early and couldn't sleep it was worse than sitting up by the fire.

The evenings were enjoyable enough. They would sit in the long living room where the open fire crackled cheerfully, and there were books and all manner of magazines to read. Often Sareeny started a book, and lost herself so completely in it she would sit and read long after the others were asleep in bed; and the story was like a magic spell that lifted her out of the lonely, wintering hills and let her live for a brief space in a strange, distant land she had never seen and would never see in her life.

The house was weirdly lonesome with the cold isolation of winter and wind, and yet all the world paraded before them on the printed and pictured pages of the newspapers that came each day to the Sarpy post office. They read of everything from paupers to kings, and beggars and great men. Little printed words told in one day of all the world's mistakes and tragedies and success stories. And day after day it repeated itself, over and over again, yet each day it was new and different. The silent newspapers were all the actual life on earth recorded swiftly as it was lived.

For no sensible reason that she could name, Sareeny felt downcast. Maybe, as the saying went, she just had a good long touch of the blues. But it seemed there was a vague, ununderstandable something in each day that saddened her. She was not worrying. It was more like she had stopped little worryings and workaday ways of things, and had reached a lull, a reckoning with herself.

As was her way, she kept all her thoughts to herself.

In December, she knew she would have another baby the next summer. And she cried over it. Not because she did not want it, but because she was suddenly tired, and foolishly felt a little old. She began to think of herself. One day when she was alone in the house she studied her face in the mirror. She decided she did not look old, but six years had surely changed her. There were tiny wrinkles around her eyes, and her lips seemed thinner, wiser; her body was not nearly so slim and straight; her breasts, that had nourished three new lives and would soon nourish another, hung loosely downward. She knew all this time passing was working a steady, subtle change in her mind and her soul, too, and never would she be able to explain it to herself even to the day she would die.

She thought: "Some day long to come I will look in the mirror and see an old woman with gray hair. And in that time between now and then a thousand thousand things will have happened. My Peg and Robert will be a grown woman and man."

She had all manner of foolish thoughts.

For hours at night she would not sleep, but lay quietly in the bed beside Case. She did not realize it, but it satisfied some hidden need, an unconscious hunger of her mind, to let herself lie there and her thoughts wear themselves out. Outside, black winter wind whispered in tune with every weary tick of time.

She would be glad when springtime came, even though she would then be heavy and cumbersome with this new baby's weight. A poor man's wife must always wish for springtime. For each year may mean another birth, and worry, and a stretch of time that is only lightened by the way she lives her own life in her own little world.

If Case turned in his sleep and his lips brushed tenderly across hers, she would be suddenly content to sleep in the curve of his arm, and her worrisome thoughts vanished behind the strength of complete peace.

On the Friday before Christmas, Jacob came walking down the road from the railway station. They had been expecting him each day, thinking he must surely be on the way, for even with the fastest trains it took several days to travel the distance from New York. Sareeny met him at the yard gate. For a minute they could hardly talk, they were that glad to see each other.

Eunice could not come, Jacob said, because she—well, it was pretty hard for Eunice to get away from New York right at this time. Sareeny sensed something strange in the way he answered her questions. He couldn't fool her. There was something about his wife he was not going to talk about.

He had a picture of Eunice in his suitcase. Sareeny made him find it, for she was as curious over what this woman would look like as she had ever been curious over anything in her life. A dozen times she had wondered, with Mom, what sort of a woman Jacob had married.

The pictured face on the cardboard seemed hardly a mature woman, yet Jacob admitted carelessly that this was her second marriage. Her first husband had been an army officer, stationed in Oklahoma. She had married and divorced and married again, all in a year's time.

Instantly, Sareeny did not like her.

A woman who could swap and juggle husbands so easily was not to be trusted. Even in this day and age, with all this loose talk of modernism and freedom of living, a line had to be drawn somewhere, and the marriage vows ought to be it. She gave the pretty pose of Eunice's pictured face and smiling eyes and long bobbed brown hair to Jacob, without another word.

At home that night Jacob gave the picture to Ellen, for her to keep.

Pleased, Ellen said: "She's a right pretty woman, Jacob. I'm sorry we cannot see her."

Frace leaned above Ellen's chair. She said openly:

"Why! She is very pretty, Jacob. You must be proud of her." She looked directly in Jacob's eyes.

"May the world give both of you everything you both want, Jacob."

And she looked as though she meant it.

He did not know what to say to answer her.

He got up and went out, taking Keith with him. Keith was a little shy of him. Jacob could not get over how Keith had grown. He talked over it as though it were a marvel, eyeing Keith proudly. At the supper table Frace spoke flatly, and then was sorry she had spoken so.

"He was over a year old when you left, Jacob. And remember you have been away nearly four years. It's a long time to grow in."

Yes, it was a long time to grow in or change in, either. Jacob sat at the supper table with them, and he thought: "Well, I'm home again." Yet he did not feel as he had expected to feel. He knew that he could never come here and settle again to live. He would hate it. He had almost

215

forgotten the exact ways of their lives, here. The large oil lamp set in the center of the table, its yellow light cast on all their faces he knew so well; and yet they had changed so greatly. Tana was half a grown, sweet girl, and half a sweeter woman, already as pretty as she could be. She sat at the corner of the table, next to Chris. Jacob had remembered Tana's flaxen hair as the way Ellen had fixed it when Tana was a child; braided and held with hairpins around her head, so that even then she had seemed amusingly like a little woman. But now—you could see Tana was a vain little vixen!—Her hair was brushed and shampooed till it was soft and silky, combed to one side of her pretty head and arranged there with a small circular blue comb, clear blue as her eyes. Jacob thought, sometime I will buy the prettiest blue satin dress that I can find, and send it to Tana, she'll be a knock-out for looks if she can have the right clothes. . . . Pa ought to have sent her on to school, out of these damned hills—what chance has she got here?

Chris was no more a gawky kid, but a man, strong and homely-looking, cheerfully sure of himself.

Pa had changed but little, turning a little more aged, a little more gruff with ill humor. Pa had always been more or less like that. Never much time for pleasant things. Just work, work, worrying over hot summer sun and hard wind and the price of wheat or cattle or what the world was coming to with its warlike, greedy ways. . . . Now when it is all summed up, what has it got you? Nothing. And look what it has done to Mom. She's old before her time to be old. . . . No, I will never live my life here, in the way you all do. . . . Not when the earth is as big as it is—

Even as they talked, Jacob felt the night loneliness of this hilly and thinly settled land. Far away yonder, in a glitter of light, in the hue and cry of a city, was Eunice. Here an oil lamp filled the room with shadows, wood fire crackled in an old stove, and wind soughed about the gray log walls of this old house where he was born. And they sat about the long table in a poor room that Mom was pitifully proud of because Chris had put cheap covering on the floor and cheap paper on the walls. And if you would but step out in the yard and listen, you could hear from the hills the long-drawn howls of wild and shaggy coyotes pointing their noses to the stars in the sky; and soon an answering call would come closer by, carried to your ears on the wind, sending a chill up your back even though you were an old man and had lived here all your life.

For some reason he did not understand, or even give a thought, Jacob was unwilling and half afraid to look directly at Frace. He would not be drawn into close talk with her, except to speak of Keith, and ask whether she planned to stay on in Sarpy. To that question she answered that she did not know. Jacob was careful never to be left in a room alone with her. He meant to go, when these few days were over, without having told her but little about himself. He owed her nothing, now. He'd let her have all of Keith, hadn't he? And he loved Keith more than anything else in all the world, maybe more than he loved Eunice, even. No one in the world knew how much his thoughts had dwelt on Keith, how he was forever wishing he could have Keith with him, his own self. Keith's mother was a good woman, and Jacob knew it— but he owed her nothing now, except friendliness and respect.

The day before Christmas, Ranny came. He and Beth herded their children into the kitchen, and as Tana said later, then the fun began. Never in all of her life had she seen such a family of spoiled brats. They stayed three days, and even Mom's nerves were a little ragged, towards the last. Beth petted and humored their every whim, and Ranny was nigh about as bad. When one of the kids set up a howl for something, it squalled till it got what it wanted. "I want it!" it would demand with a tear-stricken face. "I want it right now!" Nine times out of ten Beth would turn her eyes to Ranny and say placidly: "Let him have it, Ranny."

Beth was becoming fat, and plainer than she had ever been in her younger days. Last year she had an operation, and she told them all about it so many times the story became old and was an aggravation. They still owed the hospital bill, she said, and Ranny would be lucky if he ever got it paid, the way things looked now. It was hard enough for them to even make a living, away yonder on that God forsaken farm. Last winter when she took sick, Ranny and everyone had thought she would surely die. Beth went on to tell how Ranny had rushed her to the nearest hospital, and her appendix had burst on the way; and when the doctor cut her open, the blood popped out and hit the ceiling. She was fascinated by the memory of this experience that was all her own. Ranny, whispering slyly to Mom, said Beth was prouder of the scar on her side than she was of her wedding ring.

Now in these few days Jacob was home not one of them could have been accused of uttering one deliberate, knowing word concerning the guilty shame of Case that was shrouded in secrecy. Yet what strange thing is it that dwells in a look or manner or common conversation, forever defying the likes of such a thing to be concealed entirely? Within three days, Jacob was sure with the knowledge that now they all knew about Case and Letitia; they all knew, except Sareeny. And Jacob could not understand for the life of him how in the world Sareeny could have failed to learn of it in the face of them all. What fools were they all, to expect her not to learn of it in time? . . . when you could feel the knowledge of it in every neighbor's eyes when they looked at Case . . . and Case would turn his own eyes away like a whelping dog that will not look at you. . . . Jacob said nothing, but he pondered and mulled it over in his mind. His sister Sareeny had always been a favorite with Jacob. She yet was, too. So Jacob kept watching, his eyes and ears alert; and it struck him as a silly thing that they did not tell Sareeny, and clear the whole thing up in one way or another. Cripes! Sareeny was a grown woman able to think for her own self!

He eyed Sareeny, quietly studying her. His look dwelt on her gray eyes when she turned to look at him. Good-natured was not the word to describe Sareeny's eyes; nor was, smiling nor gentleness nor soft satisfaction complete in their meaning for them; but all these things were in Sareeny's look, together with the expression of a woman who, in life at its richest, relaxes to watch her children play. Time, and babies' nursing mouths, had loosened the firm roundness of Sareeny's breasts, and thinned the last of her girlishness from her face and skin. She was all a knowing woman now, with a remote ranch woman's skilled hands and serene face. With a woman's long silky hair—Sareeny's hair was like the dark brown color of the brown tree moss that grows deep and soft like velvet in shadowed forest places. Sareeny had a good woman's patience, Jacob thought. A woman's patience that will break and complain over little, trifling things—and endure with powerful depth and strength in the face of great and awful things. Would it not be better for some one of them to go to her and say honestly: "Sareeny, there's something we have been hiding from you. But you are bound to learn it sooner or later, so it is better to tell you now, quietly and sensibly, and have it done with. And knowing you like we do, help you to meet it sensibly your own self."

Case was the one to say it. But Case was a yellow dog, hiding behind his own self! Miserable over his own doings and afraid to do anything about it, except do his sneaking in his low lying way.

Jacob could hardly a-bear to be friendly with Case, and contempt was bold in his eyes.

They'd all hide this away—and a hidden shame grows in power!—Still it would break Sareeny's heart, that's what it would do!

Jacob made up his mind to tell Sareeny of it, himself.

He did not know that Letitia and the youngest child had burned to death. He did not even know the youngest child had ever been born. He knew only of Hosea.

In exactly the same way he had always been, Jacob did not stop to consider deeply, or weigh matters. He only sensed vaguely the vaguer feeling his folks and their neighbors were trying to conceal. He jumped to the conclusion that Case still held secret meetings with Letitia. Like a fool, Jacob formed the idea to have a good, long talk with Sareeny. He'd talk sense to her, reason with her, and see that she didn't fly off the handle and do some silly thing in the way of a woman loving Case as she did. To Jacob, just what he decided to do seemed very sensible and clear. He did not realize that you cannot in the same hour talk sense to, or reason with, a woman you have just told that the husband she loves has been gallavanting and seducing with another woman.

The morning of the day after Christmas, Case went on home with Minty and Felix, leaving Sareeny with her three young-uns to visit with Ellen and Jacob and Ranny. For Ranny and Beth would start for their own home at noon-time today.

And on the evening of today, Jacob got Sareeny alone in the yard and he told her. He told her carefully.

They were standing close by the kitchen door, where big, bare lilac bushes were higher than their heads and laden with snow. The air was heavy with frost.

All the while he was talking she did not say a word. She just stared at him and her skin turned as white as paper.

220

Jacob was sick with the knowledge of what he had done.

It was not so sane and simple as he had thought it.

Somehow, he had expected her to go into a cold rage. She did not. He had expected he would have to reason with her, a little sternly, arguing and pleading.

But when he had finished, and she fully understood, she put out one hand a little blindly and braced herself against the house. She was dead white, and though she was not crying, her breath came as in sobs, and she trembled so that her muscles jerked.

Her voice strained, tight in her throat—

"I know why it was, now . . . when they talked about the Indian woman and the little boy burning . . . It was that Letitia woman—and it was Case's own boy . . . Case knew it all and they all knew it. And it burned to death only two weeks ago. . . ."

She told Jacob of it.

Jacob put his arm tightly around her shoulders. There were tears in his own eyes. He spoke with love and tenderness.

"I only told you, Sareeny, because I thought it was best. You would have learned anyway, and I wanted you to tide over it . . . to help you . . . knowing how you love Case. . . .If Letitia is dead and the boy is dead it is all over and finished. Had I known that I would not have told you."

She said: "But it is not over. It is not finished. Birdie spoke of another boy, a six-year-old boy who did not die in the fire. And Case is its father, too.

She broke suddenly. She looked up at him, her eyes wide and stark with feeling. She started to speak and did not. She turned and walked swiftly into the house, through the kitchen, and into Ellen's bedroom.

Jacob followed her.

Ellen was alone in the kitchen. She took one look at Sareeny's face, and then at Jacob's face, and at once she understood. She dropped the work she was doing and dried her hands on her apron, saying:—

"You have told her. You should not have let her know. She'd be happy with him, not realizing the kind he is—"

She went in the bedroom with Sareeny and closed the door. In less than an hour, just before twilight, Case came driving the sleigh down the road to take Sareeny home again.

Sareeny had made up her mind she would not go with him.

Had Case not came for her so soon, never would Sareeny have gone home with him, either.

It was Ellen who pleaded and argued with her.

Sareeny stood by the bedroom window and watched Case come driving down the cold winter road to fetch her. Her face was hard, her eyes neither crying nor clear in their expression of hurt, or anger, or bitterness. As yet she truly felt only shock. Hurt had not had time to come, nor any definite or clear reaction. She had just learned of this thing, unexpected, and tinged with the horror of the thought that a child of Case's, an unclaimed little unwanted, secreted boy of shame had died a terrible death—in the agony of fire; a little boy as much Case's child as Peg, or Robert, or this little-est baby fretful in her arms—or even the one not yet lain in her arms. Birdie had said: Oh it was the pitifullest thing . . . the little boy screamed, stretching his little arms out towards them, his clothes all a-blaze and the whole house was in flames and rolling smoke

Ellen was saying:—

". . . He loves you. You know in your heart he loves you. You know it ever' time he looks at you."

Sareeny said in a low voice:—

"I love him—and would I slip away into the hills and let another man take me—would I hide a lie in my face ever' time I looked at any one of you—?"

Ellen broke in on her talk and spoke without thinking.

"Even a good man is—" She stopped. She was going to say, even a good man is carnal-minded and full of lust. But such was not true; or if a good man feels such things he controls it within himself. To say what had been on her tongue was blasphemy. There was no excuse for Case Gyler in this thing. And yet Case was a good man. They had all thought he was a mortal good man till this hidden thing had come to light. One cloud in the sky does not darken the whole sun, nor if one lamp burn out in a room of many lamps it will not plunge the room in darkness. She thought: "I am only an old woman and I am about to die. If I cannot pass judgment on Case in this thing, how can any other of you, even though you be his wife Sareeny . . . more and more I know that we cannot be lofty or too strictly just in judgment, for surely our own lives track through the same mud to the same end, though we are not all so soiled by it. . . ."

She stood in the half-darkness of the room, looking at Sareeny. She did not know what to do, except that she must make Sareeny hush her mouth over this, and go back and live with Case.

It had all happened so quickly that it was unreal.

A few minutes later they heard the sleighbells of Case's horses, and the bells grew louder, to stop in the dark and snowy yard of the house.

Sareeny was trembling. Now she was close to crying, too. She thought, and said aloud: "He is here, but I don't want to have to look at him. I can't stand to have to see him now." But Ellen went and brought her coat, and the blanket for the baby. She took Sareeny's face in her hands, and her tears wet Sareeny's face. She said so low that it was almost a whisper:—

"Go back to your home and your man, Sareeny. Brood and hold this in your mind if you must, but keep it in your own mind. After all, you still have him . . . it is not as losing something in death . . . and he loves you. Now that you know, keep your mouth hushed over it, till you see what a few months teaches you."

Frace came in from her work at the chicken house. Old Jim and Jacob and Case came in with loud talk behind her, stomping their feet to jar off the snow.

Case came to the door of the bedroom that Ellen had left open. His eyes greeted Sareeny. Her glance shot at him, and then away again. He went to the bed and helped Ellen wrap the baby in its thick blanket, and he noticed nothing different in Sareeny. Frace had come in with a lamp. Chris entered the kitchen with the big steaming buckets of milk. Tana came down the stairway with Peg and Robert, and helped Frace get them into their warm outdoor clothes.

Everything was outwardly the same as it had always been when she and Case made ready to go home.

Only that Ellen came and kissed her with a different meaning. And when they went out through the kitchen Jacob was standing by the door and he stopped her, his brown eyes pleading and sorry. He kissed her quickly and only she understood.

Never could she thank Jacob for telling her this.

But looking up into his face she understood how he felt. She squeezed his arm with trembling fingers.

In the yard, Case tucked her and the children in the sleigh with blankets and robes against the cold wind. He lifted her feet and wrapped a heavy robe around them, and tucked a blanket snug around her body. Something in her, a silent voice, struggled to say and struggled not to say, "I hate you, I hate you—I know you now as I never have before."

He shouted good night to her folks and drove away on the home road. The sleigh rode smoothly, with never a bump. The sleighbells were loud in the thin air. The night was black and bitter cold with wind.

In a week's time Jacob was gone again, on his way to New York. He had been as restless as a young caged buck. From the way he acted you would have thought that Eunice was made of solid gold, and likely to be stolen away if he was parted from her too long.

Mom was the only one he had talked to, over Eunice. When he had gone away again she told Sareeny what he had said.

Sareeny promised never to repeat a word of it to her Pa or Frace.

Jacob was in misery because he loved his wife so much and could not be happy with her. They were married on the spur of a moment, in a drunken revel, and he half-believed Eunice would never have married him had she been with a clear head.

When Jacob told all this he had walked back and forth around the room, and there were tears in his eyes. At times his voice broke, and he stopped talking until he could go on and tell her more. Three times Eunice had left him, and twice he had hunted and found her in a speakeasy so drunk with liquor he had to half-carry her home and to bed. He didn't want his mother to think Eunice was a no-good woman. He said Eunice shouldn't be judged by the quiet ranch home way of living. Eunice had lived nearly all her life in the big cities of the East and West and South, where there was a different way of everything. In cities girls drank liquor and smoked cigarettes and proudly called themselves, modern. Yes, Eunice was a city-bred woman. But she was more than that. To him, she was different from any and all other women. In her changeable ways she was likened to a dozen women all in her slender body and smooth white face. She could be gay and lightsome as a carefree girl; or tender with a woman's tenderness; or moody with stormy days of blue sadness; she could be wise, wise. He loved her. Eunice had come into his life and changed it as bright colors meet and mix and change in hue. He loved her so much that when he was not actually with her she was ever in his thoughts, anchored in his mind with doubt and tenderness and hope.

A poor man, living in a big city and depending on a job that is never certain, could be compared to a fellow lost in a crowd of clutching hands that demand money! money! For rent, light, heat, water, every morsel of food, every stitch of clothing. Expenses eat into a weekly wage like a swift cancer. They roll up like a black cloud, if a man is not careful, and smother him with the eternal need for money.

(Within two hundred years' time, the earthly world has changed, till now the clink of silver must be heard at every birth, and all through life and even at the last rites of death.)

Eunice hated the sea, and except for Jacob's work on the sea he was experienced only as a rancher and at farming. He had at best knowledge only of tilling the soil and making it give him food and clothing and a place to live. He did not fit in with a stilted job and a boss above him. But Eunice was not a ranch woman and would never be. And Jacob could no more stay away from her than an eagle shot in flight can keep from falling to the earth.

Ellen worried over Jacob as though his troubles were her own. So they were. When a woman bears a child a new life is given her in more ways than one. As long as they both shall live, the good mother lives the life of her child, too, over and over, as he lives it. When the child is young, he steps on her toes, so to speak, with his mischief and aggravation and daily

226

care. But when the child is grown, he steps on her heart, with his mistakes and troubles and separate sorrows.

Many a time in day and night Sareeny mulled over Ellen's words: "Now that you know, keep your mouth hushed over it till you see what a few months teaches you."

The winter persisted, its snow and wind and below-zero weather penning them in. The time was long.

How Sareeny kept her mouth hushed she did not know. Surely it was not because of any goodness in her, or patience, or forbearance. Case was in the house so much now, and she could hardly force herself to talk to him at all, and that little she did say was in the nagging, nasty way of a shrewish woman. She wanted to be mean to him. She wanted to open her mouth and put all her thoughts into awful words and lash out at him and let him know she was not such a simple, trusting fool as he believed. There were whole days when she loathed the very sight of him; and one wrong word spoken would have caused her to pick up her young-uns and walk out. In her thinking it seemed to her that would not have been such a sickening thing if the little boy had not died such a terrible death, with Case never going near, or speaking a word, when the little thing's charred body was buried. How in the name of God could Case have done such a thing? —even the child's death by fire had not fazed him. Oh there were no words strong enough, or vile enough to stab with meaning for him. Had Sareeny realized it, her very horror of the matter helped her to keep her voice hushed and still. She could not look at Case without seeing the little boy's hands writhing in flames, hearing his screams for his mother who was that pretty Indian woman. Sareeny could hardly bear for Case to even touch Peg, or Robert, or the baby. She had not told Case of the unborn child she was carrying now, that she would have early next summer. She could not move herself to tell him. As yet he did not know. Let him wait until he could learn by looking at her, and then let him wonder why she had not told him. Let him worry, and not know any actual reason for her to lay away from him in their bed at night, hating that his hands should touch her, hating the thought of his naked body and lips that would be tender against her lips. She thought to herself that she really knew him—she knew him now!

He was worried over her. He was even more kind and gentle-spoken than ever before. His brown eyes, wretched, followed her about through the day with sober concern. Never did he guess that she knew, because he had been so sure in his mind that she would leave him if ever she learned of it.

Sareeny had to set herself to keep from going to snatch Peg or the baby away from him, to keep from crying, from almost screaming at him: "Don't you touch them! Don't you dare put your hand on any one of them!" Was he thinking of that other son, maybe, when he loved Robert with rough play? That other son who was somewhere close in the mountains, with neither father nor mother. Why was he not man enough to come to her and tell her of all that he had done, and ask her to forgive and help him? She could see now that he was worried, too. Now she understood his spells of veiled misery and deep worry. But never would he suffer as he ought to!—As she sometimes hoped he would.

Yet she kept her mouth quiet, except for every opportunity for harsh meanness and stubborn contrariness that puzzled Case no less than it did Minty or Felix or Dorcy.

More than once Dorcy thought silently, watching her: "She knows. A fool could see she knows, and she is trying to hide it with pretense she don't. Oh Sareeny, this in its self is such a little thing. If I but dared to begin with the day I married Olen Fry and tell you all . . . this would not seem such an almighty matter."

228

Late in January Case made a strange trip to Yellowstone River. His excuse did not fool Sareeny, now that she knew him. After he returned she saw him slipping their bank-book into the box where she kept it carefully. Instantly suspicious, she waited till he had left the house, then went to look at it.

Case had drawn a thousand dollars from the bank.

Sareeny was aghast.

Long later, when she looked back to remember this moment, she knew it was the crisis. Had she given in to her rage she would have flared up to quarrel with Case. He would have lied about it, and she would have known that he was lying. But she said nothing, waiting till he came to her with his careful, lying explanation, and then she did not answer. She only gave him a quick, straight look. She guessed that he had taken the money to use in some way for that six-year-old boy in the mountains; and oddly, that guess eased some of the tension in herself. At least he was man enough to feel he owed some claim to that boy.

When spring came, Sareeny grew out of her foolishness. She understood, slowly, what the months had taught her. She had looked up to Case as a God, almost, but she had learned he was only another man. Not as good as some men, not as bad as others. She was through pondering and brooding over it, spewing petty meanness like a contrary fool. Ever she had wanted folks to say she was a good woman. Now, in the first test of her own natural goodness with her own natural spite and meanness and narrow unforgiving mind, she had come to know herself, too. Though she loved Case, never would she feel the same towards him again, for it was brought home to her so clearly that he was not such a good man, after all. He would sin and lie and deceive. And cannot any human do the same thing? In another way, she was not so truly good, her own self. Close yonder was a child of Case's that had no father and no mother, no home to bring it up right. If she were truly a good woman, she would take Case, and go and bring that child here, and she would mother it. But she could not. She could never move herself to do that. Never could she do it! Even though in that way it would always stand between herself and Case.

She reckoned this was like a second start, and each of them, secretly, was a heap more prepared and wiser for it. Yes, she had been a fool! The sooner you plum realize how surprising disgusting things can be mixed in with the natural goodness of a human being, the sooner you will be better off. There are men—and women, too!—That the world can rightfully wish had never been born. But Case was not one of them.

It might be I still am a fool, she thought.

But she got out in the bright spring sunlight and warm wind, to put her garden seeds in the ground, and help Minty plan the flowers in the yard.

It was like a tonic for her.

She was herself again. Wiser, with the same quiet and friendly goodness that you could not help but love her for, because she was so honest in herself.

And she had kept her mouth hushed.


Bright June sunlight glowed down on the red roses in Sareeny's back yard. The tiger lilies, in full bloom down by the Creek, were massed in stately dignity, their brilliant orange flowers, black-specked, a pretty sight to see. The sunlight slanted through the open window where Sareeny was looking out, and it fell upon the bed where she lay with her new child. He was three days old, and she had named him Leslie.

Sareeny was white-faced, weaker than she had ever been with any other birth. Her pain had been greater, her agony sharper, than even with that first, Peggy Ellen, born out in the hills with nothing but Case's clumsy hands to help her.

She lay back in the white pillows and clean sheets, so weak she hated to even lift a hand to still the baby's whimpering. She could not eat and keep her food. She would eat and vomit, and the pain of vomiting would cause her to drop back, half-fainting against her pillow.

Two or three times a day the doctor came down the road from the little town to do what he could for her.

Old Minty hovered around the bed, smoothing the covers, or fluffing a pillow with a deft and anxious hand. Ellen was out in the kitchen, trying to fix something light and wholesome that Sareeny could eat. Felix tromped about the yard, wishing there was something he could do. Case tried to go on with his work about the ranch, work that had to be done, and he was alone with his thoughts and his own misery and worry.

Dorcy was keeping Peg and Robert and little Alex to play over at her home, till Sareeny got better.

Ellen thought, Maybe this will be Sareeny's last.

But in April of the next year, Sareeny had another. A girl they named Nellie Ann.

And in October of the next year she had another. A boy they named Ross.

And these softly, soundlessly trumpeting years passed by into the lonely byways of a million yesterdays. Often time is like an easy unending wind, arriving with slow softness— and then is gone with the wind, leaving the weary wear of living that is never totally unpleasant, never totally happy but is ever a little of this and a little of that, like the pattern of a crazy-quilt. And like the quilt, the patches fitted together form a design that is ever new, ever different, a little startling, a little beautiful, and useful in that it does some human good.

In December of the same year Ross was born, Ellen died. It was a day in the week before Christmas. Heavy snow like floating feathers, as Peg described it, began falling early in the winter morning and continued until the end of day. There was no wind, and it was not so very cold.

On such a day, when the air is so still, twilight comes over the Montana hills like a call of peace. Gray light slowly gives way to a darkness that is more elusive than fine mist, mysterious as haze. It cups in every low place, along every winding ravine and little buxom, broad-cheeked valley, until only the hilltops stand out where day has beat a last fading retreat into the sky.

Sareeny sat in the bay window of the dining room, sewing. Minty was in the kitchen, looking after the hot supper that was all ready to be dished up; the children were there around the kitchen table, hungry and anxious for their daddy and Felix to come in from the chores to supper.

Chris came riding in a hurry down the road. Sareeny heard the horses' running feet pounding against the snow. Chris turned in at the gate, and she knew then something was wrong. The very way he sat his saddle, the strange look on his face, caused her to hurry out the front door and meet him on the porch.

He spoke quietly, yet his voice held more sorrow and grief than if he had said it with tears. He said simply:—

"Sareeny, Mom is dying."

Sareeny just stood and looked at him. She couldn't believe what he had said, or even that he had said it. Her hands stayed where they had stopped suddenly when he spoke. Her face whitened, and stared at him through the darkness of the porch until he reached out and shook her to make her listen to what he was saying. Minty came, and the children crowded out behind her. Case and Felix were coming up from the stock barns, crossing the little foot bridge of the creek.

So suddenly had all this happened that it was like a dream of torment, with Case whipping the horses along the dark road to Mom's house. Sareeny had scarcely taken time to put on warm clothing, but had snatched a heavy woolen blanket and wrapped it around baby Ross, for he, whose past months could be counted on two fingers, must have milk from his mother's breasts be there death or any calamity of life.

In her mother's house, far down the long-seeming road, the lamplight glowed like a steady signal set out in a land of lonely fore and black night and snowy earth.

Ellen was dead a half-hour before they reached her door.

Sareeny went to the bedroom where her mother lay. The doctor was there, and he had closed the old gray eyes that death had left open and unseeing of this room, where five times in her life she had labored and brought forth a child. Frace had helped him fold Ellen's stilled hands on her breast, and draw a sheet over the dead body.

Tana had been no help to them. Once she knew her mother was gone she had fled to another room, and she was in there now, living the first great hurt of her life.

Sareeny lifted the sheet from her mother's face. Not until then did she break down. For not until then could she realize her mother was really dead. Her mother's face, like a familiar symbol, was set in eternal death, as though modeled in wax.

It was the first great hurt of Sareeny's life, too. For this was not bodily pain. It was not pain at all, and yet it tore deeper than the very heart, with grief, and sorrow, and unutterable sadness of a loss that can never be brought back; or found again, less it be true that they might, in their turn, follow in her footsteps past the mystery of death and possibly meet her, face to face.

In answer to Sareeny's unspoken question the doctor said gently: "Heart failure. I told her six months ago she might go any time. She made me promise not to tell any one of you."

Old Jim walked from room to room. The blue in his eyes was brightened and cleared shining with the tears that came with his thoughts. He was silent, with no word to comfort his children's grief, but rather they tried to comfort him; and even in the midst of their sorrow they could not help but pity him, for he was old; and the woman who had stood by his side, and answered his love with her love, borne his children, and lived solely for him and his through thirty years was no longer here.

They sat up all the long winter night. It seemed strange that she was not there to talk with them. And stranger yet that she was yonder in the bedroom, silent and stilled for all time to come—yet she was not there. She could never be there again.

Past midnight, east wind came up noisily, lonely, and icy cold. It blew in a swift white blizzard that walled out all the rest of the world and made of each house and home a separate world, small and incomplete.

# CHAPTER 17

WITH the coming of the summer of '31 drought was making all the Western dryland a forlorn desert. Deep back in the hills, away from the beaten highways that threaded from city to city and town to town, woe and desolation described the earth. Almost like a scene from Biblical times, the old land scorched under the hot hell of a blazing sun, a rainless sky, and burning winds that carried the dust of a state across thousands of miles. Crops could not only refuse to grow and mature. Many seeded fields simply could not sprout in the soil that was dry as powdery ashes. Springtime brought only a faint tint of green to the grass that was as gray and dead in June as it had been in January. Creeks, and water springs dried up with a hard baked crust. The cattle and horses, milling about with mute, thirsty hope, pawed the crust to fine dust that rose up in yellow-white clouds. And the livestock died by the dozens, until their bloated, rotting bodies were scattered here and there over the rangeland, stinking the sage-brush wind.

It was no wonder poor old weather-beaten ranchers gave up, and loaded their wives and their kids into the wagon or rattling old car, and drove away. They were mistakenly hoping to find a better place. The abandoned homes swiftly donned a deserted look; for horses in search of food and water pushed over the fences and they faunched about in the shade and broke out the windows. Or else another rancher, hard up for money, came to take what he needed to repair his own house, and that could hardly be called thieving.

The forsaken home, changing owners again and again through mortgages and unpaid debts and bankruptcy, stood a shell of its former self; vacant windows and sagging doors stood open to prowling night wind and birds that nested in the walls.

The newspapers said people all over the world were in need and misery and want.

To tune in on radio speeches was interesting enough, for it was like eavesdropping at the mystery window of a road-house. With politics and the depression and the world-wide drought to talk about, politicians were more than a little hysterical. At times they allowed themselves to get quite out of control. Felix said politics was the dirtiest game on earth. Many of the men were what they were supposed to be. Good men, honest and fine. But give any political party enough rope and time and it would hang itself with lies and vote-getting promises.

The newspapers spoke truth, for they recorded life. But the radio was truth, too, for the world seemed vaguely touched with a strange madness.

Oh, these silent hills were lonely now, with empty homes; and never a green field to be seen through the long summer's heat glare. Sareeny read in the papers of mobs and bread lines, and millions of people actually starving because they could not find even a little work to do to earn a bit of food; and she could but wonder how the earth could seem still and silent with all this going on. It was as though the sky should be thick with black smoke, and the air echoing with voices of distress. Times were that bad.

Early in June, Case and Felix rounded up all their cattle and horses and drove them to the mountains. Up there the dumb critters had a chance to live, anyway. Up there the grass had not died out completely; nor the water streams dwindled away till they were dry as a bone.

Case and Felix stayed up there with the livestock, herding them around from canyon to canyon, throughout all the summer months. In a certain way Sareeny was glad Case had to be up there. He went nigh about crazy when he was home, because there was nothing to do. There were no crops to be cultivated, no hay to make, no harvest coming up. The fields were so dead it sickened your very soul to look out across them; and so bare they might have been broad highways trampled to fine dust by myriad plodding feet.

Somehow it gave them all a feeling of having their hands tied, and being unable to do anything about it. With Sareeny and Minty there was no garden stuff to can and preserve for winter. The garden was as bare as the fields. There was not even the hard-fast rule of preparing three regular meals each day, for with the menfolks gone, cooking for the children was an easy matter. There was nothing much to do, except mope around, and complain about the heat, and worry.

Yet the summer brought many things to pass.

Over at the county seat, the law courts finally decided Olen Fry was legally dead. The second week in June Dorcy was summoned before the judge. The two thousand dollars was transferred to her own name, for her to spend, or save, or leave in the National Bank, as she saw fit.

As Dorcy said, it was a grand feeling, and she was that happy she felt a little weak in the knees. Lord! what a relief to know your children won't grow up and start their own life without a penny; and what a comfort to know there is a pile of ready money waiting at your finger tips to stave off sickness or any other trouble that might pop up.

The day Dorcy came home from the law courts, Sareeny went over there to be glad with her. They sat on the low stone step of Dorcy's back door and talked and talked.

First, think of yourself as being so poor all your life that ever a silver dollar has seemed a powerful thing, that you must sweat and worry to know the hard feel of it in your hand; and you have watched your children's bare feet running through hot summers and frosty falls and you have wished—my God you have wished a million times for a silver dollar, to buy little shoes or a little young-un's fine new clothes, or a little toy that is a silly thing but not silly in a child's world. But over and above every other thing you have wished for money because it seems even a free life must be bought and paid for.

While Dorcy talked, her younger children played about the yard. The yard was a pretty place, even now, for each day she carried water from the deep new well and watered the flowers; and each year since that new well was dug, the rock garden grew and spread over and around the old well.

Dorcy's secret was buried under the rock garden's waterblue cornflowers, the poppies' mixed colors of rich red and shell-pink and California orange. She thought her secret was as dead as Olen was. It could never come to life, or speak with actual sound. It was oddly like a distant, faraway voice calling through the night; remotely heard, and yet never heard, and never understood.

In this business of the money matter, Dorcy had everything planned out, long ago. She told Sareeny of it.

She had planned, if ever she got that two thousand dollars in her own name, never would she spend one cent of it on her own self. In her mind she had divided it among her children. As each of the children reached its twenty-first birthday she would have the money ready, and it would be a gift from their old Ma. With the younger ones, time would have piled up the interest, and it would all be a tidy sum. But if ever a part of the money had to be used in sickness or any such thing, the sum used would be subtracted from the two thousand dollars as a whole.

Dorcy gloated over that money. She cried over it, because she was so happy at the prospect of giving it to her children.

On the last Monday in June, the bank "failed" and closed its doors, never to open them for business again.

Like a flash the money was gone.

With Dorcy and Frace and a thousand others, Sareeny and Case lost every dollar they had in the world, as if they had thrown it on the fire and turned away without watching it burn. Felix lost thirty thousand dollars. But even then he was far from being poor. It was not as Sareeny believed. Not all of Felix's money was in the bank. Eden and old Herman had been too smart for that. Thousands of dollars of Felix's money were tucked away in bonds and life insurance, safe beyond any "failure" of banks or greedy, thieving hands.

How could this be any different than thieving, Sareeny wondered. They had taken the money there, and left it there, because they wanted it to be in a safe place. They were saving it. Year by year they had saved a little more. Many a dollar she had gathered, her own self, by putting away nickels and dimes, even pennies. Then in the fall, when Case made ready to go to the bank to deposit the money, she brought out the can of silver and coppers, summing it up with his bills of currency. She had been prouder of that money in the bank than almost anything. Because in some way it represented her life and Case's life together. It was something they themselves had done. It was part of their home, their life, their marriage . . . just as the children were. Like the children, it came with the years and grew, with labor and worry, even pain; like the children, it had mutely seemed a long, far-reaching road wending to a time of old age warmed with peace and secured with content.

Suddenly, it was gone. Suddenly, they no longer had the cans of silver and coppers or the bills of currency; the little leather book was mockery; it might as well be dropped in

239

the fire or given to the children to play with. But she could not do that. She had kept the little book carefully put away, so long. Even now, though it would never again be worth the few cents its paper and leather had cost, she put it away and kept it for many years.

That evening she sat on the front porch and cried. What was the world coming to, anyway? Last year and this year nothing had been raised to eat. Nothing had even been raised to feed the cows and horses and chickens. All you could read about and hear about was hard times. It was like a war, that's what it was. A war without smoke and noise of guns. A battle that waged silently over all the earth-field. Even the President, behind his big desk yonder in Washington, was tormented with armies of hungry, unemployed mobs.

If you had no money to buy, you would have to go hungry, for nothing would grow in the dry dirt.

The sun and the wind could burn the earth to a dusty cinder, and nobody could stop it.

Minty could think of nothing to say to comfort Sareeny. They sat on the front porch there in the summer evening. When they did not talk they could hear a radio's melancholy music sounding softly down the dusky road from the little village. Crickets chirped along the dry banks of Sarpy. Night hawks called, and the sound floated down from the darkness of the starry sky; a tone sound, like the plucked bass string of a fiddle.

The children were asleep. Because it was so hot in the house, Sareeny had let them make their beds on the porch, and they liked that. There was fascination in sleeping in the almost out-of-doors.

Dorcy and her girl, Rose, came across the road. Rose was almost a woman now. And she would be a good woman. She was not pretty, but like every grown girl there was a certain charm in her young face and ways. In her own mind, Rose planned to become a school teacher. Where there is a will there is a way, and she wanted to earn money and do something for her mother. She wanted to do this so much that she had repeated over and over to herself: She would never fall in love with any man—not until she was thirty-five, at least. Once she had told Dorcy that, and Dorcy had smiled involuntarily and half-pityingly. Love and marriage are seldom planned, seldom avoided. They build and arrange themselves as simply and naturally as anything that is natural and supposed to be.

Dorcy sat down beside Sareeny on the porch step.

Rose spoke, and her hand still lay tenderly on her mother's shoulder:—

"I've told Mama not to worry too much about the money being lost. We can be just as happy without it."

Dorcy's homely old face was expressionless as clay. Only her eyes seemed bright with a burning look. She had not shed a tear, nor would she, for that was not her way. Her gray, thin hair, usually so neat, hung loose over her bony shoulders. Dorcy seemed taller and thinner than ever, this last year. She worked so hard, trying to manage a living for her growing young-uns.

She spoke and her words were out before she knew it:

"I was so happy I should have known somethin' would happen. You can't do a heap of wrong and get away with it. It'll ketch up with you sooner or later, before you die."

There was even a little laughter in Rose's quick voice.

"Why, Mother! I don't believe you ever did a real wrong thing in your life. And I can remember a lot of it, you know. You talk like there were two of you, and you had kept the other hidden away from everyone."

Dorcy thought, without looking up or moving her long hands clasped around her knees: "Oh Rose, who else would I hide it from first but you or any one of my children."

As Minty said, no one can ever say, "This money is mine." They can only say, "The use of this money is mine as long as I shall have it. . . . But oh, I must watch out or I shall not have it long, for people will barter and trade and steal from me as long as I have a piece of silver. For money has never belonged to anyone. It has ever belonged to the world, for the people to suffer and snatch and grapple over. . . ."

Sareeny hoped that Case would learn in some way of the bank failure. She did not want to be the one to tell him.

Almost every day Pa and Chris came driving down the road with Tana or Frace and Keith. Tana said it was so lonesome over there with Mom gone they could hardly stand it. Pa would mope around, lost because there was no work to do in the fields, worrying over how they were going to feed the cattle this winter, and worse yet, feed their own mouths. Chris was restless. Sareeny knew that was no life for a young woman Tana's age. Before this time, Tana ought to have been out going to dances, taking in neighborhood parties with young fellows, learning to flirt a little, instead of settling down with housework and washing. But you would never hear Tana complain. She hadn't changed much, either, except to fill out in places where she needed it, and look more mature like a woman. Now she and Felix were openly in love with each other. She was a sweet woman, if there ever was one, thought Sareeny. Oh, you couldn't say Tana was as pretty as a picture, or anything like that; but she was pretty enough, her eyes were so blue, her flaxen hair so light and wavy on her pert little head; she was enough to make any young man turn his eyes to look, his heart interested. But the sweetest thing about her was she could be so happy her own self. She could cheer you up and have you laughing in no time.

They were thankful for Frace, now, at Pa's house. Frace's hands had in some way filled the vacancy left by Ellen's hands. It was Frace's planning, and Frace's thought, for all of them

242

and each of them, that smoothed over their lives when Ellen's death had left them confused and bewildered. It eased Sareeny's mind to know Frace was there in Pa's old log house. For even though Mom was not there, Frace would keep alive that unnamed something that cannot be explained, yet is the spirit of the comfort of your own home and every home. Pa and Chris and Tana depended on Frace, too. It was as though Frace had been with them always and would never leave. Seldom did it come to their minds that she was an outside woman, a stranger in their house that they had learned to know and love. Chris or Tana would have done anything for her. Old Jim said little—but he would give Frace his last dollar, had she asked for it, and he would have given it humbly, with simple gladness. Old Jim was saddened, and within himself he would be glad when the time came for him to die. He had passed his sixty-ninth year. Even at best, he knew he would not see so very many more years. He did not want to live much longer. He had no money, and more and more in these last few winters and summers he had seen that he could not be so heft with work; he could not bear up under hot sun; he could not wade snow, and shoulder into cold winter wind; even now if he gathered up every last thing he owned and sold it for money, he could not garner enough to pay the debts he owed in this world. Old as he was, poor as he was, uneducated old-time Westerner as he was, what good was there in his staying on here many more years, he thought? He had not felt this way as long as Ellen was with him. He'd stay, though, till the Lord knowed his time was up, and let him go. But all his life he had worked hard and done his poor best; now an old man, he had less than nothing, the fields all around his house were bare of any growth; he soon would have nothing to feed the cattle and horses he had raised and already mortgaged for money to buy grain which he had already fed them.

And the rich and verdant land he had first loved nearly half a century ago, loved so that he had brought his young wife here with bright plans and high hopes—this land was changing. It was crumbling, moving, dying, before his very eyes.

He felt in his heart that this was no ordinary drought. No! Let the newspapers and supposed-to-be wise men talk what they would over drought cycles and rainy cycles and spots on the sun. This land was changing; and unless the Government stepped in with all its money and power to do with, this land in a few score years would surely be scant with neighbors. He would not live to see what happened. But in these last few years a feeling had grown upon him— with the deep power of a prophecy. This change in these vast Western dryland regions had come and would continue to come, with a steady creeping. You could feel it; you could go out in the hills at night and feel a loneliness different than ever before, dead loneliness akin to that of a vast tomb, and hot wind whined through the dark laden with dust powder that settled to bury even fences, so that poor dumb hungry beasts could walk right over them in pitiful search for grass and water. The dust billowed and rolled, from the ground you stood on to high aloft in the sky, so that there were no stars, no moon; and no sun by day. On such a day, it was like long hours of too dusky, unnatural twilight— yellow, brownish twilight when you could see nothing— nothing; by day and even more so by night it was awesome; if a man be alone in the hills in that wind and deep dark that was full of sting and force and feel of all these things unexplained, it struck fear in his heart. Even the wild beasts more knowing to nature than we are, were stricken with the fear of this unknown force. They crouched behind low, slowly dying bushes, and worried in their own way, maybe, even as men worried. Was not the whole world in a turmoil? Oh, there were a few folks, no doubt, to whom this was all only a rumor. A few moneyed or simple ones, who found life very solid, very credulous. A few folks who did not think very deeply, and laughed at the thought that any civilization could crash. Yet what of these stories of the fall of Babylon, and of these things you read of great cities buried, one on the other, centuries apart, each a separate civilization? Lord! how long ago men and women and growing children had lived proudly on the streets of those cities! How was a man to figure this world out, anyhow, old Jim thought? How was a man to know what to think, when it was all summed up? The more you think and read and study and learn the more flabber-gasted and in doubt you be. On one side, half of the world repeats: "Turn to the Lord, your God. He gives you life, and He takes it away. Live believing in him, and when you die, you shall not die, but shall have everlasting life. You shall go to heaven, or you shall go to hell. You will go some place, anyhow." On the other side, the other half of the world says: "Why man, you are not created by God. You are the natural development of evolution. See, we have proven it, haven't we? In the beginning, life was like a tub of jelly floating in the sea, and the sea covered the whole earth. In a few million years, or there-abouts, the jelly had evolved to things that crawled, or swam; then to things that walked and climbed trees; finally to monkeys. See, how the ape man and cave man came into life? You are but a man evolved from them, having developed—at last!—That most glorious result of all the mysteries of evolution, a *mind;* when you could think and plan, you became truly the master of all you surveyed. Now you—all of you!—Are wonderful! wonderful! But when you die your very flesh will rot swiftly as any flesh will rot when it is dead. And for you—that is the end!"

Now which, and what, was a man to believe, old Jim pon-dered. Both could not be right. And could both be wrong?

He did not know. He only knew that surely we all must die in our time, and we are on this earth no more.

And surely we are all wonderful in our own creation, however it came to be. With the mind to think and feel, to be happy, or unhappy, to love and hate . . . you and you and you!

In old Jim it was significant that no more did he argue or rail out his opinions of the Government, or ways of the world, or religion. He was hushed. In his own mind he had admitted some vague and weary defeat. Soon he would not be able to make a living for his own self. He was poor in money and things that stood for money. He knew he was ignorant. He admitted to himself how little he really knew. Take God Almighty, for example. Maybe there was a God, holding out his hand to offer everlasting life. Maybe there was not. How was a trivial man to know? After all, did it matter much? Many a man worked hard all his life, doing the best he knew how, and when he grew old and was broke, his grown sons and daughters marrying off, his wife gone, he was glad to lay down and die in peace, whether or not he had any thought of living again.

Discouraged as he was, old Jim could not help but say, as everyone else said: "This will be the last year of drought and hard times, most likely. It cain't last much longer."

For two years now, no word had came from Jacob. Many times in their talk they wondered over him, and where he might be, because his last letter had brought surprising news.

The letter had came, two years ago, in answer to the last word he had received from them; They had written again and again, since, but always their letters had been returned. No one knew where Jacob had gone.

"So Mom is dead . . ." his letter had begun—and in some way they could feel that Jacob had sat a long time before going on. . . .

I would have come home, had I the money . . . anyhow I would not want to see her that way . . . better I remember her as I saw her last when she told me good-by. . . . Tell Pa that never will I come back to Sarpy. Tell all the folks I wish them well. And you, Frace, must not hold any thought that ever I will come back to you. Someday, when I have it, I will send you money for Keith. Don't think I've forgotten him.

Frace had read the letter and folded it to push into the envelope. Chris was waiting to take the letter to Sareeny.

A tiny clipping from a newspaper column slipped from the envelope and through Frace's fingers.

She picked it up from the floor.

It said in so few words:—

Divorce granted Eunice Maylain Gore from Jacob Gore. Mental cruelty.

Now in this summer serious worry came to Frace. Not only had she lost all her money in the bank, but along with that loss came a message from the school trustees. She would have no school to teach this next winter. The school was declared closed indefinitely. Many small remote country schools were closed. The counties had no money to pay a teacher's salary for each school; and now many schools were not needed, for out of a dozen families who once lived as neighbors, often only one family remained. And for that one family's children the county would not hire a teacher even had they been able to pay her salary.

Beginning in September, a school bus would drive around each morning and gather its little load of children from the scattered ranches. It would take them all to one school twelve miles to the west. In that way the county pooled the cost of education, and pared the costs of each district down to a single upkeep. In the mornings the school bus would come down the road for Keith and Sareeny's two oldest, and Dorcy's children. In the evenings it would fetch them home again.

247

After the shock of this double loss Frace spent nigh onto a week in dazed worry. All her sense of security was gone. The money she had saved was gone. Her work was gone. Unless she could plan out some course to take, winter would bring stark need to herself and Keith. Old Jim would not let them want for anything he could give them . . . but what had he to give? What did anyone here have to give?—willing and good as they would be to give it. She would not sit calmly to depend on them, however much they had or did not have. No, she must plan something. She had Keith, and she must plan on his account, too. Just as she had planned for him, when she had saved that money so carefully.

"What shall I do?"

She spoke that thought aloud, so many times, over and over, that Tana would burst out laughing, serious as it was.

Tana said lightly:—

"Do nothing, Frace. Until the school opens again, just pretend the summer vacation is unusually long. The school will open again next year, most likely."

But really, Tana understood how greatly worried Frace was. She knew that Frace did not have a dollar. Tana thought, why does money have to be so important? . . . If you have it you are scared to death of losing it. . . If you do not have it you feel helpless . . . the world would be better off if there wasn't *any* of the blamed stuff! . . . .I'm glad I never had any.

Frace was not the kind to fret and worry too long. She knew she must do something. She must have some method of work—she must earn money.

Frace knew these were no slight "hard times" caused by a drought or any other simple, easily understood thing. This depression was world-wide, and in some vague way it was deeper with meaning than a mere depression period. It had not begun with "poor" folks. It had begun with the rich, striking them suddenly and terribly, and like slow seeping water it had spread and spread, until now no distant hidden spot of the civilized world had escaped from it. The strong, steady beat of its heart seemed centered in money. If you sought to think out its meaning and answer you arrived nowhere. People could not work because they had no money to buy with to create work, and they could earn no money because they could find no work. So they had no work, and it was as though all the money had taken wings and vanished away. Drought killed what might have grown in the fields, and even had it grown and been harvested it would not have paid the debts of growing it.

As old Jim said, folks sure did a heap of learning since history began, but there musta been some of God's mystery books they didn't read, and some paths they didn't explore . . . and I reckon we ain't mastered the world, *yet!* . . .

Frace would be mighty surprised to see the time she couldn't find work and make money once she set her mind to it!

She stopped her worrying. There was but one thing for her to do. She would have to leave Sarpy. Someone would surely have a little money to lend her. Felix Eden! He had it. And he would be glad to lend her some, until she found work and was settled.

She would take Keith and go to some warm Southern city. And you can bet your bottom dollar she would find work, too. Devil take the hard times!

Now that she had made up her mind, Frace was almost exultant.

The devil take Jacob, too!

She was even surprised at herself. The more she thought, the more she wanted to leave. A true knowledge grew in her, so that she repeated the silent words over in her mind, amazed and yet relieved. "Why, I don't love Jacob. I haven't loved him since he brought me here and I learned to know him as he truly is. I only thought I still loved him, because I did love him in the beginning. . . . Yes, I loved you then, Jacob—oh, I did love you then. Now I never want to see you again.

It is settled in my own mind, and I'm free. . . . I'm free!"

What had caused her to so willingly shut herself in this lonely place out of the world, hurt because a man had deserted her? She had so completely forgotten all the things it was pleasant to do, that she had not even missed them. All the time she had sense enough to realize Jacob Gore was a good man for no woman. . . . Yes, but in the beginning I loved him, and I thought I understood him.

She knew definitely foreverly, that she was finished with Jacob Gore. She did not hate him. She did not resent him. She would never again feel over a mild, momentary interest in him, such as where he was or how he was, or whether he still lived. She simply did not care.

She thought:—

"I will get out in the world and live. I want to be the kind of woman I was before I came here. I want to be attractive and well dressed, I want to hold my own among intelligent, modern people. I want to take Keith to theaters and libraries and museums."

But when she told old Jim her plan to leave Sarpy he was loud in his talk against it. She must not go. What would they do without her?

Never before had Frace realized just how much Jacob's family loved her. Or how much Keith loved them.

Keith would be nine years old in September. He was a handsome boy, strong, healthy. Frace had given him his clear blue eyes and fair skin and cheerful mind. But in all other ways Keith was like Jacob. With Jacob's coal-black hair, and long boyish stride—and even now, a touch of Jacob' restlessness.

Chris and Tana said so little that it was all the more plain how much it would hurt them to see Frace go.

Chris was restless, unhappy; drought gave them all too many idle hours.

And Frace did not go. She waited. Days passed. It brought tears close to her own eyes when she gradually learned of things they believed they were doing to help her, to keep her with them.

Old Jim, in his frequent, secretive talking to Chris, thought no one overheard them. He was bitter in his cursing of Jacob.

And Keith, old enough now to understand, overheard the talk. Every word clamped in his boy mind, and stayed there. He had really seen his father only that one time when Jacob had come home to Christmastime. Keith remembered him as big and strong and good—oh, so good—and his eyes had loved Keith every time he had looked at Keith. Keith had a secret worship of that memory of his father. He sulled over his grandpa's talk, and said nothing.

Old Jim grumbled with deep, aroused anger. If Jacob were only half a man, he would not leave Frace to bring up Keith alone.

Frace knew when old Jim and Tana quietly wrote the letter and mailed it away. She knew when he borrowed a little money and sent it, later. She knew they had hired someone to trace down Jacob.

Weeks passed. No word came.

Frace was sorry for them. They probably thought she loved Jacob. For her own part, she hoped Jacob was alive and well and happy, but she did not care if he was ever found, or if she ever saw him face to face again.

She had made up her mind to take Keith and leave Sarpy, and win back her own life again. And leave she would, in such time as she could go without hurting these she loved.

Bright and early one morning, Chris came alone to Sareeny's. Sareeny knew there was some deep subject on his mind, for he followed her about in her work, like some clumsy, overgrown kid. You could always tell when Chris was leading up to something. He would follow you around, getting his big feet and broad shoulders in the way.

He carried water from the shallow spring for her to wash. They were hanging clothes, when he said suddenly:

"I'm going to leave here, Sareeny."

Sareeny had her mouth full of clothespins. She looked at him with vague worry. So that was what he had come over to say. He knew she was going to tell him how foolish it was to go trailing around the country.

He went on talking.

"There's nothing for me to do here. Pa don't need me. Even if he did, do you think I want to stay here all my life? There's a few other things I want to see. And they're not hills or cottonwood trees or prickly pear cactus."

She said firmly: "Now Chris, don't you fly off the handle without thinking out the smartest thing to do. You know you couldn't get a job. You would land somewhere broke, and not knowing a soul to help you, you might starve to death. The papers are full of such stories."

He laughed, admitting her truth: "Honestly Sareeny, I believe I'd kinda enjoy it. I'm not kidding."

"Enjoy starving? Chris Gore! You never have been very hungry, or you would never say that."

His voice was filled with disgust and actual weariness: "I tell you I can't stand this any longer. We're all buried out here in the hills, away from everything. Nothing ever happens. Day after day, year in and year out, we do the same things and see the same things."

Sareeny said suddenly:

"I think you ought to go, Chris."

He stared at her. "Aren't you going to try and talk me out of it?"

"No. I'm not."

She turned the tub upside down and they sat on it. "Chris, I want to tell you something. I used to feel just like you are feeling now. I thought if I didn't get away from these ever-lasting hills and ranches I'd go crazy. I got over it, and now I'm sure—as sure as of anything in my life—that I will live here till I die. And I want to. But you are different—being a man—and I don't think you will ever be satisfied till you know a little something about the rest of the world."

He said fervently: "Gosh you are a brick, Sareeny!"

He might even go to New York City, and try to find Jacob. But down South must be a wonderful place, with warm winters, and juicy fruits growing, and drawling Southerners as good and neighborly as everybody claimed. Farther south the blue ocean's gulf rolls in waves to the sunny shores, and ships come and go from a hundred glamorous lands far across the sea. As Chris talked he forgot the hard times that were rocking the whole world, and the fierce drought that encircled the earth. And Sareeny sat and let herself listen and called herself an old fool woman letting her imagination act like a schoolgirl's. But what of it? She half-wished she were as young as Chris and had been born a boy, so that she could go, too. You don't live on this earth but once, and a little giddy spell now and then don't hurt anyone, if it helps to make you forget you are so poor the next winter may find your bottom bare to the wind.

A week passed, and Chris said no more. He just up and went. He boarded a freight train one midnight at Yellowstone River. It carried him a thousand miles to the East.

Sareeny could not help but cry when she knew that he had gone. Chris was a greenhorn. Freight trains were so dangerous. If his foot slipped when he was climbing, and he fell, he could be cut in halves, or ground to pieces. She had seen pictures of freight trains in the newspapers, loaded with bums, all kinds of people, even women and children, out of home, out of food, out of money and in misery. Likely in all those people there were some mighty fine ones, and many good ones; and among the bad there might be the lowest scum of human beings. Murderers and bestial men who would hesitate at doing nothing that entered their minds. Oh Chris would learn something, all right. But she could not have stopped him; anyway she would not have let herself try, because she understood.

Tana cried. But old Jim only went about his few chores with wordless worry, for he understood, too. Chris was a young man and he would go, and that's all there was to it. An old man can only let the young go ahead and learn. Maybe in a year's time, a home out here in the Montana hills would seem the most satisfying thing on earth to Chris; if he learned enough. There were droughts and this deep change, of course; but a man had to dig his heels in the ground and hang on, taking the dry with the rainy years, the good with the bad, just as he must always do with each year of time no matter where he be. He had to hang on and fight to keep his home solid as the ground itself, hoping, till good times came again.

In late summer an old Indian brought Felix down from the mountains. Felix said Case wanted Sareeny and Minty to pack up some food and come there for a week's vacation. They had earned a week of rest and quiet. The kids certainly could fare, a week without their Ma and Minty. Dorcy or Frace wouldn't mind playing foster mother for a few days.

Sareeny did want to go. Yet she hated to leave the children, too. They had never been parted from her. But she wouldn't take them. She reckoned she would rather stay home than spend a wild week of herding a half-dozen lively young-uns away from steep cliffs and out of canyons. Minty settled the problem. Minty was the doggonedest woman to get away from home. Felix said in aggravation that if the moon fell out of the sky and landed in the hills ten miles away, Minty would rather stay home with Sareeny's kids than go and look at it.

While she was making ready for the mountain trip the thought came to Sareeny: "Case's other boy by that Indian woman is up there. Has Case seen him, I wonder? But what if he has? I will never again let any thought of that matter worry me."

It had not worried her, either. She had shut it out of her mind, so completely that her very actions had dulled even the memory of it in her neighbor's minds. Time had smoothed over the memory of it, like smoothing over rough trampled sand. Now Sareeny made herself look upon it as a remote happening, past, and never would that child bother her, because she would not let it. No, she would never let that half-Indian boy in her house, with her own children! It was Case's if he wanted to claim it. But not in her house! She would not be able to bear the sight of it, wicked as it was to feel that way. No trouble would ever come of it, and it was shut out of their home, and life, to only a raw remembering.

Case sent word he knew about the bank failure, and for Sareeny not to worry too much about it, but come up and take life easy for a week.

Tana wanted to go, but she said nothing. If she went it would be only right to insist that Frace and Keith go. And that would leave Pa all alone in his house for the first time since he built it, many years ago. Old Jim hated being alone with himself. But as so often happens . . . a little look, an unknowing action, may speak louder than words. One morning at breakfast Frace said unexpectedly:—

"I'm going to fetch Minty and Sareeny's children over

here for this week, Tana. Now why don't you go with Sareeny and Felix up to the cool mountains? I know you want to go. So don't speak any reason why you should stay at home. You are going."

A quick brightness leaped to Tana's eyes.

Tana wanted to go because Felix was going, and because she loved him. Minty and Frace knew it, and Sareeny saw it. Tana's eyes loved Felix's face every time she looked at him. She did not try to hide it because Felix could not see her expression and therefore it was not boldness. Minty watched and waited with quiet satisfaction. Sareeny thought if ever Tana married Felix it would be a happy day, that not even drought and hard times could darken.

Felix's blue eyes held a quick tenderness when they turned to Tana's glad voice; and if ever his arm in a movement brushed against hers, their hands clasped as though it was predestined and meant to be.

Up among the mountains summer was a pleasant thing. The days were never hot. No matter how intently the sun shone down, its bright warmth seemed only able to light happily the piney slopes and sheer canyons winding to the base of peaks. Rainless as the year was, there were trickles of soft snow water, pure as the air itself, sparkling over colory pebbled beds. Where ancient boulders blocked the way the water was caused to rise in depth as it sought and found a way around. These deeper pools were like crystal rooms where rainbow trout retreated and lived in cool silence.

There is no more peaceful place on earth. High and deep in the mountains there is an aloneness; a world untroubled. Peaks a mile high, or higher, rear majestically with ore and earth and iron and snow, into the sky—but for the casual people these are only to look at. Bulging out of the slumbering earth to swift and defiant heights, they give a man the feeling if he scaled the overhanging cliffs and dangerous slopes of snow and shale to reach the crest, he would be a-top of the world, with his head in the clouds. And the clouds were rightfully put in the heavens . . . mystic creations of Comus beauty, tufted and silvery white, yet changeable with every lift of breeze and every ray of light.

Case had been kept tolerably busy every day of the summer. It was no little job, looking after meandering herds of horses and cattle. He had to shift them in rotation from one little meadowy mountain valley to another, and see that no old fool cow or dumb mare was lost. Sometimes an old grizzly would lurk near a grazing band of cows, waiting for a straying calf to lag behind. And cougars crept to the edge of canyon walls and looked down, stretching their tawny lengths out like the great cats they were, their yellow eyes watching with lazy calculation the frisky play of a colt far below. But usually, if a cougar or bear were near, the horses could smell them or sense their dangerous presence in some way. An old mare would snort and paw up dust, and bring her young colt running to her with a shrill neigh.

Fishing for trout was great sport. With the weather so dry and the water so low, the rainbows came at the bait like a flash of colored light. This was one sport Felix could enjoy even though he could not see. It never failed to thrill and excite him when the reel sang out suddenly and the rod jerked in his hands, with the fighting force of the game fish at the other end. It was work landing a trout. With a strength amazing, and a speed breathtaking, they fought and darted this way and that.

Thus on many days Case saddled his horses and rode alone through the wooded valleys, looking after the cattle.

But he was not alone.

Hosea, his son by Letitia, followed after him in hiding,

ever staying just so far behind, stopping when Case stopped, and going on as Case went on.

Unknown to Case, Letitia's father had camp in a canyon less than a mile away. While the old grandfather was shepherd to the little band of sheep, the boy was free to play and roam the forest.

For a week Hosea said nothing of his doings to his grandfather. Then one evening after dark had come, and the sheep were safely corralled for the night, and the old man was dozing before the fire, the boy said:

"I saw my father today."

Letitia's father was old and failing in health. All unknowingly his brown, leathery old face told so much. The staunch, silent Indian soul of him had lived through so much tragedy and change. Of late years he liked to sit bunched on the ground before the fire, apparently dozing, and yet his thoughts were like the smoke moving lazily from things that had been to far off time to come. He made no answer except to open his eyes sleepily and look long at the boy . . . but the expression in his old eyes was wide-awake and keenly interested.

Throughout all the first month of summer there were whole days when Hosea followed Case along the mountain trails. His bright brown eyes watched every move Case made. With cunning curiosity he hid many a time in thick cedars, and Case passed so close he could have reached out and touched him with his hand.

Hosea was now eleven years old.

He was a handsome youngster. Cleverness was expressed in the quick knowing look of his brown eyes that were so like Case's. His hair was black and straight as his mother's and never trimmed neatly, for such things were seldom noticed by his old grandfather. He wore scuffed boots with little specially made spurs, and a frayed, fringed pair of black leather chaps over his blue overalls. Often his face was dirty, with grime, or greasy from the meat stew he had eaten with his fingers. But he was healthy with every meaning of the word, and handsome with a little boy manliness; stealthy with the innocence of a stalking puppy or kitten. Occasionally, he paused to wash his face half-seriously at some mountain brook. Often as he followed Case, his jingling spurs caused him to pause in aggravation lest Case hear them; and he would carelessly rip bits of cloth from his shirt or overalls to wrap the rowels before going on.

His strong, sturdy little legs found a way up steep mountain sides as easily as a mountain goat.

After a week's time, he stopped being so stealthy. There was no need of slipping along the path and hiding so much, he thought. This man who was his father would not see him, or even guess that he was there watching. Besides, there would only be a time or two more that he would bother to follow along the trail. He only wanted to know a little of what his father was like, and what he was doing.

Suddenly one day, Case turned and caught him by the arm.

The boy struggled in Case's grasp only a minute. For Case, looking down, recognized the face he had seen that winter day in the old Indian's buggy. There were marks of Letitia there, too, in the rounded cheeks and well-shaped mouth. And looking into the boy's eyes was like looking at his own. The boy saw the expression changing slowly on Case's face. He brushed off his sleeve and looked up with a side glance of sober brown irritation.

Case's voice held none of the threatening bluster he would have used on this ragged, brown-faced young-un who had been following him all day.

"What's your name, young feller?"

Hosea looked up with actual surprise.

"Don't you know? I'm your boy."

Case stood and looked at him, his eyes taking in every-thing about the boy's torn and dirty clothes and shaggy hair and soiled face. . . . Hosea backed away a few steps, his eyes determined with spiteful bravery when he spoke again.

"I'm not afraid of you, either. My name is Hosea. And what'd you grab a-hold of me for?"

Case said slowly, carelessly: "Well, Hosea, I'm sure glad it's you. Of course you aren't afraid of me. No reason why you should be, is there? Let's sit down awhile here in the shade of this old cedar, and talk."

Hosea's suspicion melted slowly.

He said with indecision:—

"I oughtn't to do it. You're a no good devil."

"Who said so?"

"The man who is my grandfather. He only talked about you once. But he said enough. He said you was like all white men—you thought the big earth was made for your kind — he meant people who wasn't Indians."

Hosea sat down under the tree and crossed his legs. He turned his eyes to Case, looking so quizzical that Case would have wanted to laugh had he not felt the way he did his own self.

Never after could Case have explained in his own mind how he was feeling now. He did not know whether he was ashamed or proud or glad. Case was a man loving all his children with such pride that he was prone to humor their every whim; and now this unclaimed son sat beside him, as bright, as lovable, as perfectly formed as any other of his children. Hosea's clothes and face and hair told very plainly that no one ever looked out after him—that he did very much as he pleased—like a healthy little animal. Case was afraid to reach out and touch him, for it would bring suspicion and distrust quickly to the boy's eyes; he asked gently:—

"How old are you, Hosea?"

Hosea sighed with resigned surprise. "My gosh, you don't even know that. I'm more than eleven years old. I'll bet you don't even know when my birthday is. I was born in the best time of all . . . there—that ought to tell you it musta been in summer."

"Do you go to school?"

He laughed and gestured with childish arrogance: "Of course. I'm in the sixth grade." He sobered and said very seriously: "They think I'm awful smart."

Case could not help smiling. He was a little proud.

"Have you got any other kids?" Hosea demanded suddenly.

Case was so taken aback he could not answer until he had thought a moment. Somehow he had never *actually* thought of this boy as one of his children. At home there was Peg, and Robert, Alex, Leslie, Nellie Ann, and Ross. Yes, he had six other children, he said; and he called off their names aloud.

"I make seven," Hosea said in a satisfied tone. He added: "I had a little brother, too. Did you know he and my mother burned to death?"

He told Case of it. It was as bright and vivid and terrible in his young mind as though it had happened only yesterday. He had been away at school he said, and his grandfather came to take him away all of a sudden. They came home and his mother's house was nothing but ashes and smoke. There had been a funeral—and after that his grandfather had taken him down to Sarpy. . . . Hosea remembered that trip very clearly. He had been glad when his grandfather took him home again, for he had not wanted to live in Case's house. Of course, he added quickly, it would be different now, because now they knew each other.

They talked on. Hosea's trust in his father grew swiftly. When at last he started a way, he turned to Case and said "I'm gonna come here again, tomorrow." And he stopped again before the turn in the pathway hid him from sight, and shouted:—

"Now I'll be here again, when tomorrow comes."

And Case met him, day after day, and talked to him, winning his trust and confidence. He loved the boy no less than any other of his children. Ever at sundown, Hosea would hurry down the trail to his grandfather's camp. Case felt no different about this boy leaving him every night than he would have felt at Peg's or Robert's or any of his children leaving him to hurry down a mountain path to spend the night in a strange place.

He knew he was a fool. Better never to have seen Hosea, than to be wishing he did not have to see him go. Better to have sent him scampering back to his grandfather's camp that first day, with a harsh word.

Case thought to himself: "If the devil made me deceiving enough to beget this boy, what is it makes me proud of him and makes me want to keep him and raise him up to a man like I would if I could lay open claim to him?"

He lay awake nights, thinking, thinking. If he had been the right kind of man, living the right kind of life, all this would not be, and Hosea would never have been born. To think over it all, was torment. Torment that was like dry burn, because he would picture in his mind Letitia burning, and the little-est boy dying in fire. Case knew now that no matter how long he lived he would never be able to forget that picture entirely. He just couldn't. It would be forever the one awful thing in his life that he would regret the most. He had kept it hidden as you can hide some small secret thing in your closed hand. Living on as though no untoward thing had happened. As he lay awake thinking, he could have likened a man's life to a dozen things; for deep under the surface it is not just a matter of breathing and living, working and loving as you will. It seemed much more serious, much more sacred and terrible and beautiful. He likened it to a finely spun web a man weaves unknowingly with every act of good or bad. The bad are strands that tangle him in his own weaving, so hard to straighten out. He likened it to a picture painted with all life's colors; a good life makes a beautiful picture, and bad colors mar so that the ruin can be seen even long before it is completed.

His worrying and pondering brought him all manner of strange thoughts. He would wake at day, with the light bringing sight to the world, the bright sun slanting above the mountains' tops, and wonder how such queer thinking could come to his mind. But there was the problem of Hosea brazen and unforgettable as ever.

Only one thing he was sure of. He would never let this be known to Sareeny. He could in no way imagine what she might do if she knew. Over and above everything else on earth and in his life, he loved Sareeny. To have Sareeny with him as long as he lived, loving him, trusting him, depending on him, that was what he wanted and felt he had to have to make his life worth living.

Why, where were all the things he had planned long ago to do with his life? Where were all his plans and mistakes and hurts forgotten—even memories of war fields in France, seeing so many dead men whose bodies lay open to stinking rot until they could be picked up . . . and men torn to bits by shells or strangled by poison gas, till he and a million others had nigh about lost faith in everything in the world. . . ? It was all forgotten in Sareeny, that's what. Forgotten in her quiet face and goodly ways and the children she gave him from within her body. Case knew he was a fool. A man ought not to think too much, over anything. . . . Thinking too much will soften a man . . . it may easily get him only into more trouble. . . . laying his mind open for too many confusing thoughts. . . . bewildering him with what is sentimental and what is real, and what is right and what is wrong. . . .

The problem of Hosea would work out in time. Case was sure it would. But he wouldn't let it hurt Sareeny. Over and over he had drilled Hosea till he was sure Hosea would never let the secret out to Sareeny should he chance to meet her. It was a bittersweet secret, because it must be hid in shame; and because he was proud of Hosea, who came to meet him with worshiping brown eyes and happy lips, loving his dad proudly as only a boy can do.

From now on, Case meant to see Hosea as often as he could find time to ride up from Sarpy. There was no harm in that.

Frost came earlier in the mountains. Thus when Felix returned with Sareeny and Tana, this most colorful season of year had bright splashes of tinted leaves in every canyon. Low spread bushes of darkest red and cottonwoods' saffron yellow contrasted sharply with the piney forest's somber green. The tang in the air made the night's open campfire a pleasant thing. . . . But there was danger, too. Every bush and twig and tree was dry as tinder. A heedless spark could send destruction and death roaring with the speed of wind. Such fires were burning now, away off somewhere, for the keen odor of vast fires' smoke was in the wind.

Sareeny and Tana kept close watch, with buckets of water handy, as they cooked each meal.

Say! it was a week of fun—no matter if the bank had failed and lost every dollar, the droughts made the fields as bare as the palm of your hand. As Case said, worrying couldn't help matters any. You just had to take a deep breath and go on doing the best you knew how; making the best of things. What else could a person do, if they had any sense?

Tana and Felix couldn't a-worried overmuch, nohow. They were too taken up with themselves. Half the time they were off down by the creek, casting for trout; and no bank failure or no drought in the world could keep them from laughing or being so happy that everything on earth seemed simplicity and easily explained. It is odd how all the gladness and all the tenderness in life can seem to be in the hearing of a voice or the touch of a hand, Sareeny thought. Elusive something, unknown and unexplainable, born in the soul by sight and sound and touch, and called love.

Twice Sareeny came upon them unawares, and she was that aggravated with herself she felt like a blundering snoop. For Tana was held close in Felix's arm. Unwillingly Sareeny hurried away, not wanting to spy upon them.

Then if Case started down that path, she would call him back quickly and send him another way for wood.

One day, when they were all eating their lunch at the crude camp table Case had made, Hosea crept through the underbrush close by and watched. His little brown face peered out through the cedar branches like a curious kitten's. He spied a chocolate frosted cake that Sareeny had baked at home and brought with her. Hosea could not keep his eyes off of that cake. Cunningly, he waited his chance, and stole it.

And he crept away again.

Sareeny was plum put out over what had become of that cake.

Case said nothing, but secretly he was tickled pink, because he guessed that Hosea had taken it.

On the twenty-ninth day of November old Jim died on the operating table, even while the doctor was confidently working to save his life. The doctor was puzzled. An appendicitis operation is serious enough, but without complications it need not be overly serious.

But it is hard to save a man's life, if he is not anxious to live some more. When a man is old and poor it is so easy for him to grow weary when great trouble darkens the world. It is not easy to make a fresh start, when his home is broken up; or to go on trying in the face of great discouragement.

Old Jim had just closed his eyes and let go. He was not needed any more. He had lived the usefulness of his life, and done his do. He would be missed, but year by year the busy life web of all the people who knew him would weave over the vacancy he had left.

And Frace knew that now was her time to take Keith and leave this place.

One early December morning she and Keith waved a last good-by to them. Sareeny wept when Case drove away with them in the buggy, taking them to the nearest station. For trains had stopped coming to this dead place.

She knew by some feeling that she would never again see Frace.

Now these hills were a lonely land, indeed.

Frace wept and was sad, too, knowing this part of her life here was finished, and she would never return. But she slipped an arm around Keith's small shoulders and hugged him against her side, and her blue eyes loved him, while she smiled at his own excitement. For she was happy, too, because it gave her a sense of freedom to travel away completely from all this she loved and all this that had hurt her. She felt that she was coming back to life again, with a life of her own and with Keith's life. Her thoughts were already alive and bright with planning. There were many things to do in a great city, and until she had come here, she had been a city woman. Very likely, she thought, it was all for the best that her little country school had closed. She had needed something to wake her up to herself. What future could there be in this remote dry land, for either Keith or herself? She was going where there was every opportunity, and when she arrived she would not sit down and wait for it to knock, either.

Within two weeks' time, Sareeny had a letter from Frace saying she and Keith were settled; and Frace had found work that was dependable and steady, that would keep them until she found work that paid more. . . . New Orleans was very, very interesting—she loved it—and you ought to see Keith! . . . We miss you, Sareeny. . . . We love every one of you so much. . . .

Sareeny was pleased and proud. There was a smart woman for you!

The very next day a letter came for old Jim. It said briefly that "contained herein are the reports and information, complete as you desired, and for which you have paid the fee, concerning the whereabouts and activities of your son, Jacob Gore."

Sareeny read carefully the attached, closely typewritten pages.

The first paragraph said:—

Jacob Gore, immediate whereabouts, Flosin's Hotel, Seattle, Washington. Occasionally employed along waterfront, or by boats on the Sound. At present, unemployed. Penniless. Poor character. Disreputable. Drunkard. Rowdy. Apparently desperately unhappy.

*New York report*: Divorce recorded. November, 1929. . . . Divorce granted wife, Eunice Maylain Gore, grounds, mental cruelty.

And from there the reports followed Jacob up to the present time. They were like a brisk, brittle story, smirched, sad,

267

and all too human. Sareeny cried over them, hurt and ashamed, and sorry for Jacob.

Oh Jacob you poor weak fool, never will you change, I reckon. What makes you the kind of man you are? . . . What would it take to purge you clean and start you fresh? Better you come home to this lonely backwoods place and live out your life here. . . .

Sareeny put the letter away.

Someday, maybe, she would send it to Frace.

It was comforting to know that Chris would never be like Jacob.

And it was comfortable to feel that there would be no more changes in Sarpy's ways of life for a long time to come, except changes for better things.

To Sareeny, the saddest task of all her life was going home to sort and pack away the things Mom and Pa had used. For Tana would live with Sareeny now. They packed the dishes and the furniture and clothing that were dear because a thousand times Mom had used them or Pa's hands touched them. They locked the doors and barred the windows. When they drove away, the forlorn old home, with dead curtainless windows, seemed already retreated silently into time gone by, as though worn with lonely defeat.

Felix and Tana were married on Christmas day. Old Jim would not have wanted them to wait.

The year had brought many things to pass.

# Chapter 18

Snow did not completely cover the ground until after Christmas, and that is a slowness almost unheard of in a Montana winter.

The last night of the old year, a storm came. It was strange. The day before and the day after that night were bright and clear, hardly cold enough to redden the children's cheeks as they played in the yard. The storm came after dark, and dawn found the sky clear and muted blue, with no smallest wind or cloud.

It was the kind of snow that sticks. Every inch of every tree, even to the smallest twig, was coated with this frosty, alabaster white. Every curving branch of bush was like a proud plume growing large and showy from the winter earth. The fence posts were like pillars of white marble, evenly spaced, and the barbed wires were like fancy festoons stretching from pillar to pillar. When Case looked out the window at dawn and saw how the world was, he called Sareeny to come and see.

Even the telephone wires were like crusty little white ribbons reaching from white pole to white pole away into the distance. Everything on their earth was white. When winter plays a trick like this, never is there a more beautiful sight. There were no highways, no paths, no mark of man.

Later in the morning Tana came in from a hike with the children, and said walking down the dry bed of Sarpy was like a passage through a winter wonderland.

With all the hard times, life was not so bad. As old Jim

would have put it: "If a feller can keep warm and keep his belly halfway full, he can't complain." The womenfolks scrimped and saved to prepare food as good as they could. There was plenty of fuel for warmth. Tana was as handy with a needle and putting on patches as anybody could want. And hard times couldn't last forever, Sareeny reckoned; even though it did seem the price of cream and eggs would never go up. Eggs were as low sometimes as five cents a dozen— Felix said that was likely to give even the old hens the discouraging blues. And it was worth more to use cream than to trade it for the money it brought.

But imagine poor Dorcy, whose only way of making a living was by selling cream and eggs.

Everything seemed dirt cheap. Even feed for livestock. But where was the money to buy it with?

Felix and Tana were too recently married to do much worrying over the times. All they could think of was each other. If Tana came to where Felix was sitting she could not keep her hand from resting on his strong shoulder, and Felix wanted her with him all the time.

The whole family was about as proud over these two being joined in marriage as Felix and Tana were proud themselves. Old Man Mills had come to marry them on Christmas day, and he had prayed for a blessing to come down on this house. Minty was secretly doubtful over any result of prayers, but there was already a blessing, she thought . . . for it was a home. A good home, with people living in harmony with one another, working together for the good of all. And for any of them that believed in God Almighty, there was a church right down the road where they could go each Sunday and thank Him they were as well off as they were in this day and age.

Halfhearted winter faded out for an early spring. In no time at all, so to speak, Case was plowing the garden, and

Felix counting out hatchings of plump yellow chicks with Tana's help. Sareeny and Minty went about the yard dropping seeds of poppy and musk-rose.

It would no doubt be another dry year, for there had not been enough snow all winter to moisten the soil three inches down. Case could hardly plow the garden, and unless it rained he knew it would be senseless to plan for a harvest of feed for the livestock.

It happened that on Easter Sunday Dorcy decided to make a twenty-mile trip across the range, to get a cow that a neighborly rancher had been wintering for her. With cream as low-priced as it was, Dorcy needed every ounce to buy food and clothing. This cow had come fresh last month, and there would be a fine frisky calf to haul home in the wagon, too.

Dorcy took all her children, because they so seldom had a chance to go anywhere. At the last minute, Minty took a sudden surprising whim to go with them.

They drove away, down the graded highway, with Dorcy guiding the horses and turned off on the faint grassy road that threaded over the hills and basins of the open range. Dorcy and Minty sat on the flat board seat. The children sat flat on the straw in the jarring wagon box, and the younger ones were happy as only young children can be over going somewhere.

The morning was soft and warm. Coats were hardly needed.

But Montana weather can change with the swift passing of the wind. And that it did this day.

A blizzard roared in on a high east wind that afternoon. And Dorcy, returning home, lost her way on the range.

Night came down early. Cold wind, seeming able to drive right through the body, brought the snow darting down to earth, and then whirled it up again in swift white clouds that made the maze of hills a bewildering, senseless sameness no matter where they looked.

Hours passed in the night. After so long a time the fury of the storm slowed, and the sky cleared slowly. The stars shone glittering, cold, cold. The wind still blew, softly now, moving as a vast sigh over the lonely land. The hallowed crystal quiet of the winter night was all about Dorcy's wagon.

At home no one was greatly worried, because they believed Dorcy and Minty must have turned back to spend the night in the rancher's house.

The next afternoon, Dorcy's team that had been hitched to the wagon was pawing at the gate of the barnyard. They had broken loose from the wagon and found their own way home.

At three o'clock that afternoon, Case and a party of searching men found the women and children miles out in the open range. They had spent the greater part of the night huddled in the loose straw of the wagon box.

Dorcy's two youngest children, June and Inez, were frozen to death.

For weeks after that, Dorcy nigh about lost her mind. She repeated to Sareeny and Tana over and over how it had happened, and Minty too, though Minty had lived through it all her own self and knew how it was.

I knew they were freezing to death right there before my eyes and I couldn't do a thing. I wrapped my coat around them . . . and tried to keep the cold off of them . . . but it was no use. It was no use. And all that day before the men found us I would go to their dead faces and I could only look at them. . . ."

Dorcy aged twenty years in those few weeks. She wept until she could cry no more, and her suffering was a terrible thing that left her eyes dazed and almost unseeing in their expression. She moved with her shoulders hunched, and the stoniness in her thin white face belied any feeling whatsoever. Sareeny and every neighbor was so sorry for her they would have done anything on earth to comfort her, but there was nothing they could do except every act of kind neighborliness.

She kept repeating over and over that this was her punishment. This was her punishment.

Her own long, bony hands had been frozen, as had the hands or faces or feet of her other children, and Minty, too. The doctor worried over them, coaxing back the living flesh.

Unknown to everyone, Dorcy did lose her mind at times. No matter how many times she would say over and over to herself, "I did not see him. It is only my imagination. It cannot be"—Olen would come to her in the long dark hours she could not sleep.

He would enter the door of her bedroom and creep silently towards the bed. She would lie there wide-awake and terror-stricken. He was as real as he had ever been alive, only now he was dead and yet he moved. He was dead and yet his eyes were as alive as ever with mockery, gloating veiled in unspeakable horror. He could lift his hands and talk, laughing at her hysteria.

Trembling so she could hardly breathe, Dorcy would get up from bed and light the lamp with jerking hands.

With a fear she could not control, she would go back to bed. Maybe, then, before she even saw him she would suddenly hear his voice:

"Oh, you can't sleep, Dorcy. You can't sleep. You can't sleep."

She took to going to bed with the light burning. She would not imagine things so easily, unless it was dark.

Suddenly one night she woke and saw him leaning over her face, so close she saw every horrored detail in the expression of his eyes. She shrieked. He moved and vanished into the very wall above her bed.

273

Rose came running, with Denver and Sid close behind. Silver trailed in a moment later, her bare feet stumbling in her little long white nightgown, her eyes still asleep. They sat all around Dorcy's bed, comforting her, even though they were frightened, themselves, and did not know why. Silver was crying because her mommy was crying. Over and over Rose and Denver asked Dorcy what was the matter.

Sid started towards the door. His voice was resolute: "I'm gonna go get Sareeny."

Dorcy's look jerked to him. She said almost sharply:

"No. I'll be all right, son. It's just that I had a bad dream and it scared me."

After a while, the children slept across her bed, and she covered them with blankets. Except Rose, who watched Dorcy with worried eyes. Rose stayed up with her mother— till finally Dorcy made her go lie down, at an hour before dawn, and sleep.

The night was not dark, for a full moon showered down its light that is the softest of all lights. When Dorcy made sure that Rose was sleeping, she went out of the house and walked down the road towards town.

She wanted to be completely alone, and think. As she had thought in time gone by; driving away with the very force of her mind every bit of fear and torturing worry. She could do it again, if she was strong enough. She had two boys and two girls sleeping yonder at the house to think of.

But she could not reason. Inez and June crowded into her mind as crowding water will rise in a pond, hurting her too much for reasoning argument with worry.

Three of her children lay now buried under the dirt of this hillside cemetery. The three graves—Benson's had sunken and been mounded again three times—were not even marked with a marble stone such as she wanted so much to buy but had not the money.

Dorcy paused at the cemetery gate, but would not let herself go in.

And back yonder at the house these children's father was buried—three feet from her very kitchen door—where none on earth knew of it but herself.

How still and dead the night seemed! Like as though every last human in life was in bed asleep, except herself. The moon was yellow and a warm bright—for winter was over. The east wind and snow and freezing were gone, till another year should roll around.

Winter spring summer fall. That's the way it was. Winter spring summer fall. Over and over, when you looked ahead or when you looked into the past. And time does never end.

She was losing her mind, else she would never be haunted with something all common sense told her could not be.

Dorcy realized at last that she could not go on like this.

Her secret had mastered her.

She came to the edge of the town. A dog ran out and barked excitedly. What dog likes a lonely figure walking along the road at night? A half-dozen others joined the fray, raising a racket that jarred on sleep with sledgehammer vibrations.

A window went up with a bang. Old Man Mills thrust his head and shoulders out, shouting at the dogs. His voice sounded unnaturally loud in this strange hour. His white hair and beard and nightshirt were almost luminescent in the light of the moon.

He demanded gruffly: "Who's out there?"

Even when she answered, Dorcy did not know why she was saying the words. It was like her mouth opened and spoke involuntarily, without her mind. Her voice sounded strange in her own ears.

"It's me—Dorcy Fry. I want to talk to you."

Old Man Mills was only a second in answering:—

"I'll have the door open in a jiffy, soon as I get my pants on. You stay right there."

While Dorcy waited at the door she realized why she was doing this. It was because she had sat in this old man's church, Sunday after Sunday, and listened to him preach of hope, of peace, of happiness, and all the things a human mind is bound to seek for but not sure how to find. It was because Sunday after Sunday she had heard him repeat words until the words hung in her mind, in some way unforgettable. "Come unto Me and I will give ye peace, for I am yore strength, yore eternal friend, yore only hope at death."

Dorcy opened her heart and her mind to Old Man Mills and told him her story from beginning to end. He listened amazed, yet as a friend.

He asked at last:—

"Why have ye come to me? But wait—I'll tell ye. It's because ye have come to somethin' in yore life that is too big for ye to handle—too big for any human to handle. Ye don't know what to do, or where to turn. If there is a God Almighty, He is the only one that can do ye any good. For yore fellow humans would only cry out that ye be punished."

They were in the kitchen of Old Man Mills's home. He had built a fire in the old cookstove, and more from force of habit than anything else he set the coffee on. His white hair was fluffed uncombed over his head. His old blue eyes, looking at Dorcy, were as honest as anything could be.

"Dorcy, I've believed in God ever since I can remember, for my own mother taught me to. She was a mighty good woman and I'd trust her judgment even if I didn't have sense enough to see for my own self. My own wife died believin'. Oh, I know people as a whole are gettin' to laugh at such things more and more in their turnin' to scientific learnin', but shore is the truth they are gettin' to feel kinda lost, too. Ye take a person that's average smart, and after so many years of jest workin' and makin' money to show the world how smart he is, and bein' proud of his wife and kids—that ain't enough. He knows he's gonna fold up and die on some day or night, no matter who he is or what he's made his self to be. That's where God comes in.

"Now ye jest sit there and listen to me," he said placidly to Dorcy. "Ye won't have no real rest as long as ye live, and ye will drive yore self to the insane asylum if ye don't get yore mind set at peace. God is for them folks what come to know they need Him. Now if a person can talk to God and know above everything else in the world that He is listenin' and that He is goin' to help, they're comforted. Because if they believe in God, with no doubts in faith in Him, they know He can put over anything."

He looked at her and grunted.

"Right now ye are ready to turn to anything that will help ye. Ye have killed and done murder, Dorcy. And God won't refuse to help the mind of ye, if ye have faith in Him. He'll let ye go home with all yore mind cleared of worry and torment, if ye will just believe it."

The air was quieted as if all the world was waiting for the dawn. The moon was dimmed ever so slightly by the far-off approach of the brilliant sun. No dog was barking. No fires lit and burning, except in this secluded kitchen. And no sound except that of the singing steam from the lazily boiling coffeepot.

Dorcy sat hunched in gray gloom by the stove. Old Man Mills sat by the kitchen table near the oil lamp's glow of yellow light.

When a person gives way completely to worry and sorrow and overwhelming trouble, all the weary defeat in the world can be expressed in the way his head droops into his hands. Old Man Mills, looking at Dorcy sitting there with her head bowed, her poor woman's clothes, the mud from the road on

277

her old shoes, knew no other than a God can judge all the whys and wherefores of a human life.

He said in a voice that was quiet and gentle:

"I won't ever speak a word of what ye have told me, Dorcy. I'm goin' in the other room, now. And ye talk to God. Don't try hard for words to explain what ye mean or what ye want to say. Ye jest talk to him."

Strangest of all things of life, yet it happens again and again. More beautiful in its own way than a rainbow flung across the sky, or the music of a song that lives from generation to generation.

Dorcy came down the road home and her children met her at the gate. She wept for joy of freedom, of peace, and the heavy weary of a load that is washed away.

Even Sareeny and Minty and Tana and every neighbor from that day on sensed a deep change in Dorcy that they could not explain and could only vaguely understand.

# CHAPTER 19

DOWN along the Rio Grande, on Mexico soil, there are vast regions of high rounded hills, treeless as a volcanic crater and almost as barren of any grass or vegetation; suited only for what it is, a gloomy waste, with now and then a herd of half-wild cattle eking out their living in some way.

It is one of the most lonely spots on earth. You have heard of purple twilights, and whispering sands, and nights of loneliness when homesickness seems actually in the voice of the wind. There you find them. There you find graves a thousand years old, like bits of ancient history buried under layer upon layer of clay. And little unbelievable villages, hardly more than hamlets, are scattered here and there, with poverty-stricken Mexican people that have not changed greatly from the ways of one hundred years ago. Many of them yet grind flour for tortilla by hand, and cook it with frijoles and meat in the round adobe ovens built in the yards of their adobe huts.

To one of these villages, in the first month of spring, Chris came. He had little money, and was trying to travel the distance to Texas as quickly as possible. There was work in the Texas cotton fields, maybe.

But it was nine weeks before he could leave the village.

He took sick with a fever that left him so weak he thought he would surely die.

An old Mexican woman nursed him back to health. She had a daughter, Juana. Chris might have fallen in love during those weeks of quiet rest, but he did not. Juana was temptation enough, with her pretty face, and eyes as black as charcoal. Chris had never seen anyone like her. She was mischievous as a quick-witted child, fiery-tempered in the way only a woman of her race can be, and yet so tender her eyes could woo with a gentle invitation to kiss or take her in his arms. She brought Chris food and waited on him as though he were a personage of high honor. And young Mexican men came to Juana's gay home like bees to honey in a hive.

As time went on Chris could not help but feel a pleasantness in the place, even though he was anxious to be up and on his way again. Juana and her brown-faced mother were so good to him, poor as they were. Mexicans seemed to have little worry. Every evening found the street gay, with laughter and dancing, and music of guitar or accordion. There was no loneliness, unless it came in sudden, swift, and passing moods, such as Juana sometimes had.

The room where Chris lay on his straw tick looked out upon the street, and the afternoon sunlight was as warm and lazy as August summer would be in Montana. Directly beyond the narrow width of the street was a schoolroom, and many an afternoon Chris lay and laughed at the teacher and the little brown-faced pupils.

Juana was teaching him her Mexican language. As he learned the words and meanings, the conversation and voices he heard told him many things. There was much talk of over-throwing the Government, if there was only a wise man to lead them.

One day he was mildly startled to hear the teacher saying:

"Repeat this after me. *There is no God.*"

And as with one voice all the children said: "There is no God."

"Again—" the teacher said. *"There is no God."*

"There is no God," the children repeated.

Then the teacher talked, with such deadly seriousness that Chris sensed something more than strange in the whole happening. There truly was no such a being as God. It was only a yoke, a dead weighted belief that kept people from getting and doing what they wanted when they grew up to be men and women. They must learn, and grow up to throw off this yoke of nonsense. God was only a fable. A myth. A legendary tradition.

Suddenly one afternoon, a group of Mexican fathers swarmed into the schoolroom and seized the terror-stricken teacher.

They dragged him out. Someone brought a rope.

All night long the body swayed from the breeze where it dangled on a protruding beam of the school hut. The street was quiet that night. The shadow of the body lurched across the wall of Chris's room. He could not sleep for staring at it.

And Chris longed to be home again.

He had worked in Chicago, and known the experience of being absolutely alone in a city of three and a half million people. He had traveled down the Mississippi by earning his way on a contentedly moving steamboat, with a friendly captain and a crew of good and bad. Well he had seen the tall corn, and the sunny South, and the sanded bleak deserts, and the salty ocean that wasn't always blue; and he had seen a heap more than that, he thought. You can bet your life there is no place like home. Not because it is felt as home-sweet-home or anything like that . . . but because it's the people you know, the roads you know, the land you know— well, just because it is home. Even if Mom and Pa were dead and gone.

He lay awake, wide-eyed, thinking. I wonder where Jacob is and what has become of him. Never did one of us see or meet Eunice, that strange woman Jacob loved. It was best that we did not learn to know her, since she only passed through his life and is gone again. There is Case, and that heathenish little Indian boy that is alive yet. Ho Sareeny, Case sure pulled the wool over your eyes. Odd how all people's lives are. What about Frace? And Keith? Gee whiz, thought Chris. It was dawn before he slept.

By the start of summer, Chris, cured of his fever, was crossing the great plains of west Texas.

He found a job at hoeing cotton.

The work was hard. Up and down the long rows, in the hot sunlight, from sunup till sundown. Men, women, and children worked there with him. Poor Southern folks, who had lived all their lives in shacks from farm to farm, working for the other fellow; owning no land, ignorant in the ways of schooling, happy-go-lucky, and as good in their hearts as the day was long. They made Chris feel he was nearing home. At the end of each day's work he was always welcome in any one of their shacks that set at the edge of the cotton field, away from the fine white house of the boss.

The way these folks could enjoy themselves! No long day of labor under the hot sun, no lack of money, no meagerness of living, seemed able to change the old good way of common friendliness and goodness from family to family or neighbor shack to neighbor shack. Chris knew little of the life that went on in the big white house of the boss. Down here at the edge of the cotton field he was a part of the life. He knew the corn pone and the sorghum syrup, the greens boiled with salt pork; the way the women dipped their snuff, no less accurate than the men with the aiming of tobacco spit.

When supper was over, these menfolks would sit around in the dark on the hard-packed earth of their narrow yards and talk. When the dishes were washed, the women would come, so tired their bodies ached, but relishing this little spell of rest before the sleep and the field and the hoe again. Many a child went to sleep with its head on its mother's lap, while a story was being told, or a song being sung. Many a brush of snuff was dipped and spit. These people were a funny lot, to Chris. They were mostly ignorant when it came to reading or writing. They were plain and common to the last degree. But as long as they remain on earth their life gives of its own goodness in its own way.

Chris forgot about going home.

For there in the cotton fields he met Avo.

She was hardly more than a girl. Yet for as many years as she had fingers she had worked in the cotton fields beside her father and mother and older brothers. Her slender girl-woman hands could move a hoe just as swiftly; in cotton-picking time they could fill a cotton sack just as quickly. Her mother and father would look at each other with knowing eyes when her row of hoeing and Chris's row of hoeing would lag behind.

. . . And the days were like drowsy contented summers, pulsing with a secret life that needs no explaining to be understood.

Her name was Avo Sullivan.

Somehow, each day Chris was a little more glad to have her working beside him; a little more jealous if she waved to some passing fellow on the country lane.

She was a womanly little person, pretty in a quiet way; for the hard work and the understood worry of her parents' life had made her quiet. She was a little brown-faced woman, sweet to Chris as only love could make her be. With bright calico dress, and rough shoes, her blue-gray eyes shaded gently under the wide brim of the sunbonnet that framed her face and brown hair; always beside him in the fields, leaning in her work over the flowering pink-white of the blossoming cotton.

A change, so slow that Chris was hardly aware of it, and yet conscious of it with each breath he took, came to the world for Chris. The corn pone tasted better, the sorghum syrup sweeter. The yellow Southern moon was brighter; the neighborly gatherings in the shack yards friendlier.

Summer was not yet over, when Chris wrote to Sareeny. He labored long over the letter, but when it was finished and mailed it said so few of the things he wanted to say. Thunderation! He just couldn't say things on paper like you sit down and talk.

We'll be coming up to see you someday—Avo and I. You will like Avo, she is like Mom was, so good and quiet. I reckon we will live here, for a year's time or so, anyway. If you and Case ever get a few silver dollars handy you buy yourselves an old tin Lizzie and drive down and see us.

The corn pone will be waiting, with plates on the table, and chairs drawn up and ready.

# CHAPTER 20

NOW Frace had lived two years in New Orleans.

A letter she wrote to Sareeny brought strange news.

Always, when a letter came from Frace, Sareeny felt it was as though Frace, herself, had come to sit, talking, friendly and good, unseen, but with them in the house. The things she talked of were so different than all the life on Sarpy. Sareeny was fascinated. Yet she kept it all to herself, never letting Case, Tana, or anyone know exactly how she felt. Many a time she went about her work, her mind clouded with thoughts of Jacob, or Frace, or Chris. From the window she would look out at the hills, barren and dry, conquered only by the road that cut over them. The same fences, the same mountains in the distance, the same lines away yonder where the sky came down to meet the earth.

She would think: "How can it be that nothing has changed here when so much has changed? No one at Mom's old house. Jacob lost away out God knows where. Chris gone. Frace gone. All this drought and hard times. Yet everything is the same when you look out the windows except that a death has settled in the land."

Sometimes when she was thinking, Sareeny would sigh to herself and wish she could be very very wise. Then maybe she could understand so many things that happen in this world and in all people's lives. All people are just folks, no matter if some are rich, and some poor, some a little wiser, a little better, a little meaner, than others. Some are vicious or cruel, others are downright ornery in a certain quiet way,

285

and she reckoned she ought to be glad she had never bumped up against the worst type of human being. Anyway, no matter who you are, or where you live, you are only a tiny part of all life. And all life, and time, and creeping awesome change, is like the soundless blowing of bugles throughout the world. Use your imagination in thinking over the past and you could almost hear them, calling your attention to some important event, while ever the stage is set and those soundless bugle notes herald the unfolding of a new happening. She liked to think of it in that way.

December was dry and blustery cold, without snow. High wind pommeled up dust and tore through the yard, rattling the windows with indignant frustration. The open fire crackled and sparked on the hearth. The nights were black as clouds could make them; as lonely as the wind could sound. Sareeny let the children pop corn over the open fire. Tana said the only exciting thing that had happened was one night when Peg spilled a whole pan of hot corn, and quick as a wink there was corn popping all over the living room. It was in the air, on the floor, and jumping like something alive as it popped into great flakes white and fluffy. Such a mess to clean up, for even when swept into a pile the kernels burst and leaped with sudden white mischief.

Tana and Minty were knitting rag rugs, vying with each other for bright color and design. Felix was never far away from Tana.

Case, unmindful of the children's chatter, would read, silent and absorbed near the fire.

After reading Frace's last, surprising letter, Sareeny gave in to a whim and went and found all the others that had come before it. Tana had them put away, a neat bundle held with a rubber band.

For Sareeny these letters were like a glimpse of a different land. She read them all from beginning to end. The first, two years past:—

New Orleans welcomed us silently . . .

That was like Frace, smiling.

. . . early morning. At once I bought a newspaper from a street urchin. Read the "For Rent" column. Small apartment, cheap rent . . . Sareeny, already it is home. A narrow, quiet street. An old, old house with many windows and many doors and quaint stairways. Secluded by a high street wall. A wide yard only half cared for, so that it is overrun with long grass and huge careless trees and flowers that grow to color where they will . . .

Six months have passed. I shall not move to a finer street, even though, I could afford it now. Keith says, "Let's never leave New Orleans, Mother."

A Sunday by the sea. Winter in the north, warm sunlight here. People so genuinely good. We go down by the levee at dusk—just sit, made lonely by the river. Why does a great river at dusk affect so many people in that way, causing them to think and remember, serious, sad?

At last I agreed to let Keith take me camping in the swamp. . . . [There was a page about the swamp.]

. . . The stagnant odor of swamp water, glossy and black. A wilderness of trees and undergrowth, all shades of green. Moss, everywhere, banging, draped, fantastic and beautiful. Far away into the swampland the twilight spread, gloomy and dark and mysterious. Keith, of course, was fascinated over the fact it might be alive with snakes and alligators and creeping wild life of all kinds. Oh that lonely night. Frogs singing. The lights of widely separated forgottenlike homes. As Keith said, some human beings choose to live and make their homes in the oddest places. Close by in the darkness sudden little flits of light like tiny single bright eyes that open swiftly to close again. Fireflies. Keith wanted to catch some and mail them to you in a jar.

Nearly two years. How Keith has grown. The advertising firm

287

I work for have raised my salary again. "Smart woman," he said, smiling across his desk towards me. "Some day you will be managing one of our branch offices." I was so pleased. A convention to be held here, next month, December, by the firm. Banquets and a ball. I must have a new gown.

Sareeny thought, surely no one of us really appreciated Frace for her true worth when she was here. Least of all did Jacob appreciate her.

Now, away down there in New Orleans, Frace was being paid more money than she could ever have hoped to earn at any work here. She had sent photographs to Sareeny, and Sareeny admired and was proud of them. For these photographs revealed a new Frace, dressed in fine clothes of style and good taste and beauty. Sareeny had always known Frace had a flair for fine clothes. These were expensive. Frace was really beautiful. Tana said you would almost imagine these were photographs of bright handsome women you read about in smart magazines.

Keith, in his photos, seemed a regular dandy. A tall long-legged boy, dressed like a man. In the photograph his eyes were black, looking direct and straight from the cardboard picture. How like Jacob in the tilt of his head, the quirk of his lips, the contour of his face!

Sareeny looked sadly at that photo.

In a page of this last letter, Frace said simply:—

Soon I shall meet Eunice Maylain, whom Jacob loves.

I have learned she is coming to the convention, next week. From New York. She works in the firm's main offices, which are located there. Now how shall we greet each other, we two? I admit I am curious about her. What type of woman is she, whom Jacob loved and married, so influencing his life. She was strangely woven in all our lives, across a great distance, and we wondered over her, for even though she was the woman Jacob loved so much, never did we see her face.

What will she say to me? Or has she ever had a thought of me?

Sareeny said nothing, though Tana talked with keen interest about it and could hardly wait until a week would bring another letter from Frace.

No letter came.

Slowly the week passed.

A cold afternoon brought heavy snow.

And late in that afternoon Sareeny was busy preparing supper in the kitchen, when she heard Tana, in the living room, cry out suddenly. . . .

Sareeny hurried after her to the door.

Jacob and Keith were coming in at the yard gate.

Keith ran towards them through the white gloom, and Tana met him halfway. Jacob came on to Sareeny, and he could not have spoken had he tried when he put his arm around her shoulders.

It was the night of the ball. Frace, dressed in soft blue satin, held up her arms and walked slowly across the small apartment, smiling for Keith's approval. He sidled critically around her, his dark brown eyes proud, yet serious. Silent laughter moved Frace's lips. The look in her eyes loved him. She knew he was just a little worried that Eunice Maylain might come to the ballroom better dressed, more beautiful than his own mother. Why, she thought, the boy's jealous. In plain words, he hoped his mother would show this Eunice woman up as less superior. He had not said so, but Frace could read him in certain off-guard remarks he made. She was startled. Who would have thought the boy had so many thoughts in his young mind over his father and Eunice Maylain?

She rode alone downtown. The city was curiously quiet. People were indoors, at the theater, in cafes, at home. Frace had many things planned. She was quietly proud of the progress she had made in her work. She meant to go even farther. And there were many things she wanted to do where Keith was concerned. He was an intelligent boy and she meant to see him equipped for his own life with every advantage she could give him or help him to acquire. As her salary grew she had invested heavily in life insurance. That was safe and sane, beyond all loss. Oh, Frace had her life planned. She had set a goal for herself and she meant to reach it.

The high, wide ballroom was filled with music and a soft, yet brilliant light. Frace, who was watching for Eunice, saw her entering finally: a tall, cool, graceful woman dressed in black velvet. "Now I understand a little," she thought. "How Jacob must have loved her. More than she knows, more than anyone knows probably."

Later, at the end of a dance, Eunice came over to Frace, smiling and holding out her black gloved hand.

"Need we be introduced?" she asked simply. "I know who you are, and I can see you know me too."

"How did you find out I was Jacob's first wife?" said Frace, puzzled.

Eunice took in all of Frace with one glance of her lovely gray eyes.

"First I saw your name on the bulletin board as one of the convention members," she said. "I repeated the name to myself: Frace Gore. Then I learned you had once lived in Sarpy Creek, Montana, and I was positive. You can't blame me for following up my interest. What I know about you has made me admire you, Frace."

For a time the two women stood quietly looking at each other. It seemed to Frace that Eunice had not changed a bit from the picture of her Jacob sent to Sarpy Creek so many years ago. And she bore out in her person all that the picture had suggested of beauty and a nervous, restless vitality.

"Let's get away from this crowd and go for a nice, quiet ride," Eunice suggested suddenly. "I want to get acquainted. Perhaps we could be friends."

They drove through the empty streets and along the river in a fine rain that suddenly began to fall. On the way home they stopped in a restaurant. Eunice talked of her marriage to Jacob, which she admitted had been a mistake. She was only attracted to Jacob, though she knew he had loved her, truly and deeply. They had never been happy together. "But I was often sorry for him," she added thoughtfully, "even when I knew I was making him miserable."

The two women spoke honestly to each other. Neither had any recent word of Jacob, except that he was in Seattle with no work, unhappy, his world the waterfront. Only one thing did Eunice keep from Frace: the fact that Jacob had often spoken of Keith, had often dwelt moodily and fondly on the thought of the boy. Except for this one thing, Eunice was frank. And she was strangely pleased with Frace, as Frace was with her. Each sensed in the other some quality unspoken, unseen, that brought understanding. Finally they got back into a car and were driven home, stopping first across the street from Frace's apartment building. Frace said a warm goodnight to her companion. The meeting with Eunice had satisfied some long suppressed uneasiness in her heart, and she was happy, a little dazed with the success of the evening. Then she started gaily across the wet street.

There was a sudden screaming of wet tires on pavement as a car that had been rushing along the dark street tried to stop. Frace stood in the center of the open space, paralyzed with fright, and the car hit her, knocked her down. One of the wheels ran over her breast. Later on, the doctor said she had died instantly.

Eunice did not remember all that she had done and seen at that time. She heard her own screams, and the drunken cursing of the man who had been driving the car, and shortly afterwards the possessed voice of a policeman who came stalking up and took charge of things. A small crowd collected around the still body of Frace, but Eunice could not look. She thought of the boy Keith, waiting for his mother in the building opposite. At last she pulled her scattered wits together and spoke to the policeman, explained to him as coherently as she could just what had happened. He had already put in an alarm for an ambulance. Eunice took the name of the hospital, and crossed the street. She felt that somehow or other she must see Keith herself and tell him that his mother had been hurt.

The elderly woman whom Frace had hired to stay in the apartment with Keith for that evening admitted Eunice after a moment's parley. Then she went to fetch the boy, who appeared in the tiny living room with tousled black hair and eyes squinting from the light. Eunice felt a sudden tug of remembrance as she saw him. Those looks were Jacob's, and the coal-black hair, and the straight, proud carriage of the body. But she was unprepared for the hostility of the boy's attitude when she told him who she was. Plainly he knew about her, blamed her in his mind for something. And she knew that her dimly formed plan of looking after him if anything serious should have happened to Frace was in vain.

Keith accepted her story calmly, almost as if he did not believe it. Afterwards they sat across from each other without speaking. Finally she called the hospital and learned that Frace was dead.

It was two days later when Eunice located Jacob, still in Seattle.

She had thought the whole matter over carefully—staying with Keith in the small apartment. Never in all her life had she been so touched by anything as Keith's grief. The boy was utterly lost without Frace. Now he belonged to Jacob.

It was Jacob's right to have him. No need wonder whether or not Jacob would want him. Eunice knew Jacob wanted him. It was deep and silent in Jacob, beyond the comprehension of words, how much he needed Keith and all that Keith would mean to him.

She had questioned Keith about Jacob's people in Montana, and the sort of surroundings they lived in. Keith told her as best he could. Eunice had a horror of lonely, remote places. Certainly she would not willingly send this boy there. As she questioned Keith, Eunice formed the impression "Aunt Sareeny" must be an ignorant, isolated ranch woman who had lived all her life in that backwoodsy place, apparently accepting poverty as natural and matter-of-course. What a lonely and desolate land for a boy to exist in! No, certainly she would not send Keith there.

True, Jacob seemed worthless and weak and of little good. But Eunice knew what the adventure of Keith's coming to live with Jacob would mean and grow to mean in Jacob's own life.

She telephoned the Chief of the Seattle Police, briefly told him the facts and the little she knew of where he might possibly locate Jacob.

Within twenty-four hours a return long-distance telephone call told her Jacob was found. He was unemployed and he had no money, but Eunice had expected that.

She sat by the telephone in Frace's New Orleans apartment, talking to the Chief of Police in Seattle. She was not so sorry for Jacob as she was sorry because she had wronged him. Jacob had loved her. She knew she had not deserved it, nor been worth the honesty in Jacob's tenderness for her.

She asked slowly:—

"You are sure he wants the boy?"

The Chief of Police in Seattle laughed.

"No doubt about it."

293

"When you first called I understood from your talk Jacob Gore is in your office, now. Do you have him there?"

"Yes. He is here. Do you want to talk with him?"

Eunice said quickly: "No, No, I really have nothing to say to him." She went on hurriedly talking to the Chief. She would send Keith to Seattle by early morning plane. He would arrive in Seattle tomorrow noon. There were a number of insurance policies, payable to Keith, and Keith's father would have to collect payment and attend to them. The policies would be packed in Keith's luggage.

Eunice hesitated, and then said:—

"I don't want to push your good nature too far. But I am going to telegraph a hundred dollars to you, immediately. I want you to find that man a job—even if you have to buy it. Will you do that?"

Far away in Seattle, the Chief of Police sat in silence a long moment. He might have been wondering over the whole matter, or perhaps he thought she was only a sympathetic and foolish woman.

He answered with good humor.

"Well, that's a bit out of my line, but I'll try. If I can do it without the money you send I'll do it gratis. You need not pay me."

He hung up the receiver and sat silently looking at Jacob, who stood by his desk, shabby and dirty, and needing a shave.

The day of Frace's funeral was the most distressed and serious in all of Eunice's lightly lived life. She was so sorry for Keith she would have done anything to soothe him, when, directly after the early morning rites, she put him on the plane for Seattle. He was pathetically brave.

In her hotel, Eunice could not help but watch the clock all through the morning, until finally in the noon hour she said to herself: "They are together, now. Oh I hope. . . . I'm sure it was the right thing to do by Keith. . . ."

In her hotel rooms that night, she again telephoned Seattle and its Chief of Police.

His laugh came across the distance.

"Oh, it's you again, Miss Maylain. Yes, the boy arrived. O.K. You may think I did wrong with your hundred dollars, Miss Maylain. But I got pretty well acquainted with this whole matter, and when Jacob Gore said he wanted to take the boy and go home to Montana I knew it was right."

Eunice was suddenly sick with something stronger than disappointment. Jacob had used the hundred to buy tickets on a plane to Montana. He and Keith would have reached Sarpy Creek by this time.

The Police Chief's last words were confident.

"Don't you worry about that boy, Miss Maylain. Why, Jacob Gore was so happy to have the kid with him it was a blessing."

Eunice thanked him and hung up the receiver. Her hotel room seemed very still and silent. She hated stillness and silence.

So Jacob and Keith were home in that wilderness. And for them it was a new beginning. Eunice tried to imagine that land of hills, lonely in the dark night, homes in exile with windows alight by oil lamps. A place of wind and solitude, Jacob had said, changed only by winters and summers. She shuddered. She could not imagine life in such a place.

Anyway, her part was definitely finished, forever. She dressed to go out and telephoned some friends.

# CHAPTER 21

THERE simply would be no crops this year in Montana. Though it was not so dry as '31 and '30, there was another thing just as bad. The grasshoppers came in swarms, as in ancient legends of hungry pests. They were everywhere. They could settle in a field or garden, and in a week's time eat it to a patch of leafless stalks that resembled sticks pushed in the ground. In one day they could leave great gashes in a head of cabbage, or a leafy plant looking like it had stood out in a battering hailstorm.

Case scattered poison, trying to check the pesky things. The Government furnished poison free for the asking, and even sent men with airplanes to help the dryland ranchers scatter it. The planes roared low over the ground, leaving a poison cloud to settle down. But for every hopper that died there seemed to be a thousand more to take its place. Nothing would check them except a long cold winter that would freeze the soil deep down and kill the eggs waiting latent for the next spring warmth.

It was mighty discouraging.

More and more Sareeny and Case were learning to live up to the way of living they had set for themselves. To just do the best they could when able to change nothing of things as they come. There was no help in worrying too much, or letting it make them disagreeable. They'd be old soon enough.

Only once in the summer was Sareeny over at the old home. She went over with Case and stayed there three days, while Case cut what hay he could from Pa's old pastures.

In a way, it was nice over there. The old log house set in the silent sunlight, stilled with a myriad haunting memories, a mellowed home, that to Sareeny would ever be unlike any other. The yard was thick with half-dead weeds. Only the great lilacs and yellow roses bloomed on defiantly in the face of drought. Thin, scraggly blossoms, unlike the ones that came when Mom was here to water and enjoy them, but with the same sweetness of color and perfume. It was quiet in the house, because Sareeny had brought none of her children except her youngest, Ross. And he played in the yard where she had played, long ago, with Ranny and Jacob and Chris.

It was odd how being here made her remember so many little unimportant things that had happened here in some day of life, long ago. It must be that the mind is a storeroom, never filled, though every act and thought is stored there and forgotten, to pop up in memory someday when you least expect it. Like when she went to take Case's lunch to the hayfield, each of those three days. It was late in the month of June. The cactus were blooming, and they are a pretty sight. Yellow flowers of glory, tinged with a warm red, with a vague suggestion of having been sprinkled with finely powdered silver. God caused them to flower in the West. And the wild larkspur was like gaudy splotches of purple color on the hillsides of the pasture. She liked going across there with Case's warm dinner, little Ross tagging at her heels. And it was stored in her mind, forgotten and unthinking, yet in some day long off to come, remembering.

In such a way old Minty's thoughts would sometimes come, unbidden, and she could not drive them away, for they were in her mind. Her memories could not be touched or dropped or discarded. They were the records of her life, and ever they hinged upon the coming of each new day or night. Once she had lived in a little house on

297

a dark street. . . a light marked the door with a red glow. Many a lowly man had stepped across the sill with silver in his hand. One man was well along in years, white-haired, and a little broken, like an old stone wall crumbling with time. Strangely, his frequent visits were like a friendly interlude. He talked much of his wife who had died, the good woman she was, and of his own loneliness her going had caused. His word pictures of her were so real that Minty came to feel she had known the gentle woman even as he had, and loved her these many years.

No, Minty's memories were not forgotten. They were only pushed into the background by the completeness and satisfying happiness of this home. She loved Sareeny as she would a daughter. Felix's joys were her joys, and Tana seemed a deep well of it. Minty wanted nothing more than to live here with them all until her last day came. Never more in her remembering thoughts did she place blame, for the futility of blaming had faded away, dead as Felix's father was.

The long summer seemed to poise in time, lazily hot. Now and then there was a shower of rain, but scarcely enough to settle the dust. Some one of these days there would be an awful storm, for in some vague, ununderstandable way they could feel forces piling up, gathering, threatening, as on a hushed evening when heat lightning lights the whole sky and thunder growls like a warning dog.

Word came from Chris in Texas, saying when the cotton matured and was picked, that harvest over, he was coming home. He would bring Avo. Sareeny felt a singular pity for this young wife who would then leave home and all its familiar life to live with a young husband in a strange land.

With Chris here, the picture would be complete as ever it could be again.

Down the road, Jacob had leased the little brick garage. He worked every day, puttering with old cars and tractors the ranchers brought there for him to doctor. He made little money. Sunday was usually his busy day. Keith, anxious and happy to help, would crawl on his belly under a car to do this or that thing, and his face would be greasy and stained black as Jacob's. They were always dirty, when compared to those rare occasions they really dressed neatly in better clothes, and then the contrast was startling. Sareeny thought Jacob was plum foolish over that boy. Keith worshiped Jacob. They lived in those two rooms above the garage, untidy rooms, except during intervals of what Keith called "cleaning streaks." From the top of the bookcase in the front room Frace's photograph watched them sweep and dust and gather from the floor all the dirty dishes where they had fed Samson, the dog. Sareeny was careful never to correct or advise or criticize. If the grease spots were hard to wash from their shirts, she just rubbed harder and said nothing. She knew they were having a magnificent time.

Secretly, Jacob looked ahead and planned definite, positive steps in the years to come.

Case went about his work silent as an old man, sometimes. Often when Sareeny looked at Case she thought he was growing old much faster than herself. But Lordy me! hadn't there been enough trouble in the world these last few years to worry any man half to death, when he was poor and had six growing young-uns to clothe and feed and educate?

If this dry weather didn't break its tight heat and rain pretty soon, with all its threatening it might crack loose and hail. That would about finish the puny crops and sparse range grass. But if it had to do it, let it do it. There weren't no way of making the weather do what you wanted. Let it do its do. Next year would be a good year, Sareeny told

Minty. She knew it would be a good year. She could feel it in her bones.

The storm broke. Not one storm, but two.

It was on a Sunday. Nigh about everybody in the country was there for dinner. Even old Pop Carlson from way out in the hills, who could make a habit of dropping in at meal time, invited or not, seeming able to smell chicken a-frying ten miles away.

It rained all afternoon, a slow drizzle that made the cooking fire a pleasant thing. All the women were in the kitchen, chattering and busy, when the door opened.

Hosea stepped in, as wet as though he had been doused in the creek. He had a bundle of clothing tied up in a gunny sack, all as wet as himself.

The woman shut up their talking like a hand had been clapped over their mouths, and stared at him.

"Who is that?" Birdie demanded with sharp curiosity.

Under the united intensity of all their eyes Hosea backed away and looked towards the door. Plainly he was suddenly wishing he had not come, and was half-decided to go quickly out the door and leave. He pulled off his cowboy hat that dripped with rain. His coal-black hair, shaggy and wet, had not been trimmed in many weeks. It fell over his forehead, so that he reached up with a quick hand and brushed it away without ever turning his look from these strange women. They continued to stare at him, and though it was only a few startled seconds it seemed much longer. He trembled and was shaken with nervous confusion.

Dorcy guessed who he was, and she was the first to go to him. A pity for him and what he was feeling caused her to drop her arm across his shoulder. He was quivering with wet chill and nervousness. Dorcy said at once:—

"You are wet clean through to the skin. Come over by the stove."

300

The strange expressions of the other women's faces revealed that they, too, half-suspicioned who he was. Hosea looked like an Indian, and yet there were a dozen reminders of Case in the look and shape and color of his eyes, and his mouth, and his face. Dorcy spoke to the women a little sharply, yet not unkindly.

"You can see if he don't get his clothes dried out he is liable to catch a good touch of the flu—it's cold outside— he's shaking all over. . . ."

The women parted away from the stove, and Minty set a chair by the oven door. And suddenly Hosea began to cry, and he was ashamed because he cried. But he could not help it.

There was not one woman there but what crowded close around, then, reaching out with inquiring hands to feel his cold wrists and wet forehead. They all talked at once. Get him out of his wet clothes. Feed him something hot. One or two of them, even though they all suspicioned who he was, asked with make-believe innocence, "Who is he, anyway?"— They all relished the fact that they were here when this happened, and they stole quick inquiring looks at Sareeny's face, and Sareeny's face was white when she leaned to pull Hosea's muddy little boots from his feet. Birdie bustled up with a piece of chocolate cake big enough to choke a horse, before someone took it away from her. Cake was the last thing on earth he should eat—and him having a wet chill!—He needed a hot liquid food like soup or milk.

Hosea stopped his crying by sheer force. To all their questions he answered:—

"My grandfather died. My grandfather is dead."

So quickly had all this excitement flamed in the kitchen that hardly had five minutes passed before Hosea turned his brown eyes to Sareeny. He had a look akin to fear, as though he had done something very wrong and was caught in the act. His voice was a pathetic apology. He murmured directly for her:—

"I'm goin' in a few minutes . . . sure, I just stopped to get warm . . . I reckon I can go now."

Birdie was taking his wet clothes from the gunny sack and hanging them by the stove to dry. She stopped with a pair of ragged and dirty overalls in her hand, and looked at him when he spoke. Her eyes were narrowed. Tears came to her eyes and she steadied her underlip with her teeth. She knew definitely, now, who Hosea was. And things were going to be said, if that child walked out of this house into the rain. Things were always going to be said when Birdie looked like that. She turned suddenly and hung up the dirty shirt.

There was no time for any of them to say anything, for the men were crowding through the dining room door, curious over what all this sudden bustle and loud talk was about. Case started forward like he had been shot, and Hosea left Dorcy's side to go to him.

The boy's voice was strained and apologetic:—

"I'm goin', in a minute—I got wet and cold so I just stopped to dry my clothes and get warm by the fire. That's all." He suddenly realized his quick mistake in speaking directly at Case, and he looked at the other men who were staring at him. It was so still in the room it seemed no one breathed. Everyone looked from Hosea to Case and then to Sareeny, wondering.

Birdie said with sharp accusing anger:—

"This is the one that was not in the fire. I reckon he's been living with his grandfather—and now his grandfather is dead." She looked at Case. "Case Gyler, I have hated you ever since I learned how you treated and neglected them two poor little young-uns you was ashamed to claim! Well, you can't hide it no longer! And God help me I won't let this one be neglected no longer! I'll take him home with me before

302

I'll let him go out God knows where. I'll raise him up to live down the shame of you!"

The neighbors' eyes turned in quick glances among themselves. Husbands and wives exchanged looks of mutual understanding, and reached for bats and coats, making ready to leave.

Case looked up and spoke with quick recklessness. His eyes were stricken, yet stubborn and defiant:

"Yeh, you are right. This is my boy. I'm his father. That makes me about everything you will say I am as soon as your back is turned."

The men said nothing, but only went on fitting their hats on their heads with unwonted care, plainly anxious to be gone, if their wives ever got the kids rounded up.

A neighbor woman said simply:—

"Well, I reckon I speak for everyone here, when I say it's all you and your wife's business. We'll get out and let you settle it. I know what I'd do, if I was her."

Sareeny slipped by quietly into the dining room and up the stairway. Case's misery-filled eyes tried to see her face as she passed, but her head was bowed down. Tana followed her a moment later, her face flushed with agitation and shame.

Dorcy and Minty pulled Hosea away, kindly, to the kitchen table, where they seated him with a bowl of soup and hot milk. But he would not eat. He pushed the dish away and looked at Case with fear-worried eyes.

Old Man Mills came in the kitchen suddenly from the dining room.

He said incisively:—

"Now, listen to me. All of ye, cause I ain't speakin' to jest some. Ye are all members of my church and I reckon ye are all God-believin' people or ye wouldn't come. Don't go way and run off at the mouth about this, with a heap of talk. And don't forget we all got to sit in the same church at meetin'

303

tonight, and we ought to set there as neighbors and friends."

Birdie came in from the bedroom, dressed and ready for the trip home. Her only look at Case Gyler said more than she could have said in a half-day of scorching talk. To old Herman she said flatly:—

"Come on. We're going home."

"We are not," he said just as flatly. "Now you go take off that hat and coat, and that high and mighty air along with it, and help Minty find some dry clothes for this kid. And don't you open your mouth again. I may be needed here to keep a mighty fine little woman from doin' something foolish. Git along with you, Birdie!"

Birdie hesitated, and seemed about to lash back at him, but she did as he said.

When Old Man Mills had herded the last neighbor out the door, he turned and said simply in a low voice: "Come on to prayer meetin' tonight jest as if nothin' had happened. I knowed Case was the father of that boy, before any other of ye knowed it, and I still ain't refusin' to be his friend." He went out and shut the door.

Herman and Case and Felix were alone in the big kitchen. Dorcy had taken her own children and gone home. It was three o'clock. The drizzling rain and the heavily clouded gray sky made the rooms as dark as early twilight.

Old Herman sat looking at Case.

"Case, you are a fool. But I reckon a no bigger one than has been or will be. Don't you think you ought to go talk to Sareeny?"

Case was standing at the rainy kitchen window. He did not look around.

"I guess there is nothing I could say to her that would sound right. Do you think I should go talk to her?"

Herman leaned over to poke the fire. He said cheerfully:

"Well, there's never yet been a man that understood just

304

what to do over a woman, least of all when he's in the wrong, and in as bad as you are. Danged if I know what I'd do. If you go upstairs she probably would rage at you cause you came. Yet she is probably expecting you to come. I reckon she will be down after awhile. But I wouldn't wait too long. And I'd stay here in the house till you see if she comes down. Felix can go do the milking and some of the chores."

Minty's low voice could be heard in the dining room, as she answered some saying of Birdie's. The children's chatter, Peg's sharp questions, and Hosea's answers. . .

"Did you ride your grandfather's horse all the way down from the mountains in this rain?"

"Yes. It's not so far. I've been out in the rain before."

Robert asked curiously:—

"Are you going to live here?"

Hosea did not answer. Peg said very seriously:—

"We're awful hard up. But I guess everyone is."

Hosea struggled away from his embarrassment. He said a little importantly, because he knew it would impress them:—

"I've got a thousand dollars."

Peg's reaction was not what Hosea expected. She looked at him with wide and disbelieving eyes. What a lie for him to tell!

"Phooey!" she said at once. "That is a pile of money and where would you get it? I don't believe it!"

Hosea got up from the table, and went towards the kitchen.

"Then I'll show you," he said simply.

Birdie and Minty, wondering, followed the open-mouthed children to the kitchen. They all watched while Hosea held the gunny sack bottom-side-up and dumped all his miscellaneous boyhood belongings on the floor. The money came out last. Birdie gasped—a few minutes before she had held that sack right in her hand, not knowing it had a thousand dollars in it. Every one of them watched while Hosea separated the wet bills and counted them, arranging them in neat stacks on the floor.

Not one of the older people said a word when Hosea explained that Case had brought the money a long time ago, for Hosea's grandfather to keep; and the grandfather had hidden the money. When Hosea had come away after his grandfather died, he had only to get the money from where his grandfather had hidden it, and put it in the sack and bring it with him, that's all. The money was his, and he had thought he might need it.

Peg stared, fascinated, at the wet currency.

For nearly an hour there was no sound from upstairs. Minty and Birdie busied themselves preparing supper. Old Herman just sat by the stove, poking the fire occasionally, apparently not even bothering to do much thinking, but now and then making some remark to Case.

Finally Case said:—

"I guess I'll go up and talk to her. It's got to be done—I'll have to straighten it out some way, if I can straighten it out."

They heard footsteps on the stairway. Sareeny came down through the dining room and into the kitchen.

They all looked at her.

She had tidied herself up, putting on a smoothly starched, fresh housedress. Somehow she looked younger than she had looked within years, when she walked through that door. She did not seem old at all, but only a mature woman, a little more plump than she used to be.

She said simply:—

"Robert, you take Hosea and his clothes up to your room. No, you had better leave the clothes here. They're wet and dirty, and I will have to wash them. He will have to room with you . . . and you two boys better get along with each other."

306

Birdie just stared at her. Minty smiled suddenly, though there were quick tears in her eyes. Herman made out he was only coughing to clear his throat, but he nigh about got up and kissed this grand little woman.

Of a sudden Case was across the room and Sareeny was in his arms crying her own self. Case knew that never would he be able to deserve her, or be as good a man as she was a woman.

Indignation was rising in Birdie like fire catches to a pine stump. Her voice was angry.

"So that's all you are goin' to do about it. Pout for half an hour."

Sareeny said quietly:—

"I didn't pout. And I didn't go in a rage. I went through all that before, when I first learned of it . . . when Hosea was six years old. All I had to do now was think a little."

"Not very deep, I dare say," Birdie snapped. "Let a man make a fool of you before every neighbor within ten miles!" Her look at Herman was poisonous. "If Herman ever did a thing like that to me I'd bash his head in, and then I'd leave him."

Herman opened his mouth to speak and then thought better of it. It would be too easy to quarrel with Birdie now.

Oddly, the very thought of Herman doing such a thing to her made Birdie furious. She went on stirring the pan of gravy on the stove, with a quick movement that shook her whole fat body. Her face was crabapple red.

"Why, you have got supper about ready!" Sareeny said, just to make talk.

Birdie would not shut up.

She reckoned this was like a second start, and each of them, "Ever' time I look at you, after this, I'm going to think you are not only softhearted but softheaded."

Sareeny managed to laugh, but it was a little shaky, she was that close to losing her own temper. She would have liked to slap Birdie's round fat face.

When Sareeny spoke, her voice was calm and quiet and easygoing as it ever was.

"If I am a fool, it's what is best for me. Case is one half of my life, my children are the other. As for Hosea, some one of these days I'll be someone just remembered, and if he remembers me as mothering him, it's something I did that was worth doing."

She brought out her words without studying them, and it was a long speech for her. Never before had she spoken innermost thoughts so point-blank.

And old Herman spoke a thought just as point-blank, when he said to Birdie:—

"You thought you had a ringside seat to a big ruckus, and it didn't turn out that way. You're disappointed, that's all."

The storm was over, when after supper they all went down the road to church. The rain had left the earth a place of cool pleasance. Tomorrow would be a clear day, for the way of the sun's setting forecast it. All the sky was dove gray, except in the west, where old-rose color was spread like a great fan and every cloud was fringed with living, burning gold.

They were late to the prayer meeting, and they heard the people singing as they neared the church. They entered just as the song was ended. Old Man Mills looked down upon them with quiet satisfaction. Maybe, possibly, partly because the soothing melody of the hymn was still upon them, nary a neighbor's face was turned away or unfriendly.

Old Man Mills bowed his white head to utter the Lord's Prayer, and all the neighbors murmured it with him. Sareeny spoke the words, but in her secret mind was another prayer, too. For guidance to the end of her days, and strength to stand long year by year of life, with patience to endure hurt that may come mixed in with pleasant things so that they are often hard to tell apart.

Upon the farthermost bench to the front, Hosea had sat down. His coal-black head rested very still on the back of the seat. His brown eyes, so like Case's, were wide and bright with the interest of this little adventure of the life so new to him.

The End

# AFTERWORD

*On Sarpy Creek* was published in 1938 by an author Little, Brown and Company called a "real discovery." The discovery was to be short-lived and doomed to decades of obscurity, since Ira Stephens Nelson only published this one work of fiction in his lifetime. The manuscript made a real impression on all of the publisher's readers, one of whom said, "I have seldom been more moved by a book. The simple unadorned style, the singleness of the point of view, the closeness to the earth, give the story a rare quality." Almost 70 years later, the publishers of this reprinting of *On Sarpy Creek* share this reaction. The book deserves a chance to claim its place in the rich tradition of Montana literature.

There is very little known about the author. The dust jacket of the 1938 edition reads:

> A native of Hominy, Oklahoma, where he was born in 1912 [it was later learned that Nelson's birth was in 1909], Ira Stephens Nelson was educated in the country schools of Montana and at the Polytechnic Institute, Billings, Montana. He determined at an early age to become a writer, but in order to support himself he has held many jobs, some for a length of one day and others for as long as two years. His wage-earning career has been a varied one from typist to truck driver; at one time he was night nurse in an asylum for the insane. He has travelled all over the

West as well as parts of Canada and Mexico, and has lived in Oklahoma, New Mexico, Montana, Wyoming, Iowa, and California. When he was five years old his foster parents settled on a ranch in Montana, the scene of his novel, and he lived there until he was twelve years old. Mr. Nelson, now a widower, was married at the age of eighteen. His present home is in California.

Optimistically, the publishers go on to say: "*On Sarpy Creek* is his first book."

*On Sarpy Creek*, published with high expectations, received brief mention in two national newspapers, but no review in its hometown newspaper, the *Billings Gazette*. The novel then virtually disappeared. Authors' prestige is subject to booms and busts, just like the Montana economy, or the Montana landscape with its cycles of drought and abundance. The last public mention of *On Sarpy Creek* was in Joseph Kinsey Howard's 1946 landmark anthology, *Montana Margins*, where he said of the excerpt he included, "Here, in a glance into the mind of an aging and beaten man, is an unusually moving study of the bewilderment and despair born of relentless drought."

Sarpy Creek is a tributary to the Yellowstone River in south-central Montana. It flows north out of the Spray and Little Wolf mountains. In 1857 a St. Louis fur trader, Peter Sarpy, had a trading post built on the Yellowstone at the mouth of the creek, and his men named the post and creek for him.

*On Sarpy Creek* is not the author's autobiography. It is a work of fiction and imagination. There *was* a Sarpy Creek school. If there was a community like the one Ira

Nelson describes, it has disappeared like countless other small towns that came and went on the northern plains early in the twentieth century.

Nelson died in 1994 in a veteran's hospital in Georgia where he had been living and working as the caretaker of a large estate. He was reportedly working on an autobiography, but no manuscript has been found.